George C. Mason

Annals of Trinity church

Newport, Rhode Island. 1698-1821

George C. Mason

Annals of Trinity church
Newport, Rhode Island. 1698-1821

ISBN/EAN: 9783337380700

Printed in Europe, USA, Canada, Australia, Japan

Cover: Foto ©Andreas Hilbeck / pixelio.de

More available books at **www.hansebooks.com**

OF

TRINITY CHURCH,

NEWPORT, RHODE ISLAND.

1698-1821.

BY

GEORGE CHAMPLIN MASON.

GEORGE C. MASON,
NEWPORT, R. I.
1890.

At a meeting of the Vestry of Trinity Church, held August 28th, 1888, the following action was taken :

"The Vestry, having learned that the Senior Warden, Mr. George C. Mason, has written the Annals of Trinity Church, covering the most interesting periods in its history : Voted: that a committee be appointed to extend to Mr. Mason an invitation to publish in book form the material he has collected with so much assiduity, and to take such steps as they may deem expedient, to raise by subscription the means necessary to carry out the wishes of the Vestry, as here expressed ; that body having no power to appropriate money for this purpose."

Voted : That the Rector and V. Mott Francis, M.D., be that committee.

Geo. C. Mason, Esq.

Dear Sir : Having received by subscription the amount which you deemed necessary for the publication of the Annals of Trinity Church, we desire to carry out the wish of the Vestry of the Church, as expressed at their meeting, held on the 28th of August, 1888, and ask you to proceed to the work of publication.

Very sincerely yours,

G. J. Magill,   } Committee.
V. Mott Francis, }

Newport, Dec. 12th, 1889.

PREFACE.

THIS volume, prepared as time and opportunity offered, is a transcript of the records of Trinity Church, Newport, Rhode Island, from its infancy at the close of the Seventeenth Century, down to Easter Monday, 1821, and covers the most interesting periods in its history. With the text, which is given with fidelity, there are copious explanatory notes and short sketches of the men who, in their day and generation, were in some way connected with the Church.

In the earliest book of records there are gaps, the result of inexperience on the part of those who kept them, and which now cannot be filled. A more serious loss was that of a volume, covering the years just preceding the Revolution and the time the British troops were on the island. When the war broke out the minister was the Reverend George Bisset—a good and faithful pastor, who had evidently entered upon .his duties as his life-work. In common with other clergymen of the Church of England in America, at that date, he held that allegiance was due to the king, and remained on the island when the enemy took possession, preaching to the troops as he had preached to his own people. When the British left he went with them. It is probable that not knowing with whom to leave the record book he took it with him for safe keeping, and in this way it was lost. The other records have been preserved. While they are of great value, particularly to those who have occasion to search for confirmation of marriages, baptisms and deaths, there does not appear to be anything in them to warrant the printing of minutes of a later date than are here given.

The edition is limited to three hundred and fifty copies.

CHAPTER I.·

DOWN to the closing years of the seventeenth century no footing had been obtained in America by the Church of England, nor had any attempt been made in New England to gain one, till May 30, 1686,[1] when the liturgy was read in public for the first time in Boston. Ten more years elapsed before there was much promise of a church there.

Rhode Island was even more backward. The founders of the State, and the first settlers of the island of Rhode Island, were Baptists, who were divided among themselves; and when Quakerism was introduced it met with great success. Here was the field the Quaker had looked for, but which, till then, he had not found; here there was no persecution, no whipping at the cart-tail, or other methods to extort obedience to spiritual rulers. The heads of the people, the Coddingtons, Cranstons and

---

[1] The Rev. Robert Radcliffe came over in the ship that brought a commission for Joseph Dudley as Governor of Massachusetts, and landed in Boston May 15, 1686. He made application for a place in which to hold religious service, and was allowed the use of the library room in the Town House. There he held the first service, and on the 15th of the following month a church was organized.

Wantons were Quakers when the first missionary of the Church of England was sent here, and the statutes had been so framed as to give freedom to all in matters of conscience. The consequence was, that in 1700 one-half of the inhabitants were Quakers, who owned nearly one-third of the meeting-houses.

But the church had a zealous advocate in Sir Francis Nicholson, who found a field white unto harvest when he came to America, on a mission quite apart from it. He was Lt.-Governor of New York, under Sir Edmund Andros, successively Governor of Virginia and Maryland, and, later, the active agent of the Crown in the effort to wrest Canada from the French. But with all his public duties, he had time and means to give to the church, and his influence was exerted in her behalf. He had occasion to come to Newport, and it is the received opinion that he secured the services of the Rev. Mr. Lockyer, who began to preach here about 1694, and soon drew around him a little flock. For four years the work had gone on under Mr. Lockyer, of whom it is to be regretted that we know so little, and the desire to have a church edifice and a settled minister had steadily increased.

May 26, 1699, Richard, Earl of Bellomont, arrived at Boston, as Governor of Massachusetts. He soon took up his residence in New York. A few weeks after his arrival he came to Newport, and although he was received with the respect due to his rank, and every hospitality was extended to him (for which he returned thanks in a letter to Governor Cranston), he, evidently, had but very little respect for a people who entertained so many conflicting views on the subject of religion. But those who were hungering for spiritual food, knowing he was a good churchman, did not hesitate to address to him the following petition, September 26, 1699:

"To his Excellency, Richard, Earl of Bellomont, Captain-General and Governor-in-Chief in and over the province of the Massachu-

setts Bay, New York, New Hampshire and the territories thereon
depending in America, and Vice-Admiral of the same:

The humble Petition of the people of the Church of England
now residing in Rhode Island:

Sheweth,

That your Petitioners and other inhabitants within the Island,
having agreed and concluded to erect a church for the worship of
God according to the discipline of the Church of England, and
tho' we are disposed and ready to give all the encouragement we
possibly can to a pious and learned Minister, to settle and abide
amongst us, yet by reason we are not in a capacity to contribute to
such an Hon[ble] maintenance as may be requisite and expedient:

Your Petitioners, therefore, humbly pray your Lordship will be
pleased so far to favor our undertakings as to intercede with his
Majesty for his gracious letters to this Government, on our behalf,
to protect and encourage us, and that assistance towards the present
maintenance of a Minister among us may be granted, as your Excellency in your great wisdom shall think most meet, and that your
Excellency will also be pleased to write in our behalf and favor, to
the Lords of the Council of Trade and Plantations, or to such
Ministers of State as your Excellency shall judge convenient in and
about the premises.

And your Petitioners, as in duty bound, will ever pray, &c.

GABRIEL BERNON,[2]	WM. BRINLEY,
PIERE AYROULT,[3]	ISAAC MARTINDALE,[4]
THOMAS FOX,	ROBERT GARDNER,[5]
GEORGE CUTTER,	THOMAS PAINE,
WM. PEASE,	THOS. MALLETT,[5a]
EDWIN CARTER,	ROBT. WRIGHTINGHAM,
FRA. POPE,	ANTH'Y BLOUNT.
RICHARD NEWLAND,	THOS. LITTLEBRIDGE.

---

[2] *Gabriel Bernon* was born at Rochelle, France, April 6,
1644, which place he left just before the
revocation of the edict of Nantes, and fled
to England, where he resided some time—was there as late as 1687—and
came to America the following year. After a residence of about ten

The petition was forwarded to the Board of Trade by Lord Bellomont, October 24, 1699, and was read on the 5th of the following January. In his letter to the Board, endorsing the petition,

---

years in Boston, where he landed, he removed to Newport, and was here active in founding the church; his name appearing first in the above list of petitioners. He was twice married. His first wife, Esther LeRoy, died in Newport, June 14, 1710, aged 56 years. From Newport Mr. Bernon removed to Providence, where he was equally active in founding a church. His next remove was to South Kingston, where he resided for a time. He died in Providence, February 1, 1736, where he was then making his home, in his ninety-third year, and was buried under St. John's Church. He was a good man—one whose whole life was given to the extension of Christ's Church on earth. Arnold, in his history, says: "He was buried with unusual marks of respect." Gabriel Bernon's second wife was Mary Harris, granddaughter of William Harris, the friend of Roger Williams. She died February 1, 1735–6, aged 92 years.

[3] Pierre Ayrault was also a Huguenot, a native of Angers, France. He was a physician, one of the settlers of French Town, East Greenwich, and was recognized as a man of influence. He died about June 4, 1711.

[4] Major Martindale had command of the Island Regiment in 1702. He was true to the Colony, as appears by his reply to Governor Dudley, who, claiming that Rhode Island was included in his Vice-Admiralty jurisdiction, demanded that the troops of the Colony should be placed under his command; but was told by the Major that he should not call out his men without an order from the General Assembly or the Governor —an answer so foreign to the one that was expected that Dudley immediately left the Island.

[5] *Robt Gardner* was Naval Officer and Collector of the Port of Newport. His gravestone in the churchyard bears this inscription:

"Here lieth interred the body of Mr. Robert Gardner, Esq., who was one of the first promoters of the Church in this place; he survived all his brethren, and had the happiness to see this church completely finished. He was Naval Officer and Collector of this Port for many years, also employed in the affairs of this Colony, and discharged his trust to satisfaction. He died ye 1st of May, 1731, the day of his birth, aged 69 years."

Lord Bellomont says: "I send your Lordships the petition of several persons in Rhode Island for a Church of England Minister, and a yearly maintenance for him. I hope your Lordships will please to patronize so good a design, and will obtain his Majesty's allowance of a competent maintenance for such a minister. It will be the means I hope to reform the lives of the people in that Island, and make good Christians of 'em, who are at present all in darkness." [6]

That the application was favorably received and acted upon, is shown by the following reply to some other communication sent to the Society at about the same time:

Rhode Island, 29th Sept., 1702.

Honored Sirs:

We cannot forbear expressing our great joy in being under the patronage of so Honorable a Corporation through whose pious endeavours with God's assistance, the Church of England hath so fair a prospect of flourishing in these more remote parts of the world, and amongst the rest of her small branches, ours also in Rhode Island. We therefore, Honored Sirs, beg leave to tell you that we look upon ourselves as under your pious care, and accordingly presume to trouble you with small account of our affairs. Our Church is but young: it not being four years yet compleat since we began to assemble ourselves together on that occasion; upon which account

---

[5a] Near the centre of the graveyard there is a stone, the oldest in the grounds, bearing this inscription, under a skull and cross-bones:

"Here lyeth interred the body of Thomas Mallett. He came from Great Marlow, in ye County of Buckingham, Old England, and departed this life in the year of our Lord 1704, on ye 16 day of January, and in ye 56 yeare of his age.

"He was a father to the fatherless."

In his will, dated December 8, 1703–4, Mallett gave to the church forty shillings, and twenty shillings to the minister, to preach a funeral sermon.

[6] "Arnold's History of Rhode Island."

the number of such men as can be relied upon to defray the charges of it, is but small at present; altho' there is a good many that constantly attend our worship regularly. The place wherein we meet to worship is finished on the outside, all but the steeple, which we will get up as soon as we are able; the inside is pew'd well altho' not beautified; we have also got an altar, where we have had the communion administered twice to our great joy and satisfaction, chusing rather to partake of that Holy Sacrament without those necessary conveniences that the tables in England are furnished with, (well knowing that they add not to the worthiness of the guests) rather than be without it, not but we are sensible they add much to the decency and order of it. The place wherein we live is one of the Chief Nurseries of Quakerism in all America, but now we have some reason to hope that the Reverend Mr. Keith,[7] by God's assist-

---

[7] Reverend George Keith, who travelled through parts of the country between 1702 and 1705, had been himself a Quaker, but was now in Holy Orders.   He had arrived in Boston in June, 1702.   Of a visit to Newport he makes record August 2d of that year:

"I preached again at the Queen's Chapel, and next day set out from Boston, accompanied with the Reverend Samuel Myles, one of the Ministers of the Church of England congregation there, and we arrived in Newport, in Rhode Island, the next day, where we were kindly received.   Mr. Lockyer, the Church of England Minister there, and divers others of the Church, came from Newport and met us at the ferry, and conducted us to the Town and place of lodging.   Mr. Talbot stayed at Boston, to officiate in the Church there for Mr. Myles, until his return.

"August 6, I went to the Quaker Meeting at Newport, on Rhode Island, accompanied with Mr. Myles, Mr. Lockyer, and many other persons belonging to the church there.

"After one of their Preachers had spoken a long time and came to an end, having perverted many Texts of Scripture . . . . I began to speak, standing up in a Gallery, opposite a Gallery where their Teachers were placed, who were many. . . . . But I was instantly interrupted by them very rudely, and they were very abusive to me with their ill Language, calling me Apostate, &c., and they threatened me with being guilty of the breach of the Act of Toleration, by which they said their Meeting was authorized.

ing his skill on that disease hath pretty well curbed (if not quite stopped) so dangerous a gangrene. Their behaviour to us outwardly is almost as civil as is consistent with their religion. Although slily and underhand, we are sensible they would pinch us in the bud. But thanks be to God who hath putt it past their power; in that he hath not only raised up a queene that is truly a nursery mother, but hath blessed us also with the protection of so honorable a Corporation; two such encouragements as (by the assistance of God's grace) are able not only to invigorate our endeavours towards the promotion of God's true Religion and Worship, but flushed us likewise with the hope of our Success. Thus, Honor'd Sirs, we have

---

"Mr. Myles said I ought to be heard, I being a Missionary unto these American parts, by the Society for the Propagation of the Gospel in Foreign Parts, and sent on purpose to endeavor to reduce the Quakers from their Errors; the whole Society hath a Patent from the Crown of England, and not to hear me, nor suffer me to speak, was a Contempt of Supreme Authority.

"Mr. Keith then appealed to Governor Cranston, who was present, but who avoided the difficulty.

"The Governor at this went away, and Civily said to me he thought I had done better to have stayed till they were done. I told him then they would be gone, as they had served me at Lynn, at Hampton and at Dover." [Then] "one of the Speakers who was the Deputy-Governor . . . . took out of his Pocket a Printed abusive Paper, full of lies, having no name to it, and began to read it in the Meeting on purpose to drown my Voice, that I might not be heard. The title of it was *One Wonder more; or, George Keith, the Eighth Wonder of the World.* . . . Mr. Myles said it was an Infamous Libel, without a name to it, and it was a shame for such a man as he, being Lieutenant Governor, on purpose vilely to defame him. After he had done another Quaker Preacher, who had been formerly their Governor, began to preach. . . .

"At last the first speaker made a long Rambling Prayer, full of Tautologies and vain Repetitions and presumptuous Boastings, as their manner is." . . . . [Then] "all the Preachers went away and many of the Quaker Hearers, but many of them also stayed. . . . I had now full liberty without any interruption to speak, perceiving the Auditory generally desirous to hear me."—*Annals of King's Chapel.*

laid before you the circumstances of our Church, delivering them into your hands to do for us what you think best, only begging Leave to assure your Honors that whatsoever favors you are pleased to bestow upon us towards the Promotion of our Church, shall be accepted with the humblest Gratitude and seconded with the utmost of our abilities, and so we remain Honor'd Sirs.

Your most Obedient Servants to command,

JOHN LOCKYER.

WM BRINLEY ⎰
ROB'T GARDNER ⎱ *Wardens.*

The outgrowth of this letter was the sending of the Reverend James Honyman to Rhode Island, as a missionary, in 1704, by the Society for the Propagation of the Gospel in Foreign Parts.

In "An Historical Account of the Incorporated Society for the Propagation of the Gospel in Foreign Parts," mention is thus made of the sending of Mr. Honyman to Rhode Island:

"The Church Wardens of Rhode Island wrote to the Bishop of London, and to the Society, in the year 1702, declaring their early zeal, that tho' they had not assembled themselves to worship God after the manner of the Church of England above four years, they had built a handsome church. The Society resolved to send a missionary hither, both on account of their being the first, and also a numerous people, settled on a flourishing island. The Reverend Mr. Honyman was appointed in 1704. He discharged the duties of his mission with great dilligence, 'tho' the Island was full of persons of many persuasions, especially Quakers, the Governor himself being such ; yet by his prudent behavior he gave offence to none and gained many to the Church. He continued there till the year 1708, and then came to England upon his own private affairs, but returned soon to his cure again. There were three little towns on the continent, Freetown, Tiverton, and Little Compton, which had requested a Missionary of the Society. Mr. Honyman was directed to visit them by turns on week days till they could be supplied with a minister. Mr. Honyman frequently crossed over to them, and preached to them in a meeting house which he obtained the use of and which was commodiously situated in the centre of the three towns.   He said that the people at first, tho' very ignorant and rude in religious matters, were yet very grave and attentive at Divine Worship.   He performed this laborious duty for several years."

The next entry in order on the records is " A List of Persons Baptised by Mr. Honyman before he went to England last." [1708.]

Grown Persons.—Robert Lawton, Benj. Shearman, Gorsham Wooddell, John Brown,[8] Robt. Hicks, Sam'l Albro, Sam'l Davis, James Little, Wm. Barker, Jeremiah Wilcocks, Isabel Albro, Penelope Cuttler, Eliz[th] Brown, Mary Shearman, Eliz[th] Lawton, Ruth Wooddel, Penelope Stanton, Mary Carr,[9] Sarah Pope, Bethia Beer, Bethsheba Banks, Susannah Wooddel, Katharine Thurbor, Sarah Bull, Hannah Bowdish, Mary Goulden, Deborah Hicks, Mary Hicks and Elizabeth Head."

To the above there is added a list of thirty-five children baptized within the time named.

Mr. Honyman had apparently no difficulty in preserving harmony in the church while in the immediate charge of the parish; but during his absence in England there was evidently some discord that was only removed on his return, as appears by the following entry :

" A Vestry Held at Trinity Church In Newport on Rhode Island, June y[e] 20th 1709, The following Resolutions were Agreed to.

---

[8] John Brown was Captain John Brown, who settled in Newport in 1661, and died here October 20, 1731.   He married Elizabeth Cranston, daughter of Governor Samuel Cranston.   She was born in 1661 and died June 3, 1756.   After the death of Captain Brown she became the second wife of Rev. James Honyman.

[9] Mary Carr married Wm. Gardner, and was the mother of Caleb Gardner.

"That to Prevent Any Contrivance that may tend to y⁰ Defeating or Disapointing Any of y⁰ Councils or Designs of this Vestry that Nothing Concluded in it Be Discovered by Private Whispers or open Cabals but that all business Relating to the Church be transacted with a becoming Secrasie. That as far as Possible both y⁰ Names and Nature of Factions and Parties Be Banished and forgotten.

"That no Member of this Vestry as such shall for y⁰ Future Espouse Any Private Quarrell.

"That all Persons belonging to this Vestry being Summoned by y⁰ Minister to Convene and Absenting themselves shall be Punished in A fine for y⁰ use of the Poore to be Inflicted at y⁰ Discretion of y⁰ Vestry unless Reasonable Cause of such Absenting be Assigned of which y⁰ said Vestry is to be y⁰ Judg.

"That all Letters sent by y⁰ Vestry or Received by them upon y⁰ Account of y⁰ Church be Preserved in A Common Register.

"That y⁰ Queen's Most Excellent Majᵣ be Addressed in favor of y⁰ Expedition to Canada. That y⁰ Lord Bishop of London be most Humbly thanked for His Great Care of our Bell, that a Proper Person be Employed About seting up y⁰ Bell.

"That y⁰ Money Left by Collᵉᵗ Nicholson in y⁰ Goverʳˢ Hands be forthwith Received by y⁰ Church Wardens for y⁰ use of y⁰ Church at y⁰ Appointment of y⁰ Vestry.

"That y⁰ Money in y⁰ Hands of y⁰ Revᵈ Mr Miles of Boston Given by Collᵉᵗ Nicholson for y⁰ use of this Church be forthwith demanded by y⁰ Church Wardens And Receipts ordered by them upon Payment which money is Also to be Immediately Laid out for y⁰ use of y⁰ Church at y⁰ Appointment of y⁰ Vestry.

"That there be immediate Care taken of y⁰ Glass for y⁰ Church Windows now in y⁰ hands of y⁰ Glasier be put in Without Delay.

"That ye Books[10] belonging to y⁰ Library of y⁰ Church which have been Lent out be all called in & Public notice of this be given to those who have them By Placards Affixed to the Church

---

[10] Many of the books that made a part of the library at that day are in a fair state of preservation, and all that are left of the collection are stamped on the cover in gold letters, "Belonging to y⁰ Library in Rhode Island."

Dores & when they are come in a Survey be made of y⁰ said Library.

"That untill a Vestry Room is fitted up Wherein to keep y⁰ Vestry Books & utencils of y⁰ Church they be Committed to y⁰ care of y⁰ Church Wardens."

JAMES HONYMAN
NICHO^s LANGE } *Church*
THOS. LILLIBRIDGE } *Wardens.*
WILLIAM GIBBS.

Whatever this disaffection may have been, some account of it must have gone to England, for on the same day the Minister and Wardens addressed the following letter to the Bishop of London:

Newp^t on Rhoad Island
June y⁰ 20th, 1709.

May it Please your Lordship.

We Being Extremely Sencible of y⁰ unhappie Consequence of those Devisions which have like to have Prove so fatall to our Infant Church Have Agreed that Nothing Relating to this Church shall be transacted nor Representations made but by y⁰ Joynt Consent of ye Minister Churchwardens and Vestry of this Church And of this Agreement we most Humbly beg your Lordship to take Notice to Prevent all future Differences & Private Applications.

" We have by Your Lordship's Good Care our Bell safely Brought to our Hands for which we Return our most sensible Acknowledgement, And which will Not Only be A Most Beautiful Ornament to our Church But A Lasting Monument of Your Lordship's Pious & Parental Care of your Hopefull Nurseries Abroad. We most Humbly Beg y⁰ Continuance of your Lordship's Countenance & Pious Encouragement unto

May it Please Your Lordship
Your Lordships Most Obedient
And obliged Servants

JAMES HONYMAN
NICHO^s LANGE } *Church*
THOS. LILLIBRIDGE } *Wardens.*

To y⁰ Righ Rever^d Father
In God y⁰ Bis^p of London.

At the same time a letter was addressed to Queen Anne.

To y⁰ Queen's Most Excellent Majestic The Humble Address Of the Minister & People Belonging to y⁰ Church in Rhoad Island In America.

Most Sacred Sovereign

Amidst the Acclamations of Dutifull Subjects Attending your Maj⁰⁰ Glorious Reign Adorn'd with y⁰ Bright Carracters reducing Tyrants to Reason & uniting Mankind in Interest & Affection we Beg Leave to Appear before your Maj⁰ With our Most Loyal Regards And Most Humble thanks for y⁰ Design your Maj^y has been Pleased to Encourage of Adding y⁰ Conquest of Cannada to ye Glory of the British Empire In America this is a Design so Wise in y⁰ Contrivance, Carrying so benefitial A Prospect in its Consequences And Above all so Admirably founded upon y⁰ Noblest & Most Perfect Principall Your Maj⁰⁰ Most Ardent Zeale of making your Religion Eaqually with your trophies that we think ourselves In Duty Bound upon y⁰ Illustrous Occation to testify both our gratitude and Just Esteem of your Sacred Person & Administration May Conquests & Laurels Incircle Your Head & triumphs Attend your Glorious Arms till y⁰ King of Kings translate your Victorious Soul & seat it upon An Immoveable throne as y⁰ Reward of Your Vertuous Person While Incence is offered Your Memory upon Earth to Perfume & Preserve It fragrant During y⁰ succession of time

        Your Majesties Most Dutifull &
        obedient Subjects.

JAMES HONYMAN, *Minister.*
NICHO^s LANGE   ⎫ *Church*
THO^s LILLIBRIDGE ⎭ *Wardens*
WILL^M BRIGHT   ⎫ *Vestry.*
WILL^M GIBBS   ⎭

Newport Rhoad Island
  June y⁰ 20th 1709

To ye Queens Most Excellent Majestie

The Humble Address of the Ministers & People
belonging to ye Church on Rhoad Island in
America

Most Sacred Sovereign

Amidst the Acclamations of Your Dutifull Subjects &
tending Your Majes Glorious Reign [illegible] ye Bright Attractions of
[illegible] by grants to Reason and Christning Mankind in [illegible] an [illegible]
[illegible] Power to appear before Your Majes With our Most [illegible]
the Most Humble Thanks that [illegible] Your Majes has been Pleased to
[illegible] of adding ye Conquest of [illegible] to ye Glory of [illegible]
[illegible] will is at Design to [illegible] in ye [illegible] Carrying to Complete
the Prospect in its [illegible] [illegible] at [illegible] [illegible] upon ye
Noblest and Most Perfect Principall Your Majes Most Ardent Zeal of
Making Good Religion Equally [illegible] with true Prophet & [illegible] we [illegible]
the Island [illegible] Duty bound upon ye [illegible] occasion to [illegible] not our
Gratitude can Suffer Esteem if good [illegible] and ordinary [illegible] May ye
[illegible] and [illegible] Your Flag an triumph attend Your Glorious Arms
[illegible] ye King of Kings Crown Your Victorious [illegible] And [illegible]
an [illegible] Throne as ye [illegible] of Your [illegible] Pious [illegible]
[illegible] offered Your Memory Upon Earth to [illegible] and [illegible]
A fragrant [illegible] ye [illegible] of [illegible]

from Rhoad Island
June ye 20 1709

Newp^t Rhoad Island June y^e 30th 1709

Hon^b S^r

We beg Leave to Embrace this Occasion Most Humbly to thank your Hon^b for all your Kind Donations to our Church & more Espetially for y^e last because it is Most seasonable to Assist us in setting up our Bell Given by Her Maj^y & safely brought to our Hands We most Hartily Say ye Continuance of your favour & Encouragement to us Hopeing & Praying that Providence may Again Establish you in a capasity Eaquall to your Inclinations to Advance ye Interest & Hon^r of these Infant American Churches which Already owe so much to your bounty & Charity. We presume to transmit you ye Inclosed Address to ye Queen of Which we Intreat your Hon^{rs}. Care as well as Conveyance of this Letter to ye Lord Bishop of London which we have sent open to your Perusal to Inform your Honour of ye Resolution we have taken to Prevent all future Differences we are now to ask Pardon for this trouble & leave to subscribe,

May it Please your Hon^r
Your Hon^{rs} Most Obedient &
Obliedged Servants

JAMES HONYMAN
NICHO^s LANGE   } *Church*
THOS. LILLIEBRIDGE } *Wardens.*

To ye Honble Coll^d Francis^{ll}
Nicholson Att New York.

Sir Francis Nicholson is credited with being "the original founder and first principal patron of Trinity Church." He certainly was active and prominent in establishing the Church, and there is ample evidence that he was liberal in his gifts. In this respect, so far as is known, he quite surpassed all of its other benefactors, and the Minister and Church Wardens showed their grateful appreciation, not only of his gifts, but also of his ready aid, when they wished to reach the ear of the Queen, or of the Bishop of London.

The bell referred to hung in the tower from 1709 to 1740, when it cracked and was sent to London to be recast.

Newp^t on Rhoad Island.
June 30th 1709.

Revr^d Sir.

We having Present Occasion for that Money which was Left By Coll^{ot} Nicholson In your Hands some years since for ye use of our Church, We Desire you will order ye Payment of It as soon as Possible & when we know what it is & how & when Paid we shall transmit you a Receipt under our Hands.

We Expect your order this Post, & subscribe ourselves.

Your Very Humble Servants

JAMES HONYMAN
NICHO^s LANGE   } *Church*
THOM^s LILLIBRIDGE } *Wardens.*

To ye Reverend Mr. Sam^{ll} Myles,[12] Minister of Boston.

The desire to conquer Canada was not checked by the previous

---

[12]

Rev. Samuel Myles succeeded Rev. Mr. Radcliffe as minister of King's Chapel, Boston, June 29, 1689. He graduated at Harvard in 1684, officiated in King's Chapel for nearly thirty-nine years, and died in March, 1727-8. His father was Elder John Myles, who came from Wales and was a Baptist preacher. An Assistant, who was sent out to Mr. Myles from England, named Dansy, died on the passage, and Mr. Myles comforted the widow by marrying her.

"He was the oldest Episcopal minister of the town [at the time of his death]. The Rev. Mr. Honneyman, of Rhode Island; Mr. Plant, of Newbury; Mr. Piggot, of Marblehead; Mr. McSparran, of Narragansett; Mr. Miller, of Braintree; and Mr. Watts were bearers. The Rev. Mr. Cutter led the widow, the Rev. Mr. Harris walked before the corpse and buried it. The corpse was also followed by his Honor the Lieut.-Governor, and Council, the Justices and the Dissenting ministers of the town, with a vast number of gentlemen and merchants."—*The New England Weekly Journal.*

wants of success, and with enthusiasm a new expedition was fitted
out under Sir Francis Nicholson. It sailed for Port Royal September
18, 1710, and was crowned with success.   Letters of congratulation
were addressed to the Queen, and the commander of the expedition ;
and the Minister, and Church Wardens and Vestry were not behind-
hand in this grateful office.   They at once sent the following letter
to her Majesty :

To the Queen's Most Excellent Majesty
   The Humble Address of the Minister & Vestry of the Church
of England In Newport on Rhode Island In America

May it Please Your Majesty
   To Suffer us Your Majesties Most Loyall Subjects to Press the
throng of those who Dutifully Approach Your throne, With Ex-
ultations of Joy upon that uninterrupted series of Glorious success
Wherewith Heaven Has Crowned Your triumphant Arms Against
y* Common Enemy & Oppressor By Congratulating your Majesty
upon y* Reduction of Annapoles Royall to your Majesties Obedience Which as it is A very Great Enlargement of your Majesties
territories Abroad so it is so Valuable in itself that not so much the
Present Generation as unborn Posterity will Reap y* Happie Advantages of it, this new Conquest However Great In itselfe or Considerable with Regard to future Prospect Is Under y* Blessing of
Heaven in A Particular Manner Owing to y* Conduct & Resolution of y* Honble Coll^ot Francis Nicholson Whom Your Majestie
Wisely Chose to Command your troops on that Expedition For as
his very Name was y* Hope & Encouragement of His Followers so
His Presence & Wise Management struck such A horror in y*
Enemy as Made them Bow & tremble before Your Maj^es Victorious
Arms & Make A tame Surrender of so Strong A fortress as Ren-
dered all former Attempts Against it Fruitless & Unsuccessfull
We Desire Humbly to Adore y* Goodness of God In Blessing your
Majesties Forces With this success and Also to Acknowledg it y*
Peculiar Favour of Divine Providence to that Worthy Gentleman

Who had y* Honour to Command who has not Only Been y* Pious
founder of our Church but y* Most Generous & Munificent Patron
that Ever Religion Had In America May y* God of Peace Crown
all Your Majesties Designs With such success & Honour that the
universall Peace of Europe may Acknowledg You its umpire & Its
Guardian May y* Hosts of Heaven Encamp As Guards About
Your Majesty May y* secresie of y* Divine Presence be your Protection & Pavilion & May your Hands be Adorned with Eternall
Palms of Victory these are y* Incessant fervant supplications of

      May it Please Your Majesty
      Your Majesties Most Loyall Most
      Dutifull & Most obedient Subjects.

           JAMES HONYMAN, Min^r
           NICHO^s LANGE }
                           } *Churchwardens.*
           JOHN BROWN }
           WILL^M BARBUT
           JOHN BARKER

Newport on Rhoad
  Island in America
    Decr 12th 1710

There is nothing to show to whom the following letter was addressed, but there is internal evidence that it was to Sir Francis
Nicholson. The Altar Piece asked for was obtained, and had a
place in the Church. When the new church edifice, the present
structure, was raised in 1725, the altar piece was transferred to it,
and it remained within the chancel till after the evacuation of the
British, 1779, when some young men of the town, to whom the
arms of Great Britain (woven in with the design and made a part of
the carving) was an offence, tore it from its place, and took it to the
north part of the town, where it was set up for a target and demolished.

Newpt on Rhoad Island
Dec^b 12th 1710

Honble Sr

The Reflection on Your Former favors to us who Could Never Either Claim or Deserve them and ye unwearied Delight you Have of Doing Good forbid us to Doubt of Being forgiven for ye trouble we now Presume to Give You of Laying the Inclosed Address before Her Most Sacred Majesty With our Most Dutifull Regards for Her Person & Government. It is not any Flattering Panegyrick on Your Virtues but A tribute Due from us unto your Merit & ye only Monument of Gratitude we can Erect unto It.

to your other Kind Appearances for ye Interest & Honour of our Church we Also Most Humbly Intreat that this may be Added Namely that you Would Interceed with ye Honble Society for an Altar Piece for it [is] ye Only Ornament thats Wanting to finish & Compleat its Beauty we have Already sent ye Dimentions to Mr Chamberlain who It seems has Either Neglected or forgotten both it And us Which If you Will Procure & Assure us that you Continue your Favour to us as it Will be such A Durable Instance of your Piety as no time shall ever be Able to Efface so will it impress y^e Most Sensible & Most Lasting Signature of Esteem & Respect upon y^e Minds of

Honble S^r
Your Hon^s Most Obedient Humble Servants

JAMES HONYMAN
NICHO^s LANGE
J^o_n BROWN
Wm BARBUT
JOHN BARKER

July 26, 1713. John, Walter and Mary Cranston were baptized.[13]

November 29, 1713. Richard Munday[14] was married to Martha Simons by Rev. Mr. Honyman.

---

[13] They were the children of Governor Samuel Cranston.

[14] But little is known of Richard Munday other than that he was a most excellent builder. He built the Colony House (now State House) in

[The Church in Rhode Island in common with other offshoots of
the Church of England in America, desired to have a Bishop settled
in the Colonies, and early addressed both the Crown and the Society for the Propagation of the Gospel in Foreign Parts on the
subject. November 16, 1713, they wrote to the Queen:]

To the Queen's most Excellent Majesty, the Humble Petition &
address of the Minister & Church Wardens & Vestry of the Church
of England in Newport on Rhode Island in America.

Most Sacred Sovereign.

As Religion is your Majesties Greatest Ornament & Greatest
love, so you have given the World the most convincing Demonstra-
tions, that the advancement of it is your greatest care: which Happy
thought encourages us in these remote parts of your Dominions, to
the promoting the Great Interests of Which nothing can have a
Greater tendency than the Establishing among us that primitive form
of Church Government by Bishops, for were we so Happy as to
have them they would be of the Greatest Service to Religion, not
only by the necessary exercise of their sacred functions, in Conferring Holy Orders, Confirming our Children, Settling of Churches &
blessing us all in their master's name & by His Authority, but by
their presence influencing the Several Governments into the faithful
discharge of that part of their office, the Restraining of vice, &
encouraging virtue, awing the multitude into an observance of Religious duties, & Giving a Check to those licentious practices that
are so frequent abroad & which by reason of their distance are so
seldom observed and Condemned at Home, and therefore since Religion & virtue seems to languish in these Countreys, for want of
Bishops, We hope your Majesty in your Royal Wisdom & Goodness
will provide the proper Remedy, whereby it may revive & flourish.
We also embrace this opportunity of expressing our satisfaction &

1739, and a number of other buildings; and, as his name frequently appears in the records of the Church in connection with the care, repairs
and alterations of the present Church, erected in 1725, we may reasonably conjecture that he was its master builder.

returning your Majesty our most humble thanks for Giving it in
Commission to the Honble Francis Nicholson Esq.—to enquire into
the state of these American Churches.   For, as many of them owe
their very foundation to his pious Generosity, so we in a peculiar
manner must with a very deep sense of Gratitude acknowledge Him
our Chiefest Benefactor.   We beg to assure your Majesty that we
are with the most profound esteem

May it please your Majesty
Your Majesties most dutifull most loyall
& most obedient subjects.

JAMES HONYMAN
NATH : KAY
WILL : BARBUT
NICH : LANGE
THO : LILLIBRIDGE
DAN : AYRAULT
WILL : GIBBS.

Trinity Church in Newport,
    Novr 16th 1713.

[The same day the same committee addressed the following letter
to the Society for the Propagation of the Gospel in Foreign Parts :]

Right Honble & Right Reverend.

"Since our Church receives no Countenance or encouragement
from the Civil Government in this place, it's in vain to expect that it
will arrive at its Wished for Happiness without the Superintendency
of a Bishop in these parts, & therefore we join the other American
Churches, in their earnest desire for so Great a Blessing to us.

We return our most humble thanks for the care that is taken of
this place by the Supporting Religion in it.

"We shall pay the utmost deference to the power committed to
the Honble Francis Nicholson, Esq, Our most Generous Benefactor
& that not only in Obedience to your Commands, but out of a Re-

gard to that Gentlemans merit, which the Churches in these parts
are so much bound to value.

" We are with all possible respect & esteem

Right Honble & Right Reverend
Your most obedient humble servants

JAMES HONYMAN
NATH: KAY[15]
WILL: BARBUT
NICH: LANGE
THO: LILLIBRIDGE
DAN: AYRAULT
WILL: GIBBS

Trinity Church in Newport,
    Novr 16th 1713.

    Subscribed
To the Right Honble & Right Reverend
The Society for propagating the Gospel
in foreign parts.

---

[15] At the accession of Queen Anne Nathaniel Kay was sent to Rhode
Island as Collector of Customs, and took up his residence at Newport.
Here he built a house (on the lot next east of the Jewish Cemetery and ex-
tending to Catharine Street) and here he passed the remainder of his days,
dying in 1734, greatly beloved and deeply regretted. He was a benefactor
of the church while he lived, and at his death he made the following
bequest.:

I give and bequeath my dwelling house and coach house to my wife during her natural life: after which I bequeath both with my lots of land in
Rhode Island, and £400 in currency of New England, to build a school
house, to the Minister of the Church of England (Mr. Honyman) and the
Church Wardens and Vestry for the time being—that it is to say, upon
trust and confidence, and to the intent and purpose, benefit and use of a
school to teach ten poor boys their grammar and the mathematics gratis:
and to appoint a master at all times, as occasion or vacancy may happen,
who shall be Episcopally ordained, and assist the Minister, Episcopal, of
the Town of Newport, in some proper office, as they shall think most useful.

[The first volume of the Records of the Church is missing. The record of baptisms and marriages from 1709 has been preserved. On the first pages of that book the preceding letters have been recorded. From this point there is a break, with the exception of here and there an item of interest, down to 1731, when the records, though often scanty, appear to have been regularly made.]

December 1, 1716. Dr. Henry Hooper[16] was married to Mrs Remembrance Perkins.

December 20, 1716. Daniel Updike[17] was married to Sarah Arnold.

June 3, 1717. Franklin Morton[18] was married to Bathsheba Hunt, by Rev. Mr. Honyman.

Mr. Kay lies buried in the churchyard. On the side of the slab of slate that covers his remains are these lines :

"Joining to the south of this tomb lies Lucia Berkeley daughter of Dean Berkeley, obit the 5th of September 1731."

[16] This was Dr. Hooper, senior. He was a surgeon on board a privateer in the French War, and died February 17, 1757, aged 70 years. His son, of the same name and also a physician, died October 15, 1745, aged 29 years.

[17] was of Narragansett. He was Attorney-General of the Colony from 1722 to 1732, and King's Attorney for Kings County (now Washington County) from 1741 to 1743. Attorney-General from 1743 to 1757, and died on the 15th of May in that year. Updike in his " History of the Narragansett Church," says he married the daughter of Richard Smith, the first white person who settled in Narragansett ; but does not give the date or say whether it was a first or second marriage.

Col. Updike studied law and began to practice in Newport. He was the first signer of the constitution of the society out of which grew the Redwood Library.

[18] Dr. Frankland Morton, as his name should be written, was a physician in successful practice when he died, July 25, 1720, at the age of 34 years.

At a Vestry held at Trinity Church, in Newport, on the 18th day of September, 1719, present:

The Rever[d] Mr. James Honyman, *Minister.*

Mr. Daniel Ayrault,[19]
Mr. William Gibbs. } *Church Wardens.*

Mr. Adam Powell,[20]
Mr. Nathaniel Newdigate,[21]
Mr. John Brown,
Robert Gardner, } *Vestrymen.*

The underwritten instrument was presented and received.

Whereas, there has been no record made of the disposition of the pews in the above-mentioned church, which has been the cause of some misunderstanding among the members thereof, and to the end that all heats and animosities might be prevented for the future, and that we might keep the unity of the Spirit in the Bond of Peace, it is thought fit by this present Vestry, that there be due regulation made of all the pews in the said Church that are already taken up

---

[19] *Daniel Ayrault* son of Dr. Pierre Ayrault, was born about 1676–7, and, with other members of the family, came to Rhode Island from Rochelle, France. He was one of the settlers of French Town, East Greenwich, and from there removed to Newport. He married Marie Robineau, and the following is a copy of their marriage contract:

"Saturday, the seventeenth day of April, 1703. We the subscribers, Daniel Ayrault and Mary Robineau, do certify in the presence of the undersigned witnesses, that we are promised and do mutually engage each other the faith of holy matrimony. And to that end we engage all that we have or hope to have in this world, for the performance of our promise; desiring that God Almighty will give his blessing on our design, which is for His glory and the edification of our neighbors. Wherefore we are determined to consummate our marriage as soon as possible, according to the order of our Holy Discipline, and to be published the first time to-morrow in our church, according to custom, that all the congregation may

and disposed of; and also a standing rule for the disposition of those pews that are not yet disposed of, and in order thereunto it is voted and ordered as follows:

That there be a due record kept in the Church book of all the

---

be witnesses of the promise which we have made in the presence of Elias Neau, Mary Paré, Judith Robineau, the mother and daughter, Susannah Neau and Ezekiel Graziellier, the day and year above written.

DANIEL AYRAULT,   [SEAL]

MARIE ROBINEAU.   [SEAL]

" Signed and sealed in our presence,

    ELIAS NEAU,

    SUSANNA NEAU,

    JUDITH ROBINEAU,

    JUDITH ROBINEAU,

    EZEKIEL GRAZIELLIER."

The officiating clergyman was the Rev. Mr. Peret, probably a careless spelling of the name of the pastor of the French Church in New York, Peiret, who died in 1706.

Elias Neau was a vestryman in Trinity Church, New York, from 1705 to 1714. In 1704 he was appointed Catechist by the Society for the Propagation of the Gospel, with special reference to the education of Indians and Negroes in New York. He and his wife, Susannah, lie buried in Trinity Churchyard in that city.

Daniel Ayrault died June 25, 1764, and Marie, his wife, born June 28, 1684, died January 5, 1729.

[20] Adam Powell, a vestryman, was a merchant in Newport. He married, May 30, 1713, Hester Bernon, daughter of Gabriel Bernon In 1733 their daughter Elizabeth became the second wife of Rev. Samuel Seabury, who had been a Congregational minister, but who, through intercourse with Rev. Dr. McSparran, had become an Episcopal clergyman, and was appointed missionary to the church at New London, then in its infancy.

[21] The name of Nathaniel Newdigate first appears on the records in 1709. In 1728 he was one of the commissioners to revise the laws of the Colony. On his tombstone, in the old burying ground, there is this inscription:

"Here lieth Interred the Body of Nathaniel Newdigate Esq, late of Warwick in this Colony, who was born in Great Britain and died at War-

pews that are disposed of, to whom they are disposed to, for what sum they have been sold for, upon what condition they are disposed on, and that each pew be numbered and placed upon record, together with the person or person's name owning each pew, and the same method to be used for all pews that shall be disposed of in the said Church, from time to time ; and that there shall be a man appointed to keep the book of records, such as the Vestry shall think fit, and that he shall have the fee hereafter named, for his fidelity in the premises.

And to the end that all persons might be ascertained, on what account they hold their pews, it is ordered by the above said Vestry, that each pew that shall be purchased from the Minister, Church Wardens and Vestrymen, shall be his own right of inheritance, to him and his heirs forever, provided that him and his heirs are members of the Church and Constant Attendants on the services thereof: but if himself, or his heirs, should leave the Church, by any alteration of his or their opinion, or any other pretence whatsoever, for the space and time of seven years, then the said pew (at the expiration of the said seven years) shall return to the Church, and shall be disposed of as above said, for the benefit of the Church, and his, her, or their former right and property to the said pew, shall be wholly lost from him, her or them that were the former possessors thereof. Or if any family that is possessed of a pew, as above said, shall be wholly extinct ; in such case the right and property of the said pew shall wholly return to the said Church, and be disposed of as above said.

And if it should so happen that any person who is possessed of a pew in the said Church should die and leave an infant, whether son or daughter of his own, the executor or guardian of the said child, if he or they be a member of the Church, and has no pew of his own or their own, shall have the use of the said pew, for him or themselves to sit in till the child comes to the age of eighteen

---

wick the —— day of January, Anno Domini, 1740, in the 83d year of his age. He was a Noted and Famous Attorney at Law in this Colony, and acquitted himself in said Profession like an able, skilled and learned Gentleman."

years : provided that the child is brought up and educated according to the principles of the Church of England ; but if the executor or guardian of the child has an pew of his or their own, then, on the death of the parent or parents of the said child, the said pew shall be hired out by the Vestry, and the profits thereof be to the use and benefit of the said Church till the orphan arrive to the age above said. And if the said orphan should not be educated in the principles of the Church of England, and that he or she should arrive to the above said age, and then doth not declare him or herself to be a member of the Church of England, and attend constantly on the services thereof, or if the said orphan or orphans before he, she or they arrive to the aforesaid of eighteen years, then, and in all such cases, the right and property of the said pew shall return to the said Church, and be disposed of as the Vestry shall see fit, for the benefit of the Church.

And also that no person, nor persons that has purchased any pew in the said Church, shall have the liberty to let or hire any part thereof to any other person or persons whatsoever, for their own benefit but for the benefit of the Church, and the money for which it shall be let shall be paid to the Church Wardens, for the use aforesaid, and that no person or persons having a pew, shall sell or exchange his or their property in the said pew, but by the liberty and consent of the Vestry.

October 18, 1719. George Wanton,[22] son of Willian and Ruth Wanton, was baptized by Mr. Honyman.

October 25, 1719. Elizabeth and Abigail Wanton, daughters of George and Abigail Wanton, were baptized.

The following was the disposition of the pews in the Church in 1719.[23]

---

[22] George Wanton, son of Governor William Wanton, born August 24, 1694. Married Abigail Ellery, daughter of Benjamin Ellery, December 15, 1715.

[23] No plan or dimensions of the church have been preserved, but from the above it is evident that it was of very limited capacity. Allowing five persons to a pew, it afforded sittings for less than two hundred on

No.

No.		No.	
1.	Set apart for use of the Governor.[24]	17.	Madam Gidley.
2.	Mr. Neargrass.	18.	Madam Elizabeth Carr.
3.	Mr. Gibbs.	19.	John Martindale.
4.	Dr. Morton.	20.	Mr. Mackintosh.
5.	Benj. Shearman.	21.	Mrs. Margaret Wrighington.
6.	Geo. Goulding.	22.	Mr. Bull.
0.	The Minister's pew.	23.	Mr. Matthews.
7.	Mr. May.	24.	Daniel Ayrault.
8.	Thos. Lillibridge.	25.	Samuel Haydon.
9.	Gabriel Bernon.	26.	
10.	Richard Munday.	28.	
11.	Samuel Pike.	29.	Thomas Jones.
12.	Col. William Wanton.	30.	Robert Gardner.
13.	Mr. Neargrass.	31.	Jahleel Brenton.
14.	Capt. John Brown.	32.	Mr. Bright.
15.	John Cranston.	33.	Augustus Lucas.[29]
16.	Nathaniel Kay.	34.	Mr. Brinley.[27]
		35.	Capt. Joseph Arnold.

the lower floor, and that in a town with a population of 4640.* The gallery was probably confined to the west end of the building. The Governor's pew at that time was occupied by Governor Samuel Cranston. In the " Annals of King's Chapel," I., 377, there is this extract from the records of the church.

" Boston, April 29th, 1728, *voted:* That the Governor's pew be new lined with China, that the Cushions and Chairs be covered with crimson damask, and the curtains to the windows be of the same damask.

" The Governor's pew remained a unique property of King's Chapel."

The records of Trinity Church show this to be incorrect.

[24]

Gov. Samuel Cranston was elected governor in March, 1698, and remained in office up to the time of his death, April 26, 1727. He was the son of Governor John

* Census of 1730.

GALLERY.

Mr. Lange.	John Dickerson.
Mr. Paul.	Mr. Place.
Captain Flower.	John Davis.
Captain Freebody.	Adam Powell.

Cranston, elected 1678, and who also remained in office up to the time of his death, 1680.

"The death of Governor Cranston was no ordinary event in the history of the Colony. In the strength of his intellect, the courage and firmness of his administration, and the skill with which he conducted public affairs in every crisis, he resembled the early race of Rhode Islanders. Thirty times successively chosen to the highest office, he preserved his popularity amidst political convulsions that had swept away every other official in the Colony. He was the connecting link between two centuries of its history, and seemed, as it were, the bridge over which it passed in safety, from the long struggle with the royal governors of Massachusetts, to the peaceful possession of its chartered rights under the House of Hanover. The piratical period, the strife about the acts of trade, the desperate efforts of Bellomont and his successors, a long and exhausting foreign war, and two bitter boundary disputes, involving the largest portion of the Colony, one of which he lived to see favorably and finally settled, were some of the perplexing questions of his administration."—*Arnold's History of Rhode Island.*

[26] Augustus Lucas was a French emigrant, who settled in Newport. His first wife died here in 1698. His second wife was Barsheba, daughter of Joseph Eliot, and granddaughter of Eliot the Indian apostle. Their daughter Barsheba married Augustus Johnston, who was later Attorney-General of the Colony. After the death of Johnston she became the wife of Matthew Robinson, who was known as a man of erudition and a skilful lawyer.

[27] *Fras. Brinley* the first of the name who came to America, was born in England in 1690. His grandson, Francis Brinley, educated at Eaton College, came to Newport by the invitation of his grandfather, who made him his heir. He was admitted a freeman June 20, 1713. From Newport he removed to Boston, where, in 1723, he was a Warden in King's Chapel.

CHAPTER II.

1719–1731.

In the proceedings of the Society for the Propagation of the Gospel in Foreign Parts there are these entries under date of 1720 to 1721.

" Mr. Honyman, missionary at Newport, Rhode Island, reported that he preached twice every Sunday, catechises twice a week, and administers sacrament every month, and has baptized in about two years seventy-three persons, of whom nineteen are adults.

" The Rev. Mr Honyman, minister of Rhode Island in New England reports, ' That he had been lately to preach at Providence, a town in the Colony, to the greatest number of people he ever had together since he came to America ; that no house being able to hold them, he was obliged to preach in the fields ; that they are getting subscriptions for building a Church, and he doubts not there will be a considerable congregation."[25a]

May 14, 1721.   James Cranston was married to Mary Ayrault.[26]

[25a] At this time Mr. Honyman occasionally performed Divine service in the Narragansett Church, and administered the rite of baptism, and the Lord's Supper.   Rev. Mr. Gay had been appointed missionary in this section, but did not remain long, and the Society in England, in compliance with the petition from the people in Narragansett for a missionary, sent them Rev. James McSparran in 1721, who entered upon his duties with zeal, and soon acquired great influence for good.

[26] Mary Ayrault was the daughter of Daniel Ayrault, born at East Greenwich, February 16, 1704, and died in Newport, March 25, 1764. After the death of Cranston she married George Goulding, and survived him.

At a Vestry sitting in the Church, May 15, 1721, Nathaniel Newdigate and Adam Powell were elected Church Wardens; and Nathaniel Kay, Robert Gardner, Captain John Brown, Daniel Ayrault,
and George Piggott, Vestrymen.

It was ordered that a letter then and there subscribed by the Minister, Church Wardens and Vestry, be sent home to the Society's
Secretary [Society for the Propagation of the Gospel] for encouragement for a schoolmaster.[28]

At a Vestry sitting in the Church, March 22, 1722, Adam Pow-
ell and William Coddington were elected Church Wardens, and
Henry Bull, Thomas Flower, George Wanton, Godfrey Malbone,
John Freebody and Edward Neargrass, Vestrymen.

It was ordered that the Church Wardens have the pavement before the Church completed; they were also to see that leather
cushions were provided for the altar. Further instructions embraced the putting of " a post and rail fence at the end of the lane[30]

---

[28] As early as 1710 the people of Newport gave attention to the education of their children by establishing a public school, and placing it
under the Town Council; and a Latin school was opened in 1716. Portsmouth, " having considered how excellent an ornament learning is to
mankind and the great necessity there is in building a public school-
house," appointed a committee to put up such a building and obtain a
subscription to furnish it. Mr. Kay, one of the Vestry (and probably
other members were of the same mind), took a lively interest in the subject of education, and when he died he made a liberal bequest to the
Church to promote so good a cause.

[30] Church street, from Thames street to Spring street, is defined on the
John Mumford map of Newport, 1713; but for more than seventy years
after that date it was known as Honyman's lane, and was so designated
on deeds of conveyance. Rev. Mr. Honyman occupied the house on the
south corner of Thames and Church streets, and his widow resided there
after him. James Honyman, the son, owned real estate on the north
side of Church street, which descended to his heirs. We may reasonably
believe that Rev. Mr. Honyman bought a tract running through from

leading up to the Church," and in the fence there was to be a turnstile.

Ordered that Mr. James Martin have the pew that was Mr. Neargrass's, he paying.

May 22, 1722. The Rev. James McSparran[31] was married to Miss Hannah Gardiner, daughter of William Gardiner, of Boston Neck, in Narragansett, by the Rev. James Honyman, in St. Paul's Church.

October 11, 1722. William Coddington[32] was married to Jean Bernon.

January 3, 1723. William Ellery[33] was married to Ann Almy.

Thames street to Spring street, bounded on the south by Frank street, and on the north by the Brenton estate; that a part was set off for the Church, and that the remainder was disposed of from time to time by himself and heirs. The records of that period are lost.

[31] For an interesting account of Rev. James McSparran, and his labors as missionary in the Narragansett Country, see Updike's Narragansett Church. Mrs. McSparran died in England, June 24, 1755, of smallpox, and was buried in Broadway Chapel burying-ground, Westminster. Dr. McSparran, in making entry of her death, said of her: "She was the most pious woman, the best of wives in the world, and died, as she deserved to be, much lamented."

[32] was the son of Thos. and Mary Coddington, and a grandson of Gov. Wm. Coddington. He was born January 1, 1690, and was accidentally killed with others, by a gunpowder explosion, September 17, 1744, in Newport. His first wife was Comfort Arnold, eldest daughter of Gov. Benedict Arnold; his second wife was the above Jean Bernon, daughter of Gabriel Bernon. The following year he was elected Senior Warden of the Church. It was to Col. Coddington that Rev. John Callender dedicated his Century Sermon, 1738.

In August, 1737, Col. Coddington and his wife, on their removal from Newport, were admitted to St. Paul's, Narragansett, by Rev. James McSparran.

[33] William Ellery was born at Bristol, October 31, 1701, and died at ·

The Church prospered; the labors of Mr. Honyman to advance its interests and increase the number of its adherents had met with the most gratifying success, and the subject of a larger and more imposing Church edifice naturally engaged their attention. A subscription paper was started, headed by Mr. Honyman with a subscription of £30 (his stipend was but £70), which must have excited the emulation of his followers, for they were not long in raising a sufficient sum to warrant them in breaking ground. How the work went on may be gathered from the following minutes of the proceedings of the Society for the Propagation of the Gospel in Foreign Parts, on which alone we must depend for the facts, the Church record of that period having been lost.

In 1721 Mr. Honyman " reported that he preached twice every Sunday, catechises twice a week, administers sacrament every month, and has baptised in about two years past seventy-three persons, of whom nineteen are adults."

The following year he reported: " That he had been lately to preach at Providence, a town in that Colony, to the greatest number of people he had ever had together since he had came to America; that no house being able to hold them, he was obliged to preach in the fields; that they are getting subscriptions for building a church, and he doubts not but there will be a considerable congregation."

In 1723 Mr. Honyman reported, " that within two years past he hath baptised eighty-two, of which nineteen were adults, three of them negroes, two Indians, and two mulatos; that there are properly belonging to that Church above fifty communicants, that live in that place, exclusive of strangers; that the people growing too numerous for the church, and others offering to join them if they could be ac-

Newport, March 15, 1764. He was the father of the patriot of the same name, who was his third son. His wife, Ann (Lawton) Almy, was born in Portsmouth, August 1, 1703, and died in Newport, July 13, 1783.

commodated with room, he proposed the building of a new church, and has obtained near £1000 subscriptions for that purpose, though it is supposed the building will cost twice that money ; that the materials are getting ready, and the workmen will begin upon them in the spring."

In 1725 he reported to the Society "that his congregation has very much increased; that they are now building a large new church ; that in the year 1724 he baptised forty-three, among which were eight adults, six of them negroes and Indians, and one Indian child."

In 1746, when some litigation was going on between the Church and a pew owner, Rev. Mr. Honyman furnished the following information, drawn from the records then extant.[34]

Monday, Dec. 6, 1725.

" At a meeting of the Minister, Church Wardens and Vestry of Trinity Church, in the new Church this day, it was agreed that the said work should be carried on with all convenient despatch, and that a Plaisterer should be sent for from Boston for greater certainty of having it handsomely Plaistered, and that the best and most practical method of raising Money to defray the necessary charges of the s[d] building was by laying out the Pews that may amt. in the whole to the sum of money wanted to complete the whole Church as near as possible : and, further, that the whole congregation should meet in s[d] Church on Wednesday morning next, where every one desirous of a Pew may be accommodated, he paying the price set upon s[d] Pew, at least one half in hand, or in two months from that date, and the other half at or before the compleat finish of the Pews and the whole Church : according to which resolution all those who do not pay their Money down for the Pews are desired by the

---

[34] This paper was lost by some accident, and was not recovered till 1798, when it was found by Mr. Christopher Champlin, who gave it to the Vestry, which body had it attached to the records of the Church, reference being had to it, with the above statement, on page 231 of the records.

Committee to sign their names against the number of the Pews they choose, to prevent disorder and misunderstanding, as well as to ascertain the payment of the several sums mark'd on their Pews, as followeth :

"Wednesday, December 8, 1725, the Majority of the males of the Church Congregation being present, was read in an audiable voice the Committee's last resolution, and also the s^d Conditions upon which the pews in said Church were to be disposed of and bought, viz.:

" 1st. That the Pew purchased shall belong to the purchaser and his heirs forever, he and they adhering to the Doctrine and discipline of the Church of England.

" 2^d. That in case the purchaser or his Successor, in his own or any other right, shall desert the Church, or join himself to any other Society, shall forfeit all title or claim to that Pew, which in such case shall revert to the Church, for a new disposition.

" 3^d. That if a purchaser or his heirs shall leave the Town, they shall be allowed to dispose of their Pew to such as the Minister, Church Wardens or Vestry shall approve of, he or they having first given the offer to them at the first cost.

" 4th. That in case of the death of a purchaser, without heirs of his body, or name in his will, the Pew shall revert to the Church for a new disposition.

" Last. That the aforesaid rules shall be recorded in the Church books and become binding Laws to all concerned.

" This may certify that the aforewritten is a true Copy of the regulation of the Pews in Trinity Church in Newport, in the Colony of Rhode Island, made on the 6th and 8th days of December, 1725, as the same now stands recorded in the Church Books, which was compared this 24 day of June, Anno. Dom., 1746, by me."

James Honyman

July 21, 1725, the New England clergy met at Newport to confer together and take council of each other, when a letter to the Secretary of the Society was prepared and forwarded to him, making known the difficulties under which they labored, and urging that a Bishop might be sent to them.

" We humbly conceive," said they, " nothing can more effectually redress these grievances and protect us from the insults of our adversaries than an Orthodox and Loyal Bishop residing with us, and at this time are awakened to such a thought by the coming over of Dr. Welton, late of White Chapel, who has privately received the Episcopal character in England, and from whose influence and industry we have reason to fear very unhappy consequences on the peace of the Church and the affections of this Country to our most excellent constitution, and his most sacred Majesty's Person and Government.   Not only those who profess themselves Churchmen long and pray for the great blessing of a worthy Bishop with us, but also multitudes of those who are well-wishers to us, but are kept concealed for want hereof, and immediately appear and form many congregations too.   If once this happiness were granted, this would supply us with many useful Ministers from among ourselves, whom the hazards of the sea and seasickness, and *the charges* of travel discourage from the service of the Church and tempt them to enlist themselves as Members or Ministers of Dissenting Congregations. Our people might receive the great benefit of Confirmation, the usefulness whereof we preach and they are deeply sensible."

" Signed by Messrs. Cutler, Honyman, McSparran, Plant, Pigot and Jopson.   Mr. Myles was absent, not being able to bear the fatigue of the journey, and Mr. Usher [35] not only failed to sign the letter, but abruptly left the convention."—*Annals of King's Chapel,* I., 338.

---

[35] Rev. Mr. Usher was sent as missionary to Bristol, and he was to have a stipend of £60 per annum.   At Bristol he was cordially received, and entered upon the duties of his mission with zeal and faithfulness.   But he was not permitted to enjoy the emoluments of his office to the full; for it appears from a vote passed in 1731, that he was required to support all the widows of the Church (St. Michael's) from what he received as his own salary.   **Mr.** Usher's ministry was very successful.

In 1726 word was received by the Society, from Rev. Mr. Honyman, "Acquainting that the new church there is nigh finished, and will be ready for the Society's present as soon as it can be sent (which present is a plain purple communion cloth, pulpit cloth, and cushion), and that the people had given the old Church, with all its furniture, to a neighboring place, where they conceive it will be of great use."[35a]

[35a] The building was given to a congregation gathered at Warwick, but having no Church of their own. Although it was taken down and carried there, it does not appear that the materials were ever put together again. There is a tradition that it was floated from Newport to Warwick, but for this there is no warrant.

The following interesting letter from Rev. James McSparran is taken from Rev. Dr. Hallam's "Annals of St. James's Church," New London:

Narraganset, March 21 1725–6

Gentlemen. Pursuant to y* advice of Feb. 25th, I went to Newport y° next monday & the Committee for building their new Church being acquainted with my business, met y' evening at Mr. Honeyman's house, to whom having Proposed when & upon what Terms they would Part with the old Church, they came to the unanimous Result, that Provided the Gentlemen of New London would take down, Transport, Erect & Finish the Church at New London, & Expect no assistance from them, they should have it & all its appurtenances Gratis: except the altar piece, which was expected to be given to Narraganset. Next day one or Two at most y' are not of the Committee objected against parting it with it upon Terms: w^t Those Terms will be when their Congregation meets (if ever it meets) to Consult upon y' affair, I am as yet unable to advise you. In y* mean time Gentlemen, I would have you make no offer: for should the few y' are for parting with y° old Church upon Terms Prevail (wch I can hardly think) yet must the price they Set be governed by y° advantage their old Church will be to themselves, if you have it not; & not by the Benefit it will be of to you if ye have it. These things, therefore, Let me Propose to be distinctly & maturely Considered by you the Committee.

(1.) If you have their Church you must Send the Carpenters you Intend to Raise it to pull it down for the Timber must be marked all anew, & some

[At the Convention held in King's Chapel, Boston, this year, 1726, Rev. Mr. Honyman preached the sermon, which sermon was printed in Boston in 1733.]

---

new ones there will be wanting in the roof & other places; & although the Carpenter I Consulted, viz. Monday, Said the Charge of pulling it down would be £50, yet the Gentlemen themselves concluded it will be more, & I believe you may Venture to Lay the Charge of taking Safely down, Carting to ye water, putting aboard and Transportation at £500.

(2.) You will by this Church, whether Given or Sold, save no Boards, Nails, Plank Nails, Clift Boards & Nails, Shingles nor Lath Nails. Its like a few, & but a few, Plank & Boards will be Saved; it will save you no Shingles Clift Boards, Laths, lime nor Window Frames.

(3.) If you have the New Port Church you will then be under an absolute necessity of conforming to ye dimensions of said Church, both as to the House & Belfry. Now, it may be, Gentlemen, you will think a less Fabrick will do ye Turn wch if Built Square, may in time be Lengthened & Enlarged.

(4.) By this Church you will Save Something in the Pews, Pulpit, & Communion Table. You will do well, therefore, to Consider of the Dimensions of ye Church (in case you Cannot obtain this) & See w^t ye frame & materials of all Sorts will Cost, and w^t the workmen will demand to finish ye same, without wch you cannot know when you are well offered, Should the Gentlemen here send you up their Terms. As to a Subtreasurer, I have determined Mr. Shackmaple for y^t Trouble, & you will wth all Convenient Speed, I hope, Pay in the Several Sums annexed to your Names, y^t there may be a beginning; you have given a good & Encouraging Example in ye Subscription, & the like is Equally needful in paying them In to the Treasurer; by this others not of ye Committee will be animated, not only to Subscribe, but to make ready pay, for I must beg leave to tell you y^t I think it absolutely necessary there be some money Lodged before the building is begun, Leest if Some Consequences y^t may Reflect Dishonor upon ye undertaking in So Captious a Country as yours is. The motion made by the Committee hindered me from any Farther Progress then, you See, with ye Subscription Paper, but I may Venture to assure you y^t should the old Church be denied you Gratis, Severall of ye Gentlemen will think themselves bound in honor to Contribute to ye Assistance, &, for w^t I know, y^t method may be Equally beneficial to You.

September 1, 1726–7. Thomas Wickham, adult, was baptized, and June 3, 1730, his son, bearing his name, was baptized.

July 30, 1727. George Johnson[36] was married to Bathsheba Lucas.

August 3, 1827. Richard Mumford[37] was married to Sarah Newdigate.

October 10, 1728. John Gidley[38] was married to Mary Cranston, daughter of Colonel John Cranston.

I have Enclosed the Deed, there being no Difficulty in Drawing a proper Conveyance from Mr. Mumford to the use of the Church, for the Deed from him must be to 3, 4, 5, or 6 of you by name, in trust, for said use; with a Clause therein inserted, obliging the Gentlemen therein named, y^t so soon as a Minister of the Established Church comes & is Settled amongst you, & has Erected & Incorporated a Vestry, they make Conveyance of said land & Edifice thereon built to the Church Wardens by name, & their Successors for Ever in Said Office for said Use. I should have Waited on you My Self the Last Sunday of y^t Instant, but having no Horse, & being shortly to go to Boston, hope you will Excuse my Absence. I have no more to add, but the tender of my Best Respects, wch please to Accept from, Gentlemen, y^r most Obedient Humble Servant.

JAMES McSPARRAN.

[36] The name should be Johnston. Their son, Augustus, became the Attorney-General of the Colony.

[37] Richard Mumford was given the command of one of the companies raised in 1745 for the reduction of Louisburg, but dying in October of that year, the command passed to his First Lieutenant, Edward Cole, who became a distinguished officer.

[38] John Gidley was the son of John Gidley, Judge of the Vice-Admiralty Court, who came to Newport from Exon, in Devon, and died here in 1710. John Gidley, the son, was accidentally killed in September, 1744, His first wife was Sarah Shackmaple, daughter of John Shackmaple, of New London, where he was a man of prominence. She died May 12, 1727. His second wife was the above-named Mary Cranston. She died October 3, 1733, aged 24 years. His third wife was Elizabeth Brown, daughter of Captain John Brown. In 1742–3 the Judge of Admiralty having gone to England, John Gidley was appointed in his place till the king's will could be known.

[The year 1729 opened with an event of great interest to the Church—the arrival in America of Rev. George Berkeley, Dean of Derry, who, on his return to England, after a stay of nearly three years on this Island, was made Lord Bishop of Cloyne. The object of his visit to America, and the events connected with his life on this Island, are so well known that I need not here recall them. The circumstances attending his landing at Newport, January 23d, after a passage of five months, are thus given in " Bull's Memoir of Rhode Island ":]

" The ship ran into the west passage, and came to anchor. The dean wrote a letter to Mr. Honyman (Rector of Trinity Church), which the pilots took on shore at Conanicut Island, and called upon a Mr. Gardner and Mr. Martin, two members of Mr. Honyman's Church, informing them that a great dignitary of the Church of England, called Dean, was on board the ship, together with other gentlemen passengers. They handed them the letter from the dean, which Gardner and Martin brought to Newport in a small boat, with all possible dispatch. On their arrival they found Mr. Honyman at Church, it being a holyday on which divine service was held there. They then sent the letter by a servant, who delivered it to Mr. Honyman in the pulpit. He opened it and read it to the congregation, from the contents of which it appeared the dean might be expected to land in Newport every moment. The Church was dismissed with a blessing, and Mr. Honyman, with the wardens, vestry and congregation, male and female, repaired immediately to the Ferry Wharf, where they arrived a little before the dean, his family and friends."

[Dean Berkeley found in Newport a congenial society, and a residence here delightful. He bought about one hundred acres of land, built a house and called the place Whitehall, a name that it still retains. How well pleased he was with his surroundings, within three months of his landing, is shown in a letter to Thomas Prior.]

Newport, on Rhode Island, April 24, 1729.

I can by this time say something to you, from my own experience, of this place and people. The inhabitants are of a mixed kind, consisting of many sects and sub-divisions of sects. Here are four sorts of Anabaptists, besides Presbyterians, Quakers, Independents, and many of no profession at all. Nothwithstanding so many differences, here are fewer quarrels about religion than elsewhere, the people living peaceably with their neighbors of whatsoever persuasion. They all agree in one point, that the Church of England is the second best. The island is pleasantly laid out in hills and vales, and rising ground; hath plenty of excellent springs, and fine rivulets, and many delightful landscapes of rocks, and promontories, and adjacent lands.

The town of Newport is the most thriving place in all America, for business. It is very pretty and pleasantly situated; I was never more agreeably surprised, than at the first sight of the town and harbor.

March 12, 1729. Major Fairchild[39] was married to Bathsheba Palmer.

May 27, 1729. William Mumford[40] was married to Elizabeth Honyman by Dean Berkeley.

------

[39] The "Major" was Fairchild's Christian name, and not a title. In an old deed he is styled "cooper." He was engaged in trade, chiefly commercial, and his daughter Ann became the wife of Metcalf Bowler. With Bowler he was engaged in commercial enterprises. October 28, 1764, he married Katharine Malbone, daughter of Godfrey Malbone, who became his second wife.

[40] William Mumford was put in command of Fort George in 1756, and he was also in command in 1759. Elizabeth Honyman, who became his wife, was the only daughter of Rev. James Honyman. Her married life was short, for she died on the 21st of July, 1730, in her 24th year. Her remains lie buried in the churchyard, by the side of those of her father and mother. This is the only entry in the Church records of a marriage by Dean Berkeley during his residence on the Island, and it was a graceful tribute to him on the part of Mr. Honyman to ask him to marry his daughter.

June 12, 1729. David Chesebrough was married to Abigail Rogers.[41]

September 21, 1729. Henry Barclay [Berkeley] son of Dean Barclay, was baptized by his father, and received into the Church.

September 25, 1729. Captain Robert Oliver[42] was married to Mary Dunbar.

There are no entries for 1730, and, in fact, much of the material brought together in these pages up to this date was gathered from other sources than the Church records. The record of baptisms and marriages is fairly well preserved, but there is no record of deaths up to this period. From 1731 the records go on regularly, but are far from minute in their details; and when we come down to the revolution there are gaps that cannot now be filled. The services of the Church were kept up, and when the town was taken possession of by the British they were continued the same, for the minister, Rev. George Bisset, was a loyalist. Other places of worship were desecrated and turned into stables, but that of the Church of England was kept from such defilement.

An interesting event connected with the stay of Dean Berkeley on the Island was the formation, in 1730, of the Philosophical Society, out of which, ultimately, grew the Redwood Library. The influence of Berkeley was felt long after his departure. His personal friends, who joined him in the formation of the society, were Daniel

----

[41] Mrs. Chesebrough died in Newport in 1737. Mr. Chesebrough's second wife was Margaret Sylvester, of whom there is a portrait extant painted by Blackburn, the second artist who came to America. Mr. Chesebrough removed to Stonington, and died there in March, 1782. His daughter Abigail, by his first wife, married Alexander Grant, oldest son of Sir Alexander Grant, of Scotland. In the Newport *Mercury* of September 11, 1775, it was announced that " The Hon. Mrs. Abigail Grant, lady of Sir Alexander Grant, arrived at Newport from London *via* New York."

[42] Captain Robert Oliver was an active and widely-known commander, in his day, in the mercantile marine.

Updike, the Attorney-General of the Colony, James Searing, Judge Edward Scott, Henry Collins, Nathan Townsend, Jr., James Honyman, Jr., Jeremy Condy, Samuel Wickham, Thomas Ward, Josiah Lyndon, John Callender, Jr., Sueton Grant, Dr. John Brett, Captain Charles Bardin, Hezekiah Carpenter, Joshua Jacobs, Joseph Sylvester, John Checkley, Jr., William Ellery, John Adams, Daniel Hubbard, John Wallace, Stephen Hopkins and Samuel Johnston, nearly all of them men whose influence was commanding.

Dean Berkeley, realizing that in all probability there would be some delay in securing the grant that would enable him to establish the projected college at Bermuda (the object of his visit to America), prepared to make himself comfortable during his stay by buying a farm of ninety-six acres and building thereon a modest house, which he called Whitehall. There he resided till the autumn of 1731, when, in September, he embarked from Boston for England. After his return to England he gave Whitehall to Yale College with a valuable collection of books, a list of which may be found in an article on "Bishop Berkeley's Gifts to Yale College," by Daniel C. Gilman, Vol. I. of "Papers of the New Haven Colony Historical Society." He also gave valuable books to Harvard College and Trinity Church, Newport. To the Church he gave seventy-five volumes, some of which are still in the possession of the Church, with many of the volumes sent out by the Society for the Propagation of the Gospel in Foreign Parts when the parish was in its infancy.

WHITEHALL.

CHAPTER III.

1731–1737.

THE officers of the Church on the 5th day of July, 1731, were:

Rev. James Honyman, *Minister.*
Captain William Wanton, } *Church Wardens.*
Captain Jonathan Thurston, }

Vestry.—Nathaniel Kay, Col. William Wanton, Capt. John Brown, Col. Wm. Coddington, George Goulding, Daniel Ayrault, Col. William Whiting, Capt. John Freebody, Capt. Henry Bull, Capt. Godfrey Malbone, Capt. John Brown, Jr., Capt. John Chase, Jahleel Brenton, Jr., Daniel Updike, John Gidley, Peter Bours, and James Martin.

James Martin was appointed Clerk of the Vestry.

Ordered: that the Church Wardens do all things necessary for the repairing of the bell, and have the fence and gates painted.

Ordered : that Captain Robert Elliot[43] be invested with the property of the pew No. 30, for the consideration of £50, he paying the same within a month, or else the pew to be returned.

Thomas Salter to have pew No. 20 in the gallery, he paying for the same £12.10.

Voted : that the Vestry meet the first Tuesday in every second month ensuing.

On the 11th of June of this year, Dean Berkeley baptized three of his negroes, " Philip, Anthony and Agnes Berkeley."

August 27, 1731. Nathaniel Kay, Esq., is desired to write to Mr. Richard Munday to meet the Vestry on Monday next at 11 o'clock, in the forenoon, at the Church, to consider about repairing the steeple.[44]

---

[43] Capt. Robert Elliot was married to Almy Coggeshall, by Mr. Honyman, January 1, 1730. His second wife was Abigail Searing, to whom he was married July 21, 1765. Immediately after the Declaration of Independence, he was appointed a Captain of Artillery, and did service in that capacity. He was a Deputy from Newport to the General Assembly; subsequently he was appointed Intendant of Trade for Newport, and died in 1781, while holding that office.

[44] There is nothing to show who built the Church edifice, but, apart from the prominence of Richard Munday as a builder, his connection with the Church, and the manner in which he was frequently called upon to examine the structure and make good the defects that from time to time appeared, leads to the conclusion that the edifice was built under his supervision. The plans were evidently sent out from England. The general features of the interior are not unlike those of St. James, London. The details are of the colonial period ; the groined ceiling is remarkably fine ; the pulpit, reading desk and clerk's desk stand out in the body of the Church, the pulpit being reached by a high flight of stairs, with spiral newel and balusters. Over the pulpit there hangs a graceful sounding-board. The chancel, elliptical in form, is shallow, and not more than nine or ten can kneel at the rail at a time. The organ is in the gallery, at the opposite end of the Church. The pews are square, with high, straight backs.

Voted: that the Church Wardens do forthwith have an air-hole made in the under-pinning of the Church, to prevent the same from rotting.[44a]

Voted: that Capt. John Chase and Mr. George Dunbar be desired to assist the Church Wardens in providing and getting materials for repairing the steeple, and other things necessary for the Church.

August 30, 1731. Voted: that the committee appointed for the repairing of the steeple do agree with some person for the doing thereof as they shall think proper, with the advice of Mr. Richard Munday, and provide materials for the same.[45]

September 5, 1731. Lucia Berkeley, daughter (an infant) of Dean Berkeley, died, and was buried in the churchyard, just south of the grave of Nathaniel Kay. She was baptized by her father on the 24th of the previous August.

Voted: that Sarah Velvin be invested in the property of the northwest corner pew of the five new pews lately built, she having paid for the same the sum of £10 to Capt. William Wanton.[46]

[44a] No provision was made for a cellar when the Church was built, and the only means of ventilating the beams is by "air-holes" in the low foundation. A few years ago so much of the earth was removed as was necessary to admit of setting a couple of furnaces, now used to heat the Church.

[45] From this and other like entries from time to time it is evident that, while the edifice was so far finished when it was said to be complete, in 1726, as to admit of its being used for services, only pews enough had been provided for the actual wants of the congregation at that day, and that from time to time other pews were built and disposed of to applicants.

[46] Captain William Wanton, the Senior Warden, was, like many other members of the Wanton family, a distinguished man. The manner of his becoming an Episcopalian is a tradition, one that is generally received as correct. The son of a Quaker preacher, Edward Wanton, he was himself a Quaker. He fell in love with Ruth Bryant, the beautiful and accomplished daughter of Deacon John Bryant, of Scituate, Mass., an

September 23, 1731.   James Honyman[47] was married to Elizabeth Goulding.

March 21, 1732.   It is agreed that Capt. John Chace, Capt. George Wanton, and James Martin do audit and inspect all the ac-

uncompromising Presbyterian, who would not listen to such a connection. When out spake William Wanton, and said: "Ruth, I am sure we were made for each other; let us break away from this unreasonable bondage. I will give up my religion and thou shalt give up thine, and we will go to the Church of England and the devil together."

The public services that William Wanton rendered the Colony, and his valiant deeds in his early manhood, have been recorded.   To the Church both he and his wife became devoted.   In 1732 he was elected Governor of the Colony, and died while in office, in January, 1733, aged 63 years.

[47] J. Honyman was the son of Rev. James Honyman, Minister of Trinity Church.   He was born at Newport, and was educated for the Bar.   In 1732 he was elected Attorney-General of the Colony, which office he held till 1741, when the election of County Attorneys was introduced, when he held the office of King's Attorney for two years.   He was one of the committee on the boundary question between Rhode Island and Massachusetts, and was appointed, with Governor Hopkins and George Brown, to attend the Congress of Governors and Commissioners of the Northern Colonies, called by Lord Loudoun, and held in Boston, to devise measures for the defeat of the enemy.   In 1756 he was elected First Assistant of the Colony, and was re-elected up to 1764; but when the Legislature remonstrated against the rule of 1756 (which rule occasioned great losses and great irritation in the Colonies) he declined a re-election.

Shortly after this event, Mr. Honyman was appointed King's Advocate for the Court of Vice Admiralty in Rhode Island, and retained the appointment up to the breaking out of the revolution.   In that struggle and when hostilities began, he offered to give up his commission, if the Legislature desired him to do so.   The Legislature so desired, and his commission was delivered to the Governor, to be lodged in the Secretary's office.

Mr. Honyman had an extensive and lucrative practice when the war broke out.   He did not leave the Island on the approach of the British, but remained here, and here died February 15, 1788, aged 67 years.

counts, beginning with the committee for building, and pass accounts from one to the other, and to make a final end thereof, with a return of the same to the Vestry next Easter Tuesday.

It is agreed and ordered that Mr. Edward Scott and Mr. James Honyman, Jr., be desired to go about, in order to collect what money they can for and towards the support and assistance of Mr. Beach,[48] a gentleman of Connecticut, who is going to London to have Episcopal ordination, and make a return of their doings herein next Easter Tuesday.

At an Annual Meeting of the Vestry, for the choice of Church officers, on Easter Monday, being the 10th of April, 1732, Captain Jonathan Thurston and James Martin were chosen Church Wardens.

Voted: that Mr. James Allen, Captain Samuel Wickham, and Mr. Edward Scott be admitted members of the Vestry for said Trinity Church.

Adjourned Meeting, April 11, 1732. William Weston has agreed to take £44 for the balance of his account for the fence around the churchyard, and gates thereto, in full.

It is the opinion of the Vestry that he allow to the Church the sum of thirty pounds for the ground where he has erected his vault in the churchyard.[49]

Mr. Peter Bours, Capt. Godfrey Malbone,[50] Mr. Edward Scott [51]

---

[48] Mr. John Beach went to England to receive Holy Orders, returned in September, 1732 and began his labors as Missionary, at Newtown, Ct. He had been a preacher sixty years when he died, in 1782. In 1772 he stated that in forty years he had lost but two Sundays through sickness.

[49] There is no trace at the present day of any such vault.

[50] *Godfrey Mallbone* was a native of Princess Anne County, Virginia. He came to Newport about 1700, and here settled. The tradition is that he had a strong desire to follow the sea, and to this end bound him-

and Captain George Wanton do agree to gather in the subscriptions
quarterly, as they become due, each man in his turn, as they are
above named.

Ordered: that John Barzee [the sexton] be paid his half year, end-
ing the 29th of March, 1732, the sum of £5.

John Barzee has engaged for sexton another year, for £15.

Ordered: that the money belonging [52] to the poor be delivered to
the eldest Church Warden, he giving a bond for the same, payable
to the Minister with lawful interest, and the bond to be renewed
every year.

---

self to some captain. While serving out his time, he came into possession of
a valuable estate in Virginia, which enabled him to shape his own course.
Here he became eminent as a merchant, and was active in fitting out privateers in the French and Spanish wars. At the request of Governor
Shirley, he was commissioned to raise a regiment of three hundred and
fifty men in Rhode Island, to join the expedition against Louisburg.

In 1766 Col. Malbone's beautiful country seat was destroyed by fire.
He died February 22, 1768, and was buried under Trinity Church.
October 18, 1719, he was married to Katharine Scott, who survived him,
and died in Boston in 1817. Her remains were brought to Newport and
interred in the churchyard. The autograph at the head of this note was
taken from an old deed, but the name as generally given has only one "l."

[51] *Edward Scott* was the granduncle of Sir Walter
Scott. For more than twenty years
he was master of the grammar
school in Newport, the first classical school in Rhode Island. He was an
active member of the Philosophical Society. On the tombstone of his
father, Edward Scott, there is this inscription:

"This Monument Is sacred to the Memory of Edward Scott, Esq., Who
departed this life June 30, 1708, aged 65 years. Having for many years
served His country By a faithful life & discharge of several important
offices of government, preserving throughout his life That noblest of
characters, AN HONEST MAN."

[52] Lacking other modes of putting money out to interest, it was the
custom to put funds in the hands of some person of known probity
engaged in business who could use it, and who gave bonds, as above, for
its return with interest.

April 25, 1732.   Benjamin Brenton[53] was married to Alice Barker.

May 2, 1732.   John Norton paid James Martin ten pounds for the middle pew of the five new pews lately built at the west end of the gallery, for which he is to account, and the said Thomas Norton is to be invested with the property.

November 20, 1732.   Voted and resolved: that every person that has subscribed anything towards discharging the Church debts, and every person that is indebted otherwise to the Church, pay in their subscriptions and debts on Thursday the 30th instant, and that Capt. John Freebody and Mr. Daniel Ayrault be desired to attend them with their bonds in order to have them discharged.

November 30, 1732.   Mr. Ayrault[54] has discounted, in part of his bond, thirty pounds for the vault in the churchyard, which is in full of what he was to give for it.

Mr. Ayrault's bond discharged in y[e] Vestry.

Mr. John Lance is desired to set the Psalms in the Church.

December 22, 1732.   Ordered: that Capt. John Chace, Mr. Edward Scott and James Martin be a committee to draw up an instrument, to be put on the public record, for the dedication of Trinity Church, and that the same be prepared for the next Vestry.[55]

---

[53] Benjamin Brenton died April 1, 1766, and was buried on his farm in Narragansett.

[54] This was Daniel Ayrault.   The vault is under the tombstone that bears the name of his wife, Mary Ayrault, who had died January 5, 1729, and whose remains he placed in the vault when it was completed.   The entrance is under the flagstones of the walk leading to the north door of the church, and is reached by steps under the walk.

[55] The following document is all that is now known in regard to the above movement.   It is recorded in the City Clerk's office, and not on the records of the Church:

"To all People to whom these Presents shall come, Greeting: Whereas, Francis Brinley, of Boston, in the County of Suffolk and Province of the

February 25, 1733. Voted: that the Church Wardens write to
Mr. Charles Theodore Perchival, in Boston, to acquaint him that the
organ is arrived for the Church, and that he is desired to come up
here and assist us with his advice, in putting the same up, and that

Massachusetts Bay in New England, gentleman, & Deborah his wife did
by their Deed of Sale, bearing date the Third day of October, in the year
of our Lord one Thousand seven hundred & twenty, Grant, bargain,
sell, alien, convey & confirm unto Daniel Ayrault & Wm Gibbs,
both of Newport, in the County of Newport, & Colony of Rhode
Island, &c., the then Church Wardens of Trinity Church in Newport
afores^d, & to their successors in said office forever, A certain piece, parcel, or lot of land, situate lying & being in Newport afores^d, butted &
bounded as follows: East on land belonging to Peleg Sanford, late of s^t
Newport, Esq', deceased, South upon a way between the land of the said
Francis Brinley & the land of Caleb Carr, late of s^d Newport, Esq', deceased, West on land belonging to s^d Francis Brinley, & North partly
on land belonging to said Trinity Church, & partly on land belonging
to the Reverend James Honyman, of s^d Newport, Clerk: The said Premises measuring & containing one hundred & one feet on the south
line, ninety-three feet & a half on ye north line, forty-six feet on the
west line, & fifty feet on the east line, or however otherwise butted &
bounded, as in & by the s^d recited Deed, reference thereto being had
will now fully & at large appear; And Whereas, the Minister, Church
Wardens & Vestry of said Trinity Church, did at their meeting held in
s^d Church, on the Tenth day of September in the year of our Lord one
thousand seven hundred twenty & three, unanimously agree to erect
& build a new Church on the afores^d Piece or Parcel of land with the
free & voluntary subscription of well disposed persons, & then nominated & appointed Wm Wanton, Wm Coddington, Henry Bull, Godfrey
Malbone & John Chace, all of Newport, afores'd, & the s^d Daniel
Ayrault to be a committee for the overseeing & superintending s^d work,
which building has been perfected & named Trinity Church: Now
Know Ye, that we, the Rector, Church Wardens & Vestry (represent-
ing the congregation) of s^d Church, do hereby dedicate & devote s^d
Trinity Church to the Publick worship of God, according to the Liturgy
of the Church of England as by law established.

In Testimony whereof, we, the said Rector, Church Wardens & Ves-

he shall be satisfied for his assistance in the affair.   And also to Mr.
Richard Munday, to desire him to come here forthwith, to advise
and assist us in preparing a plan to set up the organ [56] in this Church.

trymen have hereunto subscribed our names & affixed our seals at a
meeting held in said Trinity Church on Easter Monday, being the twenty-
sixth day of March, in ye sixth year of the reign of our Sovereign Lord
George the Second, by the Grace of God of Great Britain, France &
Ireland, King, defender of the Faith, &c., Anno Domini 1733.

JAMES HONYMAN,   [L.S.]
JAMES MARTIN,   [L.S.]
JAHLEEL BRENTON,   [L.S.]
NATH¹· KAY,   [L.S.]
Wᴹ· CODDINGTON,   [L.S.]
GODFREY MALBONE,   [L.S.]
Wᴹ· WANTON, Jᴿ·   [L.S.]
JNO. CHACE,   [L.S.]
JNO. BROWN,   [L.S.]
GEORGE WANTON,   [L.S.]
JONᴺ· THURSTON,   [L.S.]
EDWARD SCOTT,   [L.S.]
J. HONYMAN,   [L.S.]
RICᴰ· MUMFORD,   [L.S.]

Signed & sealed in sᵈ meeting,
  in the presence of us.
    WILLIAM JONES, JUNᴿ·
    JOHN LANCE.
Recorded, June 27, 1733,
    per Wᴹ· CODDINGTON, T. C. K.

[56] The gift of an organ to Trinity Church from Dean Berkeley quickly
followed his departure from Newport, and the receipt of it must have filled
the hearts of the congregation with joy. Some change had evidently to
be made in the gallery at the west end of the church, to receive it, but to
what extent cannot now be shown. The pipes, etc., were long since so
worn as to make it necessary to replace them, but the case of English
oak, beautiful in design and as beautifully made, remains as of old; sur-
mounted in the centre by a crown, and on either hand a Bishop's mitre.
  To meet modern demands and to secure a larger compass, the organ has

The Rev. Mr. Honyman is desired to draw up a letter of thanks to the Rev. Mr. Dean Berkeley, for his generous present of an organ to this Church, and likewise a letter of thanks to Mr. Henry Newman, for his care about and shipping the same; in order to be sent to England as soon as conveniently may be.

Voted: that Capt. Jonathan Thurston and Capt. Richard Mumford are appointed to go about to get subscriptions for £250 to defray the charges of setting up the organ and satisfying Mr. Perchival and Mr. Munday for their assistance in said affair, painting ye Church and securing the tower from injury from the weather.

Adjourned till the arrival of Mr. Perchival.

March 8, 1733. Voted: that the letter of thanks to the Rev. Mr. Dean Berkeley for the present of the organ to this Church, and likewise the letter of thanks to Mr. Henry Newman for his care and trouble in getting the same done, and shipping thereof, drawn up by the Rev. Mr. Honyman, is approved of and signed in the Vestry, and ordered to be sent home forthwith.

At a Vestry held at Trinity Church, in Newport, on Easter Monday, being ye 26th day of March, 1733:

Capt. Jonathan Thurston, having served as Church Warden for two years, was dismissed with the thanks of ye congregation, and James Martin elected in his room as eldest Church Warden, and Jahleel Brenton, Esq., chosen in ye room of said Martin to serve for ye ensuing year.

Mr James Honyman is admitted a vestryman, and Capt. Richard Mumford is admitted another.

Voted: that John Lance is allowed his pew that he sits in, in the gallery, for his past service done the Church, upon the same footing of those who purchased it.

in recent years been greatly enlarged, by adding wings, attached to the old case, which latter is made the central portion.

Voted : that John Grelea is allowed £10 for his past services when he went to sea, and is chosen clerk for the year ensuing at the salary of thirty pounds.

John Grelea paid the £10 in the Vestry.

Voted : that for the ensuing year the Church Wardens receive the contributions and the money collected for the subscriptions, and to pay the Rev. Mr. Honyman £200^N for ye ensuing year by quarterly payments of £50, and the subscriptions to be gathered in by Mr. Richard Mumford for the two first quarters, Mr. Edward Scott the third quarter, and Capt. Jonathan Thurston for the last quarter.

Voted and ordered : that the poor's money be put out at lawful interest for the benefit of the poor, except £10, to be left in the Church Warden's hands.

Ordered : that Jahleel Brenton, Esq., and Capt. Godfrey Malbone be empowered to purchase oil and colors for the painting the Church without and [illegible] within, as soon as they conveniently can, and they agree with a workman for that purpose; and likewise to get a frame for an altar piece.

Voted : that John Barzee be allowed £20 for the ensuing year, and to ring the bell at 9 o'clock at night, and for ye same to get what subscriptions he can.

Ordered : that the legacy of James Cranston, deceased, of £100, be paid to Mr. Daniel Ayrault, and that the same be in his hands till further orders of the Vestry.

August 27, 1733. Jahleel Brenton,[58] Esq., having presented the

---

[57] Paper money was then so depreciated that it was not worth more than three to one of silver.

[58] the donor of the clock, was a staunch friend of the Church. He married, May 30, 1715, Frances Cranston, daughter of Governor Samuel Cranston, who bore him fifteen children. His second wife, to whom he was married April 25,

Church with a clock,[59] the Vestry, in behalf of the Church, do return him thanks for so generous a donation.

Voted: that the Church Wardens have a case erected over said clock forthwith, to secure it from the wind and weather.

Voted: that the one hundred pounds given to said Church by Mr. James Cranston, and now in the hands of James Martin, be put out to interest till the Vestry calls for the same, and the Church Wardens are hereby empowered to do it.

May 14, 1733. Voted: that Captain Richard Perkin's legacy to the Church be appropriated for the purchase of a flagon for the communion table.

Nathaniel Kay, Esq., agreed to purchase another of the same value.[60]

Voted: that James Martin forthwith draw up a proper instrument, in order to collect by subscription money sufficient to defray the charge of painting the Church, and that Mr. Peter Bours and said Martin go about therewith.

September 10, 1733. Benjamin Wanton was baptized.

1744. was Mary Scott, daughter of Stephen Ayrault, and widow of George Scott, by whom he had seven more children. His son, Sir Jahleel Brenton. who was the author of a number of books, died an admiral in the British navy. One of his nephews also became an admiral. One daughter, Susannah, married Dr. John Halliburton, January 4, 1767, and went with him to Halifax, and another daughter married Rev. John Eliot, of Gilford, Conn., son of the Indian apostle. Mr. Brenton died in 1767. He was an original member of the artillery company, and one of the committee to build the State House, 1739.

[59] The clock was made by _William Claggett_, the electrician and friend of Franklin. His early and successful experiments with electricity were remarkable. He died in Boston, December 15, 1736, aged 75 years.

[60] These two flagons have been in use until a very recent day. They are massive, are alike in design, and are eleven and a half inches high.

November 25, 1733.   Mary Honyman, daughter of James Honyman, Jr., was baptized.

At a Vestry held at Trinity Church in Newport, on Easter Monday, the 15th day of April, 1734:

Jahleel Brenton, Esq., and Mr. John Gidley were chosen Church Wardens.   Vestrymen : Col. William Coddington, Capt. Godfrey Malbone, Capt. Henry Bull,[61] Mr. Peter Bours, Mr. John Gidley, Col. Daniel Updike, Capt. Samuel Wickham, Capt. Richard Mumford, Mr. James Allen, Mr. James Honyman, Jr., Mr. Edward Scott and Mr. George Dunbar.

Voted : that £200 be allowed the Rev. Mr. Honyman for the ensuing year.

That given by Mr. Kay appears, from the date upon it, to have been made first.   The inscription in each case is on a mantling.

The flagon given by Mr. Kay bears this inscription :

An Oblation

from Nathaniel Kay a Publican

for the use of the blessed Sacra-

ment in the Church of England

in Rhode Island.

1733.

Lux perpetua

Credentibus Sola.

[61] *Henry Bull* grandson of the first settler of that name, was born November 23, 1687.   He was a man of strong character and attained to an influential position—a Representative to the General Assembly, Attorney-General in 1721, Speaker of the House of Representatives in 1728-9, and one of the Commissioners to settle the boundary dispute between Massachusetts and Rhode Island. And when the Court of Common Pleas was established, he was appointed Chief-Justice for Newport County.   He died December 24, 1771, aged 85 years.

Voted : that £40 be allowed Mr. John Grelea as clerk for the ensuing year.

Ordered : that Robert Oliver and Miller Frost have the pew No. 20 in the gallery, in lieu of the pew that was formerly said Oliver's and Alexander Brown's, taken up for placing the organ.

Ordered : that the pew in the gallery, No. 23 (that was Nathaniel Norton's) be for Mordecai Dunbar, in lieu of his pew that was taken up for the placing of the organ, and the Church to pay the said Norton the money he gave for the pew.

Ordered : that Capt. Samuel Wickham, Capt. Jonathan Thurston, Mr. Peter Bours and Mr. Edward Scott, are appointed to get in the subscriptions for the Church officers, and Mr. Charles Theodore Perchival, as the same shall come due quarterly.

June 24, 1734. Lawrence Langworthy[62] was married to Mary Lawton.

July 8, 1734. Mr. John Gidley has complied with the legacy left by Capt. Richard Perkins to Trinity Church, in full as executor.

Ordered : that the Minister and Church Wardens receive of Mrs. Ann Kay, the £200 left Trinity Church by her late husband, Nathaniel Kay, Esq., deceased : viz. £100 to and for the poor of said Church and the other £100 for the use of said Church, and that the same be applied accordingly.

James Martin paid the sum of one hundred pounds (which he received of the executors of James Cranston, deceased, and passed by his receipt to the same) to Jahleel Brenton, which was paid by said Brenton to Mr. Charles Theodore Parchival, for his services, &c., in setting up the organ in the Church.

—

[62] Lawrence Langworthy was of Ashburton, County of Devon, and died here October 19, 1739. His wife, from the same county, died before him. The name was perpetuated in Newport for some time. Jonathan Langworthy died here April 13, 1800, aged 84 years.

April 7, 1735. At a meeting held in Trinity Church; present, the Rev. Mr. James Honyman, Rector; Jahleel Brenton, Esq., and Mr. John Gidley,[63] Church Wardens, and some part of the congregation.

Mr. John Gidley chosen eldest Church Warden, in the room of Jahleel Brenton, Esq., and Capt. Samuel Wickham chosen younger Church Warden, in the room of Mr. John Gidley, for the year ensuing.

Mr. John Grelea chosen clerk for the year ensuing at his former salary.

John Barzee chosen sexton for the year ensuing at his former salary.

Ordered: that the widow Norton have the south pew in the upper gallery at the west end of the Church, in lieu of the pew that her son formerly purchased, which was taken from her by the placing of the organ.

April 8, 1735. The Vestry made an offer to Mr. Charles Theodore Parchival of the same salary that he had for the preceding year, which he declined to accept of, whereupon he was desired to officiate in the service of the Church as organist during his stay in this place, and agreed that he should be paid for the same in proportion to the allowance made him for the last year, for the time he

---

[63] John Gidley was a prosperous and enterprising merchant at the time that he was killed by a gunpowder explosion in 1744. In the churchyard there are monuments to the memory of a number of the Gidley family. The first is that of John Gidley, "of Exon, in Devon, Great Britain," a "Fuller," who died April 28, 1710. In the same grave rest the remains of his wife, Sarah, who died May 9, 1742, and of Sarah, his daughter and wife of John Vine. On the stone there is this further inscription:

"This tomb I desire may not be opened until it is demolished by time, it being filled up."

shall perform such service; and that the Vestry did then agree to take proper methods for the supplying the said Church with an organist.

May 14, 1735. Elizabeth Martin, wife of James Martin,[64] died, in her 33d year.

September 18, 1735. Charles Bardin[65] was married to Ann Carr.

Ordered: that the pew in the northwest corner, in the gallery, the property thereof is invested in Mr. Thomas Huxham, according to the rules of the Church, he having paid £20 for the same to Mr. John Gidley, Church Warden.

December 26, 1735. Ordered: that the two Church Wardens and James Martin be appointed to write (with the assistance of the Rev. Mr. Honyman) to Mr. Henry Newman, in London, to procure an organist for said Church, and that he be empowered to offer to a proper person for such a purpose the sum of twenty pounds sterling per annum.

[64] William Gardiner was a descendant of Joseph Gardiner, one of the first settlers of Narragansett. He married Elizabeth Gibbs, daughter of William Gibbs, April 16, 1719, and his sister, Hannah, became the wife of Rev. Dr. McSparran. Gibbs's widow married James Martin April 9, 1732, and died as above stated. Martin was born in Houston, Devonshire County, England, and was a man of some prominence. He was Secretary of the Colony from 1733 up to the time of his death, in February, 1746. His second wife was Mary Kennedy, to whom he was married December 28, 1741, by Mr. Honyman. William Gibbs was not connected with the family of George Gibbs.

[65] *Charles Bardin* was born in London, July 13, 1700, and died in Newport June 3, 1773. Ann Carr, his wife, died August 29, 1805, aged 92 years. Capt. Bardin had some knowledge of music, was competent to play on the organ, and occasionally served as organist, as will appear.

.Ordered: that Capt. Charles Bardin is ordered to assist Robert Mason in instructing him in playing on the spinnet.

Ordered: that the Church Wardens are desired to advise with John Proud[66] about the clock, in order to have it in better order.

Easter Monday, April 26, 1736. At a Vestry, Capt. Samuel Wickham and Mr. Edward Scott were chosen Wardens.

May 10, 1736. Adjourned meeting. Voted: that Capt. John Brown and Capt. Godfrey Malbone be desired to agree with Mr. David Wyatt, or some other person, to paint the Church, and that Capt. Samuel Wickham and Mr. Edward Scott get subscriptions for discharging the same.

Voted: that Messrs. George Scott and Daniel Ayrault be desired to collect the subscriptions for the Minister, &c., for ye ensuing year.

Ordered: that there be lent to Mr. John Grelea the sum of £40, without interest, for one year, out of the poor money, he giving a note for the same to the Church Wardens, and to serve for the ensuing year, or to return the money again; and in case of any accident the Vestry to make good the money to the poor at the year's end.

May 22, 1736. William Tate[67] was married to Mary Iverson.

June 24, 1736. Adjourned meeting after prayers.

Voted: that Mr. John Owen Jacobi [who had been induced to come out from England as organist, and had just arrived] be allowed the sum of £25 sterling, as organist for the Church, for the year ensuing if he thinks proper to accept thereof, and that the Church Wardens wait upon him to acquaint him with the result of this Vestry.

[66] John Proud was a clockmaker. He was succeeded in business by his son Robert, who eked out a living by adding to his calling the extracting of teeth.

[67] William Tate was a blacksmith, who, in his will, gave his estate, after the death of his wife, to the Church, and which will be noticed in place.

Voted: that the two east doors,[*] on the north and south side of the Church, be shut up and pews made there, and that two pews be made of each side of the steps of the altar, and that any person that purchases the side pews shall pay for the ground-rent £50 each, and build the pew and make the window at each of their respective charges; and the other two end pews to be valued at £50 each likewise, and the purchasers to build their own pews.

September 21, 1736. An account of £18.15 exhibited by Mr. John Owen Jacobi, for the amount of his passage and expenses more than the 10 guineas advanced by Mr. Hay in London, is allowed and ordered to be paid out of the money arising from the new pews.

Ordered: that the £10.10 sterling, advanced by Mr. Hay in London for Mr. John Owen Jacobi, be paid to the Rev. Mr. James Honyman, at the rate of four hundred and fifty per cent., for the use of said Hay.

Ordered: that an abatement of £10 be made to Capt. Robert Oliver, his pew being smaller than that on the north side of the altar.

[*] There was at that time no vestry room where the vestry room now stands, but a door leading directly to the street, with a similar door on the south side of the chancel, also opening upon Spring street. These were the doors ordered to be closed up. Windows were set in their places and new pews were made there. The two pews at the side of the chancel steps are the ones there now—one under the monument to Rev. Marmaduke Browne, and the other under the one to the Rev. Salmon Wheaton, D.D.

CHAPTER IV.

1737–1745.

EASTER MONDAY, April 11, 1737. Mr. Edward Scott and Mr. Daniel Ayrault, Jr., elected Wardens.

Capt. Charles Bardin, Dr. John Brett[69] and Capt. Caleb Godfrey are admitted Vestrymen of the Church.

Voted: that the officers of the Church be continued for the ensuing year at the same salaries.

Mr. Ninyan Chaloner, Peleg Brown, Esq., and Capt. George Scott are admitted Vestrymen.

At an adjourned meeting, the following day. Ordered: that the tower be repaired, for the preservation of the clock, and that the account of Mr. Claggett, amounting to £5, be paid.

Mr. John Grelea and John Barzee, refusing to serve this year for their former salaries, ordered that the Church Wardens speak to Mr. John Lance, in order to agree with him to officiate as Clerk, and to Mr. Jeffers to officiate as sexton.

Capt. Charles Bardin is desired to go about with a subscription, to raise money to make up what was borrowed of ye poor money, repair the steeple and make up the fence, being about £100.

May 2, 1737. Ordered: that Mr. John Lance be continued as clerk for this year, 'till next Easter Monday, unless he of himself declines in the meantime.

---

[69] But little is known of Dr. John Brett, other than that he was a native of Germany and a graduate of the University of Leyden. He was a scholarly man and early contributed to the collection of books for the Redwood Library. He was married, by Mr. Honyman, to Mary Howland, February 10, 1739.

[Rev. Mr. Honyman began now to show signs of failing health. In a letter to the Society, under date of July 6, 1737, he made it known "that he had been very much weakened by a long disposition, but he had not omitted his duty in preaching twice every Sunday; in observing every festival; in reading prayers and catechising twice a week in Lent; and he may affirm with great truth, that his congregation was the largest and most flourishing of any in those parts."]

Easter Monday, April 3, 1738.   Mr. Daniel Ayrault [Jr.] chosen eldest Church Warden, and Mr. William Mumford the other Warden.

George Dunbar, Esq., and Mr. Lawrence Langworthy are admitted Vestrymen.

Voted: that the salary of the clerk, Mr. John Grelea, be £30 and Mr. John Lance was allowed £30 for his last year's service.

April 7, 1738. Ordered: that the Church Wardens advise with Mr. Munday about making a pew in the northeast part of the gallery, for Capt. Nichols White, and that they agree with the said Mr. White for the value thereof; and in case they can't agree with him, to accommodate any other person therewith that has a mind to purchase.

Easter Monday, April 23, 1739.   Mr. William Mumford and Mr. Joseph Wanton chosen Wardens.   The Vestry remains the same as last year, with the addition of Mr. Jonah Bailey.

The organist, clerk and sexton are continued for the ensuing year upon the same salaries.

May 8, 1739.   Ordered: that the Church Wardens, with the assistance of Capt. John Brown, agree with Mr. John Allen to finish the painting of the Church on the outside, and that the Church Wardens collect the subscriptions in that are signed for that end.

Ordered: that the Church Wardens advise with Mr. Munday and

desire him to inspect into the state of the tower, and that the same
be repaired forthwith.

Ordered : that there be a pavement of flat stones, from the west-
ernmost gate to the Church door opposite to it [the present walk
from Church street to the north door] and that Mr. George Goulding be desired to speak with Mr. Johnson, of Connecticut, about the
stones.

Ordered : that £10 be added to the salary of Mr. John Grelea, for
the year.

August 14, 1739. Ordered : that the subscriptions be continued,
and that the Church Wardens carry the boxes round to receive the
contributions below stairs, and that Capt. Charles Bardin, and Mr.
James Gould be appointed to do the same above stairs in the galleries.

August 18. Penelope Honyman[70] was baptized by her grandfather, Rev. Mr. Honyman.

December 23. Isaac Stelle[71] was married to Penelope Goodson.

[Towards the close of this year the bell, the gift of Queen Anne,
that had hung in the tower since 1709, and which was prized not
only by the congregation, but by the whole town, was found to be
cracked and no longer fit for service. Measures were at once taken
to replace it.]

December 26, 1739. The Church Wardens are desired to write
to the Rev. Mr. Caner, of Fairfield, and inquire at what price the

[70] Penelope Honyman, the daughter of James Honyman, Jr., became
the wife of Rev. George Bisset, Minister of the Church, April 26, 1773,
went with him to New Brunswick, and died there August 2, 1816, aged 70
years.

[71] Isaac Stelle was engaged in commercial pursuits with John Mawdsley and other merchants in Newport, and was one of the syndicate, 1761,
that sought to control the manufacture of spermaceti, then largely carried
on in Newport. Mr. Stelle was the owner of " the crewless vessel " that
came ashore on the beach. See Bull's Memoir of Rhode Island.

founder there will cast our bell for, of 800 lbs. w^t, and likewise to
the correspondent at New York, to inquire whether the new bell
that was brought there from England sometime since, will be disposed of or not, and find out what it will be disposed of for.

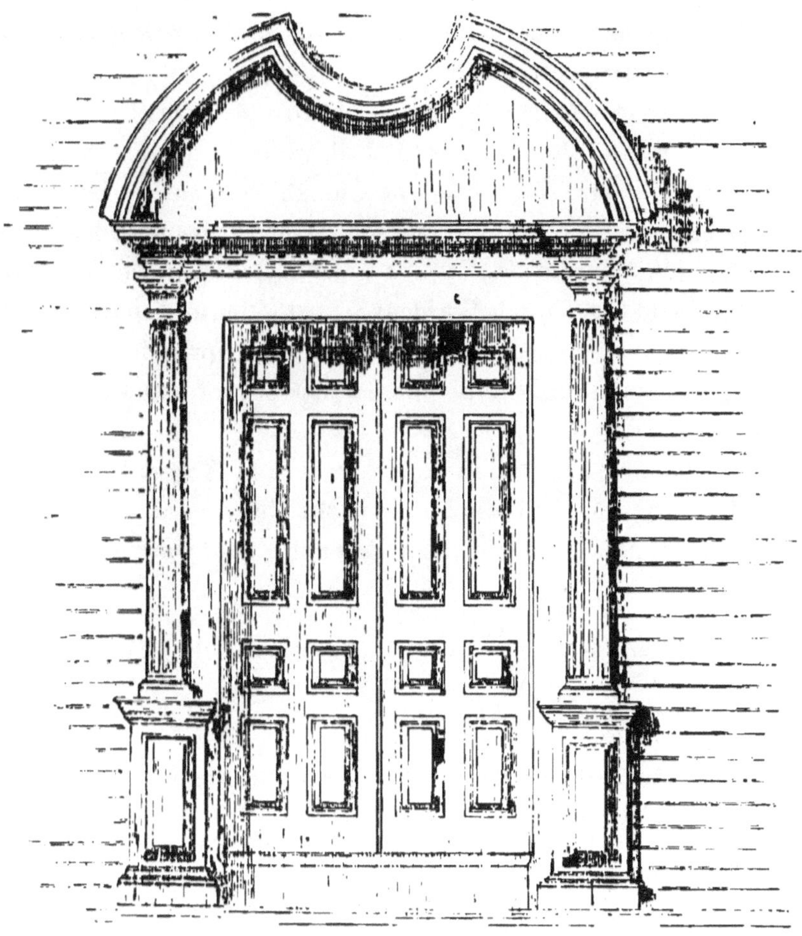

Easter Monday, April 7, 1740.   Joseph Wanton, Esq., and Mr.
John Bannister, chosen Wardens.   No change made in the vestry.
April 24, 1740.   Voted: that the house and lot where Nathaniel

Kay, Esq., dwelt, together with the lot of land let to Mr. John Bennett, be let out for the sum of £130 per annum, and that whoever shall have the same, shall give security for the payment of the rent quarterly.

Ordered: that the £400 given by Nath¹ Kay, Esq., for the building of a grammar school house, be let out to such persons as shall hire the same with sufficient sureties.

May 24, 1740. Oliver Beer[72] was married to Mary Brownell.

July 17, 1740. Voted: that the bell, which is cracked, be taken down forthwith, and shipped by the Church Wardens, on board the ship *Newport Packet*, Wm. Jackson Bonfield, commander, consigned to John Tomlinson, Esq., in London; and that the Rev. Mr. Honyman and the Church Wardens write to him to dispose of said bell, and such money as shall be raised by subscription and remitted to him, shall be in order to purchase a new bell, of about one thousand pounds weight.

December 2, 1740. Sarah Robinson, wife of Robert Robinson,[73] died, aged 56 years, and was buried in the churchyard.

December 23, 1740. Stephen Ayrault[74] was married to Ann Bours.

---

[72] Oliver Beer was mate of the brig William, Capt. Benj. H. Rathburn, captured by a letter of Marque, from St. Domingo, and was taken to France, where he died. For a long time it was supposed that he had been lost at sea.

[73] Robert Robinson, Searcher of the Customs in Newport, held offices under Queen Anne, George I. and George II.

[74] Stephen Ayrault, third son of the first Daniel Ayrault, was born at East Greenwich, December 11, 1709. His parents removed to Newport the next year, and here he continued to reside. Ann Bours, his wife, was the daughter of Peter Bours, by whom he had four daughters but no sons. "A pious, Christian, upright merchant and honest man; uniformly discharging the various official and relative duties," says the inscription on his tombstone, "through a long life." He died April 16, 1794, aged 84 years.

December 29, 1740.   Capt. Jonathan Conkling having agreed to leave the differences between the Church and him to men, and proposed Mr. Thomas Ward, whom the Vestry approved of; and they nominated Mr. James Honyman on their behalf, whom Capt. Conkling approved of.   And it is further agreed between the Vestry and said Conkling, if Mr. Ward and Mr. Honyman cannot agree, that they shall choose a third man.

Voted: that the pew lately belonging to Nathaniel Kay, Esq., be hereafter the property of Capt. Philip Wilkinson[75] and Capt. Jon' Conkling, upon their paying for the same £125.

Voted: that Capt. Ezbon Sanford be employed by the Church Wardens to repair the tower where it is defective.

Voted: that Messrs. Philip Wilkinson, Daniel Ayrault, Jr., Peleg Brown and Edward Scott be a committee to inspect all accounts relating to the Church and to audit the same; to discourse with Capt. Ezbon Sanford about sashing the Church windows, and building a school-house, and letting the lands belonging to the Church.

January 12, 1741.   Ordered: that the Church Wardens collect

[75] *Philip Wilkinson* was a merchant, and was engaged with Daniel Ayrault, Jr., in many commercial transactions.   Updyke, in his "History of the Narragansett Church," says he was a well-educated and intelligent gentleman, who emigrated from the north of Ireland to this country, and resided in Newport, and that "his first wife died after migrating to this country."   Of her death I find no other mention.   Capt. Wilkinson married Elizabeth Freebody, daughter of John Freebody, April 26, 1736.   She died October 24, 1759, aged 46 years, and lies buried, with members of her father's family, in the common ground.   October 30, 1763, he married Abigail Brenton, daughter of Jahleel Brenton.   He died in 1782.   June 24, 1787, his widow married Capt. Charles Handy, and died September 10, 1809.   She was distinguished for her beauty.   Her portrait, greatly admired, long adorned the walls of the Redwood Library, where it was deposited.   It is now in California.

the interest due on the bonds for the poor money, and that their
successors do the same every year hereafter.

Ordered: that the money belonging to the poor, in the hands of
Mr. William Mumford, be delivered to Joseph Wanton, Esq., in
order to be distributed.

Ordered: that the committee appointed to discourse Capt. Ezbon
Sanford about building a school-house do agree with him, or some
other proper person, to build the same, and call in the money that
was left for the poor to do it with.

Easter Monday, March 30, 1741. Mr. John Bannister and Mr.
Peleg Brown chosen Wardens. The Vestry remained the same as
last year.

April 5, 1741. Peter James [a successful shipmaster] was married
to Sarah Harding.

April 6, 1741. Ordered: that the Church Wardens collect the
rent due for the house, &c., left to the Church by Nathaniel Kay,
Esq., and that they repair said house as far as it is requisite, and
rent the lands.

September 2, 1741. Voted: that the old subscriptions be gathered in, to defray the charges of hanging the bell and repairing the
lead of the tower, and that Messrs. Peleg Brown and Richard
Mumford collect the same and make report to the next Vestry, to
be held on Friday, the 11th instant.

September 9, 1741. Thomas Vernon was married to Jane Brown.

September 11, 1741. Voted: that the Church Wardens immediately employ proper persons to repair the tower and leads, and
that they speak to John Proud to enlarge the hammer of the clock.

Voted: that the Church Wardens inform Capt. John Rouse that
it is the desire of the Vestry that he take the lock off his pew, and
admit some person to sit therein, who will allow him something for
it, and also contribute weekly.

Voted: that Messrs. Peleg Brown and Stephen Ayrault be desired to go about with a subscription, in order to see what they can raise towards paying an organist.

Voted: that Major Lockman be allowed £10 out of his rent towards hanging the great room of the house where he now dwells [the Kay estate], he leaving the hangings when he quits the house.

September 21, 1741. Capt. Charles Bardin is chosen organist for the year ensuing at £120 [inflated paper currency] per annum, to be paid half-yearly.

October 1, 1741. Matthew Robinson[77] was married to Bathsheba Johnston.

October 19, 1741. The Rev. Mr. Honyman is desired to acquaint Mr. Cornelius Bennett that if he is willing to take the school upon the following terms, he may enter as soon as the school-house is finished, viz., upon the donation given by Nathaniel Kay, Esq., deceased, amounting to ———— per annum, upon condition of schooling ten poor children, and that the gentlemen belonging to the Church will put their children to him for his further encouragement, and the same to continue until a school-master, Episcopally ordained, shall be admitted, according to the intent of said will, which is proposed to be done as soon as conveniently may be.

[77] was born in Newport in 1709. He was the only son of Robert Robinson, Searcher of Customs in Newport. He studied law in Boston, and opened an office in Newport about 1735. He was a prominent member of the Bar. He removed to Narragansett in 1750, and died at South Kingston November 4, 1795. Bathsheba Johnston was the widow of Augustus Johnston, and daughter of Augustus Lucas. She died soon after their removal to Narragansett.

Messrs. Scott and Bours are desired to speak with the gentlemen belonging to the Church, and endeavor to procure as many scholars as they can for the school-master that shall be admitted into the new school-house.

January 7, 1742. The Vestry agreed that the Church should make application to the Society for the Propagation of the Gospel in Foreign Parts, to procure a school-master according to the tenor of the will of Nathaniel Kay, Esq., and send them home a copy of the said will; and likewise what encouragement he may expect for said service; and likewise to request said Society to make some addition towards ye support of said school-master.

Meeting of the Congregation and Vestry, Easter Monday, April 19, 1742. Mr. Peleg Brown and Capt. Philip Wilkinson chosen Church Wardens.

All the vestrymen remain as before, and the organist, clerk and sexton are continued for the ensuing year upon the same salary.

April 22, 1742. Ordered: that the money belonging to the poor, now in the hands of Capt. George Wanton, he be desired to pay the same; and that it be appropriated towards repairing the dwelling-house for the school-master, and bonds to be given to the Church Wardens for the payment of the same, with interest.

[The following is from the Abstracts of the Society for the Propagation of the Gospel in Foreign Parts, 1742-3-4:]

" By letters from Rhode Island government, we are informed that the Church continues to flourish at Newport, under the care of the Rev. Mr. Honyman, and at Narragansett, under the care of the Rev. Dr. McSparren, where seventy negroes and Indians attend on it in public, whom the Doctor frequently catechises and instructs for an hour before divine service begins; and by him the people of Conanicut, mentioned in the abstract of last year, return their thanks to the Society for a folio Bible and Common Prayer Book for the public, and the pious tracts sent them for their private use; and propose the building of a church for the more decent celebration of divine worship.

"The Rev. Mr. Honyman, by his letter of June 13, 1743, blesses God that his church is in a very flourishing and improving condition; there are in it a very large proportion of white people and an hundred negroes, who constantly attend the public worship of God. Mr. Honyman hath eighty regular communicants, and he hath baptised within the preceding two years one hundred and fifteen persons, of whom twenty were adults and seven were negroes—while seventy negroes and Indians, with a large congregation of our own people, fill the neighboring church of Narragansett, under the care and administration of the Rev. Dr. McSparran."

Easter Monday, April 4, 1743, Capt. Philip Wilkinson chosen y⁰ Elder Church Warden, & Mr. Stephen Ayrault chosen y⁰ Younger Church Warden. Mr. John Grelea, Clerk, Thos. Jeffries, Sexton.

Voted: that the money now resting in the hands of Mr. Peleg Brown,[78] of the rent rec⁴ and what will be due the 25th day of July next, on the house where lived Nathaniel Kay, Esq., with the money due on a note of hand from Messrs. Joseph Wanton and William Mumford, and £30, due from Edward Perkins, and what is due from John Whitehorne and Thos. Vickers, the whole amounting to £239.5, be applied towards discharging the debt contracted in repairing the dwelling-house belonging to the school.

Voted: that a record be made, that the pew No. 10, in the south gallery, which formerly belonged to Mr. Joram Place and returned to y⁰ Church on the removing of said Place to Bermudas, is now given to Mr. John Grelea, in consideration of his good service to the Church.

---

[78] Peleg Brown, son of Capt. John Brown, was born in 1709, and died in 1756. His wife was Sarah Freebody, daughter of John and Sarah Freebody, to whom he was married February 20, 1745-6. She was born in 1721, and died in 1806.

May 22, 1743. Walter Chaloner[79] was married to Ann Almy.

October 10, 1743. Voted: that Mr Cornelius Bennett, the present master of the school founded by Nathaniel Kay, Esq., be allowed £60 per annum out of the revenue of the estate left for the support of sᵈ school, to commence from yᵉ 24th of July last, in consideration of his schooling ten poor children, and the remainder of the income of the said estate be appropriated to the repairing the buildings belonging to said estate, until the same be completely repaired.

December 25, 1743. Benj. Wickham was married to Mary Gardner.

January 10, 1744. Voted: that the Church Wardens request the several persons indebted to yᵉ Church for the rent of the house and land left by Nathaniel Kay, Esq., to pay their respective debts forthwith, and acquaint said persons that unless they comply therewith, they must expect to be sued.

----

[79] was one of the committee to run the lines between Massachusetts and Rhode Island. In 1747 he was in command of Fort George. The commissioners sent to the council called in Boston, in 1756, by Lord Loudoun, "were instructed to recommend to his Lordship, Capt. Chaloner, who had held a commission in the expedition against Carthagena, as a person deserving favor."

On his tombstone at St. John's, New Brunswick, are these words:

" Beneath this stone lie interred the bodies of Walter Chaloner, Esquire, formerly High Sheriff of Newport, the then British Colony of Rhode Island, and afterwards one of His Majesties Justices of the Peace for Kings County, in the Province of New Brunswick, who departed this life on the 16th day of November, 1796.

"Also of Ann Chaloner, his wife, who died on the 16th day of April, 1808."

Voted: that George Gibbs[80] be invested with the property of one-half of the pew he commonly sits in, he paying the Church Wardens for the same the price that Capt. Nicholas White gave for the other half.

Easter Monday, March 26, 1744. At a meeting of the Congregation of Trinity Church, Mr. Stephen Ayrault was chosen eldest Church Warden, and Capt. Thomas Wickham, younger Church Warden.

Voted: that the number of vestrymen for the ensuing year, to be chosen, be sixteen.

Vestrymen: Capt. Wm. Coddington, Jahleel Brenton, Esq., Mr. Godfrey Malbone, Capt. John Brown, Capt. Philip Wilkinson, Peter Bours, Esq., Samuel Wickham, Esq., Capt. Jonathan Thurston, Joseph Wanton, Esq., Edward Scott, Esq., Mr. Daniel Ayrault, Jr., Mr. William Mumford, Mr. James Honyman, Jr., Mr. Peleg Brown, Mr. William Paul, John Gidley, Esq.

Mr. James Martin chosen Clerk of the Vestry.[81]   Mr. James

---

[80] *George Gibbs* was the founder of the house of Gibbs & Channing, one of the most influential commercial houses in New England in the closing years of the last century. He was born in Newport, and died here October 11, 1803, aged 68 years. His first wife, Susannah Scott, daughter of Joseph Scott, died June 24, 1767, in her 22d year. His second wife was Mary Channing, daughter of John and Mary Channing, and sister of his partner, Walter Channing, to whom he was married, November 19, 1768. Their eldest daughter Elizabeth, became the wife of Thos. William Moore, at one time British Vice-Consul at Newport. Eliza married Luther Bradish, of New York, and in 1814 Ruth married her cousin, the Rev. William Ellery Channing, D.D. Sarah, who died single at an advanced age, erected in her lifetime St. Mary's Church, Portsmouth, and gave at her death, the glebe now improved by the parish. William Channing Gibbs, the son, was governor of the State from 1821 to 1824.

[81] The Clerk of the Vestry kept the records of the Church, and served

Wady chosen Clerk for the year ensuing, at the same salary that Mr. John Grelea had. Mr. Thomas Jeffries chosen sexton for the year ensuing.

April 17, 1744. Voted: that the Church Wardens call upon Major Lockman for the rent due from him for the house he lives in to the 24th of this instant, and in case he doth not pay that he be sued to May Court, and that he give security to pay the rent quarterly as it shall become due, for the future, or be sued out of the house.

April 24, 1744. Voted: that there be a new fence around the churchyard; that Messrs. Thomas Wickham and William Paul go about with a subscription to raise money for that purpose, and that the Church Wardens employ a proper person to build said fence and mend the Church tower.

Voted: that Henry West and George Owen have a pew built in the southeast part of the gallery, they paying for the same £20.

Voted: that the Church Wardens let out at interest the sum of £120, part of the money in the hands of Mr. Stephen Ayrault for the use of the poor.

---

in that capacity, as did the Wardens and Vestry in their several offices, without compensation. The Clerk of the Church ("Clark," as he was called) held a more important position than the Clerk of the Vestry, and for his services drew a stipend. It was his duty to lead in the responses, from the small desk directly in front of and under the reading desk, and also to give out the psalms and hymns and to set the tunes. There were men at times who filled this office who were not always what they should have been, as will be shown further on. The Clerk's desk has remained unchanged in form and position since the time when the Church was built.

CHAPTER V.

1745–1750.

EASTER MONDAY, April 15, 1745. Messrs. Thomas Wickham and William Paul chosen Church Wardens.

Mr. George Wanton chosen Vestryman in the room of Mr. John Gidley, deceased, and Mr. Stephen Ayrault added to the Vestry. Mr. James Martin, Clerk of the Vestry. Mr. James Wady chosen Clerk for the year ensuing; salary the same as before. Mr. Thomas Jeffries chosen sexton.

Voted: that the Church Wardens, with Mr. William Mumford, be a committee to repair the house belonging to Trinity Church, and that Mr. William Mumford be a tenant if said house, as soon as it is repaired, at one hundred and thirty pounds per annum, for y* house and lot belonging to it.

February 4, 1746. At a Vestry, held at the house of Mr. Honyman. Voted: that there be allowed to Mr. John Jones the sum of £75, old tenor, being the prime cost of the pew[82] that formerly be-

---

[82] The above pew, as appears by a vote of the Vestry, May 19, 1744, was ordered to be sold for the benefit of the Church, the late owner having died, and there being no representative of the family willing to occupy it. By the rules of the Church, when the owner of a pew died, and no one member of his family came forward and expressed a desire to occupy it, it was to be sold and the proceeds were to go into the treasury. The order of sale, of May 14, 1744, was resisted by a brother of the deceased, and an attempt was made on the part of the Church to secure legally what was believed to be its rights. In this it was stayed by the opinion of Hon. Thomas Ward, set forth in the following letter; hence the action of the Vestry on the 4th of February, 1746 :

longed to his brother, Mr. W. Jones, deceased, said Jones withdraw-
ing his action commenced for said pew, at November Court last,
and giving a discharge in full for said pew.

February 10.   James Martin died, aged 55 years, and was buried
in the churchyard.

Easter Monday, March 31, 1746.   Capt. William Paul chosen the

---

Sir, I will give you my sentiments concerning the case of Jones and
Almy about a pew in Church as well as my Circumstances & Temper of
mind will admit.

1ˢᵗ. Trinity Church, altho' the Parson has recᵈ Orders from the Bishop
of London, altho' its Worship be according to the Forms &c. of the established Church in England, and altho' it has Church Wardens, a Vestry,
&c. cannot in my opinion be looked upon as the Churches in England
are, for there is no Patron nor Glebe Land, neither has Mr. Honyman
ever been presented, instituted or inducted according to the Laws of England.   And, in fact, this Church was built by private persons by way of
subscription, as is notorious.   So the Property or Fee remains vested in
the first Proprietors, or their Heirs or Assigns.

2ᵈ. Mr. William Jones, by the Consent of the Proprietors, shut up the
north-east Door, put a Window in yᵉ place of the door & erected this
pew, whereby he became possessed of it in his own Right, & continued
so till his death, for which you have the Evidᶜᵉ of Messrs. Bours, Martin, Jos. Wanton & Capt. John Brown, who are summon'd.   I expect
they will say on the other side, Jones did not by these Things become
seized in Fee.   I say he did, because by the Articles he had it to him &
his pew forever.   Coke, lib, fo. 1.   N. B.   There is no occasion to allow
the Articles are binding, but to insist that from the Tenure of all other
Pews in Ch'h., Jones had the Fee of the Pew sued for.

3ᵈ. Wᵐ. Jones, by his Will, made present Pl't. his Residuary Devisee
& Legatee, as you see by the Devise in yᵉ 3ᵈ page of the Will, marked.

4ᵗʰ. This proceeding is ungenerous, because yᵉ same Wᵐ. Jones gave the
Ch'h £150; see yᵉ Article next Preceeding the Devise just referred to.
And it is likewise repugnant to the Principles of Com'on Justice to take
away a man's Right who hath committed no crime nor violated any Law.

5ᵗʰ. The Articles of the Ch'h are void in themselves, not being signed,
&c., but had they been signed they would only oblige the Signers, for

Elder Church Warden, and Mr. Walter Chaloner the Younger Church Warden. The Vestry remains the same as last year.

Voted: that Samuel Wickham, Esq., be, and he is hereby appointed in behalf of the Church, to settle a dispute between the Church and Mr. Cornelius Bennett, the late school-master, and to meet with Mr. Peleg Brown, chosen by Mr. Bennett for this purpose; and that if Messrs. Wickham and Brown cannot agree, they choose a third person, to settle the dispute, and that the parties give bonds to abide by the determination of the arbitrators; the Church Wardens to give bonds in behalf of the Church, and Joseph Wanton, Esq., offering to give bonds in behalf of Mr. Bennett.

Voted: that Mr. Nathan Coffin, the present school-master, be allowed £60 per annum, out of the rent of the estate of the late Nathaniel Kay, Esq., and also the rent of the dwelling-house in the school-house yard, from his first coming to the school.

May 19, 1746. Voted: that the note given by Mr. Joseph Wanton to Capt. John Freebody, for the sum of £36, in behalf of Mr. Edward Pigott, shall be discharged out of the money belonging to the poor of the Church.

July 14. Voted: that Nath' Coffin be paid at the rate of £100 per annum, for teaching the ten charity boys at his school: the same to commence at this time.

altho' in England the parson has the Freehold of the Church, & he with the Vestry have power to elect Church Wardens, &c., yet they have no such right in this Country, & consequently their action cannot be binding on the whole.

6. By the 4th of the Ch'h Articles we have a Right to the Pew.

I have not referred you to any Authorities, knowing Jacob's Dictionary will be at Hand, and supply you with what is necessary. I am Sir your hum. Servant

Nov. 28th, 1746.
For Mr. Robinson.

Voted: that the cross alley, from the north to the south door, be shut up, and that four pews be built for some gentlemen whose families are destitute of pews.

Voted: that the Minister and Church Wardens forthwith address the Society for Propagating the Gospel in Foreign Parts, for a person capable of teaching school, and that they send over to them an exact state of Mr. Kay's donation, with an account of the annual neat produce of the same, and request of them that such school-master be Episcopally ordained, and sent to act in the capacity of a catechist, and that they would be pleased to settle £20 or £30 sterling, per annum on such person; that the yearly income of Mr. Kay's donation, with that settlement of theirs may be proper encouragement for such a person to reside among us: and that Messrs. Samuel Wickham and Peter Bours be a committee to draw up a state of the circumstances and annual neat produce of Mr. Kay's donation.

February 9, 1747. Voted: that Messrs. Samuel Wickham and Peter Bours draught a letter to Mr. John Tomlinson,[83] merchant in

---

[83] The action of the Society is set forth in the following from the "Abstract of the Proceeding of the Society:"

"The Rev⁴ Mr. Honyman, the Society's missionary, and the Church Wardens and Vestry of the Church of Newport, in Rhode Island, by their letter dated August 2ᵈ, 1746, petition the Society to send them over a proper person, Episcopally ordained, to take on him the office of school-master, to teach grammar and the mathematics, pursuant to the will of the late worthy Mr. Nathaniel Kay, who bequeathed an house and lands to the value of about twenty-five pounds sterling per annum, in trust to them for that purpose. And that the Society would be graciously pleased to appoint such person catechist to their Church, under the direction of Mr. Honyman, and to be assistant to him in the care of that very numerous congregation. To this the Society, out of regard to the advancing years of Mr. Honyman (who has been more than forty years their faithful and diligent missionary there), have consented; and they have given him directions to consult the Rev. Dr. Johnson, of Stratford, and to choose out of the young gentlemen educated at New Haven, whom,

London, requesting him to use his interest with the Hon[ble] Society for Propagating the Gospel in Foreign Parts to procure a school-master Episcopally ordained, with some annual allowance in addition to the generous donation of Nath[l] Kay, Esq., deceased, to assist the Minister of the Church and keep school.

March 26, 1747. Walter Cranston was married to Frances Ayrault, daughter of Daniel Ayrault.

April 19, 1747. George Wanton[*] was married to Sarah Hazard.

Easter Monday, April 20, 1747. Capt. Walter Chaloner chosen Elder Church Warden and Capt. Evan Malbone chosen the younger Church Warden.

April 20, 1747. John Moldsley [Mawdsley] was married to Sarah Clark.

May 12, 1747. Robert Crooke[**] was married to Ann Wickham.

---

upon their own request, Dr. Johnson hath recommended for employment to the Society, a fit person for these offices; and to send him over to England for holy orders, of which, if he shall be found worthy, the Society, after his ordination, will appoint him catechist and assistant to Mr. Honyman, in the care of his very large and increasing congregagation, not of whites alone, but of blacks also; no less than twelve of the latter sort having been admitted members of it, by the holy sacrament of baptism, within twelve months."

Mr. Jeremiah Leaming was selected as the candidate for holy orders, and was sent to London, at the expense of the Church, to be ordained.

[*] George Wanton, born May 10, 1724, was the son of the third George Wanton, and Sarah Hazard, his wife, was the daughter of George Hazard.

[**] Robert Crooke came to Newport from Kingston, N. Y., settled here and had an honorable career as a merchant. His son, William Crooke, was educated for the bar; but, under the advice of his physician, he found more active employment in mercantile pursuits. He built the large brick building recently razed on the corner of Thames and Pelham streets. From 1797 to 1801 he was the Senior Warden of the Church. July 25, 1796, he was married, by Rev. William Smith, to Mary Malbone, daughter of Francis and Margaret Malbone. She died February 16, 1852, and he died in 1832.

June 17, 1747. there was a convention of the Episcopal Clergy at Trinity Church. The Rev. James McSparran preached the sermon from Romans I., 16.[85]

August 6, 1747. Rev. Dr. McSparran baptized Mrs. Elizabeth Wilkinson, wife of Capt. Philip Wilkinson, in Petaqamscutt Pond: Witnesses, the doctor, his wife and Mrs. Jane Coddington.

August 10, 1747. Voted: that Capt. Walter Chaloner have the property of the pew formerly belonging to Capt. Richard Mumford, he paying to the Church the sum of £70, old tenor, for the same, and giving up to the heirs of said Mumford all his right to the pew formerly belonging to Nath' Newdigate, deceased, which right he acquired by purchasing said pew of Mr. Newdigate in his lifetime.

---

[85] Rev. Dr. McSparran's sermon before the convention was printed in Newport the same year. In it he thus speaks of St. Paul:

"Learning was there [Rome] in all the glory and beauty of its fullest bloom, which must make every attempt to introduce a new and unadorned doctrine the more desperate and romantic among so inquisitive and discerning a people as the Romans were. In contrast to this, it has been observed of one Apostle (and as it should seem) objected to him, that besides his having no grandeur of person, no gracefulness of air or mien to recommend him, his speech was also contemptible, rude and unadorned with the rhetorical paint, so taking at that time. How then could he expect to make a figure at Rome, where poets and orators vied with each other, whose speech should the most sparkle with the glistening drops of Grecian dew.

"Indeed, as to eloquence, he disavows all ambition of aiming at the first, and less principal part, consisting in the nice choice and beautiful arrangement of words, but in *that*, which lies in a chain of clear and strong reasoning, famous figures, a becoming ardor, and an amazing art of persuasion; sure, no *one* ever outshone *St. Paul.* He surely had a masculine and flowing *eloquence*, a certain majestic *simplicity* of words, that entered the hearts of his *hearers*, whenever he had a mind to admonish, exhort, or warn their passions—doubtless he had *divine* and *useful eloquence* that enabled him always to speak with an emotion *adapted*, and in a style suitable to his subject. Had there not been a majesty in his speech, whereby he spoke greatly of great things, it is not likely the Lystrians would have mistaken him for Mercury, the God of Eloquence, or Jove's Interpreter."

From the Abstracts of the Proceedings of the Society we gather:

"The Rev. Mr. Honyman continues his usual diligence in his mission at Newport, in Rhode Island—it appearing by his letter of May 14th, 1747, that he had baptized eighty-three persons, eleven of whom were adults, and properly instructed, sixteen negroes and two Indians."

January 4, 1748. Voted: that Mr. Honyman be desired immediately to send for Mr. —— Ogilvie, that he may be sent home to y° Society for Propagating the Gospel in Foreign Parts, to receive orders as a Catechist, and school-master, to receive the donation of Nathaniel Kay, Esq., deceased.

Voted, also: that the depreciation[56] of the money be considered with respect to the Rev. Mr. Honyman's salary, and that there be a general contribution of the whole congregation on Easter Sunday, next, in order that the deficiency may be made good.

February 24, 1748. Present, the Rev. Dr. McSparran[57], vice the Rector, and the members of the Vestry.

Voted: that y° encouragement given by Mr. Kay, in his will, with y° expectations of an addition from the Society, be represented to Mr. Joseph Cleverly, of Braintry: by the Rev. Mr. Honyman, & that he be acquainted that the Church Wardens & Vestry have chosen him for a school-master, upon y° foundation of said Mr.

----

[56] "The committee [appointed by the General Assembly] to whom the sale of bills of exchange on England was intrusted, reported, February 27th, 1748, the sale of £7800 at an exchange of £1050, currency, for £100 sterling, showing the great and rapid depreciation in the paper money of the Colony."—*Arnold's History of Rhode Island.*

[57] Rev. Dr. McSparran was probably here on a visit to Mr. Honyman, who had been stricken with paralysis, and whose rapidly failing health told that with him the time was near at hand when he must give up his charge altogether.

Kay's will, & that a messenger be sent forthwith, with this advice, desiring him to come, & this be done at the cost of the Church.

April 4, 1748. Mr. Jeremiah Leaming having been recommended to the Minister, Church Wardens and Vestry, as a suitable person to be a school-master and an assistant to the Rev. Mr. Honyman, it is therefore unanimously voted that he be accepted and received as such, pursuant to the last will and testament of Nathaniel Kay, Esq., deceased; and that he be forthwith sent to London, at the expense of the Church, to take Holy Orders, and thereby, on his arrival here and entering on his office, be entitled to the profits of the donation of the aforesaid Nath' Kay, Esq., from this time, and the bounty given by the Honorable, the Society for the Propagation of the Gospel in Foreign Parts."

And it is agreed between the Minister, Church Wardens and Vestry, and the said Mr. Leaming, that if he should have an offer of settling with any other people after he has entered into Holy Orders, that he may judge more advantageous to him than the income and profits he may make at Newport in his capacity aforesaid, that in such case if the gentlemen of this Church will make up to him as much yearly as such offer he may have, that he be obliged to tarry with them, and discharge the duties of a school-master and an assistant as aforesaid; but if the gentlemen of the Church shall not incline to come up to such offer as he may have, yet, nevertheless, he shall be obliged to stay with them and act in his capacity aforesaid, till they be furnished with another proper person to supply his place; and also, on leaving them, he shall be obliged to refund

<hr>

" The difficulty experienced in securing a competent teacher for the school on the Kay foundation seems to have been great from the start, and it does not appear that any efforts were wanting on the part of the Vestry, for many years after the above date, to carry out the wishes of Mr. Kay, as expressed in his will.

whatever money may be advanced for the defraying his charges to London, to be admitted into Holy Orders, as aforesaid.

April 10, 1748. Voted: that the Church Wardens go among the congregation with a subscription to collect money to purchase a pall and two surplices, and for repairing the tower.

Easter Monday, April 11, 1748. Capt. Evan Malbone chosen the elder Church Warden, and Capt. Charles Wickham the younger. Vestrymen: Messrs. Wm. Coddington, Jahleel Brenton, Godfrey Malbone, John Brown, Peter Bours, Samuel Wickham, Jonathan Thurston, George Wanton, Joseph Wanton, Edward Scott, James Honyman, Jr., Wm. Mumford, Peleg Brown, Wm. Paul, Thomas Wickham and Walter Chaloner.

September 29, 1748. The Rev. Jeremiah Leaming, having produced his orders as Deacon and Priest, and a letter being produced from the Rev. Dr. Bearecroft, Sec'y to the Hon'ble Society for the Propagation of the Gospel in Foreign Parts, signifying that the said Society did approve of the said Mr. Leaming for a school-master, catechist and assistant to the Rev. Mr. Honyman, this Vestry is fully satisfied with the vouchers produced, and does admit and receive the said Mr. Leaming" in his capacity aforesaid.

Rev. Jeremiah Leaming, D.D., was born in Middletown, Ct., in 1719, graduated at Yale College in 1745. and was ordained in 1748. He resided in Newport eight years. From here he removed to Norwalk, Ct., where he remained in charge of the Church in that town for twenty-one years. From there he removed to Stratford, where he was in charge of the Church in that town for eight or nine years.

August 19. 1750, his daughter, Ann Kay Leaming (probably named after Ann Kay, maiden sister of Nathaniel Kay), was baptized in the Church, and July 22. 1752, his wife, Ann Leaming, died in her 22d year, and was buried in the churchyard.

Choice was made of Rev. Dr. Leaming as the first American Bishop;

Easter Monday, March 27, 1749. Capt. Chas. Wickham was chosen the elder Church Warden, and Mr. Walter Cranston, the younger.

No change was made in the Vestry. Mr. John Grelea, appointed Clerk, and Thomas Vickars, sexton.

March 28, 1749. Voted: that Thomas Wickham and Evan Malbone have the Christening Pew, to be divided into two pews, they paying what the Minister, Church Wardens and Vestry shall think proper, either annually or as their property.

March 29, 1749. Voted: that a lot of land, formerly belonging to Nathaniel Kay, Esq., and by him put under the care of the Minister, Church Wardens and Vestry, above named, joining easterly on land belonging to John Gibbs, southerly on a lane, and westerly on Thames Street, be divided into equal lots, and let out for

---

but enfeebled health, and great bodily infirmity (hip complaint, the result of the severe treatment he received as a Tory, in New York, in the Revolution, which left him a cripple) he declined, and choice was made of Rev. S. Seabury. He died at New Haven, Sept. 15, 1804. On his tombstone in the old cemetery, in that city, there is this inscription following his name:

"Long a faithful minister of the Gospel in the Episcopal Church, well instructed, especially in his holy office, unremitting in his labors, charitably patient, and of primitive meekness. His public discourses forcibly inculcated the faith illustrated by his practice. Respected, revered and beloved in life, and lamented in death, he departed hence, Sep^t. 15, 1804, aged 87."

The *Newport Mercury*, in announcing his death, said of him;

" He was formerly school-master and Assistant Minister of Trinity Church, where he is still recollected with sentiments of affectionate regard by many of his pupils, parishioners and others, as the engaging and faithful preceptor, the pious and humble Christian, the zealous divine and the exemplary good man."

He published a number of works. "Defence of the Episcopal Government of the Church, 1766. A Second Defence, 1770;" "Evidence of the Truth of Christianity," 1785; and "Dissertations on Various Subjects," 1785.

a fifteen year lease; the westermost to Peter Bours, for twenty-one shillings, sterling, per annum; the next easterly to Mr. Evan Malbone, at fifteen shillings, sterling, and the other three at the same rate, to such persons as the Church Wardens shall agree with.

Voted: that Mr. William Mumford have the house and lot he now hires, at the rate of £160 per annum.

December 29, 1749. The following entry was made in the Records of St. Paul's, Narragansett:

"The bans of marriage between Martin Howard, Jr.," and Ann Concklin being duly published in Trinity Church, Newport, and certificates thereof being under the hand of the Rev. James Honyman, Rector of said Church, said parties were joined together in holy matrimony, at the house of Major Ebenezer Brenton, father of said Ann, by the Rev. James McSparran, D.D., incumbent of St. Paul's, in Narragansett, the parish where the parties do now reside."

Easter Monday, April 16, 1750. At a meeting of the congregation, Mr. Walter Cranston was chosen eldest Church Warden, and Capt. Robert Shearman the younger Church Warden.

———

[94] *Martin Howard* may have resided temporarily in Narragansett at the above time, but his home was in Newport, where he had studied law under James Honyman, Jr., and was then practicing at the Bar. His father, who was admitted a freeman in 1726, at Newport, was evidently a man of but little prominence. Martin, Jr., is chiefly remembered for his connection with the Stamp Act, under which he accepted office with Dr. Thoms Moffat, a Scotch physician, and Augustus Johnston, Attorney-General of the Colony. It resulted in their being burnt in effigy, in front of the Court House, by an ungovernable mob. The following day their houses were rifled and they were forced to seek protection on board the Cygnet sloop-of-war, then in the harbor. The next year Howard was made Chief-Justice of North Carolina. In 1778 he went to England, and died at Chelsea, March 9, 1782. The name of his second wife, Abigail, is mentioned in his will. She died in Boston, in 1801.

The Vestry continued, except that Jonathan Thurston departed this life since our last election, and Capt. Charles Wickham is elected in his stead.

John Grelea appointed Clerk, and Thos. Vickars, Sexton, and his salary raised to £40 per annum.

April 17, 1750. The Vestry met according to adjournment. Present, the Rev. James Honyman, Jahleel Brenton, Godfrey Malbone, Capt. John Brown, Joseph Wanton, Wm. Mumford, Peleg Brown, Thos. Wickham, Chas. Wickham, Jas. Honyman, Jr., Col. Wm. Coddington, Geo. Wanton, Walter Chaloner and Wm. Paul.

Voted: that the Church wardens, with Joseph Wanton, Esq., Mr. Walter Chaloner and William Paul, be a committee to procure an organist, provided he can be had at or under £30 sterling, per annum : and that they also be a committee to pay the salary of said organist, Joseph Wanton, Esq., promising to pay what cannot be collected from the congregation, for said organist's salary.

April 23, 1750. Voted: that the Church Wardens view the house and lot Mr. Mumford now occupies (that was formerly a part of the estate of Nathaniel Kay, Esq., deceased) and report to the Vestry what repairs they need, and that they also prepare a lease for five years, at £40 sterling,[91] per annum, for said house and lot : Mr. Wm. Mumford agreeing to take one for s⁴ term : said Mumford by said lease being obliged to deliver up the said house and lot (at the expiration of his lease) in as good repair as when he received them.

July 11, 1750. At a meeting of the congregation at the Church, voted and agreed: that William Paul should be clerk of the Vestry and congregation, to record their votes, give copies of them, and to do whatever else of that nature [that shall] be required of him.

----

[91] This was the last Vestry meeting at which the Rev. Mr. Honyman was present.

CHAPTER VI

1750-1753.

VOTED and unanimously agreed: that the funeral expenses of the Reverend James Honyman[92], deceased, be defrayed by said congregation, and the Church Wardens are to collect the money for that purpose by subscription.

The death of Rev. Mr. Honyman was a severe blow to the Church. The people had been so long guided by him, had so long placed their trust in him, that they knew not how to get on without his guiding hand. He had been sent a missionary to Rhode Island in 1704, at a time when the inhabitants were swayed to and fro by all manner of doctrines: the Quakers owned more than half the meeting-houses; the Baptists were divided among themselves, and the friction, the outgrowth of varied disquisition, checked the growth of religious belief everywhere. But the factions, however quarrelsome among themselves, united in opposition to the Church of England, with which they had nothing, and could have nothing, in common. To battle with such a state of things required tact and great discretion—a patient waiting for the growth of the seed he was daily planting was all the worthy missionary could hope for. He was never aggressive to a degree that aroused opposition: in a simple, quiet way, he taught those who could be brought together, to love, respect and venerate the Church: and little by little, he made them feel sure of the ground on which they stood. He had a way of putting things in a light that commanded attention, and his 12mo. volume " Faults on all Sides; the Case of Religion Considered; showing the substance of true Godliness, and presented to the Inhabitants (especially of Rhode Island) printed at Newport by James Franklin," in 1728, is said to have seen three editions. But when, the following year, Bar-

Voted: that the Rev. Jeremiah Leaming officiate as Minister of
Trinity Church, above s^d, and that he receive from the Church
Wardens out of the weekly contributions £4 per week, for officiating as minister of said Church, during the time he performs that
duty; and when he takes an usher into his service at school, he

clay's "Apology for the True Christian Divinity, as the same is held forth
and preached by the People, called in scorn Quakers," he simply put in
circulation the tracts of George Keith and others, and more prayer-books.

It resulted in men of all beliefs coming to hear him, in Newport, at
Tiverton, Little Compton, Portsmouth, Narragansett, and frequently at
Providence. The means of communication were restricted and the mode
of travelling was fatiguing, but he seems never to have tired; and not until
his vigorous constitution began to give way did he relax in the least degree
his efforts to do his Master's bidding. Dissensions in the Church there
were none, and when, at the expiration of nearly fifty years in the ministry
on Rhode Island, he was called home, he saw his congregation in the enjoy-
ment of a stately and becoming place of worship, their numbers steadily
growing, and they a happy and united people.

The remains of Mr. Honyman, with those of his wife and daughter, lie
buried in the churchyard, just by the Church door. On the tombstone
there is this fitting tribute to his memory; and in Middletown, just over
the line, one of the most picturesque hills on the Island bears his name:

" HERE LIES THE DUST OF

JAMES HONYMAN,

OF VENERABLE AND EVER WORTHY MEMORY,

for a faithful minister of near fifty years in the Episcopal Church in this
town, which, by divine influence on his labors, has flourished and exceedingly increased. He was of a respectable family in Scotland—an excellent scholar, a sound divine, and an accomplished gentleman. A strong
asserter of the doctrine and discipline of the Church of England, and
yet, with the arm of charity, embraced all sincere followers of Christ.
Happy in his relative station in life, the duties of which he sustained and
discharged in a laudable and exemplary manner. Blessed with an excellent and vigorous constitution, which he made subservient to the various
duties of a numerous parish, until a paralytic disorder interrupted him in

shall have as much more from said congregation as (with the above £4 per week) will pay said usher's salary, until we are supplied with a settled minister for said Church.

Voted: that application be made to the Society for the Propagation of the Gospel in Foreign Parts to send us a minister, and that Dr. Samuel Johnson be recommended.[93]

the pulpit, and in two years, without impairing his understanding, cut short the thread of life on July 2d, 1750."

The adjoining stone bears this inscription:

IN MEMORY OF

MISTRESS ELIZABETH.

the wife of

the REVEREND MR. JAMES HONYMAN.

She departed this life

February 28th, 1737, aged 48 years."

Mr. Honyman's second wife was the widow of Captain John Brown. Her maiden name was Elizabeth Cranston, daughter of Governor Samuel Cranston. She died January 3, 1756, aged 65 years, and was buried by the side of her first husband's family. The only evidence that she was Mr. Honyman's widow at the time of her death is found on her tombstone, for no mention is made of their marriage in the Church records—a singular omission.

The portrait of Mr. Honyman, hanging in the Vestry room of the Church, was painted by an artist named Gaines. In 1774 it was engraved in mezzotint, one of the earliest specimens of the art in America. The portrait was given to the Church by Mrs. Frances Sophia Malbone, widow of Francis Malbone, and grand-daughter of Mr. Honyman.

[93] The following fragment of the draft of a letter has been preserved:

Newport, R. I., Sept. 1750.

Revd Sir.

The Church Wardens and Vestry of Trinity Church, in this Towne, beg leave to address the Honble Society for Propagating the Gospel in Foreign

A list of the persons who voted that some gentleman might be recommended, and of those who voted not to recommend anybody ; also who they voted who should be recommended after they lost their first vote.

Those who voted to recommend, and who they would recommend:

Mr. Thomas Wickham,	for	Mr. Robert Carter.
" Edward Scott,	"	Dr. Johnson.
" Chas. Wickham,	"	Mr. Robert Carter.
" Robert Shearman,	"	do do
" Martin Howard,	"	Dr. Johnson.
" Thomas F. Taylor,	"	————
Capt. James Allen,	"	Mr. Robert Carter.

Parts, and to inform them that it hath pleased the Sovereign Disposer of all things to take to himself our late worthy Minister, the Rev. Mr. Honyman, who, after a life well spent in promoting true religion and virtue among us, yielded up [his] soul to God on the second of July last, in full hope and expectation of a glorious immortality.

We have too deep a sense of the great and pious care of the Venerable Society in planting and supporting the Church of England in this country, not to acknowledge their favors, which, as they ought, so they do, excite in us the highest strains of gratitude, and notwithstanding we have enjoyed these favors for so long a time, yet we have hope we may be indulged the liberty of soliciting the continuation of their benevolence, when it comes to be considered that our congregation are really and truly unable to support a minister to live in so decent a manner as the dignity of such a station requires.

It is true that we have a considerable number of persons that frequent our Church, but there are but few of them whose circumstances will allow them to contribute towards the necessary expenses of it. As the town is a seaport, and depends entirely on trade, so there are in it a large number of widows and orphans, left by seafaring men who have suffered in the late war and died abroad ; a great share of which belonged to our Church, and are unable to bear any part of the charges.

We would also beg leave to observe that the greatest part of our present congregation came from the various sects of dissenters amongst us, and many of ——

Dr. John Brett,	for	Dr. Johnson.
Mr. Walter Chaloner,	"	do do
" Thomas Vernon,	"	do do
" John Chaloner,	"	do do
" George Wanton,	"	do do
" Stephen Ayrault,	"	Peter Bours, Jr.
" William Coddington,	"	Mr. Robert Carter.
" Charles Bardin,	"	Dr. Johnson.
" John Thurston,	"	do do
" John Sowdey (?),	"	do do
" Godfrey Malbone, Jr.,	"	——————
" Samuel Wickham,	"	Dr. Johnson.
" John Archer,	"	——————
" James Honyman,	"	Dr. Johnson.
" Peter Bours,	"	do do
" Thomas Vickars,	"	do do

Those gentlemen who voted not to recommend any person to the Society to be sent as a missionary, having lost their vote, joined with the others in recommending such persons as they thought proper:

Mr. Thomas Freebody,	for	Mr. Robert Carter.
" Samuel Freebody,	"	do do
" Joseph Whipple,	"	do do
" Philip Wilkinson,	"	do do
" Daniel Ayrault, Jr., did not recommend any one.		
" Andrew Hunter,	for	Mr. Robert Carter.
" Peleg Brown,	"	Dr. Johnson.
" Jeremiah Clarke,	"	do do
" Edward Cole,[94]	"	Mr. Robert Carter.

[94] *Edwd Cole* was in command of a company before Louisburg in 1745, and in 1755 he had a company in the regiment under Col. Harris, sent against the same stronghold. In 1757 he held the rank of Lieutenant-Colonel under

" Wm. Coddington did not recommend any one.

" John Tweedy,[95]   for   Mr. Robert Carter.

" Jahleel Brenton did not recommend any one.

Capt. John Brown,   for   Dr. Johnson.

Mr. Wm. Mumford did not recommend any one.

" John Barzee,   for   Dr. Johnson.

" Walter Cranston did not vote to recommend.

" William Paul,   for   Mr. Robert Carter.

" Henry Willis,   "   Dr. Johnson.

" Moses Howard,   "   do   do

[96] For Dr. Johnson,   20 votes.

[97] " Mr. Robert Carter,   13 votes.

" Mr. Peter Bours, Jr.,   1 vote.

Not voting,   8

—

42

Col. H. Babcock in the expedition against Crown Point, and was subsequently in command of the regiment. He was also present at the taking of Havana, in 1762. In the Revolution, Col. Cole took sides with the Crown, and raised a company against his country. For this his property was confiscated. A tanner by trade, he was born in North Kingston, and died at St. John's, New Brunswick, in 1793.

[95] was at the head of the house of John & William Tweedy, of Newport, the largest importers of drugs in the colonies. They had a branch office in New York, where dealers could learn the prices they had established to the trade. John married Mary Tillinghast July 10, 1732, and his second wife, Freelove S. Crawford, he married July 28, 1735. He died in 1782.

[96] Rev. Samuel Johnson was born in Guildford, Ct., October 14, 1696. He graduated at Yale College, and became a Congregational minister; but soon left that denomination, studied for the Episcopal ministry, went to England to be ordained, and returned to America in 1723. He labored

Voted: that the Church Wardens, with Samuel Wickham, Peter Bours, Edward Scott and James Honyman, be a committee to write to Dr. Samuel Johnson, to acquaint him with the proceedings of this meeting, and to request his answer.

July 30, 1750. At a meeting of the congregation, Voted: that the Church Wardens desire of Mr. James Honyman a particular account of the expenses of his deceased father's funeral, to be laid before the Vestry, or congregation, at their next meeting.

Voted: that the committee appointed to invite Dr. Samuel Johnson to supply the place of the late Reverend Mr. James Honyman, in this Church, be also a committee to answer Dr. Johnson's letter and to repeal their invitation to him.[96]

A motion for the evening service to begin at three o'clock was postponed till we have a settled minister.

August 26, 1750. Jabez Champlin[99] was married to Hannah Gibbs.

in the Church for thirty years, chiefly at Stratford, Ct., from which place he was called to the presidency of King's College in 1754. In 1763 he resigned that office and returned to Stratford, where he resided during the rest of his days, dying January 6, 1772.

A warm intimacy sprang up between Dr. Johnson and Dean Berkeley, and before the Dean returned to England Dr. Johnson visited him at White-hall.

[97] Of Rev. Robert Carter but little is known. He must have gone to the West Indies soon after the death of Rev. Mr. Honyman, for in 1752 he was missionary and school-master at New Providence, where he was spoken of as an Englishman.

[98] No copies of these letters have been preserved.

[99] *Jabez Champlin*, son of the second Christopher Champlin, was born August 31, 1728, and was admitted a freeman May, 1758. He was High Sheriff from 1775 to 1780, and the duty fell on him, in 1776, to take the Charter of the

August 27, 1750. The committee who wrote to invite Dr. Johnson; are now desired to write to the Rev. Mr. John Beach[100] to know of him if he is willing, on proper encouragement, to remove here to be the Pastor of this Church.

September 17, 1750. Solomon Townsend[101] was married to Rebecca Sturgis.

January 30, 1751. Voted: that application for an organist should be suspended till we hear from the Society respecting a minister.

Easter Monday, April 8, 1751. Capt. Robert Shearman was elected the elder Church Warden, and Mr. Jonathan Thurston the younger.

Vestrymen elected: William Coddington, Jahleel Brenton, Godfrey Malbone, John Brown, Peter Bours, Samuel Wickham, George Wanton, Joseph Wanton, Edward Scott, James Honyman, Peleg Brown, William Paul, Thomas Wickham, Walter Chaloner, and Charles Wickham.

Colony out of the house of Governor Wanton, who had refused to take the oath of office. He was made a prisoner in the war, and was exchanged. In 1780 he was appointed Barrack Master. He died in January, 1805. Hannah Gibbs was the daughter of George Gibbs.

[100] In 1732 Trinity Church contributed to the fund to send Mr. John Beach, a young student of theology, to England, for Holy Orders. He returned to America in September of that year, and began his work in the ministry at Redding and Newtown, Ct. Rev. Mr. Caner was then at Fairfield, the elder Seabury at New London, and Rev. Samuel Johnson at Stratford. He died in 1782, after a ministry of sixty years.

Dr. John Brett wrote of him from Nassau, New Providence, November 6, 1752: "The People of our Church at Newport I think will be quite happy with the indefatigable labors of the ever industrious Mr. Beach, and he will be somewhat assisted by Mr. Leaming, to whom I have again wrote a consolatory letter on his great loss."

[101] Solomon Townsend was a merchant, largely interested in commerce, and was associated with John Mawdsley in many ventures on the sea. He married Rebecca Sturgis, September 17, 1750, and after her death, Frances Brenton became his wife, January 12, 1764.

John Grelea elected Clerk and Thomas Vickars sexton.

May 13, 1751. At a meeting of the congregation Mr. Samuel Bours, Peter Bours and Edward Scott were appointed to send to y' Rev. Mr. John Beach, a copy of the Society's letter to us, of y' —— of March, 1751, as also a copy of a paragraph of theirs to y' Rev. Jeremiah Leaming of the same date, and to acquaint him that the congregation still continue their good opinion of him, and desire his immediate answer.

May 22, 1751. Benjamin Almy,[102] of John and Anstiss, was married to Sarah Coggeshall by James Searing, P. E.

June 10, 1751. At a meeting of the congregation of (and at) Trinity Church, it was voted and agreed: that Samuel Wickham, Peter Bours and Edward Scott, be a committee to answer a letter from the Society for Propagating the Gospel in Foreign Parts, dated 5th of March, 1751, and recommended the Rev. Mr. John Beach; and also to send him [Rev. Mr. Beach] a copy of the letter they write to the said Society.[103]

[102] Benjamin Almy was not a man of much force of character, and for many years was content to keep a boarding-house, run chiefly by his second wife. His first wife, the above Sarah Coggeshall, was the daughter of Thomas and Sarah Coggeshall. She died February 22, 1756, and October 22, 1762, he married Mary Gould, daughter of James Gould and great-granddaughter of Governor Walter Clarke. She favored the efforts of the Crown to retain the Colonies, and remained in Newport during its occupation by the British. She died March 25, 1808. The journal that she kept during the siege of Newport, an interesting document, has been published in the Newport *Historical Magazine.*

[103] "The Society, at the earnest request of the Church at Newport, hath consented to the removal of the worthy Mr. Beach, their missionary at the Church at Newtown, to that numerous congregation; and they will endeavor to provide the Church at Newtown with a worthy successor, as soon as they shall be informed of Mr. Beach's removal thence."—*Abstracts of Proceedings of the Society.*

September 26, 1751. Stephen Decatur[104] (a native of Genoa) was married to Priscilla Hill.

Easter Monday, March 30, 1752. Mr. Jonathan Thurston was appointed eldest Church Warden, and Capt. John Jepson, youngest.

The Vestry remained the same as last year, except that George Wanton retired, and Daniel Ayrault, Jr., was elected in his place.

John Grelea elected Clerk, and Thomas Vickars, sexton.

April 13, 1752. At a meeting of the Vestry, Rev. Jeremiah Leaming,[105] the Church Wardens and Vestrymen being present, voted: that the pews be handsomely numbered with paint on each door, and that Mr. Bours' lease be lengthened three years.

July 20, 1752. Thomas Vernon was chosen Church Warden, in place of Capt. John Jepson, who was going to sea.

July 19, 1752. David Thomas Leaming was baptized. The sureties were Capt. [John] Brown, Joseph Wanton (Collector) and Jerusha Thompson.

August 27, 1752. At a meeting of the congregation at the Church, voted: that Samuel Wickham, Peter Bours and Edward Scott, be a committee to advise Mr. Beach that we have received a letter from Dr. Bearcroft, by which we learn that he has leave to be our minister, and to invite him to come to us.[106]

---

[104] Capt. Stephen Decatur died at Frankfort, Pennsylvania, November 14, 1808. His son, who became a distinguished officer in the American navy, was baptized June 7, 1752. He married a lady named Wheeler, of Virginia, celebrated for her beauty, and at the time a reigning belle.

[105] The Rev. Jeremiah Leaming, as already shown, by a vote of the congregation, July 11, 1750, received a temporary appointment as minister, he having previously officiated as Assistant Minister. He was still filling the pulpit.

[106] No copies of the correspondence with Rev. Mr. Beach have been preserved, and no reason is given in the Church records for his declining the call; but from the *Abstracts of the Proceedings of the Society*, the following particulars have been gathered:

"The Rev. Mr. Beach, the Society's missionary at Newtown and Read-

Voted: that Jahleel Brenton, Esq., Capt. John Brown, and Joseph
Whipple, Esq., be a committee to collect by subscription a sufficient
sum of money to purchase a house and glebe for a minister of the
Church for the time being, and that they appropriate the same to
that purpose.

Voted: that the vestry-room and Church Wardens' pew be con-
verted into private pews, and that John Whipple, Esq., and Mr.
John Baninster have the offer of them. Samuel Wickham, Peter
Bours and James Honyman were to draw up an instrument to regu-
late the tenure of the pews.

Voted: that £40 per annum be allowed the Rev. Mr. John Beach
as soon as he is settled as our minister.[106a]

October 2, 1752. Voted: that £10 sterling be added to the £40
allowed Mr. Beach at our last meeting.

December 26, 1752. Voted: that Messrs. Samuel Wickham,

ing, in Connecticut, having declined, through want of health, to accept
of the great care of the Church at Newport, in Rhode Island, which, at
the earnest request of the inhabitants thereof, had been offered to him,
the Society hath appointed the Rev. Mr. Pollen, M.A., late curate of St.
Antholins Church, in London, but then curate of the Episcopal Church
of Glasgow, to that mission, upon his own request; and it is hoped that
he is by this time safely arrived, and to good purpose employed in the
duties of his holy function there."
    This is the first mention of Mr. Pollen in connection with the Church.
    [106a] In the diary of Rev. Ezra Stiles, D.D., there is this entry:
" When, in 1755. I had a formal invitation from the Episcopal Church
in Stratford to conform and succeed Dr. Johnson, with at least £100 sterling a year; and before that, in October, 1752, when I sustained a vigorous application to take orders and become a minister in the Episcopal
Church in Newport, then representing a living of £200 a year; I thank
God none of these things moved me."
    No mention is made in the records of the Church of the above appli-
cation, which must have come from individuals, and not from the Corporation or Vestry.

Jahleel Brenton, Edward Scott, James Honyman and Peter Bours, Esqrs., be a committee to draw up a letter to the Society for the Propagation of the Gospel in Foreign Parts, and desire them to send us a minister, and that they assure the Society we will give £50 sterling per annum, exclusive of his improvement of our house and glebe.

Voted: that £50 sterling per annum be settled as a salary of a minister of this Church, as soon as one shall be appointed by the Society, and that it shall commence from the time of his appointment.

Easter Monday, April 23, 1753. Thomas Vernon[107] was chosen eldest Church Warden, and Edward Cole the youngest.

Vestrymen: Wm. Coddington, Jahleel Brenton, Godfrey Malbone, John Brown, Peter Bours, Joseph Wanton, Edward Scott, James Honyman, William Mumford, Peleg Brown, William Paul, Thos. Wickham, Walter Chaloner, Chas. Wickham and Daniel Ayrault.

[107] Thomas Vernon, born May 31, 1718, married, September 9. 1741, Jane, daughter of John Brown, merchant, of Newport. She died April 28, 1765, aged 43 years. He next married, May 20, 1766, Mary Mears, who died in August, 1787. He was a merchant of the firm of Grant & Vernon; was royal port-master, at Newport, from 1745 to 1775, registrar of the Court of Vice-Admiralty twenty years, and secretary of the Redwood Library. While holding the office of Senior Warden, Dr. John Brett, then at Nassau, New Providence, wrote to him on his appointment: "The streams of honor are greatly diffusive and convey their influence to the most distant regions; consequently when I am congratulating you upon your late ecclesiastical preferment, I am in some measure partaking of the honors thereof. Dignities and distinctions are due to merit, consequently I must think the second dignity in the Church was not conferred on my good friend, Mr. Vernon, had he not been worthy of it. Make my congratulations to the Church Warden's lady, who certainly has as just title as any one to partake of the honor."

Mr. Vernon suffered imprisonment for his principles as a Tory. His journal while so confined, now belongs to the Newport Historical Society.

John Grelea Clerk, and Thos. Viekars Sexton.

August 15, 1753. Voted: that the application made to Mr. Brown,[105] of Portsmouth [New Hampshire], by Jahleel Brenton, Esq., Capt. John Brown, Mr. Honyman and Peleg Brown be approved of, and that those gentlemen be a committee to address him again, in answer to his letter of 10th of August, instant, and inform him that the letters between him and them have been laid before the congregation, and the contents unanimously approved; and that they desire a visit, or, in case he can't come, to beg that he will be more explicit in his answer.

[The following document was evidently prepared at this time. It is without date, and is in the handwriting of Daniel Ayrault, Jr. No mention is made of it, or of the circumstances connected with it, in the Church records:]

Whereas the Society for the Propagation of the Gospels in Foreign Parts, in consideration of the present circumstances of the Congregation of Trinity Church, in Newport, have thought fit to withdraw £20 sterling, per annum, of the salary which they formerly allowed to the Minister of the said Church, whereby it has become absolutely necessary for the Congregation to augment the allowance which they heretofore made for his better support; and whereas it is found by experience that the weekly contributions are insufficient to answer this purpose, it has been therefore thought necessary, at a meeting of said congregation, that the weekly contributions should be continued as usual, and that in addition thereto a moderate tax should be laid upon the pews in the said Church, in order as well to make up the deficiency as to pay the salaries of the other Church officers, and other incidental charges. Wherefor we, the present owners and possessors of the said pews, duly considering the necessity and duty of supporting our Minister in a comfortable and decent manner, do freely and voluntarily consent and agree to the

---

[105] The Mr. Browne above referred to was Rev. Marmaduke Browne, son of Arthur Browne, then a missionary at Portsmouth. New Hampshire.

following taxation, to commence the first day of January, Anno
Domini, 1753, which we do hereby oblige ourselves, our heirs and
successors to the said pews, to pay yearly and every year over and
above our weekly contributions, for so long a time as the congregation shall judge the same to be necessary ; and we further consent
and agree, that in case that we or our successors in the same pews,
or any of us or them, should hereafter refuse or neglect to pay the
respective sums at which each pew is rated, for the space of three
months after the same becomes due, that then it shall be in the
power of the Church Wardens and Vestry of the said Church, for
the time being, at their discretion, to place one or more persons in
the said delinquent's pew, as shall be willing to pay the yearly rent
it is set at ; and that such person or persons so placed in such pew,
shall continue therein for so long a time as the said Church Wardens
and Vestry shall think fit ; or, until the owners of the said pews
shall comply with the covenant and agreement ; provided, nevertheless, that no person or persons who shall be placed in any such pews
for the reason aforesaid, shall be from them displaced in less time
than one whole year after their entering therein, and that they shall
not be obliged to pay the rate or tax of such pews for any longer
time than they continue to have a place in them.

In testimony of our free consent to the foregoing exaction, and of
our obligation to comply therewith, we have hereunto subscribed our
names :

Henry Bull,	Elis. Jepson for J. Jepson,
John Brown,	Content Rogers,
M. Goulding,	Walter Cranston,
W. Coddington,	Godfrey Malbone,
Jas. Honyman,	Daniel Ayrault,
John Brown,	Edward Cole,
P. Wilkinson,	Aug[st] Johnston,[108]

[109]

Augustus Johnston was born at Amboy,
N. J., about 1730. He showed himself to be a man of talents, came rapidly
into notice, and on June 13, 1757, he
was elected Attorney-General of the Colony ; an office that he held

M. Howard Jr.,
Jos. Wanton,
D. Coggeshall,
Jer. Clarke,
Jahleel Brenton,
John Whitehorn,
    Wright,
E. Cole for A. Cole,
Edw. Scott,
Peter Bours,
Samuel Bours,
Rob' Elliot,
Benj. Wanton,
Mrs. Munday,
E. Gidley,
W^m. Gardner Wanton,
Thos. Wickham,
Joseph Whipple,

Jon. Thurston,
L. Payne,
Wm. Mumford,
M. Brett,
M. Bowler,
Walter Chaloner,
W^m. Paul,
John Bourke,
John and Jos. Thurston,
Dan' Fortaine,
D. Updike,
Silas Cooke,
Samuel Wickham,
Isaac Stelle,
G. Dunbar,
Thos. Jeffries,
Rob' Shearman.

IN THE GALLERY.

M. Phillips and M. Bowler,[110] Chas. Bardin,

for nine years. His popularity was so great that the town of Johnston was named after him. In 1765 he was appointed Stamp Master by the British Government ; an office that brought him into trouble—his house was beset, his furniture destroyed, and at the hands of a mob he suffered many indignities, even to being burnt in effigy [with others associated with him in the Stamp Office] on the Parade. In 1766 he was appointed Judge of the Vice-Admiralty Court, in South Carolina, and in Charleston he resided a part of each year ; holding in that city a number of offices. He died suddenly, at the age of 49 years.

[110] Metcalf Bowler was for many years one of the most active and enterprising of the merchants of Newport, and, with the Malbones, Wantons and others, fitted out and kept at sea many privateers in the French and Spanish war, from 1756 to 1763. He had both his town and his country house ; the former

Henry Taggart,
Jas. Cahome,
Samuel Ayrault,
George Gibbs,
Jas. Hasting,
Jon[a] Ingraham,
John Haxham,
Rob[t] Dunbar,
Ann Pye,
John Archer,
Chas. A. Wigneron,
John Briston,
Henry Allen,

John Tweedy,
Robt. Wheatley,
Nath. Norton,
Jas. Holmes,
John Barzee,
Benj. Jefferson,
J. Beard and J. Cooper,
John Launce,
W. G. Owen,
Jas. Wilson,
Job Snell,
John Vial.

---

was what is now known as the Vernon House, on Mary and Clarke streets, and the latter was a farm in Portsmouth, where the gardens were filled with the choicest fruits and the rarest flowers. But he suffered severely under the enforcement of the rule of 1756, and was subjected to vexatious suits in England, from Dutch and other neutrals whose vessels had been taken and condemned for covering property of the enemies.

Mr. Bowler also took an active part in public life. He was Speaker of the House of Representatives from 1767 to 1776. With Henry Ward he was appointed a Commissioner to the Congress held in New York, and in 1765 he was among the foremost who opposed the Stamp Act. On the anniversary of the repeal of that Act, 1767, he threw open his house and entertained the friends of liberty right royally. In 1768 he was elected one of the Assistant Judges of the Superior Court of Judicature, and in 1776 he was made Chief-Justice of the Court. He also rendered public service as one of a committee to obtain the earliest intelligence of the acts and measures of the British Parliament that bore on the American Colonies, and to maintain a correspondence with the other colonies. But the return of peace found him in straitened circumstances; his property was depreciated; he was too old to enter upon his old pursuits again, and in 1787 he was keeping a boarding-house, the "Queen's Head," in Providence, where he died in 1789.

CHAPTER VII.

1753–1762.

AUGUST, 20, 1753. Voted: that the Church Wardens be a committee to repair the steeple of the Church, roof and gates, and whatever else belonging to the Church that may want it ; and to partition off a part of the belfry for a vestry-room.

Voted: that the half-yearly tax or rent on the pews, now due, should be immediately collected by the Church Wardens, and Mr. Leaming's demand for payment of his usher satisfied out of it.

August 27, 1753. At a meeting of the congregation, voted: that John Grelea, for his ill-behavior in absolutely refusing to sing the tune played by the organist in the morning service yesterday, and also refusing to read the first line of the Psalm he proposed to be sung after he was desired to do so by Mr. Leaming, then minister, be, and he is hereby dismissed from being Clerk of said Trinity Church.[112]

September 17, 1753. Charles Handy[113] was married to Ann Brown.

---

[112] The above was the outcome of a quarrel between John Grelea, the Clerk of the Church, and Capt. Charles Bardin, the organist. Primarily the organist was to blame for playing a different tune from the one selected by the Clerk ; and the Clerk sinned in failing to lead in the singing, and then in refusing to go on when so requested by the minister. The matter was finally adjusted, as will be seen further on.

[113] Capt. Charles Handy, son of Samuel Handy, was born in Maryland, October 8. 1729. Ann Brown, to whom he was married as above, was the daughter of Capt. John Brown, an active member of the Church. She was born August 19, 1733, and died July 26, 1780. After her death he

November 12, 1753. Voted, that Mrs. Hannah Leadbethy should take possession of the parsonage-house and dwell there free, provided she was warned out and removed within three months of the time of her entering into it; and in case she remains in it three months longer, she is to pay a reasonable rent; Mr. James Honyman engaging she shall remove immediately when required, and leave the house in as good repair as she finds it.

Voted: that Mr. George Owens be sexton for the remainder of the year.

January 17, 1754. Benjamin Mason[114], was married to Mary Ayrault.

February 11, 1754. Voted: that Richard Beal and Metcalf Bowler be a committee to collect the remainder of the subscription to the parsonage house, in the room of Jahleel Brenton, Esq., and Capt. John Brown, who have desired to relinquish that office.

It was also voted: that Joseph Wanton, Esq., Godfrey Malbone, Jr.,[115] and Martin Howard, Jr., be a committee to procure an organ-

---

married Mrs. Abigail Wilkinson, widow of Philip Wilkinson and daughter of Jahleel Brenton. His daughter Ann became the wife of Major Thomas Russell, a Revolutionary officer, and his son, Major John Handy, was also an officer in the Revolution. Capt. Charles Handy died July 25, 1793.

[114] Benjamin Mason born in December, 1728, and died January 7, 1775, was a merchant extensively engaged in trade in Newport. Mary Ayrault, his wife, was the daughter of Daniel Ayrault, Jr., born in 1735, and died March 17, 1792.

[115] Godfrey Malbone, Jr., was the eldest son of Godfrey Malbone. He was educated at Queen's College, Oxford, and returned to Rhode Island in 1744. In 1756 he commanded a regiment of 400 men, and marched for Albany, but his orders were countermanded before he reached that point. After the war

ist as soon as may be; for the payment of whose salary they are to raise money by subscription.

Easter Monday, 1754. Edward Cole was elected elder Church Warden, and Metcalf Bowler, the younger.

The Vestry remained the same, with the addition of Evan Malbone.

William Allen chosen Clerk, at £60 per annum, and George Owen, sexton, at £40 per annum.

May 13, 1754. The Rev. Mr. Pollen[116] having delivered us a letter from Dr. Bearcroft, Secretary of the Society for Propagating the Gospel in Foreign Parts, advising us of his, the Rev. Thomas Pollen, being appointed a missionary of our Church, it was voted: that it is agreeable to us, and he is received accordingly; and that Edward Scott, Peter Bours, and James Honyman be a committee to return our thanks to the Society for their care in sending him.

Voted: that Edward Cole be a committee to collect what money remains unpaid of the subscription for purchasing the parsonage house, in place of Richard Beel, who refuses to act.

he retired to Pomfret, Ct., and resided there. His wife was a sister of Francis Brinley. He died without issue, at the age of 60 years, November 12, 1785.

[116] "Rev. Thomas Pollen. Dr. Berriman, in a letter to Dr. Samuel Johnson, dated London, February, 1754, says: 'Mr. Pollen is appointed a Missionary to Rhode Island. He is a worthy clergyman, and esteemed a good scholar. He was cotemporary at Christ Church College, Oxford, with your friend Dr. Burton, who is now Vice-Provost of Eton College. I would beg leave to recommend him to your favorable notice and that you would advise and assist him in any case that may need your helping hand. He is a traveller and has seen the world, and has been lately employed in an Episcopal Church at Glasgow, but was never in your parts; and being quite a stranger to such a kind of settlement, may often have occasion to consult you, who are so much known and so well esteemed by all around you.'"—*History of the Narragansett Church.*

Voted: that £400, old tenor, be given the Rev. Mr. Pollen, a present, for the payment of his passage, &c."[117]

May 27, 1754. Voted: at a meeting of the congregation, that the salary we voted to the Rev. Mr. Thomas Pollen, should be paid him from Christmas day, last; at fifty [pounds] sterling per annum, agreeably to a former vote of ye 26th December, 1752.

Voted: that the proceedings of the Church Wardens and Vestry, at their last meeting, should be, and are hereby confirmed.

---

[117] " By a letter of thanks to the Society, from the Church Wardens and Vestry of the Church at Newport, in Rhode Island, bearing date the 28th of May, 1754, for the appointment of the Rev. Mr. Pollen to that mission [as mentioned in the abstracts of the Society's proceedings in the year 1753] it appears that Mr. Pollen arrived safely in the beginning of that month, and was very acceptable to them; not only for his general good character, but also from his good behavior and abilities in his pastoral duties, as far as they have yet experienced them; and they made no doubt but he would answer the pious and charitable design of the Society in sending him to them. And Mr. Pollen, by his letter of June the 7th, 1754, gives an account of his kind reception, and that he hath great hopes of propagating the true Christian faith, and doing much good among them, towards which he promises his best endeavors shall not be wanting." —*Abstracts from the Proceedings of the Society.*

Following his connection with the Church, Rev. Mr. Pollen became the Rector of the Church, at Kingston, Jamaica, and under date of March 12, 1761, from that place wrote to Dr. John Brett, touching the recent death of the king: "Our Church is in mourning, which, I believe, is more than you can say of yours. This, if it be true, proves we make a greater show of loyalty than you, tho' not of religion; for I cannot find there came to ye Church when it was opened one person extraordinary, either to see the new decoration, or hear me, the new preacher. The difference between the Kingston and ye Newport churchmen is this: the former take care to pay the parson, but do not care to hear him preach; the latter take care to hear the parson preach, but do not care to pay him. Whence I may likewise infer that ye former have more honesty, tho' perhaps less sanctity than the latter."

The Committee appointed to return thanks to the Society, having presented the following letter, draughted by them, it is approved of:

Revd Sir. Your most agreeable favor of the 10th of February last, we received by the Rev. Mr. Pollen, who, with his family, arrived here the beginning of this month. We shall punctually perform our engagements made to the Honble Society, and do everything in our power that may contribute to render his mission agreeable to him. From the general good character we have received, and the small acquaintance we have had with him since his arrival, we promise ourselves great satisfaction and make no doubt but he will be greatly instrumental in promoting true religion among us, and therby answer the pious and charitable design of the Honble Society in sending him ; for which favor and all others we entreat them to accept our most grateful acknowledgements, and are, with profound respect, and with much esteem, Revd Sir.

Your Most Obedient Hum^ble Svt's
Signed by the Church Wardens.

September 17, 1754. John Powell[118] was married to Jane Grant.

November 12, 1754. Francis Brinley was married to Aleph Malbone.

December 3, 1754. Henry Ward was[120] married to Esther Freebody.

January 6, 1755. Voted : that from the first day of July last, the

---

[118] John Powell was the son of Adam Powell [one of the Wardens of the Church in 1721] and Sarah Bernon, daughter of Gabriel Bernon, his wife. Jane Grant, was the daughter of Sueton and Temperance Grant. Mrs. Grant died on Long Island, where she went to be inoculated for the smallpox, in October, 1774. Mr. Powell removed with his children to England, and died at Ludlow, in 1800, aged 83 years.

[120] Henry Ward was Secretary of the Colony, and then of the State, from 1760 to the time of his death, in 1797. His brother Thomas had filled the same office fourteen years, and another brother, Samuel, was Governor of the Colony from 1762 to 1763, and from 1765 to 1767.

proprietors of the double pews should pay as a tax towards the payment of the Rev. Mr. Pollen's salary, per annum, £18; the pews and a half, £13.10, and the single pews £9, and the pews in the gallery £6.15, each.

Voted: that Mr. Pollen should be paid his salary at the rate of sixteen hundred pounds, old tenor, for one hundred sterling.

Easter Monday, March 31, 1755. Metcalf Bowler chosen Elder Church Warden, and Robert Jenkins, youngest.

Philip Wilkinson was added to the Vestry.

John Grelea was elected Clerk, at £100, per annum.

Voted: that hereafter the organist, in divine service, should play such tunes only to the psalms proposed to be sung, as the said Clerk shall direct.

George Owen was continued as sexton.

October 26, 1755. Voted: that the pew No. 27, that was formerly Captain W[m] Bell's, and that which was Capt. W[m] Gibb's, No. 19, should be sold, and that sundry persons applying for pews, should draw lots for the pews; when Mr. Robert Jenkins, in behalf of Capt. John Mawdsley, drew No. 27, at £300. Capt. John Dennis drew the southernmost half of pew No. 19, that was William Gibbs's, at £200, and Capt. Peter Harrison[2] the north part of the said pew, at £200, and that the above mentioned pews should be subject to the same tax and other charges, as the other pews in the Church.

October 13th, 1755. Jonathan Thurston was chosen one of the Vestry, in the room of W[m] Coddington, deceased.

---

[2] Peter Harrison was an accomplished architect—one who left his mark in Boston as well as in Newport. He was the architect of the front (the original) part of the Redwood Library, a beautiful and refined specimen of Roman Doric architecture, and also of the City Hall and the Jews' Synagogue; and it is probable that he designed some of the finer specimens of domestic architecture, still preserved to us.

Easter Monday, April 19, 1756. Robert Jenkins was chosen eldest Church Warden, and Joseph Wanton, Jr., youngest.

Vestrymen: Jahleel Brenton, Joseph Wanton, Godfrey Malbone, Edward Scott, John Brown, Peter Bours, James Honyman, Wm. Mumford, Jonathan Thurston, William Paul, Thomas Wickham, Charles Wickham, Daniel Ayrault, Jr., Evan Malbone, Philip Wilkinson and Walter Cranston.

John Grelea, Clerk of the Church; William Paul, Clerk of the Vestry; and Geo. Owen, Sexton.

July 5, 1756. Voted: that Mr. Proud's allowance, for weekly winding up the clock, should be augmented to £26 per annum for the future.

October 16, 1756. Mrs. Elizabeth Cole,[122] widow of Elisha Cole, was buried by Rev. Dr. McSparran.

October 18, 1756. Robert Stoddard[123] was married to Mary Pease.

----

[122] The following record was made in the books of St. Paul's, Narragansett, by Rev. Dr. McSparran:

"October 16, 1756. Being wrote and earnestly entreated to go to Newport for that purpose, I preached a funeral sermon for and on account of Mrs. Elizabeth Cole, widow and relict of the late Elisha Cole, Esq., who died many years ago in London, and buried her in the burying-ground in Newport. She was a good woman and a particular friend of the subscriber's, and she and her husband and family were baptized by me.

JAMES McSPARRAN."

Elisha Cole was the son of John Cole, an early settler of Narragansett, and grandson of the famous Ann Hutchinson. One of his sons, John, became distinguished at the Bar, was made Chief-Justice, and held other important offices. Of Col. Edward Cole, the third son, mention has been made in these pages.

[123] Robert Stoddard was a storekeeper in Newport. After the death of his first wife he married, November 29, 1767, Catharine Wanton, daughter of Joseph Wanton and grand-daughter of Gov. William Wanton.

Easter Monday, April 11, 1757.   Joseph Wanton, Jr., elected Eldest Church Warden, and Charles Handy, the youngest.

No change was made in the Vestry.

Voted: that for the future the Rev. Mr. Pollen's salary should be paid in sterling money.

April 18, 1757.   Voted: that the Rev. Mr. Pollen be allowed £200, old tenor.

May 19.   William Redwood[124] was married to Sarah Pope.

[St. John's Day, June 24, 1756.   Services were held in the Church, and a sermon was preached before the "Society of Free and Accepted Masons" by the Rev. Mr. Pollen.]

November 21, 1757.   Voted: that Joseph Wanton, Thomas Wickham and Godfrey Malbone be a committee to learn on what terms Mr. Knotchell[126] will act as organist for us, and to get a subscription for the payment of an organist.

February 13, 1758.   Voted: that Mr. Joseph Wanton, Jr., and Mr. Charles Handy be a committee to write to Mr. Marmaduke Browne to know if he will act as Catechist in the Rev. Mr. Leaming's station.

Easter Monday, March 27, 1758.   Charles Handy was chosen eldest Church Warden, and Andrew Hunter, the youngest.

Joseph Wanton, Jr., was added to the Vestry.

After the death of Stoddard she married Dr. Destailleur, a surgeon in the British army, and removed to Canada.

[124] William Redwood was the fifth child of Abraham Redwood, born at Newport, June 1, 1734, removed to Philadelphia, and died at Burlington, N. J., without issue.   January 14, 1815, he was buried in the Friends' burial ground, Philadelphia.

[126] From the time the organ was set up in the Church there seems to have been difficulty in securing the services of an efficient and reliable organist, and for many years subsequent to this date the difficulty had still to be solved.   Knotchell held the office till he died, in 1769.

John Grelea elected Clerk, and George Owen, sexton.

Voted: that Peter Bours and Edward Scott be a committee to ask of the Society a school-master, to supply the place of Mr. Jeremiah Leaming.

Voted: that Joseph Wanton, Jr., Andrew Hunter, and Christopher Champlin be a committee to have four pews built, agreeably to a vote passed in May, 1746, and that Isaac Stelle have the offer of one of them.

April 10, 1758. Voted: that the following gentlemen should have the pews, viz.: Thomas Cranston, No. 61; Francis Brinley, No. 62; Simon Pease,[17] No. 63, and Isaac Stelle, No. 64; at the rate of £200 each, subject to the same tax as the pews adjoining.

March 29, 1759. Catharine Sorento, an adult Indian, was baptized.

April 9, 1759. Voted: that the Church Wardens and their successors, with Capt. Charles Wickham, and Evan Malbone, be a committee to repair the house left in trust by Nathaniel Kay, Esq., deceased, to the Minister, Church Wardens and Vestry of the above Church, and to lease it to Mr. Robert Crooke for five years, at the rate of $111 per annum, to be paid quarterly, and that the lessee give security for the payment of the rent. The committee also to lease the land given with said house, formerly rented to Mr. John Bennett, and that they inquire in what repair the fence was when Mr. Bennett first hired it, and who was obliged to keep the fence in repair.

---

[17] Simon Pease was strongly conservative and looked well to the public interest. In 1750, when the paper money party was in power, and an effort was made to create another bank, in face of the £135,000 of paper money still afloat, he, with seventy-one other persons in Newport, signed a protest sent to the king. Bills on London were then selling at eleven hundred per cent.

Voted: that the Church Wardens pay Capt. Charles Bardin £100, the balance of his account.

Easter Monday, April 16, 1759. Andrew Hunter and Capt. Isaac Stelle chosen Church Wardens. The Vestry remained the same, and William Paul, John Grelea and George Owen retained their offices.

Voted: that the Church Wardens receive the poor money from Mr. John Baninster, or any other person who inclines to pay it in, and let it on interest, with good security.

March 17, 1760. Voted: that the Church Wardens buy, for the use of the Church, a broad-cloth pall.

Easter Monday, April 7, 1760. Isaac Stelle was chosen eldest Church Warden, and John Mawdsley the younger.

The Vestry and other officers remain the same.

Voted: that Mr. James Honyman and Peter Bours should again solicit the Society to send us a school-master.

May 26, 1760. Rev. Gardiner Thurston[128] was married to Mrs. Martha Sanford.

August 6, 1760. Voted: at a special meeting of the congregation, that as the Rev. Mr. Pollen has now told us that he is determined to leave us very soon, Edward Scott, James Honyman and Peter Bours, Esq., be a committee to write to y⁰ Society for the Propagation of the Gospel in Foreign Parts, and request them to

---

[128] Rev. Gardiner Thurston, born in Newport, in November, 1721, was licensed to preach in 1748, and became the assistant minister of the Second Baptist Church. The pastor, Rev. Nicholas Eyres, died February 15, 1759, and April 29th of that year Mr. Thurston was ordained pastor of the Church. He died August 23, 1802. A concourse from this and neighboring towns attended his funeral, for he was widely known. The funeral discourse was preached by Rev. Stephen Gano, of Providence.

send a missionary, and that they also send over ye proof of our having payed Mr. Pollen what we promised.[129]

Voted: that Mr. Bours desire of Mr. Pollen a copy of his letter respecting the instruction of negro children.

Easter Monday, March 23, 1761. Capt. John Mawdsley and Benj. Mason were elected Church Wardens.

No change was made in the Vestry, and the clerks were the same. Edmund Bell was elected sexton.

Voted: that the Church Wardens pay Samuel Bours what may be due to him for boarding Rev. Mr. [Marmaduke] Browne.

—

[129] No reason is given in the records for Mr. Pollen's determination to break the connection, but the following, from the " Abstracts of the Proceedings of the Society," throws light upon the subject :

" The Rev. Mr. Pollen, late the Society's missionary to the Church in Newport, in Rhode Island, by a letter dated there July the 10th, 1760, acquainted the Society that he had received an invitation to a parish in Jamaica, and hoped the Society would not take amiss his acceptance of it, as he should always retain the utmost veneration for them ; whether in or out of their service, gladly embrace any opportunity of promoting it ; that he was pressed immediately to embark for Jamaica, but he would stay and officiate in Newport till the beginning of winter.

" And the Church in Newport entreated the Society by a petition, dated September 23, 1760, to grant them another missionary, in the room of Mr. Pollen, then about to leave them : and they take the liberty to mention Mr. Marmaduke Browne, the Society's itinerant missionary in New Hampshire, as a clergyman of very good character, who had lately officiated to them to the great satisfaction of the congregation, and they hoped to be quite happy under his pastoral care, would the Society be so good as to appoint him to that mission. This the Society have granted, Mr. Marmaduke Browne joining in the request, together with his father, the Society's missionary at Portsmouth, New Hampshire."

The following sermons, preached by Rev. Thomas Pollen, while in Newport, were published :

" A Sermon preached in Trinity Church, Newport, Rhode Island, on Thursday, May 29, 1755. Upon occasion of the Embarkation of some of

Voted : that the Wardens repair the school-house under our care,
out of the rents of the estate left by Nathaniel Kay, Esq.

July 5, 1761. Voted : that the Church Wardens pay to Mr.
Browne what is due to him.

Voted : that Captain Northam have leave to build a pew on the
north side of the gallery.

September 13, 1761. William Hunter[130] was married to Deborah
Malbone.

------

the Colony's Troops, in order to go against the Enemy. Published at the
Desire of the Council of War, at Newport."

" Universal Love. A sermon at Newport, R. I., before a Lodge of Free-
masons, June 24, 1757."

" May 29, 1755, Upon occasion of the Embarkation of some of the
Colony's Troops, in order to go against the Enemy. By Thomas Pollen,
M.A. Published at the Desire of the Council of War at Newport. Text :
Save now, I beseech thee O Lord. I beseech thee send now Prosperity.
Psalm cxviii., 25."

" The Principal Marks of True Patriotism. A Sermon preached in
Trinity Church, at Newport, in Rhode Island, on the 5th day of March,
1758. By Thomas Pollen, M.A. And humbly dedicated to His Excellency, John, Earl of Loudoun."

[130] Dr. William Hunter was a highly educated Scotch physician, who
came to America in 1752, and settled in Newport. It is said that he was one of the devoted
band who adhered to the Stuarts, and that his emigration grew out of his
participation in the rebellion of 1745. In 1755 he was appointed surgeon
of the regiment raised in Rhode Island to go against Crown Point, a position for which he was eminently fitted, he having served as surgeon in the
British army before he came to America. It was in Dr. Hunter's tent that
the brave Baron Dieskau died. In 1756 Dr. Hunter delivered in Newport
the first course of anatomical lectures delivered in America. A ticket to
this course, printed upon the back of a playing-card, is in the possession
of one of his descendants, Dr. William H. Birckhead.

Before the Revolution, and up to the time of his death, Dr. Hunter

September 20, 1761.   Peter Bours[131] died.

[In October, 1761, a violent storm did serious injury to the Church spire.   No mention is made of it in the Church records.   The following concise account of the event is from the Newport *Mercury* of October 27, 1761 :]

"On Friday evening last came on a terrible storm from the north east, which continued increasing, with a heavy rain, and did not abate till after two o'clock in the morning. The violence of the wind broke off part of the steeple of Trinity Church, just below the second ball, which, in its direction towards the southwest, fell upon the adjacent house of Mr. John Hadwin, went through the roof and garret floor and broke the summer of the chamber floor, where it lodged, but happily for the family (who were greatly surprised by the shock) did no other damage."

espoused the cause of the Crown.   He remained in Newport when the British took possession of the place, and died in 1778, after a few days' illness, of putrid fever, contracted while attending some sick prisoners. Mrs. Hunter was the youngest daughter of Godfrey Malbone.   Many of Dr. Hunter's valuable books were given by his son, the late Hon. William Hunter, to Brown University.

[131] Peter Bours, who was at the age of 56 years at the time of his death, was an influential man, both in the Church and in the community.   He had served the town with great fidelity, and when, through failing health, he was forced to retire from active life, "The town, from a just sense of the advantages of an upright administration, and to express their grati tude, unanimously passed a vote that Col. Bennett and Mr. William Coddington wait upon Peter Bours, Esq., with their compliments, and thank him for the singular service he had done the town, and for that interested zeal and regard he has discovered on every occasion in the different characters he had maintained in the General Assembly upwards of twenty years, to promote the happiness and welfare of the Colony."—*Newport Mercury*, October 21, 1761.

Rev. Peter Bours, Rector of St. Michael's, Marblehead, from 1753 to 1762, was the son of the above Peter Bours.   He died February 24, 1762, aged 36 years.

November 2, 1761.   Voted: that James Honyman and Edward Scott be a committee to acquaint the Society for Promoting the Gospel in Foreign Parts, that the Rev. Mr. Pollen has left us, and desire they will appoint the Rev. Marmaduke Browne in his stead, and that they will also send us a school-master.

Voted: that Mr. Robert Veates have the use of the school-house under our care, and that he have from out of the donation of Nathaniel Kay, Esq., £10, old tenor, per boy, per annum, for teaching ten poor boys ; to begin from this day.

January 11, 1762.   Voted: at a meeting of the congregation, that a minister should now be chosen ; Edward Scott, Daniel Ayrault, Jr.,[132] Joseph Wanton and Walter Cranston dissented.   Voted: that the Rev. Marmaduke Browne should be our minister, and that he shall receive from this Church, annually, as his salary, £100 sterling, to be paid in payments of £50 each, at the end of each six months ; provided the Society do not continue their mission.

Voted: that said salary should be raised by a tax on the pews.

Voted: that Capt. John Mawdsley, Benj. Mason, Andrew Hunter, Thomas Cranston and Charles Wickham be a committee to assess

[132] second son of Daniel Ayrault, was born at East Greenwich, November 2, 1707, was sent to Boston, "to learn the art and trade of a merchant," and was engaged in business in Newport in 1726. In connection with Philip Wilkinson, he was largely interested in navigation. His first wife was Susannah Neargrass, to whom he was married April 17, 1737. His second wife was Rebecca Neargrass, widow of Edward Neargrass, to whom he was married March 3, 1745. His third wife was Hart Brenton, daughter of Jahleel Brenton and Frances his wife. She died January 30, 1764, aged 39 years. Mr. Ayrault died April 20, 1770. Following in the steps of his father, he was active in all works of benevolence, and was a staunch supporter of the Church.

the pews, for raising £100 sterling, for payment to the minister, and £50 for the other Church officers.

Voted: that the above-named gentlemen be a committee to consider the making of an addition to our Church, and report to us on Thursday next.

CHAPTER VIII.

1762–1771.

JANUARY 18, 1762. At an adjourned meeting, Voted: that the Church might be enlarged to the eastward, provided the gentlemen hereafter mentioned, give security to the Church, that they will make the addition without its being any expense to the other members of the Church, for which they are to have the pews, subject to a tax for defraying the expenses of the Church. The undertakers are as follows:

Thomas Cranston, Andrew Hunter, Silas Cooke, Robert Jenkins, John Jenkins, Benjamin Mason, Christopher Champlin, Samuel Goldthwait, Joseph Wanton, Jr., William Mumford, George Gibbs, Robert Stoddard, Francis Malbone, Benj. Wickham, Wm. Richardson, Peter Harrison, Samuel Mumford, Joshua Almy, John Dupee, Solomon Townsend, Isaac Lawton, Nicholas Lechmere,[133] Henry John Overing, John Magee, Sherman Clarke, Robert Crooke, Samuel Johnstone, Matthew Cozzens, George Croswell, Peter Mumford, John Miller, Ignatius Battar, Peter Dorden, Nathaniel Bird, John Chaloner, James Potter, James Drew, James Keith, James Roach, Robert

---

[133] Nicholas Lechmere was appointed Searcher and Land Waiter in Newport, by the London Custom House, February, 1761, and was holding that office when the obnoxious persons who were appointed to enforce the Stamp Act, were set upon by a mob. With his associates, he was forced for the moment to seek shelter on board a sloop-of-war in the harbor. He married Elizabeth Gardiner, daughter of William Gardiner, of Narragansett, and left Newport at the time of the evacuation by the British.

Lockwood, James Duncan, William Hunter, John Bannister, Joseph Scott, Simon Pease, Jr., and Francis Brinley.[134]

Easter Monday, April 12, 1762. Benjamin Mason was chosen eldest Church Warden, and Samuel Brenton, youngest. Vestrymen: Jahleel Brenton, Godfrey Malbone, Joseph Wanton, Edward Scott, John Brown, James Honyman, Wm Mumford, William Paul, Daniel Ayrault, Jr., Evan Malbone, Philip Wilkinson, Walter Cranston, Joseph Wanton, Jr., Charles Wickham, and Thomas Cranston.

William Paul, clerk of the Vestry, John Grelea, clerk, and Richard Durfee, sexton.

Voted: that the Church Wardens, Evan Malbone and Capt. John Mawdsley be a committee to repair the steeple by subscription, and that they consult a carpenter, and make report at the next meeting what the expense will be.

October 11, 1762. At a meeting of the congregation, Voted: that Thomas Cranston, Daniel Ayrault, Jr., Samuel Bours and Evan Malbone be a committee to examine into the Church's account with those persons who have the Church's money in their hands, and make report to a future meeting of the congregation.

Voted: that Mr. Benjamin Mason buy a book proper, in which the Church's accounts may be properly kept, and deliver it to Mr. Thomas Cranston, of the committee.

The plot of the Church given on the following page, is from a rough draught in the hand-writing of Daniel Ayrault, Jr., after the enlargement of the Church, in 1762. The owners and occupants of pews are given as follows—the numbers corresponding with those on the plot:

---

[134] The church edifice was cut in two, and the eastern part was moved east to the line of the street; the intervening space was filled in, making two bays in the interior and affording thirty-six additional pews. The points of juncture can easily be discovered by an observing eye.

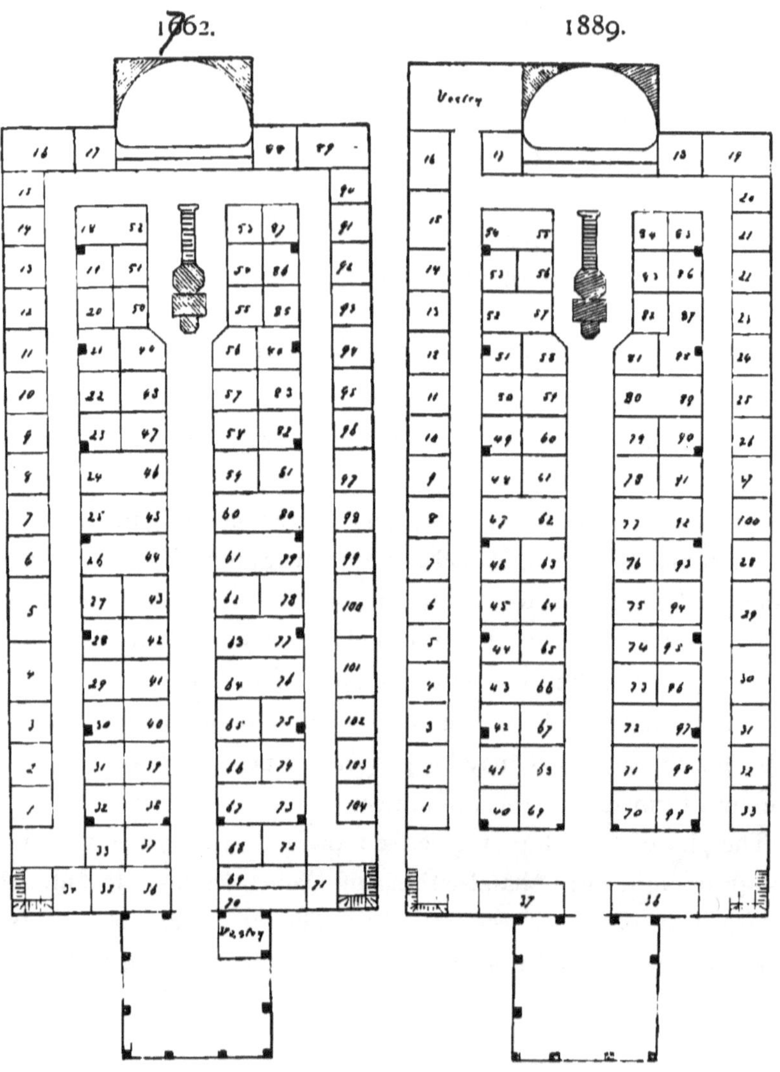

No.
1. Mrs. Munday,
2. Nathaniel Mumford,
3. Mrs. Chase,
4. Mrs. Gidley, a pew and a
   half,

No.
5. Mrs. William Coddington,
   a pew and a half,
6. Daniel Updike,
7. James Honyman,
8. Mrs. Cowley,

No.

9. Captain James,
10. Mrs. Almy and Mrs. Lawdy?
11. Captain Cook,
12. Captain Joshua Almy,
13. Dr. William Hunter,
14. Christopher Champlin,
15. Peter Mumford,
16. Jonathan Nichols, double pew,
17. Captain J. Lawton,
18 and 52. Minister's Pew, double,
19. James Miller,
20. Captain Stoddard,
21. Captain Charles Wickham,
22. Captain Simonds,
23. Solomon Townsend,
24 and 46. John and Jonathan Thurston, double,
25 and 45. Jahleel Brenton, double,
26 and 44. Captain George Wanton, double,
27. Mrs. King,
28. Mrs. Fortana,
29. Col. Daniel Updike,
30. Samuel Brenton,
31. Capt. Samuel Wickham,
32. Capt. Godfrey Malbone,
33. Colonel Whiting,

No.

34. Jabez Champlin,
35. Evan Malbone,
36. Capt. Thomas Wickham,
37. Thomas Cranston,
38. John Collins,
39. Capt. William Paul,
40. John Mawdsley,
41. Edward Scott,
42. John Bours,
43. Capt. Robert Eliot,
47. Francis Malbone,
48. Thomas Cranston,
49. Robert Jenkins,
50. Francis Brinley,
51. Capt. Samuel Sweet,
53. Matthew Cozzens,
54. Benjamin Carr,
55. Andrew Hunter,
56. Col. Joseph Wanton,
57. George Gibbs,
58. Benjamin Wickham,
59. Augustus Johnston,
62. Edward Mumford,
63. Nathaniel Hatch,
64. James Martin,
65. Metcalf Bowler,
66. Walter Chaloner,
67 and 73. John, Thomas and Samuel Freebody,
67. Simon Pease,
69. Robert Sherman,

No.

70. John Tweedy,
71. Mr. Bourke,
72. Isaac Stelle,
74. Mrs. Cupitt,
75. John Forester,
76. John Jepson,
77. Capt. Jas. Lillington,
78. Walter Cranston,
79 and 61. Godfrey Malbone,
80 and 60. Daniel Ayrault,
81. Captain Charles Handy,
82. Captain John Dennis,
83. Nicholas Lechmere,
84. John Overing.
85. Captain Keith,
86. Capt. Samuel Johnson,
87. Capt. Job Snell,
88. Capt. Robert Oliver,
89. Henry Bull,
90. Robert Crooke,

No.

91. Ignatius Battar,
92. John Jenkins,
93. Sherman Clarke,
94. William Mumford,
95. Thomas S. Taylor,
96. John Brown,
97. George Goulding, a pew and a half,
98. John Brown, a pew and a half,
99. Philip Wilkinson and Martin Howard, a pew and a half,
100. Joseph Wanton, a pew and a half,
101. Mr. Coggeshall and Mr. Clarke,
102. Mr. Brenton and Mr. Ayrault,
103. Mr. Whitehorne.

Gallery pews occupied :

No.

13. Robert Dunbar,
14. Henry Nye,
15. George Owen,
17. John Archer,
18. James Wilson,
19. Charles Anthony Wigneron[136]
20. Charles Bardin,

No.

21. John Tweedy,
22. Robert Wheatley,
23. Mark Morton,
24. Ann and John Chaloner,
25. Jahleel Brenton,
26. James Holmes,
28. illegible,
29. Benjamin Jefferson.

INTERIOR OF TRINITY CHURCH.

[February 27, 1763. Mr. Fayerweather was married to Mrs. Abigail Bours, the surviving relict of the late Peter Bours, of Marblehead, in the church at Newport by the Rev. Marmaduke Browne, and that day (an exceedingly cold day) preached on the occasion from these words: Do all to the Glory of God.][137]

Easter Monday, April 4, 1763. Samuel Brenton was chosen eldest Church Warden, and Samuel Bours, the younger.

The Vestry the same as last year, except that Stephen Ayrault takes the place of Walter Cranston.

William Paul, clerk of the Vestry, John Grelea, clerk at £200 per annum, John Ernest Knotchell, organist, at £30 sterling, per annum, Richard Durfee, sexton.

The congregation Voted: that Mr. John Ernest Knotchell shall have the use of the school-house under our care, and that he shall

[136] C. Anthony Wigneron was the eldest son of Dr. Norbent Felician Wigneron (sometimes written Vigneron), a native of Province d' Artois, France, who came to America in 1690, and died in Newport in 1764, aged 95 years. Dr. Charles Anthony (Antonio) died in New York, November 10, 1772, in his 56th year, after being inoculated for the small pox. Stephen, the second son, also trained to the medical profession, sailed on a cruise, as surgeon, in the war with France, and nothing more was heard of the vessel. Dr. Stephen, son of Dr. Charles, born November 25, 1748, practiced medicine in Newport, as the successor of his father, until the Island was occupied by the British, when he removed from the town. He died on board the hospital ship in New York harbor, August 24, 1781, in his 53d year.

[137] The above is from the records of St. Paul's, Narragansett.

Rev. Samuel Fayerweather was a graduate from Harvard. He was settled over the Second Congregational Church in Newport, in 1754, was ordained a Presbyter in the Episcopal Church in England, 1756, and entered upon his mission at St. Paul's, Narragansett, August 24, 1760. He died in 1781, and was buried under the communion table of St. Paul's.

teach ten boys we shall send him, English, Latin, writing and arithmetic, for each of which ten boys he shall have £10, old tenor, per quarter, paid him out of the rent of the estate of Nathaniel Kay, Esq, deceased, left for that purpose.

July 25, 1763. Voted by the congregation: that a place for another candlestick should be made in the ceiling of the church.[138]

Voted: that the proprietors of those pews next the pulpit, as it lately stood, may remove those in the middle alley as far as the others, at their expense.

April 17, 1764. Winthrop Saltonstall[139] was married by Rev. Mr. Leaming, to Ann Wanton.

Easter Monday, April 23, 1764. Samuel Bours chosen eldest Church Warden, and John Jenkins the younger.

The Vestry remained the same, except that John Mawdsley took

---

[138] In the ceiling, before the church was enlarged, there were two rosettes, enriched with boldly carved leaves and bunches of grapes. From the centre of each there hung a brass chandelier, fitted for candles, and they have hung in the same place since the time when they were given to the church, in 1728. One of them bears this inscription:

"THOS. DREW. OXON. 1728."

When the church was lengthened, it was found necessary to increase the artificial light for evening service; hence the above vote. Subsequently, and within the memory of the generation that is now nearly closed, it was found expedient to carry a smoke-pipe in winter, up through the ceiling and enter a chimney built there at the time. This pipe was made to pass through the centre of the rosette that had been put up in 1762. The putting in of a furnace did away with the stove-pipe, but the rosette was never restored. All traces of the brass chandelier that once hung there have been lost.

[139] Winthrop Saltonstall was the son of Gov. Gurdon Saltonstall, of New London, and was the cousin of his wife, Ann Wanton, daughter and fourth child of Gov. Joseph Wanton, of Newport.

the place of Capt. John Brown.[140]   The other officers were retained.

June 9. 1764.   The Vestry voted to write to the Society, desiring them to send out a school-master.

September 16, 1764.   George Scott[141] was married to Mary Ayrault.

October 28, 1764.   Major Fairchild[142] was married to Catharine Malbone.

December 16, 1764.   John Bell[143] was married to Mary Heatly.

[February 17, 1765.   Rev. Mr. Fayerweather preached at Newport, and baptized three children, one of Governor Wanton; all with their proper sponsors.][144]

Easter Monday, April 15, 1765.   Joseph Jenkins was chosen eldest Church Warden, and John Bours the younger.

[140] *John Brown*, son of Capt. John Brown, and an active member of the Vestry, had died January 2, 1764.   He was a merchant engaged in commercial pursuits, and with Godfrey Malbone and George Wanton fitted out privateers in the second Spanish war.   December 26, 1717, he was married by Rev. Mr. Honyman to Jane Lucas, born in 1769, and daughter of Augustus Lucas.   She died at Newport, October 13, 1775.

[141] George Scott followed the seas, and after his death his widow married Jahleel Brenton.   Mary Ayrault, his wife, was the daughter of Stephen Ayrault.   She was born in 1742, and died March 13, 1816.

[142] "Major" was Fairchild's Christian name, and not a title.   Catharine Malbone, his wife, born October 21, 1737, was a daughter of Godfrey Malbone.

The Major Fairchild, who married Bathsheba Palmer, March 12, 1729, was probably the father of the above.

[143] John Bell was a Major in the British army.   He went to England with his family, and died at Islington, County of Middlesex, May, 1779.   Mrs. Bell, whose maiden name was Mary Grant, daughter of Sueton Grant, was the widow of Andrew Heatly.   She died in England in 1781.

[144] *History of the Narragansett Church.*

The Vestry and other officers were continued. The sexton's
salary was raised to £140 per annum.

January 8, 1765. Henry Marchant[145] was married to Rebecca
Cooke.

Easter Monday, April 15, 1765. Joseph Jenkins was chosen
eldest Church Warden, and John Bours the younger.

The Vestry and other officers were continued. The sexton's
salary was raised to £140 per annum.

Voted: that the Church Wardens hire a room for Markadore, formerly a slave of Nathaniel Kay, Esq., deceased, set him free and pay
his rent for one year.

Voted: that James Honyman, Esq., be desired to inquire of the
Town Council respecting the affair of John Barzee.[146]

[The following, from the " Abstracts of the Proceedings of the
Society for the Propagation of the Gospel in Foreign Parts," should
have a place here:]

" The Rev. Marmaduke Browne, the Society's missionary at Newport, in the Colony of Rhode Island, in his letter dated February

---

[145] Henry Marchant was born at Martha's Vineyard in 1741, and died at
Newport, August 30, 1796. He became eminent at the Bar. After quali-
fying himself in the law office of Judge Trowbridge. at Cambridge, he
commenced the practice of the law in Newport. In 1770 he was elected
Attorney-General of the Colony, which office he held till 1777. when he
was chosen a delegate to the Continental Congress. In the interval he
had been sent, 1771, to England to adjust claims against the British government. When the war broke out he retired to Narragansett, but in
1784 he returned to Newport, was sent to the General Assembly as a Representative, and was a member of the Convention that adopted the Federal
Constitution. Following the adoption of the Constitution, he was appointed District Judge, which office he filled up to the time of his death.
He was highly esteemed.

[146] There is no reference to the affairs of John Barzee in the records of
the Town Council of that date.

29, 1764, writes, that notwithstanding the great enlargement of
Trinity Church, there is still room wanting to accommodate all who
would willingly attend.   In this Colony, he observes, a good harmony subsists between Churchmen and dissenters.   The Quakers,
in particular, express their regard for the Church from the experience they have had of the mildness and lenity of its administration.
And his parishioners are constant and decent in their attendance on
public worship, and unblamable in their lives.   In his letter, dated
September 19th, Mr. Browne gives a particular account of the rents
of the lands and houses left by Mr. Kay for the use of a grammar-
master at Newport, which, from the 1st of April, 1765, will amount
to the sum of £64 5s sterling, from which deducting £10 to keep
the house in repair, the estate will produce near £54 sterling per
annum.   The Society are desired to recommend a grammar-master
for this school, as soon as a proper person can be procured.   Mr.
Browne has baptized in the preceding year forty-five infants, two
white and one black adult, and has from 112 to 120 communicants."

Easter Monday, March 31, 1766.   John Bours was chosen eldest
Church Warden, and Simon Pease the younger.

The Vestry and other officers continue the same as last year.

July 31, 1766.   Voted: that the house rented to Mr. Robert
Crooke be immediately repaired, under the inspection of the Church
Wardens; the gentlemen appointed having reported that £500, O. T.
will put it into tenantable repair; but if more be needed, the Wardens
are not limited.

January 4, 1767.   Dr. John Halliburton[147] was married to Susannah
Brenton.

---

[147] Dr. Halliburton was eminent as a physician, and
socially his standing was equally high.   When the Revolution broke out
his leaning was to the Crown.   He was suspected of holding treasonable
correspondence with the enemy, escaped to New York, and from there

Easter Monday, April 20, 1767. Simon Pease, Jr. and Christopher Champlin[14] were chosen Church Wardens.

Vestrymen: Godfrey Malbone, Joseph Wanton, Edward Scott, James Honyman, Wm. Mumford, William Paul, Thos. Wickham, Evan Malbone, Philip Wilkinson, Joseph Wanton, Jr., Charles Wickham, Thomas Cranston, Stephen Ayrault, John Mawdsley, Jahleel Brenton and Andrew Hunter.

William Paul, Clerk of the Vestry, John Grelea, Clerk of the Church, Richard Durfee sexton during his good behavior.

Voted: that £4000, old tenor, should be raised by a tax on the pews, for repairing the steeple, and that the Church Wardens, with

— —

removed to Nova Scotia, where he died in 1807. His wife died there in 1818.

[15] fourth of the name, was born at Charlestown, R. I., February 7, 1731, and died in Newport, April 25, 1805. He took up his residence in Newport prior to 1753, for at that time he was a member of the Artillery Company. He joined the expedition against Crown Point, and was commissioned, May 10, 1755, a Major in the regiment raised by Col. Harris. The following year he was made Lt. Colonel. On his return to Newport he entered into business, chiefly commercial, and with other leading men, had much to do with fitting out privateers.

In 1763 a number of British men-of-war under Lord Colville, Rear Admiral of the White, were stationed at Newport, to enforce the revenue laws. For several years there was seldom a day when there was not one or more such vessels in the harbor. The Victualling Agent of the Navy was Sir Alexander Grant, in London, who had his agents in America, Mr. Champlin was his Newport agent; but when the war came on he removed to Narragansett till the return of peace. After the war he again took up his residence in Newport. He was elected an Alderman when the city government was organized, in 1784, and had other appointments of trust.

John Mawdsley, be a committee to tax the pews for raising the aforesaid sum, and that Evan Malbone, Capt. John Mawdsley and Andrew Hunter be a committee to hire and agree with proper persons for finishing s^d work, and to oversee and inspect the same till it is finished.

Voted: that the gallery pews be taxed twelve shillings per annum.

[At the June session of the General Assembly, 1767, a lottery was granted, to raise twenty-five hundred dollars for putting a new steeple upon Trinity Church, the old one being much decayed.][149]

November 16, 1767. Voted: that the Church Wardens should hire the sum of £50 sterling, at lawful interest, to pay the Rev. Mr. Bisset's passage, and his salary to the First of September last; for the payment of which, principal and interest, the Vestrymen themselves are bound.

December 3, 1767. Whereas the Church Wardens have reported to the Vestry, that they are not able to hire the money for the purpose of the aforesaid vote of the 16th of November, unless they give 8 per cent. interest for it, whereupon it was voted that the Church Wardens hire said money at said last mentioned rate, and the Vestry oblige themselves to see the same repaid.

Easter Monday, April 4, 1768. Francis Brinley and Francis Malbone chosen Church Wardens.

Vestrymen: Joseph Wanton, Edward Scott, James Honyman, Wm Mumford, Thomas Wickham, Evan Malbone, Philip Wilkinson, Joseph Wanton, Jr., Charles Wickham, Thomas Cranston, Stephen Ayrault, John Mawdsley, Jahleel Brenton, Andrew Hunter, Simon Pease, Jr., and John Bours.

The other officers were continued.

April 7, 1768. Voted: that the old tower of the Church, which

---

[149] Arnold's *History of Rhode Island*.

is reported by a survey of carpenters to be very defective, be pulled
down, and a new one, of wood, be erected in its place.

April 10, 1768.   At a meeting of the congregation, Voted: that
Capt. Evan Malbone, Capt. Charles Wickham, and Mr. John Bours,
be a committee to agree with Messrs. Charles Spooner, Jethro
Spooner, and James Tew, Jr., to pull down the old tower, and
build a new one, of wood, eighteen feet square, and sixty feet high,
and make a report to the congregation on Wednesday next.

April 13, 1768.   Messrs. Evan Malbone, Charles Wickham, and
John Bours, made report to the congregation, met by adjournment,
that they had covenanted with Charles Spooner, Jethro Spooner,
and James Tew, Jr., to pull down the old tower, and build a new
one, of wood, upon the following terms, viz.: That the said Charles
Spooner, Jethro Spooner, and James Tew, Jr., will engage to pull
down the old tower and build a new one, of wood, eighteen feet
square, and sixty feet high, they finding all and every the materials
necessary for completing the said tower, excepting what mason's
work may be wanting, the lead and leading, glass, and rigging
wanted at raising, together with the heavy iron work; the Church
paying them for the same the sum of £9000, old tenor, or eleven
hundred and twenty-five Spanish milled dollars; they to have the
old tower for their trouble in pulling it down, and some new timber
belonging to the Church.

Voted: that the report made by Evan Malbone, Charles Wickham, and John Bours be accepted, and that the said three persons,
with Mr. Stephen Ayrault, George Gibbs, and Archimedes George,
be a committee to oversee the said works, and enter into articles of
agreement with the said persons for carrying out the same immediately.

June 7, 1768.   Voted: that the Church Wardens hire the sum of
£100 to pay the Rev. Mr. Bisset what salary may be due him, and

that they be empowered to give 8 per cent. interest, per annum, for the same, provided it cannot be obtained at a lower interest.

Voted: that the persons indebted to the estate of Mr. Kay, for rents, be immediately sued for the same by the Church Wardens.

September 19, 1768.   Edward Wanton[150] was married to Frances Ayrault.

January 9, 1769. Voted: that Mr. Francis Malbone and Mr. Simon Pease, Jr., be a committee to hire a sum of money sufficient to pay the balance due from the Church to the carpenters for building the steeple, &c., and some other debts due from said Church, and that the Vestry and congregation give to them a counter security for the payment of the said money.

Voted: that Thomas Cranston, Esq., John Mawdsley, Esq., and Mr. Evan Malbone be a committee to go to Providence, to attend the General Assembly, to sit there the 27th inst., and endeavor to obtain the granting of a petition for incorporating the Church, and the said gentlemen were requested to attend the same.

February 26, 1769. In consequence of the vote of the Church Wardens and Vestry, on the inst. [ult.] to hire a sum of money sufficient to pay the carpenters the balance due to them for building the steeple, &c., $1000 were hired of Capt. Charles Handy for the term of one year, at the rate of 8 per cent. interest per annum, and $500 of John Tillinghast, Esq., at the rate of 6 per cent. per annum, for the same time.

Easter Monday, March 27, 1769.   Mr. Francis Malbone and Mr. Peter Cooke were chosen Church Wardens.

Francis Brinley chosen one of the Vestry in the room of Edward

---

[150] Edward Wanton was one of the three sons of Gov. Gideon Wanton; and Frances Ayrault, his wife, was the daughter of Stephen Ayrault. After the death of Wanton she married John Piper, of the Parish of Colyton, County of Devon, England, and with him resided there.

Scott, deceased; John Bours, Clerk of the Vestry; John Grelea, Clerk of the Church; John E. Knotchell, organist; and Richard Durfee, sexton, on good behavior.

Voted: that the sexton's salary be augmented to £20 per annum, and that he employ some person to ring the bell on Sundays, which shall be done for the future from the second story of the belfry.

April 3, 1769. Meeting of the congregation. Voted: that James Honyman, Evan Malbone, Charles Wickham, Stephen Ayrault and John Bours be a committee to draw up a set of rules and regulations for the Church, agreeably to the charter[151] lately granted by the Colony.

Voted: that the Clerk's salary be raised to £30 per annum.

May 29, 1769. The congregation voted: that a tax of $800 be assessed on the pews, towards paying the money lately hired by the Church, of Job Tillinghast and Charles Handy, for paying the debts of the Church, owed for building the steeple, &c., that the pews be rated equally, according to their bigness; that the gallery pews be rated one-third of the pews below, and that the Church Wardens collect the same.

The Rev. Mr. Browne having informed the congregation, that he is under necessity to go to Europe, and that he has obtained leave of absence from the Society for that purpose; voted: that he have liberty from the congregation also, and that his salary go on during his absence.

June 12, 1769. At a meeting of the congregation, voted: that the Rev. Mr. Browne, and John Mawdsley, Esq., be requested to procure in London, a new stop for the organ, in the room of that which is wanting; either the *vox humane*, or any other stop that

---

[151] This was the first charter granted to any religious society in Rhode Island.

may be thought most suitable, and that the congregation will pay the expense of the same.[152]

October 9, 1769. Voted: by the congregation, that the salary of Mr. Knotchell, organist of the Church, lately deceased, be continued and paid to his widow until the first day of January next ensuing ; and that the widow and family of the said Mr. Knotchell live in the house in the school-house yard, belonging to the Church, until Easter next, rent free.

Henry Bull, Esq., came into Church and agreed that the pew belonging to him, should be disposed of to Capt. Samuel Wickham,

---

[152] The following imperfect draught of a letter, found in a package of old papers, without signature, will throw light on the subject. From it we also gather the name of the builder of the organ :

"Newport. Rhode Island, October, 1755.

"Mr. Richard Bridge.

In the year 1733 you made an organ for the Rev. Doctor Berkeley. late Bishop of Cloyne, in which were the following whole stops (which he presented to Trinity Church.)

Stop Diapason, Principal Flute, 15th & Human Voice.

      ½ stops ; Cornet.)
      Trumpet.   Treble.
      Open Diapason.   )

Echo Trumpet, stop Diapason. Open Diapason—all half stops.

"We have sent a box to the care of Mr. Richard Mollineau. Iron Monger, in London. all the box H. pipes, which were never of any use here. as no organist could ever make some of them speak, and others when tuned would not stand half an hour. Now, Sir, what we desire is, that if you can so alter them as to make them answer their design, pray do : if not. we are of opinion that if we had a trumpet bass and the treble vox humane, it would be a good addition to the loudness of our organ. We waited so long in hopes an organ maker might accidentally come here, but as there is no one expected now, we hope for the credit of your organ, you'll repair this to your satisfaction, as well as to that of, Sir, ——

"P. S.—If neither of those ways above mentioned can be made use of, if you think proper, make a 12th in lieu thereof, and Mr. R. M. will pay you."

for $120, out of which sum the money due on said pew to the Church should belong ; reserving a seat for himself in said pew during his life.

October 16, 1769. Voted: by the congregation, that the tax of twenty-three shillings, sterling, on the pews in the lower part of the church, and twenty shillings sterling on the pews in the gallery, be continued for the present tax, in order to defray the incidental charges of the Church.

Voted: that Capt. Charles Bardin officiate as organist of the Church until Easter next, and that he be paid at the rate of £52 per annum.

["Yesterday, in the afternoon, we hear there was a very handsome collection at the Church of England in this Town, for the relief of Mr. Thomas Allen, of Providence, in this Colony, a very poor man, whose circumstances are really deplorable ; having a wife, who, by much sickness, has been a long time blind, and 11 children, 7 of whom were born blind."—*Newport Mercury*, January 20, 1770.]

February 26, 1770. At a meeting of the congregation, a letter from the Rev. Mr. Bisset to the Church Wardens, acquainting them that he had received an invitation to settle in Boston, as an assistant to Dr. Caner, at the Chapel there, and informing them that unless the Church would give him an additional salary of $100 per annum, and repair the house annexed to the school-house, in a decent manner, immediately, so that he might live in it, he should leave them ; was laid before the meeting. Whereupon a vote was put, whether the Church would comply with Mr. Bisset's proposal, which was passed in the negative.

Voted: that Joseph Wanton, Esq., and Mr. John Bours be a committee to write to the Rev. Arthur Browne, at Portsmouth [N. H.], and inform him that the Rev. Mr. Bisset is about leaving the Church and school, and request his assistance in supplying the Church with a minister, until the return of his son, the Rev. Marmaduke Browne, either by coming up to Newport himself, or sending up the Rev. Mr. Badger.

Voted : that the above gentlemen be also requested to write to the Rev. Dr. Miles Cooper, of King's College, in New York, and to the Rev. Dr. Smith, Provost of the Academy at Philadelphia, and enclose a paragraph of Mr. Kay's will respecting a school-master and assistant, and request those gentlemen to make inquiry for a suitable young man to go to England for orders, to supply Mr. Bisset's place.

March 8, 1770.   Abraham Redwood, Jr.,[133] was married to Susannah Honyman.

Easter Monday, April 23, 1770. Mr. Peter Cooke and Mr. Thomas Wickham, Jr., chosen Church Wardens. John Grelea, Clerk ; Charles Bardin, Organist ; and Richard Durfee, Sexton, during his good behavior.

Voted : that the Church Wardens be requested to sue immediately all persons who are delinquent in paying the pew tax, and money due to the Church by subscription.

Voted : that the house in the school-house yard be put in tenant able repairs, and delivered to the Rev. Mr. Bisset for his use, and that he keep the same in repair.

April 30, 1770. Mr. Thomas Wickham, Jr., having refused to accept of the office of Church Warden, Mr. John Bours was unanimously requested by the congregation to accept of the office of Senior Warden, which, to oblige the Church, he agreed to ; Mr. Peter Cooke agreeing to act as Junior Warden under him for the year ensuing.

---

[133] Abraham Redwood, Jr., was the eldest son of Abraham Redwood, the founder of the Redwood Library ; born January 8, 1728, and died in 1788. Susannah Honyman was the daughter of James Honyman, and granddaughter of Rev. James Honyman.

Voted: that the Wardens pay to the Rev. Mr. Bisset £8 sterling per annum for the hire of the house in the school-house yard, which, it is the opinion of the congregation, he is entitled to, and that the Church Wardens warn Mrs. Knotchell to leave the same immediately, and that they hire it out on the best terms they can.

Voted: that the Rev. Mr. Bisset's[154] demand of £8 per annum sterling, for the hire of the house in the school-house yard, for two and a half years past, be deferred to the consideration of the congregation at the next meeting.

June 25, 1770. At a meeting of the Church Wardens and Vestry, specially called. Present, James Honyman, Esq., Thomas Cranston, Esq., Mr. Charles Wickham, Col. Joseph Wanton, Mr. Stephen Ayrault, Mr. William Mumford, Mr. Frank Brinley, Mr. Thomas Wickham, Mr. Philip Wilkinson, Mr. Evan Malbone, John Mawdsley, Esq., and John Bours and Peter Cooke, Wardens.

Voted: that the house belonging to the Church, part of the estate of Nath' Kay,[155] Esq., be disposed of for $3000, and the first offer be given to Mr. Brinley.

July 9, 1770. The congregation voted: that Dr. Edward Evans[156] be chosen organist of the Church, at the annual salary of £30, sterling, to commence on his return from England to Newport,

---

[154] Rev. Mr. Bisset was a bachelor, and not wanting a house, the one in the school-house yard, the use of which he was entitled to as school-master, was rented for his benefit ; but he claimed that he should receive a rental for it from the time that he entered upon his duties. Mrs. Knotchell, widow of the organist, had been living in it rent free. How his claim was met by the congregation does not appear.

[155] This was the Kay house. The ground for this action is only conjectural—that the expense of keeping it in repair, and the difficulty experienced at times in finding a good tenant, led to the wish to convert it into money, which could be put out to interest. Later, as will be seen, the Vestry thought better of this.

[156] Dr. Edward Evans never returned from England.

and that he be requested to purchase in London the *vox-humane*
stop and other necessary additions for the organ, for which the
Church will be accountable to him at his return.

Voted: that a vote passed by the Vestry at their last meeting,
respecting the selling the house Mr. Brinley lives in, be reconsidered
and that the said house, together with all the estate belonging to
Nath¹ Kay, Esq., the house in the school-house yard included, be
leased to Mr. Francis Brinley for the term of seven years, at the
rate of £62, sterling, per annum, and that he be obliged to lay out
$100 in repairing the house he lives in, and that he keep the said
estate always in good repair, at his own charge, and that the said
house be painted at the expense of the Church, as soon as oil and
colors can be procured.

October 29, 1770. The congregation voted: that the Church
Wardens be desired to employ proper persons to take down the
spindle and scroll-work from the top of the spire, which was broken
off in the great storm on Saturday last, and that they inquire at the
same time whether it is practicable to have the same repaired this
fall, and make report to the congregation at a future meeting.

November 5, 1770. The Church Wardens reporting to the con
gregation that they had employed persons to take down the scroll-
work, &c., from the top of the mast of the steeple, and had consulted about repairing the same this fall, voted: that the spar which
is now fixed within the tower for doing the above-mentioned work,
remain, and that the necessary repairs be put off until the next
spring, for more suitable weather to do the same.[157]

Monday, March 18, 1771. At a meeting of the Vestry at the
parsonage house, the Rev. Mr. Browne having departed this life on

---

[157] In a severe blow from the north-east, the spindle broke off just below
the upper ball, and was only prevented from falling by the lightning-rod.

Saturday morning last, the 16th inst., it was voted unanimously: that he be buried in a decent manner, at the expense of the Church, and every mark of respect in their power shewed to his memory; and the Church Wardens were requested to wait upon the Rev. Mr. Bisset, and desire him to preach a funeral sermon on the day he is buried, and to officiate till after Easter.

CHAPTER IX.

1771–1780.

[" On Thursday the 21st of March, 1771, Mr. Fayerweather being invited by a letter from the Church Wardens of Trinity Church, Newport, he attended as a pall-bearer the funeral of the Rev. Marmaduke Browne,[137a] pastor of said Church, when a sermon was preached by

---

[137a] Rev. Marmaduke Browne was a native of Ireland. In 1730 he was sent to America, as missionary, and was settled at Providence for a time. From there he removed to Portsmouth, New Hampshire, where his father, also a missionary, had a parish. In 1760, on the withdrawal of Rev. Mr. Pollen, as already stated, he was elected minister of Trinity Church. His wife died in 1767, of which event the following minutes was made in the records of St. Paul's, Narragansett, under date of January 9, 1767:

"Mr. F. [Fayerweather] was sent for to attend the funeral of Mrs. Browne, the consort of the Rev. Mr. Browne, over whom he performed the funeral service in Trinity Church, Newport. An exceedingly large concourse of people attended, but no sermon, as both the lady herself, and her husband, too, had an utter aversion to pomp and show on those occasions, and utterly against all parading."

Rev. Mr. Browne left a son, Arthur Browne, who became a distinguished man of letters. Immediately following his father's death, then a lad, he wrote to Mr. John Bours, Senior Warden of the Church:

"Portsmouth, May 16th, 1771.

" Dear Mr. Bours:

It seems to me most proper to write to you concerning the following affair, both as Church Warden, and as being one of my best friends. My Grandfather declines drawing upon the Society, and thinks it would be best for the gentlemen who are Church Wardens, not to draw, but to write to the Society, informing them of my father's death, of his leaving me wholly unprovided for, by which means there was a great chance of my losing a liberal education at home, whither my father

the Rev. Mr. Bisset, colleague of the Rev. Mr. Browne, to a very numerous and weeping congregation."—*Records of the Narragansett Church.*]

Easter Monday, April 1, 1771. John Bours and Isaac Lawton were elected Church Wardens, John Grelea, Clerk, and Charles Bardin, organist, until the arrival of Dr. Evans from England. Geo. English elected sexton.

Vestrymen : Joseph Wanton, James Honyman, William Mumford, Thomas Wickham, Evan Malbone, Philip Wilkinson, Stephen

----

designed to send me. He says I may be pretty sure, if those gentlemen would be so kind as to write [obliterated] of the Society's doing something handsome for me, especially if they would represent me in as favorable a light as they think proper, as a lad of some merit, who, if properly encouraged, might turn out something.

These are his words, not mine; for not all the vanity natural to man should induce me to write thus of myself, were it not his direction. I know your friendship will excuse this trouble, which, notwithstanding after having troubled you so often, I am to give you, and I hope poor Peter was recovered before you got home. My love to Mrs. Bours.

I receiv'd Mr. Sam Bours' kind letter, and found that I must chuse a guardian as he says. I hope poor Mrs. Bours has had no more ill turns. My compliments to all friends. My Grandfather and all the family join with me in love to you and Mrs. Bours, and believe me always, your affectionate,

hum^b Servant,

Arthur Browne.

The above Arthur Browne was sent to Ireland, where he was educated and attained to a distinguished position. He was a man of marked character and high attainments, was made Fellow and Senior Proctor of Trinity College, a Doctor of Civil Law, King's Professor of Greek, &c. In his "Miscellaneous Essays and Dissertations," long out of print, he gives an entertaining account of society and manners in Rhode Island, and makes mention of many of the prominent men of that day. He also wrote a

Ayrault, John Mawdsley, Jahleel Brenton, Andrew Hunter, Simon
Pease, John Bours and Francis Brinley.

Voted: that a letter be written to the Society, informing them of
the death of our worthy minister, the late Mr. Browne, and soliciting a continuation of the mission, and that the Rev. Mr. Bisset be
particularly recommended as a suitable person to succeed Mr.
Browne, and that Mr. Honyman, with the Church Wardens, draft
the said letter.

Voted: that the Rev. Mr. Bisset be requested to officiate as
Minister of the Church, and that he be paid £50, sterling, per
annum by the congregation, the sum that was paid to the Rev. Mr.
Browne, and that he have likewise the use of the parsonage-house
until we hear from the Society; and that Mr. Dudley, with the
Church Wardens, be desired to acquaint Mr. Bisset with these
resolutions of the Church.

work on Civil Law, which is still valued by the profession. He died in
1805. In 1795 he caused a mural tablet, bearing a likeness of his father,
in relief and the family coat of arms, with the following inscription, to be
placed by the side of the Chancel in the Church:

To the memory of the Rev.

MARMADUKE BROWNE,

A man eminent for talents, learning, and religion, who departed this life
on the 19th of March, 1771, and of ANN, his wife, a lady of uncommon
piety and suavity of manners, who died the 6th of January, 1767. This monument was erected by their son, ARTHUR BROWNE, Esq., now senior
fellow of Trinity College, Dublin, Ireland, and representative in Parliament for the same: In token of his gratitude and affection to the best and
tenderest of parents, and of his respect and Love for a Congregation
among whom, and for the place where, he spent the earliest and happiest
of his days.

Heu! Quanto minus est,
Cum aliis Versari,
Quam tui Memisse,
M. D. CCXCV.

Voted: that the gentlemen who draft the letter to the Society, be requested to mention to them, in the same, the sending of a suitable person for a school-master and assistant, provided they should appoint Mr. Bisset our minister.

Voted: that Capt. Mawdsley,[158] Capt. Charles Wickham and Capt. Keith be a committee to repair the steeple, by having the spindle and vane put up again, in such manner as they shall judge best, as soon as the weather will permit.

Voted: that an account exhibited to the Church for attendance and medicine for negro Markadore in his last illness, by Dr. Thomas Eyres, be paid by the Church Wardens.

April 8, 1771.   Mr. Stephen Ayrault and James Honyman, Esq., were appointed a committee to visit Mr. Bisset's school from time to time, as often as they judge necessary, in order to see that the number of charity boys be always complete; and if there be any vacancy at any time, they are requested to look out a proper boy to fill it.

Voted: that the Church Wardens have the house Mr. Brinley lives in painted, agreeably to a former vote of the Vestry, in the best and cheapest manner they can, and the expense of the same be paid out of the money due to the Church.

Voted: that the Rev. Mr. Browne's salary be paid up to Easter.

[June 3, 1771.   the Rev. Mr. Bisset preached a funeral sermon on the death of Mrs. Abigail Wanton, wife of Gov. Joseph Wanton, to whom she was married January 26, 1756.][159]

---

[158] John Mawdsley at one time had a large capital, which he employed in navigation.   In 1776 he was one of a committee of safety, but taking sides with the crown, his property was confiscated.   His first wife was Sarah Clarke, to whom he was married April 20, 1746.   She dying, he married Mary Bardin, August 3, 1766.   He died February 21, 1795, aged 71 years.

[159] "A sermon preached in Trinity Church, Newport, Rhode Island,

June 25, 1771.   Voted by the congregation: that Mr. William S. Morgan be chosen organist of the Church for three months, provided Doct' Evans should not arrive from England within that time: But whereas Capt. Charles Bardin was chosen at Easter last, to officiate as organist until the return of said Dr. Evans from England, it is voted that said Bardin be paid one dollar per Sunday, out of the salary of £30 per annum, formerly voted by the congregation for the support of the organist, until Easter next, and that said Morgan be paid at the rate of £30 sterling per annum, after deducting said sum of one dollar per Sunday.

July 1, 1771.   Voted: that a tax of $1000 be immediately assessed on the pews, in order to discharge so much due from the Church on bond: being for money borrowed for the repairs of the Church, and building the steeple; and that those persons who are unable to pay the said tax be excused paying it, and the deficiency be made up by a subscription; and that Mr. Simon Pease, Mr. James Keith, Mr. Thos. Wickham, Jr., and Mr. Samuel Freebody be a committee to apportion said tax, to judge what persons ought to be excused, and make a report to the congregation on Monday next.

July 8, 1771.   The report made by the committee was received, and it was voted: that Messrs. Stephen Ayrault, Thomas Wickham, Jr., and Capt. Isaac Lawton be requested to collect the tax, and that they have discretionary power to excuse, either in whole or in part, those persons whom they judge unable to pay the same.

Mr. Andrew Hunter, in consequence of the infirmities of age, asked to be excused from longer serving as a vestryman ; when it was voted unanimously that the thanks of the Church be given to Mr. Hunter for his past good services to the Church, and that the Wardens signify the same to him.

Mr. Francis Malbone was chosen a Vestryman in the room of Mr. Andrew Hunter.

October 14, 1771. Mr. William S. Morgan was continued organist of the Church until Easter next, upon the same salary as was voted him when first chosen.

October 16, 1771. Resolved: that James Honyman, Esq., be requested to draft a letter, to be signed by the Rev. Mr. Bisset, the Wardens and Vestry, to the Rev. Dr. Burton, Secretary of the Society for the Propagation of the Gospel in Foreign Parts, acquainting him that the Rev. Willard Wheeler has offered to accept the school, provided there should be a vacancy, and to desire the Society, if they have not already fixed upon a person to supply that place, not to give themselves any further trouble in the affair, as they would, in that case, accept of Mr. Wheeler.

October 28, 1771. Meeting of the congregation. Whereas: the venerable Society for Propagating the Gospel in Foreign Parts, in answer to a letter wrote them in April last, to inform them of the death of the Rev. Mr. Browne, and to solicit a continuation of the mission, entirely refuse to comply with our request to give any further salary to our minister ; Resolved, unanimously : that a letter be wrote by the Rev. Mr. Bisset[160] and the Church Wardens, to the

---

[160] Rev. George Bisset during the time that he had been connected with the Church, as school-master and assistant minister, had won the esteem of the people. His election as minister opened the way for him to marry, and he made choice of Penelope Honyman, daughter of James Honyman, Esq., for a wife, and they were married April 23, 1773. His ministry was successful till the war broke

Society, to return them their thanks for their past favors conferred upon the Church.

Resolved, unanimously: that the Rev. Mr. Bisset be our Minister, and that he be allowed and paid the same salary that was given to Mr. Browne, viz., £133.6.8 lawful money of this Colony; said salary to commence on Easter day next, April 19, 1772, and that the same be collected by the Church Wardens and paid to him half-yearly;

up the congregation: but he remained at his post, and when the British took possession of the town, it was not displeasing to him, for he was a Loyalist. The services of the Church were continued, and the pews that had once been filled by those who formerly worshipped there, were now occupied by British troops. A sermon that he was to preach on the Sunday before the evacuation, had for its theme, "Honesty the best policy in the worst of times." It had for its text St. Luke, xviii, vs. 30, 31, and 32; but there was too much confusion preparatory to a hurried departure, to give heed to the Sabbath, and the sermon was put aside; for Mr. Bisset, too, was among those who were about leaving. He went without his wife and little ones, who were left to the tender care of those who remained in the place. His furniture was seized by the State authorities, but was subsequently given up to his wife, who was allowed to go to New York by act of the General Assembly, June, 1780, under the direction of the Continental troops, where she joined her husband. While in New York Rev. Mr. Bisset preached the above sermon in St. Paul's, and also in St. George's. From New York he went to England, where, in 1784, the sermon was printed in London.

Two of Mr. Bisset's sermons preached in Newport, were published:

"A Sermon preached in Trinity Church, Newport, R. I., June 3, 1771, at the Funeral of Mrs. Abigail Wanton, late consort of the Hon. Joseph Wanton, Jr., Esq., who died in the 36th year of her age."

"The Trial of a False Apostle. A Sermon preached in Trinity Church, Newport, R. I., on Sunday, October 24, 1773. By George Bisset, A.M., Rector of said Church and Fellow of Rhode Island College."

Rev. Mr. Bisset resided in London till 1786, when he removed to St. John's, New Brunswick, where he became Rector of St. John's. There he died, March 3, 1788. Mrs. Bisset died at Frederichton, N. B., August 2, 1816, in her 70th year.

The *Newport Herald*, of April 24, 1788, in announcing the death of

and that he enjoy the donation of Mr. Kay, with the £50 sterling voted him at Easter last, until said time, and that he also have the parsonage-house to live in.

Voted: that the annual tax on the pews on the lower floor be raised to nine pence, lawful money, for every Sunday in the year; or, thirty-nine shillings lawful money for the whole year; and that the pews in the gallery be at half said sum, viz.: four pence half pence lawful money; in order to defray the expenses of the Church, said tax to commence at Easter next, to be paid half yearly.

December 19, 1771. Samuel Whitehorne was married to Ruth Gibbs. [She was the youngest child of George Gibbs, and was born in 1748.]

[In Advent Mr. Fayerweather preached for the Rev. Mr. Bisset in Newport, by earnest request. On the 25th day of December, 1771, it being Christmas, attended Trinity Church again, and administered communion at the altar, above two hundred members present.—*History of the Narragansett Church.*

January 8, 1772. Rev. Alexander Keith, Jr., died, and was buried in the church-yard.

[Rev. Mr. Fayerweather, made the following entry in the records of St. Paul's, Narragansett:

" January 9, 1772. Received a letter from the Church Wardens of Newport to attend as pall-bearer to the Rev. Mr. Keith,[161] my old

Rev. Mr. Bisset, said of him: " The style of his composition was remarkably elegant, and his reasoning seldom failed to force conviction on the minds of his hearers. As a divine he was equally distinguished for the sanctity of his manners, and the liberality of his sentiments. As a scholar he was free from pedantry, and as a gentleman he possessed the social virtues in an eminent degree, and never once lost sight of his sacred functions."

[161] Rev. Alexander Keith, Jr., born in Aberdeen, Scotland, was educated at King's College. After his ordination he officiated for ten years

friend, and once my predecessor in Georgetown, South Carolina,
and to preach a funeral sermon on the occasion, which I did on the
very day after the interment, in Trinity Church, to a full auditory."

February 18, 1772. At a meeting of the congregation, voted:
that the Church Wardens be directed to make out a list of all those
persons who are delinquent in paying, and whom they judge able
to pay a tax of six and one-half dollars, assessed on each pew, July,
1771, and that they deliver the said list to William Brooks Simp-
son, Esq., attorney-at-law, and desire him to put the same in suit
immediately, unless paid; the former to a Justice Court, and the
latter to the Court to be holden in May next.

February 18. At an adjourned meeting of the congregation,
voted: that John Brown, son of the late Peleg Brown, who is heir
to $\frac{1}{3}$ part of pew No. 89, which belonged to his s^d father, have
and enjoy the said $\frac{1}{3}$ part of said pew, and also $\frac{1}{3}$ part of said pew
more, given him by Mrs. Elizabeth Gidley, said Brown paying $\frac{2}{3}$
parts of all rates, and taxes unpaid on said pew.

February 29, 1772. Agreeable to a vote of the congregation, at
their last meeting, the Church Wardens have hired of Messrs.
William Vernon[162] and Benj. Mason, the sum of $769, silver Spanish

---

in St. Paul's Chapel, Aberdeen, and when he came to America, he was
placed in charge of the Church at Georgetown, S. C., over which he
presided during a period of twenty-five years.

[162] was born January 17, 1719,
and died December 22, 1806.
His wife, Judith Harwood,
daughter of Philip Harwood
and great-granddaughter of
Gov. Walter Clarke and Gov.
Cranston, died August 29,
1762, aged 38 years. Mr.
Vernon was a distinguished merchant, a public-spirited citizen and a

milled dollars, at 6 per cent. interest, in order to pay Capt. Charles
Handy his bond: and the over-plus, with what is collected of the
taxes, be appropriated towards discharging Capt. John Tillinghast's
bond.

April 9, 1772. Pew No. 22, belonging to Mrs. Frances Townsend, widow of Solomon Townsend, by consent of the Wardens and
Vestry, was disposed of to Mr. George Rome,[163] the arrearage having been first paid to the Church.

Easter Monday, April 19, 1772. John Bours and Isaac Lawton
were elected Church Wardens. John Grelea, clerk, and George
English, sexton.

Vestrymen: Joseph Wanton, Jr., Jas. Honyman, William Mum-

---

patriot. He was an original member of the Artillery Company, 1741,
and on the death of Abraham Redwood he was elected the second President of the Redwood Library. In 1773 he was appointed by the General
Assembly one of a committee of three to prepare a letter on a bill pend-
ing in the House of Commons on the fisheries prosecuted by the merchants of Rhode Island, in and near the Gulf of St. Lawrence. The following year he was one of a committee of correspondence of the Town of
Newport with Boston, and in 1775 he was engaged with others (William
Ellery being one of the committee) in collecting statistics of the losses
sustained by Rhode Island at the hands of the British. As President of
the Continental Naval Board (elected by Congress, May 6, 1777,) he
rendered able service to the country. The war over, he returned to Newport, and here passed the remainder of his days.

[163] George Rome came from England to Rhode Island in 1761, as agent
of Hayley & Hopkins, a large commercial house in London. He divided
his time between Newport and Narragansett, where he entertained his
friends with great hospitality. In the trouble between the Colonies and
England, he sided with the Crown, aroused the indignation of the people
by his course, and was at length compelled to find shelter on board a man-
of-war in the harbor. His property was seized by order of the General
Assembly, and when sold the proceeds were turned into the General
Treasury.

ford, Thomas Wickham, Evan Malbone,[164] Philip Wilkinson, Joseph Wanton, Jr., Charles Wickham, Thomas Cranston, Stephen Ayrault, John Mawdsley, Jahleel Brenton, Simon Pease, John Bours, Francis Brinley and Francis Malbone.

Voted: that an alteration be made in the galleries, by removing the negroes to the west end of the Church, provided it be agreeable to the proprietors of the pews behind the organ to exchange their pews for those to be built at the south side of the gallery, where the negroes now sit, and the negroes can be as well accommodated as they are at present.

Voted: that for the future, a person leaving the Church with his family, shall be at liberty to sell his pew without consent first obtained from the Wardens and Vestry.

May 11, 1772. The Rev. Mr. Willard Wheeler was chosen Assistant and School-master, on Mr. Kay's foundation; his salary to commence from the first of last April.

[From the Town Records: Whereas ye Church bell rings at 9 of y* clock at night without any charge to y* Town, that for y* future John Simms, who rings Dr Stile's bell, and had nine dollars a year for y* same, be not allowed anything for ringing y* same.]

Under date of 1772, in the Abstracts of the Proceedings of the Society, there is this entry:

"Advice has been received of the death of the Rev. Mr. Marmaduke Browne, the Society's worthy missionary at Newport, in Rhode Island. The people have chosen Mr. Bisset, who used to assist the missionary, and kept the school founded by Mr. Kay. But the flourishing state and opulent circumstances of that parish having

---

[164] Evan Malbone died at the village of Long Island, March 30, 1830, aged 83 years. For many years he was a member of the Legislature of Connecticut.

been fully represented, the Society do not think it consistent with their trust to give any longer a salary from hence, as it would prevent their bounty where it is more wanted, to other Churches, which cannot be supported without their assistance."

[Rev. Mr. —— Page, Chaplain to the Right. Hon. Countess of Huntingdon, arrived here March 1, 1773, and preached in Trinity Church on the following Sunday.—*Newport Mercury*.]

Easter Monday, April 12, 1773. John Bours and Isaac Lawton were elected Church Wardens, and the clerk and sexton were re-elected. No change was made in the Vestry.

Voted: that the Church Wardens be requested to write to some proper person in London, to desire his assistance in procuring an organist as soon as may be, and that they represent the encouragement that will be given by the Church to a suitable person for that office; and that Mr. Charles Bardin officiate as organist in the meantime; and that he be allowed and paid for his services at the rate of sixty Spanish milled dollars per annum.

Voted: that the Wardens have the parsonage-house newly shingled if they find it absolutely wants it.

John Freebody[165] died, in his 67th year.

May 26, 1773. Mrs. Mary Lightfoot, consort of Robert Lightfoot,[166] Esq., died.

---

[165] "John Freebody was a gentleman of great integrity and unblemished morals, and in all his various connections, both in public and private life, he discharged his duties with that faithfulness and affection which are the true characteristics of a mind that delighted with the practice of virtue."—*Newport Mercury*.

[166] Robert Lightfoot had many friends in Newport. At the time that he held the office of Judge of Vice Admiralty in the Southern District of the United States, he came here in enfeebled health, and finding the place so attractive, he gave up his office and settled here, dividing his time between Newport and Narragansett. His daughter Frances, who died in 1800, lies buried in the church-yard.

June 3, 1773.   Charles Bardin died.

September 12, 1773.   Christopher Mardenbrough[167] was married to Rhoda Fryers.

December 20, 1773.   Meeting of the congregation.   Whereas, Mr. William Selby[168] is arrived in town from London, in consequence of an application made to him by the Wardens of the Church, and now offers himself as an organist, and the congregation having heard him officiate, and think him a suitable person to sustain said office, it is therefore voted: that he be received as organist of the Church, and that he be paid at the rate of £30 sterling per annum, to commence from the first day of October last; and that the Wardens be requested to collect by subscription, ten guineas or more, for him, towards paying his passage to America.

Easter Monday, April 4, 1774.   The officers of the previous year, were re-elected, with the addition of William Selby, as organist.

Voted: that Mr. Peter Cooke have the improvement of the lot of land adjoining the distil-house lot, and bounded upon the harbor, part of Mr. Kay's estate, at the annual rental of twenty shillings, sterling, and that the Church Wardens give him a lease of the same for the term of twenty-one years from this time; Mr. Cooke to build a stone wall before the same, to keep it from washing into the sea.

Voted: that a tax of twenty-eight shillings, lawful money, be assessed on the single pews below, and fourteen shillings on the gallery pews in order to pay off part of the bond due to Messrs. Vernon and Mason.

[167] Christopher Mardenbrough came from the Island of St. Christophers and settled in Newport.   He died October 25, 1806.

[168] William Selby advertised in January, 1774, that he had just arrived from London, and would "teach the violin, flute, harpsicord and other instruments in use," and that he intended to open a dancing school.

August 1, 1774.   Selby gave a concert of instrumental and vocal music at the Court House.

Voted: that Mr. Simon Pease be requested to write to his friend in London, for a new stop for the organ, agreeably to Mr. Selby's direction.

May 23, 1774. James Bisset,[169] son of Rev. George Bisset, and Penelope, his wife, was baptized by his father.

December 27, 1774. Brenton Halliburton was baptized.

January 22, 1775. Joseph Wanton, Jr., was married to Miss [Sarah] Brenton, daughter of the late Jahleel Brenton.

Easter Monday, April 17, 1775. The officers of the previous year were re-elected.

May 1, 1775. Lieut. James Conway[170] died, and was buried in the church-yard, aged 45 years.

Easter Monday, April 8, 1776. No change was made in the officers of the Church.

April 15, 1776. Voted: that Mr. Francis Malbone and Mr. Simon Pease be added to the Church Wardens, as a committee to wait upon the Rev. Mr. Wheeler, and acquaint him that the Vestry and congregation are greatly disappointed and dissatisfied with regard to his school, and that, as many difficulties arise from the unhappy situation of public affairs, in collecting the rents and taxes of the Church, to support the officers, they would have no objection to Mr. Wheeler's[171] being removed to another more advantageous living.

Easter Monday, March 31, 1777. The Wardens and Vestry were re-elected. James Gibbs was elected clerk in place of John Grelea.

---

[169] The child was probably named after his grandfather, James Honyman.

[170] Lieut. Conway was a Lieutenant of Marines, and was attached to the man-of-war, Rose, then stationed in this Bay.

[171] This probably closed the connection with Mr. Wheeler, for no further reference is made to him in the records.

February 1, 1778, Major John Breese[172] was married to Elizabeth Malbone.

Easter Monday, April 20, 1778. John Bours and Isaac Lawton were elected Church Wardens: James Gibbs, clerk; Thomas Lawton, clerk of the Vestry; George English, sexton.

Vestrymen: Joseph Wanton, Evan Malbone, Philip Wilkinson, Joseph Wanton, Jr., Charles Wickham, Thomas Cranston, Stephen Ayrault, John Mawdsley, Jahleel Brenton, John Bours, Francis Brinley, Francis Malbone, Isaac Lawton, Thomas Wickham, William Wanton, and James Keith.

March 29, 1779. Henry Goldsmith was married to Mary Mason.[173]

Easter Monday, April 5, 1779. No change was made in the officers of the Church.

April 27, 1780. At a meeting of the congregation, April 27, 1780. Voted: that Messrs. George Gibbs, Christopher Champlin, Thomas Freebody and John Bours be a committee to lease out all the estates belonging to the Church, upon the best terms they can, and that they make what repairs they judge necessary on the parsonage-house, the church and fence around the yard; and that they

---

[172] Major John Breese was an officer in the British Army, 54th regiment. When the British retired from the Island, he left the army and settled in Newport. In 1796 he was appointed British Vice Consul for Rhode Island, and died here April 23, 1799. Mrs. Breese, who was the daughter of Francis and Margaret (Saunders) Malbone, died May 22, 1832.

[173] This was the last marriage ceremony performed by the Rev. Mr. Bisset before he took his hurried departure with the British troops.

Henry Goldsmith was born in the County of Westmeath, Ireland, July 4, 1755. His wife, Mary Mason, daughter of Benj. Mason and granddaughter of Daniel Ayrault, was born November 9, 1759. Mr. Goldsmith adhered to the Crown. After the birth of his first child he removed to St. Andrews, N. S., from there to Annapolis Royal, then to Halifax, and, finally in 1800, to England, where he and his wife died. They had fourteen children born to them.

make some allowance, at their discretion, to Mr. George English for his past services as sexton.

Voted, also: that the said committee make inquiry relative to the estate of William Tate, which was left by will to the Church after the death of his wife, who had lately deceased: and that they make report to the Church.

CHAPTER X.

1780–1785.

MAY 5, 1780. The committee appointed by the Church, at their meeting on the 27th of April last, to lease out all the estates belonging to the Church, have this day agreed with Mr. Francis Brinley that he should pay ninety silver dollars for the rent of the house and lot he now improves, for the present year. That Mr. George Scott have a lease of the lot of about eight acres, he improves, for the present year, for forty-five silver dollars, and that Mr. Jabez Champlin live in the parsonage-house this year, at forty-five dollars per annum rent. Agreed also, that a rough fence be put around the church-yard, and that two carpenters be consulted upon the cost, and that if it should not exceed $25, silver, it be done immediately.[171]

[171] The town of Newport was at this time in a deplorable condition; its trade was gone, some hundreds of dwellings, store-houses and barns had been destroyed by the British, its people were scattered, and those who had been forced to remain at home were so impoverished that they could only secure in scanty measure means for the support of their families. To do much for the Church was out of the question; but the will was there and, step by step, they gradually brought it up to its former standard; though it was not till 1786, that they could command the services of a settled pastor. In the meantime the pulpit was filled as opportunity offered; and when a clergyman could not be obtained, the congregation were drawn together, to listen to a lay reader. For some time, beginning in 1780, while his own church was being repaired, the Rev. Gardiner Thurston, Pastor of the Second Baptist Society, occupied the pulpit and his own people were invited to worship there. The services of the Church were also conducted by Rev. John Graves, then residing in Providence without a parish, Rev. Moses Badger, who was at Newport at the time

July 22, 1780. M. de Vilernaas,[175] First-Lieut. of the French frigate Hermione, was buried in the church-yard.

August 29, 1780. Mr. James Keith[176] died and was buried in the church-yard.

Easter Monday, April 16, 1781. John Bours and Francis Malbone were elected Church Wardens, James Gibbs, Clerk, and Geo. English, sexton.

Vestrymen : Philip Wilkinson, Charles Wickham, Thomas Cranston, Stephen Ayrault, John Bours, Francis Brinley, Francis Malbone, James Keith, Charles Handy, Christopher Champlin, George Gibbs, Henry Hunter, Thomas Freebody, Samuel Freebody, Silas Cooke and John Malbone.

Voted : that Messrs. George Gibbs, Christopher Champlin, Thomas Freebody, and John Bours be a committee to lease the estates of the Church upon the best terms they can ; and that they inquire about a lot of land at Narragansett, left by will towards the support of the Minister of the Church for the time being, by Nathaniel Norton.

July 27, 1781. Heithcote Murison,[177] of Fairfield, Ct., died, and was buried in the church-yard.

---

that he was called to St. John's, Providence, in 1786, and Rev. Samuel Parker, of Boston, when he could arrange to fill the pulpit.

[175] M. de Valernaas died of wounds received in the action between the Hermione and the British frigate Iris, and was interred with military honors. The Hermione, commanded by the Chevalier de la Touch, had reached Newport, June 19, 1780.

[176] James Keith was a relative of the Rev. Alexander Keith, Jr., by whose side his remains were placed. He was born at Aberdeen, Scotland, had resided in America nearly forty years, and had attained to his 70th year. "As he lived beloved he died lamented."

[177] Heithcote Murison died of wounds received in the excursion of our allies to Long Island. He was of a very respectable family on Long Island, very attractive in his manners, and full of zeal for the cause, which latter

September 29, 1781. Francis Malbone[178] was married to Katherine Pease, by Rev. Samuel Parker, of Boston.

Easter Monday, April 1, 1782. No change was made in the officers of the Church, save that Capt. James Arnold was added to the Vestry, to fill the vacancy caused by the death of Capt. James Keith.

Voted: that the Wardens make an allowance to the clerk and sexton out of the money collected at Church on the first Sunday of every month, to begin in May.

May 23, 1782. Mr. William Tweedy[179] died, and was buried in the church-yard.

Easter Monday, April 21, 1783. The officers of the Church were re-elected, with Samuel Brenton as Vestryman, in place of Philip Wilkinson, deceased.

July 20, 1783. Mr. John Meunscher was employed as organist, at the rate of one dollar per Sunday.

August 17, 1783. Henry Edwin Stanhope[180] was married to Peggie Malbone by Rev. Mr. Fogg.

quality led him to become a volunteer in an enterprise which cost him his life. His remains, followed by the gentlemen of the town, and a great number of French officers, with a detachment of troops, were interred with military honors. He was 26 years of age.—*Newport Mercury.*

[178] Francis Malbone died in 1785. His widow died in Boston in 1817, and her remains were brought here for interment.

[179] "The Sunday following the death of Mr. Tweedy, his remains, attended by his connections and numerous friends, were carried to Trinity Church, where the ceremony and an excellent sermon, well adapted to the solemnity of the occasion, were performed by a particular friend of the deceased, after which they were interred in the church-yard."—*Newport Mercury.*

[180] Henry Edwin Stanhope, vice-admiral of the blue, was the only son of the Hon. Edwin Francis Stanhope, cousin to the Earl of Chesterfield, and the Rt. Hon. Lady Catherine, daughter of John, Marquis of Caernavon, eldest son of James, Duke of Chandos. Peggie Malbone was the

October 5, 1783. Gilbert Eames[161] died, and was buried in the church-yard.

October 10, 1783. Richard Chilcot was married to Elizabeth Thurston by Rev. Gardiner Thurston.

November 20, 1783. Thomas Russell[162] was married to Ann Handy.

November 24, 1783. Voted by the congregation : that the Church Wardens and Vestry be requested to petition the General Assembly for liberty to dispose of the lot of land left to the Church by Nathaniel Norton, deceased, late of Newport, lying in North Kingston, the same being of no use to the Church, and that the money arising from the sale thereof be invested in real estate in Newport.

December 28, 1783. William R. Robinson[183] was married to Ann Scott by Rev. Mr. Badger.

Easter Monday, April 11, 1784. John Bours and Francis Malbone were chosen Church Wardens; James Gibbs, Clerk; John Meunscher, organist; Daniel Vernon, sexton.

daughter of Francis and Margaret Malbone. She died in England, in August, 1809.

[161] Gilbert Eames was for many years one of the Honorable Council of the Island of Granada, prior to its reduction by the French in 1779. He was born in the County of Limerick, Ireland, and was in his 54th year at the time of his death.

[162] Major Thomas Russell, son of Thomas, was born September 28, 1758, and died in Newport, February 19, 1801. When but eighteen years of age he was commissioned a lieutenant in Col. Henry Sherburne's regiment, and subsequently was appointed Aid-de-camp to Brig.-Gen. Starke. In 1781 he retired from the service and devoted himself to business. His wife was the daughter of Capt. Charles Handy.

[183] William R. Robinson was the son of Rowland Robinson, and grandson of Lieutenant-Governor William Robinson. He died without issue. His wife was the daughter of George Scott. After his death she married Dr. John Preston Mann, and died October 10, 1841, aged 77 years.

Voted: that the Wardens dispose of the lot of land given to the Church by the late Nathaniel Norton, agreeably to an act of the General Assembly, for the most they can obtain for it; and that the amount of the same be laid out in a lot of land in Newport, the annual rent of said lot to be appropriated for the use aforesaid.

Voted: that Mr. Charles Handy and Mr. George Gibbs be a committee to view the lot of seven acres of land, part of Mr. Kay's donation, and that they take into consideration a proposal made by Mr. George Scott to the Church for exchanging the said lot for the same quantity of land adjoining the house now improved by Mr. Brinley, and make report at the next meeting.

Voted: that Mr. Handy, Mr. Gibbs and Mr. Champlin, with Mr. Brinley, be a committee to draw up a plan for settling a minister, and for fixing on ways and means for his maintenance; and that they propose to Mr. Bours his taking orders and becoming our minister; and that the congregation be notified to meet here again on Monday, the 19th, to receive their report.

Vestrymen elected: Charles Wickham, Stephen Ayrault, John Bours, Francis Brinley, Francis Malbone,[1] Charles Handy, Chris-

[1] Col. Francis Malbone, born March 20, 1759, was the son of Francis Malbone, of Virginia. He was in business in Newport, first with his brother, Evan Malbone, who died in August, 1784, and then with Daniel Mason, who died in September, 1797. Col. Malbone was one of the most popular men of his day. He left Newport, February 20, 1809, to take his seat in Congress, and while ascending the steps of the Capitol the following June, to attend divine service, fell and immediately expired. The Senate, of which body he was a member, voted to attend his funeral, and to erect a monument, in Washington,

topher Champlin, George Gibbs, Henry Hunter, Thomas Freebody, Samuel Freebody, John Mawdsley, Thomas Wickham, John Malbone, Samuel Brenton, Joshua Arnold.

April 19, 1784. Adjourned meeting of the congregation.

Voted: that Mr. Charles Handy and Mr. George Gibbs be continued a committee to make an exchange of land with Mr. George Scott, provided his first proposal be adhered to by him, of giving acre for acre, and if an exchange be made, that the same gentlemen endeavor to obtain a passage to it through land belonging to the Jews by making an exchange also with them.

Voted: that the rent of the house Mr. Brinley improves be affixed at the same sum that Gen. Greene gave for the hire of the estate of the late John Tillinghast, to which Mr. Brinley consented.

Voted: that Col. Malbone, Mr. Saml Brenton, Mr. Fran^c Malbone and Capt. John Northam be a committee to apply to every proprietor of a pew in the Church, with the report now made to, and accepted by, the congregation, assembled by adjournment, to receive the same, by Mr. Chas. Handy, Mr. Brinley, Mr. Samuel Freebody, and Mr. George Gibbs, relating to settling a minister, and that the said proprietors be requested to signify their approbation of the same, by affixing their names thereto.

" We whose names are hereunto annexed, being proprietors of pews in Trinity Church, do manifest our approbation of the plan for settling a minister, contained in a report made by the above gentlemen, and accepted by the congregation, assembled at the Church, on Monday, the 12th day of April, 1784.

---

to his memory. Mrs. Malbone was the daughter of William and Catharine Tweedy. She died in 1829, at the age of 66 years. Her daughter, Freelove Sophia Malbone, became the wife of Dr. Edmund T. Waring. Mrs. Malbone was the widow of Simon Pease at the time of her marriage to Col. Malbone, in September, 1782.

"Susannah Mumford, Abigail Redwood, John Cranston, Stephⁿ Deblois, John Handy, Sam' Brenton, Thoˢ Greene, Abigail Coggeshall, Godfrey Wenwood,[155] Benj. Mumford, John Northam, Chaˢ Wickham, Abʰ Wilkinson, Henry Hunter, Mary Overing, N. Bird, Mary Dupuy, Gid. Sisson, Debʳ Hunter, Phebe Champlin, Francis Mumford, Jabez Champlin, Francis Malbone, John Malbone, Fraˢ Brinley, Majʳ Fairchild, Sam' Whitehorn, William Shaw, Stephⁿ Ayrault, Thomas Arnold, Sam' Freebody, Benj. Gardner, John Mawdsley, Sarah Wanton, Eliz. Scott, Abraham All, Catharine Tweedy, Esther Morris, Thos. Halpin, Peter Mumford, David Melville, Josiah Arnold, John Banister, Chaˢ Handy, James Duncan, Richard Bourke, George Gibbs, Peleg Wood, Dan' Mason, Rob' Stoddard, Mary Thurston, Mary Coddington, John Miller, Elizabeth Lechmere, Mary Paul, Sam' Sweet, Benj. Fry, Thos. Webber, Adam Ferguson, Amy Goldthwait, Fraˢ Malbone, Jr.

May 7, 1784. Voted: that an exchange of land be made with Mr. Scott, acre for acre, and that Mr. Christopher Champlin and Mr. Peter Mumford be requested to view both the lots and allow Mr. Scott what they shall think just, for what fencing Mr. Scott's lot has more on it than the Church lot; that the said gentlemen apply to the General Assembly to ratify the exchange, and that they give the offer to Gen. Greene, of the lot exchanged.

Voted: that Capt. John Northam be requested to act as assistant Warden, under Mr. Bours.

The report of the committee to consider and draw up a plan for

— —   —

[155] Godfrey Wainwood died October 2, 1816, aged 77 years. He was married to Mary Campbell, May 19, 1775. He was a baker, on Bannester's wharf, and claimed to have been instrumental in bringing to light Dr. Church's treasonable correspondence with the enemy, in the early stages of the Revolution. Gen. Washington gave the particulars of the discovery, in a letter to the President of Congress, under date of October 5, 1775.

settling and supporting a minister, was made and accepted, and is as follows:

"We, the subscribers, having been chosen a committee by the congregation of Trinity Church, at said Church assembled, April 12, 1784, to consider on some plan to settle and support a minister, do report: that we have taken the situation of said Church under consideration and are of the opinion that it is able to support a minister, and would recommend the following plan for that purpose, viz.:

"That the late Mr. Kay's donation to said Church be improved by the Minister, for the present, he keeping the same in good repair, and instructing ten poor boys, agreeable to Mr. Kay's will; and that a tax of twenty-eight shillings, lawful money, per annum, to be paid half yearly, be assessed on each pew below, and twelve shillings per annum, in the galleries, and that £93.6.8, per annum, be paid our Minister, half yearly, out of the money so collected by the tax, to make up a comfortable support for him, in addition to what he may receive from Mr. Kay's donation.

"And whereas, it appears to be the unanimous wish of the congregation, at their meeting on Easter Monday, that Mr. Bours, who has officiated in the Church as a lay reader, to their entire satisfaction, for upwards of two years, would enter into holy orders and become their minister, would recommend an offer being made to Mr. Bours to that purpose; allowing him a reasonable time to resolve whether he will accept; and that he be requested, in the meantime, to proceed as he has done, and that he be allowed £30 per annum, and the use of the parsonage-house, for his services.

"We would further recommend that these proceedings be made known to every proprietor of pews in said Church, that their minds thereon may be known, as we are satisfied the prosperity of the Church depends on our choice of a minister.

CHAS. HANDY,
FRAN. BRINLEY,
SAM^L FREEBODY,
GEO. GIBBS."

July 11, 1784. Capt. John Grimes[156] was married to Mrs. Elizabeth Christan.

September 10, 1784. Voted: that Mr. Bours be requested to proceed in officiating in the Church, as heretofore, notwithstanding his letter of decline.[157]

Voted: that Mr. Bours invite the Rev. Mr. Badger to officiate occasionally for a few Sundays.

Voted that Mr. Christopher Champlin and Mr. P. Mumford be requested to proceed in the exchange of land with Mr. George

---

[156] John Grimes was a patriot, and was active in annoying the enemy in Narragansett Bay, in the Revolution. At one time he commanded a privateer. He died in the West Indies. His wife's maiden name was Cowley, daughter of Joseph Cowley. Grimes was her third husband. After his death she was married for the fourth time, and became the wife of Thomas Tromp Tyrrell, who died January 28, 1806. Mrs. Tyrrell died August 19, 1830, in her 77th year.

[157]   Newport, July 26, 1784.

Gentlemen :

Impressed with the most grateful sense of the honor conferred on me, at your meeting on Easter Monday last, by your unanimous vote and proposal to me to enter into holy orders, and to become your minister, I now feel myself obliged in conscience, as well as duty to the Church, to defer my answer no longer, but to inform you, that after the most mature deliberation, I am fearful that sacred office would be incompatible with my present circumstances, and therefore must, tho' reluctantly, decline the offer.

As you cannot be insensible of my having the welfare and prosperity of the Church near my heart, so you will not doubt my readiness, at all times, to co-operate with you in any eligible plan for settling a minister. In the meanwhile, if it is your desire, I will continue to keep the congregation together in the way we are in.   May heaven direct us to the best.

With every sentiment of love and affection, I remain, Gentlemen.

Your most obe.t, Hum'le Serv't,

J. BOURS.

The Wardens, Vestry and Congregation of Trinity Church.

Scott, and settle the dispute relative to the fencing the same, in the best manner they can.

October 24, 1784. John Meunscher[188] was married to Johanna Sophia Knotchell. December 13, 1784. William Atherton,[189] of Jamaica, was married to Mrs. Sarah Wanton.

The ceremony in both instances was performed by the Rev Moses Badger.

March 10, 1785. William Littlefield[190] was married to Elizabeth Brinley by Rev. Moses Badger.

Easter Monday, March 27, 1785. No change made in the officers of the Church.

Voted : that a tax of twenty-eight shillings, lawful money, be assessed on the pews below, and of fourteen shillings in the galleries.

---

[188] Knotchell, the organist, had died July 20, 1783, and his widow married Meunscher, the new organist.

[189] Mrs. Atherton, who was the daughter of Jahleel Brenton, and the widow of Joseph Wanton, Jr. (to whom she was married January 2, 1775,) died July 19, 1787, aged 35 years. Immediately after her death Mr. Atherton disposed of his household goods and went to England, where he had a tablet prepared, bearing the following inscription, which he sent to America, and had it set up in the Church, in November, 1788 :

" Sacred may this marble long remain (the just tribute of a husband's affections) to the Memory of Mrs. Sarah Atherton, wife of William Atherton, of Jamaica, Esq., and daughter of Jahleel Brenton, Esq., and Mary his wife, of Newport, who was translated from this to a happier State, on the 19th of June, 1787, aged 35 years; while her Ashes rest entombed in the Clifton burying-ground in this Town.

" If an assemblage of all the Virtues which adorn and dignify the Soul, united to Elegance of Person and Refinement of manners could have rescued her from Death, she still had lived."

[190] Capt. William Littlefield was born on Block Island. He entered the army in the Revolution, and was on the staff of Maj.-Gen. Greene, who married his sister. His son William, for a number of years, was Collector of the Port of Newport.

Voted : that Mr. Bours be requested to officiate in the Church, as he has done, for the year ensuing, and that he be paid for his services £30, lawful money, and have the improvement of the parsonage-house and lot, as the last year.

Voted : that Col. Christopher Champlin, Mr. George Gibbs, Mr. Samuel Freebody and Capt. Charles Handy be a committee to call upon Mr. Brinley, Mr. George Scott and others, who are indebted to the Church on account of the Kay estate, and receive of them the money due, and pay the same to Mr. William Vernon, in part of the bond due from the Church to the heirs of Peter Dorden, deceased ; and that said committee be clothed with power to lease out for one or more, but not to exceed seven, years, all the said estate, upon the best terms they can ; that ten poor boys, whose parents belong to the Church, have their schooling paid by the Wardens out of the rents ; and the remainder, after the necessary repairs are deducted, be appropriated towards paying the said bond.

May 2, 1785. The committee made report of their proceedings with regard to the negotiation with Mr. Brinley and Mr. Scott, and the deed of the land is agreed to be signed by the Wardens and Vestry, and the exchange completed with Mr. George Scott.

CHAPTER XI.

1785–1789.

MAY 29, 1785. Henry Sherburne[191] was married to Catharine Tweedy, by Rev. Moses Badger.

June 26, 1785. Thomas Grosvenor, of Connecticut, was married to Ann Mumford, by the Right Reverend Bishop Seabury.[192]

The Wardens and Vestry of Trinity Church received a letter from

[191] Col. Henry Sherburne was a Revolutionary officer. His first commission, dated July 1, 1775, was signed by John Hancock; and, as Major, he was attached to the regiment commanded by Col. Church. During the war he lost all his property, and needing some employment after the return of peace, he was appointed commissioner to adjust the accounts between Rhode Island and the United States. From October 1792 to 1808 he was General Treasurer of the State of Rhode Island, and he held other offices; but the one that gave him the most satisfaction was a mission to the Choctaws and Chickasaw Indians, in which he was so successful as to call forth a vote of thanks from Congress. He died May 31, 1824, aged 77 years. Mrs. Sherburne was the widow of William Tweedy, and the daughter of James Honyman, Esq.

[192] Rt. Rev. Bishop Seabury, on his return from England, landed at Halifax; from there he came to Newport, reaching here June 25th, on his way to New London. The following day he performed the marriage ceremony. This was probably the first couple that he married in America after he was raised to the Episcopate. He also preached in the Church, from Hebrews xii., 1 and 2, and this was his first sermon after his return.

Rev. Samuel Parker, under date of August 1, 1785, calling their
attention to a vote at a convention of Episcopal clergymen of Massachusetts and Rhode Island, held at Boston, September 8, 1784,
appointing the Rev. Edward Bass, Rev. Nathaniel Fisher and Rev.
Samuel Parker, a committee, with power to call a convention of the
Episcopal Churches in Massachusetts and the neighboring States,
"at such time and place as they might deem most necessary and
convenient." Notice was given in this letter that there would be
such a convention in Boston on the 7th of the following September
"to deliberate upon some plan of maintaining uniformity in divine
worship, and adopt such other measures as may tend to the prosperity and union of the Episcopal Church in the American States."
Trinity Church was asked to send one or more delegates to the
convention.

The Wardens replied, August 9th, that it was their purpose to
lay the matter before the congregation ; but that before doing so,
"several of the gentlemen of the Vestry have signified a desire to
know what was the result of the convention of the Clergy, held the
last week at Middletown," adding : "As we have the interest of the
Episcopal Church in America greatly at heart, we shall think ourselves happy in promoting any measures that may tend to forward
the same."

To this letter Rev. Mr. Parker replied :

BOSTON, August 15, 1785.

MESSRS. BOURS AND MALBONE,
Wardens, &c.,

GENTS: In answer to your favor by Mr. Mumford, I have to inform you that the Clergy of Connecticut, in convention assembled,
agreed to recognise, accept and receive Dr. Seabury as their Bishop,
and promised to render him that respect, duty and submission which,
as they understand, were given by the Presbyters to their Bishops
in the primitive Church when unconnected with, and uncontrolled

by, secular power. After which a convention assembled, a committee was chosen to attend the Bishop and wish him to propose such alterations in the liturgy as sh'd be thought expedient for the present, to be laid before the convention at New Haven next month ; which alterations I am requested to propose to the Churches in this and your State, to see if they will unite with the Churches in Connecticut in promoting a uniformity of worship. The grand object of the proposed convention will be, to see if we shall join with Connecticut and receive their Bishop ; or, whether we shall choose a deputy or deputies to attend the general convention at Philadelphia in September, or adopt any other measure to continue as one communion. To this end the convention is called, and it is hoped you will send one or more of your members to promote the design.

I am, Gents, with respect and esteem, your most ob't and very humble Serv't,

August 22, 1785. Meeting of the congregation :

The Wardens laid before the congregation two letters, of the 1st and 15th instant, from the Rev'd Samuel Parker, of Boston, advising them, that pursuant to a vote passed at a meeting of the Episcopal Clergy of Massachusetts and Rhode Island, held at Boston on the 8th day of September last, he, with the Rev'd Edw. Bass and Nathaniel Fisher, were appointed a committee to call a convention of the Episcopal Churches, in that and the neighboring States, to meet at such time and place, as they should judge most necessary and convenient ; and requesting the said Wardens to propose to the Church

---

[193] Rev. Samuel Parker, D.D., was born in 1744, graduated at Harvard College, was ordained by the Bishop of London in 1774, became Rector of Trinity Church, Boston, in 1784, was made Bishop of the Eastern Diocese, September 16, 1804, and died on the 6th of the following December before he had discharged a single duty of the Episcopal office.

to chose one or more, of their members, to meet in convention, at Boston, Wednesday, the 7th day of September next ; then and there to deliberate upon a plan for maintaining uniformity in divine worship, and adopting such other measures as may tend to the union and prosperity of the Episcopal Churches in the American States.

The congregation having taken the said letter into consideration, and duly weighed the contents of the same, do vote and resolve : that they will comply with the request of the said Committee, by sending a member to represent this Church ; and do hereby nominate and appoint Mr. Bours, and unanimously request him to proceed to Boston, and meet in the said convention, with full power and authority to join in and agree to, in behalf of this Church, any plan, or plans, that may be adopted at the said convention, or at any other that may be judged necessary by the said convention, to be holden at a future day, for promoting the interest of the Episcopal Church in the United States of America ; reserving to the members of this Church the liberty of approving, or disapproving, of any alteration that may be made in the form of prayer.

Voted : that Mr. Bours be paid the expenses of his journey to Boston.

August 28, 1785. Martin Benson[194] was married to Jane Coddington.

September 12, 1785. Mr. Bours having reported to the congregation the proceedings of the convention of clergy and lay depu

---

[194] Martin Benson, born at Newport, October 2, 1741, was the son of John Benson and Anna Collins (probably a daughter of William Collins), his wife. He was engaged in the African trade for many years, and was familiarly known as the " Governor of Goree," on which island he resided for some time. Having acquired a handsome property, he returned to Newport. Subsequently he sailed on another voyage to Africa, and died at Goree, December 24, 1811. His wife, who was twenty years younger, was the daughter of Capt. John Coddington, and the granddaughter of Gov. Joseph Wanton. She died at Newport, December 6, 1836.

ties from the several Episcopal churches in the States of Massachusetts, New Hampshire and Rhode Island, at Boston, on the 7th day of this month, and they having heard read, and duly weighed the same, do vote and resolve, that they fully approve of said proceedings, and do agree to adopt the alterations made in the Liturgy, agreeable to the plan proposed.

Voted: that Mr. Bours be requested to attend the convention, at their adjournment, on the 26th day of October, with full power, as before, to represent this Church.

The committee who were appointed at Easter last to lease out the estate belonging to the Church, late Mr. Kay's, reported that they had agreed with Dr. John Baker, of Philadelphia, to give him a lease of the house now improved by Mr. Brinley, with the garden and buildings thereon, together with the lot of land, containing upwards of seven acres, lately had of Mr. George Scott, in exchange for the same quantity of land, part of said estate, for the term of six years from the first day of January next, 1786, and to conclude and end on the first day of January, 1792, upon condition that the said Dr. Baker pay to the Wardens and Vestry of the Church two hundred silver Spanish milled dollars, per annum, for the rent of the same; three years' rent being advanced and paid down, and the remainder as it becomes due, yearly or half yearly; the said Baker to return and surrender up the said estate to the Church, at the expiration of the lease, in as good repair as he received the same.

The said report is accepted, and the Wardens are desired to give a lease accordingly to Doc[t] Baker.

December 8, 1785. Robert Nichol Auchmuty[195] was married to Henrietta Bruce, by Rev. Mr. Badger.

---

195 born in 1758, was the eldest son of Rev. Dr. Auchmuty, of New York. He graduated at Columbia College, and in the Revolution served as a volun-

In July of this year, 1785, a marble monument[196] was erected to the memory of Admiral de Ternay, who, while in command of the French fleet in these waters, had died here after a brief illness, December 15, 1780, and was buried in the church-yard, with great pomp and ceremony.

Easter Monday, April 16, 1786.   Samuel Freebody and Francis Malbone, elected Wardens, John Bours, clerk of Vestry; James Gibbs, clerk; John Meunscher, organist; Daniel Vernon, sexton.

teer in the British army.   After the death of his first wife, he married Henrietta Overing, his first cousin, daughter of John Henry Overing, of Newport.   He died January 28, 1813.

Arthur Gates Auchmuty, probably a brother of the elder Judge Auchmuty, was buried in Trinity Churchyard, but no stone marks the spot.   He was married to Ann Dickinson, by Rev. Dr. McSparran, September 3, 1734.

[196] The monument sent out by order of the French King, was intended for the interior of the Church, but as no wall space could be found for it, it was set against the exterior wall, in the church-yard, where it was gradually falling to decay, when the Marquis de Noailles, then the French Minister to the United States, had it repaired, and the Vestry found a place for it in the vestibule of the Church, where it is well cared for.   It was placed there in 1872.   It bears the following inscription:

D. O. M.

CAROLUS LUDOVICUS D'ARSAC DE TERNAY.

ORDINIS S^{ti} Hierosolymitani Eques. non dum vota professus,

a vetere et nobili genere, apud Armoricos Oriundus.

unus è Regiarum Classium præfectis,

CIVIS, MILES, IMPERATOR.

de Rege suo, et Patriâ, per 42 annos bene meritus, hoc sub marmore

JACET.

FELICITER AUDAX,

naves regias, post Croisiacam Cladem, per invios VICENONLÆ fluvii

anfractus disjectas, è cœcis voraginibus, improbo labore,

annus 1760, 1761.

inter tela postium,

detrusit, avellit, et stationibus suis restituit incolumes,

Anno 1762, TERRAM NOVAM in America invasit.

Anno 1772, renunciatus PRÆTOR.

Vestrymen : Charles Wickham, Stephen Ayrault, John Bours, Francis Brinley, Charles Handy, Christopher Champlin, George Gibbs, Henry Hunter, Thomas Freebody, Samuel Freebody, John Mawdsley, Thomas Wickham, John Malbone, Francis Malbone, Benjamin Gardiner, Benjamin Brenton.

Voted : that the house given by the late William Tate to the poor of the Church be inspected.

Voted : that Mr. Bours be requested to write the chairman of the

ad regendas BORBONIAN et FRANCIÆ Insulas, in GALDIAS commoda, et
Colonorum felicitatem per annos Septem, totus incubuit.
FŒDERATIS ordinibus, pro libertate dimicautibus.
A Rege Christianissimo missus subsidio Anno 1780.
Rhodum Insulam occupavit :
Dum ad nova Se accingebat pericula,
IN HAC URBE.
inter commilitonum planctess, inter Fœderatorum Ordinum lamenta et
desideria.
Mortem obiit, gravem bonis omnibus, et luctuosam Suis.
die 15 A x^{bris}, M DCC, LXXX,
natus annos 58.
REX CHRISTIANISSIMUS Severissimus virtutis judex.
ut clarissimi Viri memoria posteritati consecretur
hoc monumentum ponendum jussit.
M. DCC, LXXX.

This done, the Marquis de Noailles caused a heavy slab of granite, bearing the following inscription, to be placed over the Admiral's grave in the churchyard :

Hoc Sub Lapide
Anno MDCCCLXXIII Posito Jacet
Carolos Lvdovicos D'ARSAC DE TERNAY
Anno M. DCCLXXX
Decessos
Sub Proximo Templi Porticvm Restavratvm Et Protectvm Translatvm
Est.

convention, to be holden the 26th inst., at Boston, and obtain a copy of their proceedings.

Voted: that a tax of one guinea on the lower, and half a guinea on the gallery pews, be continued for the ensuing year.

Voted: that Mr. Bours, Mr. Brinley and Capt. Handy, with the Wardens, be a committee to write Bishop Seabury upon the subject of obtaining a minister.

Voted: that the thanks of the congregation be returned to Mr. Bours for his past services, and that he be requested to keep them together, as he has done, and that he receive at the rate of £30 per annum, with the improvement of the parsonage-house, as before.

Pew No. 13, the property of Thomas Cranston, was sold by him to Mr. Christopher Champlin, with the approbation of the Wardens, Jnne 29, 1786.

Meeting of the congregation, July 31, 1786.

A letter from Bishop Seabury,[197] in answer to one wrote to him

---

[197]   New London, July 17, 1786.
        Gentlemen :
        It has not been in my power to give an earlier answer to your letter of April 21st. The Convention of the Clergy at Stratford did not break up till June 12th and my duties required my absence from home for a fortnight after. I had no sooner returned than I was again obliged to go to New Haven. And, indeed, it was in this last journey, that I got such intelligence as enables me now to write to you with any degree of certainty.
        I am much obliged to you, Gentlemen, and to the whole congregation of the Church at Newport, for the favorable opinion you entertain of me, manifested by your wishing to have me reside with you, and take charge of your Church. However agreeable such an event might be to me, the state of Connecticut does not seem to permit it. Since you turned your attention towards me, we have lost five clergymen, and I believe shall lose the sixth. This makes it a matter of more consequence that I stay with them, and endeavor to remedy the inconvenience that must arise on this occasion. And, indeed, should I accept your kind invitation, my neces-

by the committee appointed for that purpose, on Easter Monday
last, being laid before the congregation, it was voted : that the same
committee be requested to write to the Bishop again, and to the
Rev^d Mr. James Sayre, of Fairfield, whom he has recommended as a
proper person for our minister, and invite Mr. Sayre to come to
Newport, and officiate in our Church a few Sundays, that the con-

sary absence from you, would leave your Church unsupplied more frequently than it ought to be.

I am, however, very sensible of the necessity there is, that you should
have a prudent and acceptable clergyman settled among you, that divine
service may be duly celebrated, and the holy sacraments administered. In
the present scarcity of clergymen, no great choice can be had ; but there
is one in this State who is not under any present engagement, and whom
I think a worthy and prudent man. He has a good understanding, and
appears to be well acquainted with and fully grounded in the principles
of our holy religion ; and is firmly attached to our Church in doctrine and
discipline. I never heard him preach; but he is esteemed a very good
preacher by his brethren, and the people to whom he has officiated. He
reads prayers much to my satisfaction. His voice is strong and, I believe,
equal to your church, and not disagreeable. His character is irreproachable, and his piety and discretion may be depended on. He is a middle-
aged man ; is married, and has, I think, three small children, and a most
amiable woman to his wife. The gentlemen is the Rev. Mr. James Sayre.
He is at present at Fairfield. I have conversed with him on the subject,
and, it appears to me, he would be pleased with a settlement at Newport,
but he has some backwardness in offering himself, or going upon trial.

I should be perfectly satisfied to have him for my parish minister, and
I persuade myself, your congregation would be happy in him. If you
think proper to make any application to him, I shall be happy to promote
it ; or to assist your endeavors to procure a minister in any other way that
shall be more agreeable to you. He, as well as I, would be glad to hear
from you as soon as the importance of the subject will permit, as we
have a number of vacancies here, and cannot afford to have him long
idle. I could say nothing to him of the living at Newport, but only that
I presumed it would be a decent one.

I ought to inform you that there are three young gentlemen, who, we

gregation may have an opportunity of hearing him, and if they approve of him, to treat upon terms of settlement.

Mr. Bours having reported to the congregation the resolution of the clergy and lay delegates, met in convention on the 21" inst. at Boston, by adjournment, voted: that the same be approved and adopted by our Church.

August 8, 1786. Dr. Sylvester Gardiner[195] died in his 80th year, and was buried under the Church.

Sunday, August 27, 1786. At a meeting of the congregation after divine service, voted: that the Rev. James Sayre, who hath performed the services of the Church this day, be accepted and settled as our Minister, and that he be paid as a salary £100 sterling money, per annum, to commence upon his arriving at Newport

---

expect, will go into Deacons' orders in September, one only of whom is engaged; but I should imagine that quite a young man would not suit you so well.

Commending you and your Church to the blessing and protection of Almighty God, I beg leave to subscribe myself, Gentlemen, with great regard, your most affectionate

and very humble serv't,

Samuel Bp. Connect.

Messrs. John Bours, Samuel Freebody, Francis Malbone, Fra's Brinley and Charles Handy, the Committee of the Congregation of Trinity Church, Newport.

[195] Dr. Gardiner was born in South Kingston. He was educated in Europe. When he returned to America he settled in Boston, where he became eminent as a surgeon, and amassed a fortune. At the opening of the Revolution he went to England, where he remained till peace was declared. Returning to America, he took up his residence at Newport. The funeral was solemnized at the Church, at which time a sermon was preached at his own request. Many marks of respect were shown to his memory on the day of the funeral.

with his family ; that he improve the parsonage-house and lot, and
be also paid the expenses of his present journey to Newport, and of
the removal of his family ; and that Col. Malbone, Mr. Champlin,
Mr. Gibbs and Mr. Brinley, with the Wardens,[199] be a committee to
wait upon Mr. Sayre, and inform him of the resolution of the congregation, and report his answer.

Voted : that Mr. Bours be requested to officiate until the arrival
of Mr. Sayre.

October 1, 1786.   Whereas, the Rev. Mr. Sayre hath this day
arrived from Fairfield, with his family, and taken charge of our
Church, voted : that a sum sufficient to defray the expenses of his

---

[199]   Newport, August 2d, 1786.

Rev. Sir :

The Right Rev. Bishop Seabury, having, in consequence of an application made to him by the congregation of Trinity Church, in this city, to
become their Rector himself, or to recommend a proper person to them,
mentioned you as well qualified in all respects to undertake the important charge.   At a meeting of the Church on Monday last, a unanimous
vote was passed empowering and requesting us to write you upon the subject, and to propose to you the taking a ride to Newport and officiating a
few Sundays, that the congregation may have an opportunity of hearing
you and making proposals for a settlement.

We would just observe that we gave our late Minister, the Rev. Mr.
Bisset, £100 sterling, per annum, and the improvement of a house and
garden.   We cannot promise more than that sum at this time, when this
city is laboring under some peculiar difficulties, but so far we may possibly
go again with proper exertions.

We shall be glad to hear from, or see you, as soon as convenient, and
are very respectfully,

Rev^d. Sir,

Your most Obed Servts,

Rev. Mr. James Sayre.

The above is from an unsigned copy of the letter, in the hand-writing
of John Bours.

removal, together with his late journey to Newport, be collected by subscription, and paid him by the Wardens.

Voted : that Mr. Sayre be requested to notify the congregation to meet after divine worship on Sunday next, that they may be desired to pay the taxes of the pews by the possessors of them ; by putting the same into the box on the Sunday, marked with the name of the proprietor, or occupier, or number of the pew, so that the Wardens may give credit for the same.

Voted : that the lease given to Dr. Baker be for eight years.

October 8, 1786. The congregation, having a grateful sense of the services rendered to the Church by Mr. Bours, in his officiating for them for the last five years, as a lay reader, do unanimously vote him their sincere thanks.

Entered by order of the congregation,

FRAS MALBONE, Warden.[200]

Easter Monday, April 9, 1787. Samuel Freebody and Francis Malbone were elected Church Wardens ; John Bours, clerk of the Vestry ; James Gibbs, clerk ; John Meunscher, organist ; Daniel Vernon, sexton.

Voted : that the sexton's salary be augmented to thirty dollars per annum.

Whereas, the shutting up of the aisles, at the west end of the Church, is found to be very inconvenient to several of the congregation, voted : that the same be laid open, and that the proprietors of the four pews built therein be accommodated with pews by the Church, whenever they apply for that purpose.

Voted : that the thanks of the congregation be presented by the

---

[200] Mr. Bours, who kept the records of the Church, was naturally disinclined to make this entry himself, and the duty was assigned to the Warden.

Wardens to Mrs. Jonas Redwood,[201] for her present of a large prayer-book to the Church.

September 4, 1787. Voted: that the Rev. Mr. Sayre[202] be requested to give notice to the congregation, that as provision is made by the Vestry, for the schooling of ten poor boys, upon Mr. Kay's donation, they are desired to make return to him of such names as

---

[201] It does not appear whether this was the wife of Jonas Langford Redwood, second son of Abraham, or of his son of the same name. The first married Abigail Godfrey, of Newport, and the latter married a Miss Holman, of Virginia.

[202] *James Sayre* This was the last meeting of the Vestry at which Rev. Mr. Sayre was present, and the marriage ceremonies, from this date to the close of Mr. Sayre's connection with the Church, were performed by Rev. William Smith, of St. Paul's, Narragansett, to which place persons wishing to be united went for that purpose. There was trouble in the Church, and the breach between the minister and the congregation was not closed till the Rev. Mr. Sayre's connection with the Church was severed. While he was cordially received at the outset, there seems to have been a want of harmony in the Church soon after his entering upon his duties. There was probably blame on both sides. Mr. Sayre was far from conciliatory (was often arbitrary), and the congregation, frustrated in some of their designs, particularly in their wish to enter into cordial relations with some of the churches of the neighboring States, were severe in their remarks against him. They charged him with "refusing to put a vote in the Vestry which he had previously agreed to do." They apprehended, from conversation had with him, " that he would never be brought to conform to any form which might be agreed upon for the establishment of union in the Episcopal Church of America, and which was then supposed to be in agitation, if it differed in any manner from the forms of England, excepting the prayer for the King." That on being asked "if the Church in Pennsylvania had been consecrated, he replied that there were no churchmen there," etc.

To make matters worse, the controversy got into print, and letter followed letter in the newspapers of the day. Then a pamphlet was put into circulation by Mr. Sayre, and was answered by Mr. Bours (who was the leader of the opposition), as he had answered some of his letters.

are proper objects of that charity, to be laid before the Vestry at
their next meeting.

Voted : that the Vestry meet on the first Monday of every month,
at 10 o'clock, A.M., at the parsonage.

It was represented to Mr. Bours at this stage that if he would retire from
his offices, as Vestryman and Clerk of the Vestry, peace would probably be
restored.   To bring about this result, Mr. Bours sent in the following
letter :

Newport, April 10, 1780.

Gentlemen :   Having been informed that an objection is raised by some
persons unfriendly to me, that my holding the office of Clerk, and being a
member of the Vestry, is an obstacle to the re-establishment of peace and
harmony in the congregation, and having the *true* interest of the Church at
heart, I had long since determined that every consideration, on my part,
should give way to any object so desirable, and therefore beg leave to assure
you that I do, with the greatest cheerfulness, resign both these offices, sincerely wishing that it may answer the end proposed. and am, with sentiments of regard,

Gentlemen, your most obed' Servant,

J. BOURS.

The Gentlemen, Wardens and Vestry and Congregation of Trinity
Church, Newport.

But the breach was now far too wide to be closed easily, and the congregation, in a letter to Mr. Sayre, thus addressed him :

" Reverend Sir : The two last meetings of the Vestry, having ended only
in an adjournment, and the disagreeable consequences that must attend
the continuance of the present division in our Church have induced a free
conversation among us. the result of which we beg leave, briefly, to communicate to you.

" It was once the hope and expectation of us all, that under your ministry we should be happy and united ; but being unfortunately disappointed
in that hope, and seeing no prospect of the wished for happiness, either to
you or us, and flattering ourselves that your sentiments and the religion
you profess. will not permit you to obstruct our happiness, especially
where you cannot yourself, in our opinion, expect to enjoy any by remaining longer our minister, we also wishing to continue on the same friendly

13

October 1, 1787.   Voted by the congregation, that Mr. Stephen De Blois be a vestryman in the room of Mr. Charles Wickham, deceased.

Voted: that £10 sterling be added to the Rev. Mr. Sayre's salary for the year ensuing.

Voted: that the Wardens have a floor laid over the ceiling of the new part of the Church as soon as possible.

----

and neighborly terms we have been on with each other; for these considerations, and others unnecessary to mention, we are induced to wish that you could so far join in opinion with us, as to be willing to fix a time for putting an end to your ministry here.   And as we do not desire that you should suffer any inconvenience by a sudden removal, if it should be more agreeable to you to remain till Easter next, we shall freely agree to it, and shall be happy, if every disagreeable circumstance that has lately taken place among us, may be buried in oblivion, if that is as much your wish as ours."

The above is from a draft of a letter, and is without date; if answered, the answer has been lost.

The appeal to Rev. Mr. Sayre not meeting with a favorable response, a letter was addressed to Bishop Seabury, as appears by a draft, also without date.

"As the Reverend Mr. Sayre was introduced here, and cordially received as Minister of Trinity Church, on your recommendation, he then being an entire stranger, and, as we believe, that many parts of his character were then unknown to you; 'though few of us have the honor of a personal acquaintance with you, yet from the circumstances just mentioned, and from our knowledge of your rank in the Church, and of the character you sustain, we beg leave to lay before you the enclosed state of the dispute at present subsisting between Mr. Sayre and a part of the congregation, and of our firm purpose in consequence of it, omitting the breach between him and Mr. Bours, of which we suppose you are already perfectly informed.

"We declare to you, Sir, that we have used all the means in our power, to prevail on Mr. Sayre to leave us, without coming to an open rupture; in confirmation of which we take the liberty also, to enclose a copy of an address, which was delivered to him after he refused to put a vote to the

November 5, 1787. Voted: that the sexton be directed by the Wardens to go to all the owners and occupiers of pews, and inform them that they are earnestly requested to put the tax on their pews into the box, on the Sunday, to prevent great and unnecessary trouble to the Wardens.

Easter Monday, March 31, 1788. Samuel Freebody and John Handy were elected Church Wardens; John Bours, Clerk of the Vestry; James Gibbs, Clerk; John Meunscher, organist; Daniel Vernon, sexton.

Voted, by the Vestry: that the necessary fencing be made by the Wardens on the lot improved by the organist, late the estate of William Tate, deceased.

August 6, 1788. Edward Mumford was chosen one of the Vestry, in the room of George Wright, deceased.

Easter Monday, April 13, 1789. John Handy and Robert N. Auchmuty were chosen Church Wardens; Robert N. Auchmuty, Clerk of the Vestry; James Gibbs, Clerk; and John Meunscher, organist, with the same salary that he had last year; Daniel Vernon, sexton. Peter Mumford was elected a Vestryman in place of John Bours.

Voted: that no records of the proceedings of the congregation shall be shown, or copies of them be given to any person, without the consent of the Wardens and Vestry.

Voted: that the new form of worship recommended by the con-

Vestry, which he had previously engaged to do; to which he has not condescended to return an answer.

" Respect to you, Sir, and to your recommendation, and the hope that, after perusal of the enclosed papers, you will be convinced that it will be for the peace and quiet of the Church, as well as of society, that Mr. Sayre should retire, are the causes of this address; and we shall suspend the publication until an opportunity offers of hearing from you, and shall be very happy to be enabled by your mediation to suppress it; as an appeal to the public, on this occasion, has ever been disagreeable to us."

vention at Boston, and adopted by the congregation the 31st of July, 1786, be discontinued, and that the service be performed in the manner that it was prior to that vote.

A separation was probably brought about through the mediation of Bishop Seabury, and Mr. Sayre was found a parish at Stratford, Ct. There he published:

" A Candid Narrative of certain matters relating to Trinity Church in Newport, In the State of Rhode Island, By James Sayre, A.M., late Minister of said Church; With a view of correcting the egregious misrepresentations of Mr. John Bours, contained in a letter addressed to the Author, in the *Newport Herald* of October 9th, 1788. Fairfield. Printed by Forgue & Bulkeley, 1788. Audi et Alteram Partem."

He also furnished for the press the copy of

" An Address Presented to the Rev. James Sayre, A.M., Minister of Trinity Church, Newport, Previous to his leaving this Town; together with his Answer, After his Arrival at Fairfield, in Connecticut. Published by Request of a Number of Subscribers to the Address. Newport (R. I.) Printed by Henry Barber, 1789."[203]

Voted: that Messrs. Charles Handy, Mr. Wickham, Mr. Mumford and Mr. Auchmuty be a committee to converse with Mr.

---

[203] The "address" was printed by Peter Edes, at the office of the *Newport Herald*, and bore this title:

" An Appeal to the Public; in which the Misrepresentations and Calumnies contained in a Pamphlet entitled ' A Narrative on Certain Matters Relative to Trinity Church, in Newport, in the State of Rhode Island,' by a very extraordinary man, the Rev. James Sayre, A.M., late Minister of said Church, are pointed out and his very strange conduct during the time of his ministration at Newport, faithfully related. By John Bours, Merchant, and one of the Vestry of said Church."

> " Honor and shame from no condition rise,
>   Act well your part, there all the honor lies."
> " Worth makes the man, and want of it his fellow,
>   The rest is all but leather or Prunella."—(POPE.)

Smith, and learn if he has any objection to conforming to the customs and service of our Church.

April 27, 1789. Meeting of the congregation. The report of the committee appointed at the last meeting to wait on the Rev. Mr. Smith, being received, it was voted: that the same committee be continued and requested to converse further with Mr. Smith on the same subject.

The exact date of the retirement of Rev. Mr. Sayre cannot now be fixed, but it occurred some time in the winter of 1788–89. In April, 1789, the congregation had under consideration the calling of Rev. William Smith, then settled in Narragansett, as Rector of the Church. Of the subsequent career of Rev. Mr. Sayre we have a brief outline in Hitchcock's *History of the Church in Woodbury*:

"At the convocation assembled at Litchfield, June 2d, 1790, a vote was taken on the adoption, or, rather, approval, of the General Convention at Philadelphia, October 2d, 1789. It was decided in the affirmative, every one of the fifteen clergymen present voting in favor of it, but the Rev. James Sayre, who entered his protest against the proceedings, and desired that it be recorded. The next day he withdrew from the convocation. He accompanied his opposition to the new prayer-book, and the General Constitution, with bitterness of feeling and personal abuse—the traits of character which he had shown at Newport, Rhode Island, where the displeasure of a divided parish fell upon him before he came to Connecticut. Speedy efforts were made by the Bishop and Clergy to neutralize his influence, and bring the people under his care into harmonious action with the Diocese.

"At a Convocation in East Haddam, February 15, 1792, this peremptory vote was passed: That unless the Wardens and Vestrymen in Christ Church, in Stratford, shall transmit to the Rt. Rev., the Bishop of Connecticut, within fourteen days after Easter Monday next, a notification that the congregation of said Church have adopted the Constitution of the Protestant Episcopal Church, as settled by the General Convention, at Philadelphia, in October, 1789, they (the congregation) will be considered as having totally separated themselves from the Church in Connecticut. The controversy was bitter and Mr. Sayre finally withdrew from his parish at Stratford, and took charge of a church at Woodbury, but with no happier results. His mind was diseased, a fact hitherto unknown, and actual insanity terminated his life, in 1798."

CHAPTER XII.

1789–1790.

MAY 25, 1789. Voted, at a meeting of the congregation: that Mr. Christopher Champlin and the Wardens be a committee to write to the Rev. Mr. Smith, and request him to visit us every other week for the present; and likewise to write to the Wardens, Vestry and congregation of St. Paul's Church, Narragansett, to know if they have any objection to his conforming to our desire.[204]

Voted: that the same committee provide decent lodgings for Mr. Smith, should he accept our invitation.

Voted: that the Wardens, Mr. Champlin, Mr. Handy, Mr. Gibbs, Mr. Wickham, Mr. Gardiner and Mr. Peter Mumford, be a committee to inquire after and endeavor to find out a clergyman that may be agreeable to the congregation.

Voted: that a notification be put in each pew requesting the congregation to contribute every Sunday, as much as their situation will permit, for the payment of Mr. Smith, the other officers, and unavoidable expenses of the Church.

June 15, 1789. The committee appointed to write to the Rev. Mr. Smith, and the congregation of St. Paul's Church, Narragansett, having reported that the Rev. Mr. Smith, and the congregation at Narragansett, had consented to comply with their request, it was

------

[204] Rev. Mr. Smith had, for some time, been in the habit of occasionally visiting the Church and preaching. In March, 1789, Mrs. Ann Baker, wife of John Baker, of this town, died, and was buried under the Church, at which time a sermon was preached by Mr. Smith.

voted: that the same committee write to the congregation at Narragansett, and return them thanks for their kindness.

September 10, 1789. A notification having been received from the Rev. Mr. Parker, of Boston, that the convention lately held at the city of Philadelphia, and adjourned to the 29th of this month, had expressed a desire that this Church should be there represented, it was thereupon ordered, that the Wardens request the Rev. Mr. Smith to notify a meeting of the congregation, at the Church, immediately after divine service, next Sunday, in the afternoon.

Voted: that the Wardens, Mr. F. Brinley, Mr. C. Handy and Mr. D. Wickham, be a committee to draw up such papers as they may think necessary to lay before the congregation.

September 13, 1789. At a meeting of the Wardens, Vestry and congregation of Trinity Church, in Newport, in the State of Rhode Island, immediately after divine service, it was voted unanimously: that this congregation will, for the future, abide by and maintain such rules and orders, respecting both the doctrine and discipline of our Church as has been determined upon by the General Convention, held in the city of Philadelphia, from the 28th of July to the 8th of August last, or which may be determined upon by the convention which is to be held by adjournment, in Philadelphia, the 29th of the present month; and that we will apply to some gentleman to represent us in the said convention.

Voted: that the Rev. Samuel Parker, D.D., be requested to represent us in the said convention, and that the Wardens, Messrs. Brinley, Wickham and DeBlois, be a committee to write to him on the subject.[305]

---

[305] The committee immediately wrote to Rev. Dr. Parker:

"Rev⁴ Sir, The extract of the letter from the committee of the convention to the clergy of Massachusetts and New Hampshire, which you favored us with, was immediately laid before the Wardens and Vestry of our Church, and as it was of great moment, the congregation was summoned to meet in

December 26, 1789. Voted: that the congregation be desired to meet in the Church, on Sunday next, immediately after divine service, for the express purpose of choosing a Minister.

December 28, 1789. Voted: that every person who regularly pays his pew tax shall have a right to vote in the choice of a Minister.

Voted: that the Wardens, Mr. Brinley, Mr. Champlin, Mr. Gibbs, Mr. Wickham, and Mr. De Blois, be a committee to wait on the Rev. Mr. William Smith,[206] inform him that we have this day chosen

---

the Church after divine service, last Sunday, in the afternoon, to take it into consideration. Having likewise read the Journal of the convention and duly considered the canons and general constitution, we were appointed a committee, not only to thank you for your communication, but to request of you, as we, unhappily, are at present without a Rector, to represent our Church at the adjourned convention, which is to be held in the city of Philadelphia the 29th of this month; and we likewise enclose you a vote of the congregation, which we hope will be sufficient to convince that respectable body of our determination to abide by any rules or orders that may be formed by them, respecting both the doctrine and discipline of the Episcopal Church in the United States.

We are sorry that from the shortness of time we have not been able to consult our sister churches in this State, and form a convention; but as by the fifth article of the General Constitution every church may be represented that shall accede to it, we flatter ourselves that your appearing in our behalf at the adjournment of the Convention will be sufficient.

Although we do not presume to dictate, yet we are desired to express a hope that the alterations [in the prayer-book] may be as few as possible.

If we were not fully sensible of your zeal for the Church in general, we should think it necessary to apologize to you for the trouble we give you.

[206] Rev. William Smith was born in Scotland, where he was educated, studied for the university, and was ordained. He came to America. His first parish was in Maryland, but he did not remain there long, for in July, 1787, he was in charge of St. Paul's, Narragansett, where he was settled at the time that he was called to Trinity Church, and remained here

him for our Minister, and request his acceptance of the office, and
that the said committee offer him such a salary as they may think,
from the present situation of our Church, we may be able to
punctually pay.

February 25, 1790.   At a meeting of the congregation, voted :
that provision be made for schooling ten poor children, agreeable
to Mr. Kay's will, as soon as possible.

Voted : that Mr. Gibbs, Mr. Brinley and Mr. Wickham be a committee to seek for some person, qualified as the will directs, to edu-
cate them.

Voted : that the Rev. Mr. Smith be appointed and requested to
undertake the education of the said children for the present ; and
that public notice be given next Sunday for all persons who have
children entitled to the benefit of the said donation, to send in their
names and ages to the Rector, prior to Easter next, that the Vestry
may select those that are proper objects of charity.

Easter Monday, April 5, 1790.   The officers of the Church then
holding office were all re-elected.

October 10, 1790.   Voted : that notice be given to the congregation to meet next Sunday, after divine service in the Church, to take

---

till April 12, 1797. He was a man of learning, and was gifted in many ways ;
but, unfortunately, he had an infirmity of temper, which frequently brought
him into trouble.   Rev. Salmon Wheaton, D.D., is quoted in Ross's
Century Sermon, as saying : "Had Mr. Smith's prudence been equal to
his talents and learning, he might, with the Divine blessing, have been instrumental in healing the unhappy divisions among his people and restor-
ing the Church to its former prosperity."   And the Rev. Mr. Beardsley
said of him, in an historical discourse : " He possessed a singular ver-
satility of talents, and was both a theologian and a scholar, a composer
of church music, and a constructor of church organs ; and but for the
peculiarity of his temperament, and the infirmity of his constitution, he
might have been more useful in his day and generation."   He died in
New York, April 6, 1821, in his 69th year.

into consideration the proceedings of the late General Convention, to consider of the propriety of writing to our sister churches in this State, for the purpose of meeting in a State Convention, and for such other matters as shall then be thought proper to lay before them.

October 17, 1790. Meeting of the congregation. Voted: that the congregation write to the sister churches in this State, requesting them to meet us in Convention at this place, as soon as conveniently may be, agreeable to the resolve of the last General Convention, held in Philadelphia, September 29, 1790.

Voted: that the Rev. Mr. Smith and the Wardens be a committee to write to our sister churches, and to represent us in Convention.

Voted: that the Revised Book of Common Prayer be used by this congregation as soon as they can be procured; previous notice of one Sunday being given.

. November 21, 1790. The delegates appointed on the 17th of October, to represent us in Convention, having reported that they had met the churches of Providence and Bristol in Convention, and having furnished the Vestry with a copy of their proceedings, it was voted: that the Rev. Mr. Smith be requested to give notice next Sunday forenoon, in church, that the congregation are desired to remain in the church in the afternoon, after divine service, to take the same into consideration.

November 23, 1790. At a meeting of the congregation it was unanimously resolved, that the thanks of this congregation be given to the Rev. Mr. Smith, John Handy and R. N. Auchmuty, our delegates to the late Convention; and the Clerk of the Vestry is desired to insert the whole of the proceedings on the records of this Church, as a testimony of our approbation.

" At a Convention held in Newport, November 18, 1790,

" The Churches of Newport, Providence and Bristol in representation :

" *Newport :* represented by the Rev. William Smith, Rector of Trinity Church.

" Lay delegates: John Handy[207] and Robt. N. Auchmuty.

" *Providence :* The Rev. Moses Badger, Rector of King's Church.

" Lay delegates: Jera F. Jenkins, John Mumford.

" *Bristol :* John Usher, Lay delegate from St. Michael's.

" After authoritative testimonials from the different representatives and approved of, the Rev. Moses Badger was chosen President, and Robt. N. Auchmuty, Secretary.

" After having read and duly considered the seventeen canons adopted by the General Convention, held in the city of Philadelphia, from the 29th of September to the 16th of October, 1789, it was unanimously

" Voted: that this Convention will adhere to and obey the above mentioned canons, and recommend to their Standing Committee the strict observance of them.

" Voted: that the following be added as an addition to the sixth canon, to be observed in this State :

" ' That no person shall be received by the Standing Committee of the Church in this State, as a candidate for Holy Orders, unless he shall produce testimonials that he hath been a regular communi-

---

207   Major John Handy was one of many patriots in the Revolution, who sacrificed private interest to the public good. In the effort to drive the British from Rhode Island, he served under Sullivan and Spencer. On the Fourth of July, 1776, he read the Declaration of Independence from the steps of the Court House in Newport ; and fifty years from that day he read it again, July 4, 1826, from the same place. Major Handy, who was the eldest son of Captain Charles Handy, died March 2, 1828, aged 72 years. His widow, who was Frances Stewart, of New London, attained to the age of 92 years, and died March 8, 1854.

cant for the two years last past, certified by two clergymen, with one or both of whom he has communicated; or, by three or more other communicants, in case of the vacancy of the Church or Churches of which the candidate is a member.'

" Voted: that this Convention approve of and will recommend to their respective Churches the use of the revised Book of Common Prayer, adopted by the late General Convention.

" Voted: by this Convention, that the Churches in this State be immediately united under a bishop.

" Voted: that the Right Rev. Father in God, Samuel Seabury, D.D., Bishop of the Church in Connecticut, be, and he is hereby declared the Bishop of the Church in this State. That the Rev. Moses Badger and William Smith be requested to write to and address him on the subject, and that the letter of recognition and Episcopal acceptance, be entered upon the journals of this Convention; and, further, that copies of the said letters be transmitted to the respective Churches of this State, to be entered on their records.

" Voted: that the Rev. Mr. Badger, the Rev. Mr. Smith, and Mr. John Usher, be the Standing Committee of this Convention.

" Voted: that the Rev. Mr. Smith[205] be requested to write to the

---

[205] The following is a copy of the letter addressed to Bishop Seabury:
Right Honored Father in God.

Appointed by an Ecclesiastical Convention, held in this place, the 18th ult., wherein Trinity Church, in Newport, King's Church, in Providence, and St. Michael's Church, in Bristol, were duly represented, as from minutes of the Convention, herewith transmitted, will appear, we take the earliest opportunity of addressing your Reverence.

Confiding in your moderation and prudence, and beholding the decency and propriety with which you conduct your Episcopal administration in your diocese of Connecticut, as also esteeming you an able defender, as well an avowed patron and propagator of Apostolic faith and practice, the aforesaid Convention has nominated and unanimously voted your Reverence, the Bishop and Ecclesiastical Superior of the Churches so represented; and of such others in this State as may in future accede to and become parts of the established Episcopacy of the United States; and in consideration of the many advantages which will naturally result from your superintendance, as well as to manifest our desire to promote and

Churches of Bristol and Narragansett, representing to them the disadvantages resulting from the want of a regular ordained minister.

"Voted: that the thanks of this Convention be given to the Rev.
Mr. Smith, for his excellent discourse, delivered this day, and that
he be requested to furnish us with a copy for the press."[20]

"The Convention adjourned *sine die*."

---

strengthen the unity of Christ's Apostolic Church, as far as in us lieth,
the aforesaid Churches promise to pay to your Reverence all due and
Christian respect and canonical obedience.

And our prayers to God are, that the most perfect unity may pervade all
the Churches in those States, that the God and Father of our Lord
Jesus Christ, who brought again from the dead that great Shepherd of the
sheep, the Supreme Bishop of our souls, and head of his Church, may
shed abroad more and more of his divine light and love upon our Episcopacy and Priesthood, and on all the Churches of our communion ; that
every one in his several vocations and ministry, may by a life of Faith
upon, and obedience to, the Son of God, glorify him in " time, and be
numbered with the Saints of the most High," when time shall be no
more.

With the most affectionate regard for your person and family, and
praying with all fervency that the pleasure of the Lord may prosper in your
hands :

We have the honor and felicity to be.

Right Reverend Father in God,

your Reverence's

Most Obedient and Very Hum[ble] Serv[t]

WILL. SMITH.

Rec[t] of Trinity Ch., Newport.

M. BADGER,

Rector of King's Church, Providence.

Newport, 20th Nov., 1790.

The Right Rev[d] Father in God, Samuel, by Divine Providence Bishop of
the Church in Connecticut.

[22] The sermon was printed, with the following title :

" A Discourse at the Opening of the Convention of Clerical and Lay
Delegates of the Church, in the State of Rhode Island, delivered in Trinity
Church, Newport, Thursday, the 18th of November, 1790. Psalm cxxii.,
7-9. By William Smith, A.M., Rector of Trinity Church, Newport."

CHAPTER XIII.

1790–1797.

At a meeting of the congregation of Trinity Church, on Sunday, December 9, 1790, a letter from the Right Rev⁴ Samuel Seabury, in answer to the letter of the convention, being received and read, was ordered first to be copied on the records, and then filed among the papers of the Church.

New London, Decb. 1, 1790.

Reverend Gentlemen :

Your letter of the 20ᵗʰ of November came to me in due time. I feel myself much obliged by the confidence the Ecclesiastical Convention held at Newport, the 18ᵗʰ of the last month, have placed in me; and by the manner you, gentlemen, have notified me that that convention had " nominated and unanimously voted " me the Bishop and Ecclesiastical Superior of Trinity Church, in Newport, of King's Church, in Providence, and of St. Michael's Church, in Bristol and of such other churches in the State of Rhode Island " as may in future accede to and become parts of the established Episcopacy of the United States."

Had I a high opinion of my own abilities, it is probable I should accept this instance of the good opinion your convention are pleased to entertain of me, with more confidence; next, however, to doing as well as we wish, is to do as well as we can.

Confiding then in the assistance and protection of Almighty God, and hoping, gentlemen, for your advice and support, and for the support of all good men, I do, in the fear of God, and under a sense of duty to the great Redeemer and Head of the Church, accept the charge your convention have thought proper to commit to me; and will exert my best efforts that their expectations from me may not be entirely disappointed.

By the divine permission I will visit your churches as soon as the
spring season shall permit, and hope then for a happy opportunity
of personally settling with you such matters as may be thought
necessary or useful to their general interest.

I most heartily join in your devout prayers for the unity and
prosperity of the church in the United States.   May it ever continue
a sound and flourishing part of the Catholic Church of Christ.

Commending you and your Churches to the blessing and protection of Almighty God ; requesting your prayers for me to the same
all-sufficient Being, by whose power the weakest abilities are sometimes made the instrument of his glory, and of prosperity to His
Church, I remain, Reverend Gentlemen, your affectionate Brother
and very humble servant,

SAMUEL BP., Connect.

February 4, 1791.   Voted : that the Rector is desired to request
the attendance of the congregation in the Church on Sunday next,
after Divine Service, to consider of the expediency of applying to
the Hon'ble General Assembly, for liberty to raise a sum of money
by lottery, sufficient to pay the debts and to repair the Church ;
which proposition was unanimously agreed to by the congregation
the following Sunday, and the Wardens, with Messrs. Gibbs, Wickham, Mumford, and Crooke as managers.[210]

Easter Monday, April 5, 1791.   The officers of the Church were
re-elected.

[June 27, 1791, St. John's day.   A discourse was delivered in the

---

[210] The right to have such a lottery was granted, and March 12th the
scheme was offered to the public.   Five thousand tickets were put upon
the market, at two dollars each.   The prizes, 1701 in all, ran from one of
$1000, down to 1598 at four dollars each, subject to a deduction of fifteen
per cent.

In a note appended to the printed scheme, the managers stated that
" from the encouragement they have already met with, they are determined
to draw the lottery by the last of May."   (See page 200.)

Newport Trinity Church LOTTERY.

THE General Affembly, at their laſt Seſſions, having granted Permiſſion to the Congregation of Trinity Church, in Newport, to raiſe by Lottery, the Sum of Fifteen Hundred Dollars, to diſcharge the Debts they unavoidably contraſted during the War, and to repair the Church and Lane, commonly called Church Lane, the Subſcribers (who have given Bond to the General Treaſurer) beg Leave to preſent the following Scheme for the Patronage of the Public.

S C H E M E.

NOT TWO BLANKS TO A PRIZE.

Prizes		Dollars		Dollars
1	of	1000	is	1000
1		500		500
2		200		400
5		100		500
7		50		350
4		30		120
10		20		200
15		10		150
20		8		160
38		6		228
1598		4		6392

1701 Prizes.   10000
3299 Blanks.

5000 Tickets at 2 Dollars.

Subjeſt to a Deduſtion of Fifteen per Cent.

_ Tickets may be had of the Managers, who will pay the Prizes on Demand, and who, from the Encouragement they have already met with, are determined to draw the Lottery by the laſt of May.

GEORGE GIBBS,
THOMAS WICKHAM,
EDWARD MUMFORD,
JOHN HANDY,
ROBERT N. AUCHMUTY,
WILLIAM CROOKE,
} Managers.

NEWPORT. March 12, 1791.

Church before the Grand Lodge of Free and Accepted Masons of the State of Rhode Island, by the Rector, Rev. William Smith, from the text: " He who built all things is God."   Christopher Champlin was that year installed First Grand Master.   The same day George Gibbs, Benjamin Bourne and Robert N. Auchmuty were appointed a committee of the Grand Lodge to wait on the Rev. Mr. Smith, with the thanks of the fraternity for his discourse, and ask for a copy for the press.

The discourse was printed in Providence by Bennett Wheeler.]

February 2, 1792.   Voted: that Mr. Champlin and Mr. Brinley be a committee to view the school-house lot, and the lot proposed for an exchange by Mr. Channing, and to report on the expediency thereof.

February 6, 1792.   Voted: that Mr. Christopher Champlin and Mr. Wickham be a committee to converse with Mr. Tilley respecting the sum he will give annually for the lot on which his [rope] walk stands, and that the Wardens be authorized to grant him a lease for a term of years, not exceeding seven, on such terms as said committee shall agree with him.[211]

Voted: that Mr. Champlin and Mr. Wickham be a committee to consult with Mr. Meunscher respecting the repairs that are wanting in the house he occupies ; that they inquire into the grievances he complains of, and that they inform themselves what Mr. Carr will demand for a passage-way to the well of water, and report to the next meeting.[212]

[211] The rope-walk stood on land acquired of George Scott in exchange for some of the Kay land ; which negotiation is referred to under date of May 2, 1785. It had its eastern bounds on the Jewish cemetery, and made a part of what is now Kay Street.   The remains of the rope-walk that stood there were burnt by some mischievous person during the excitement of the Dorr rebellion, in 1842.

[212] The house occupied by Meunscher was a small story-and-a-half gambrel roof building in the rear of the school-house (now the Shiloh Bap-

The Wardens, Mr. Wickham, Mr. Malbone and Mr. Edward Mumford, were to be a standing committee to adjust the whole business of the Vestry, and that they report their proceedings at each monthly meeting.

Voted: that the Vestry meet the Monday evening after the monthly communion Sunday, alternately at each others' houses, beginning with Mr. Champlin.

March 19, 1792. Voted: that the Wardens give Mr. Tilley a lease for the land on which his rope-walk now stands, for seven, or as many more years as he may choose, at the rate of fifteen dollars a year.

Easter Monday, April 9, 1792. John Handy and Robert N. Auchmuty were elected Wardens; Robert N. Auchmuty, Clerk of the Vestry; John Meunscher, organist; Daniel Vernon, sexton.

Vestrymen: Francis Brinley, Charles Handy, Christopher Champlin, George Gibbs, Henry Hunter, John Mawdsley, Thomas Wickham, John Malbone, Francis Malbone, Benjamin Brenton, Stephen DeBlois, Edward Mumford and Peter Mumford.

Mr. Stephen Ayrault, from old age and deafness, having resigned his place in the Vestry, it was unanimously

Voted: that the thanks of the congregation be given him for his long and faithful services, and that the Clerk of the Vestry furnish him with a copy of this vote.

Voted: that the Wardens, Mr. Thomas Wickham, Mr. Francis Malbone, and Mr. Edward Mumford be a standing committee to adjust the whole business of the Vestry, and that they report their proceedings at each monthly meeting.

---

tist Church). There was no well on the premises, and an arrangement was made whereby the occupant of the house could have access to the well on the premises next west of it. The house was occupied for many years by John Springer, into whose possession it finally came, and he died there. Old and past repair, it was razed not many years ago.

August 6, 1792. Voted: that Mr. Francis Malbone be requested to represent this Church, as a lay delegate, at the State Convention, to be holden in Providence.

At the Easter meeting, Edward Mumford retired from the Vestry, and Henry Sherburne and David Olyphant[213] were elected Vestrymen. No other changes were made.

Easter Monday, April 1, 1794. Joseph Dyer was elected Clerk of the Church, and Samuel Whitehorne and John Handy were added to the Vestry, Handy still serving as Junior Warden.

Voted: that the Wardens, with Henry Sherburne and William Littlefield, be the Standing Committee of the Church.

[214] January 13, 1795. Oliver Hazard, Raymond Henry Jones, Sarah Wallace and Matthew James Calbreth, children of Christopher Raymond Perry and Sarah, his wife, were baptized by Rev. Mr. Smith.

February 21, 1795. John Mawdsley was buried by Rev. Mr. Smith.

---

[213] Dr. David Olyphant was born in Scotland; for many years he resided in Newport, and died here, in the home of his adoption, April 2, 1805, at an advanced age. Previous to his coming to Newport, he had practiced in Charleston, South Carolina. He was eminent in his profession, and " lived universally respected and revered." October 23, 1785, he was married to Ann Vernon, daughter of Samuel Vernon, by Timothy Waterhouse (father of Dr. Benj. Waterhouse), one of the Justices of the Court of Common Pleas. Witnesses, Major Daniel Lyman and Mrs. Lyman. Trinity Church at that time was without a Rector.

[214] Capt. Christ. Raymond Perrry, then in the merchant service, resided in Narragansett. In 1798 he received a commission as captain in the navy, and his two sons, Oliver and Matthew, both of whom rose to the rank of commodore, and became distinguished officers, entered the navy as midshipmen. Oliver was born in South Kensington, and Matthew in Newport.

March 4, 1795. Died: Governor John Collins,[215] son of Governor Samuel Collins, and Hannah his wife, in his 78th year.

Easter Monday, April 6, 1795. William Crooke and William Littlefield were added to the Vestry. Standing Committee, Messrs. Sherburne and Littlefield.

Voted: that the thanks of the congregation be given to Mr. Porea,[216] for his kindness in performing on the organ, and that the Rector be requested to inform him of this vote.

June 30, 1795. Mr. Auchmuty informed the Vestry, that Richard Harrison, Esq., of New York, had desired him to make the following proposal—" That he would take a lease of the house and grounds on the hill [the Kay estate] for nine hundred and ninety-nine years, and would pay for the same yearly, and every year during the same time, the sum of three hundred dollars; and that on the execution of the lease he would make the Vestry a present of three hundred dollars, for the express purpose of new shingling the Church ; whereupon, after mature deliberation, it was " voted and resolved, that Mr. Harrison's offer be accepted, and that a lease be drafted and forwarded to him, for his approbation."

October 7, 1795. Major Anthony Singleton[217] was buried in the church-yard.

---

[215] Governor John Collins was engaged in business in Newport prior to the Revolution. In 1774 he was elected an Assistant. In 1778 he was a delegate to the Continental Congress, and in 1786 he was taken up by the paper money party, and elected Governor in opposition to Governor Greene ; but in 1790, having given offence to his party by casting his vote in favor of the Federal Constitution, he was dropped by those who had previously supported him.

[216] This is the only mention made of Mr. Porea (of whom nothing more is known) and we are left in the dark as to why or when Meunscher, the organist, retired.

[217] Major Singleton came to Newport from Richmond, Va., the previous August, with his family ; but already stricken with disease, he died in a few weeks. While here he had won the esteem of many persons.

October 15, 1795. John Malbone[218] was buried in the church-yard.

October 19, 1795. William Miller, of Turk's Island, died here, and was buried in the church-yard.

February, 1796. Thomas Hadley, late of the Island of Jamaica, died here in his 35th year, and was decently interred in the church-yard.

March 20, 1796. Felix, son of Citizen Arcambal,[219] Vice Consul of France, and Elizabeth Charles la Suganier, his wife, was baptized.

March 29, 1796.[220] Baptized Ann Isabella, daughter of Cleland and Harriet Kinlock.

[Following the death of Bishop Seabury, the Standing Committee of Rhode Island addressed this letter to the Standing Committee of Connecticut:]

Newport, March 29, 1796.

To the Standing Committee of the Protestant Episcopal Church in the State of Connecticut:

Gentlemen: Duly impressed with a grateful sense of the bless-

---

[218] *John Malbone* an eminent merchant, was Brigadier-General of the State militia at the time of his death. His remains, attended by the Marine Society, of which he was an honorary member, were interred in the church-yard. He was the father of Edward G. Malbone, the distinguished miniature painter. On his tombstone there is this inscription:

"A gentleman whose sense of honor, liberality of sentiment, philanthropy and benevolence, reflected lustre on his character as a merchant, citizen and friend, and justly gained him universal esteem."

[219] L. Arcambal succeeded M. Augustus Berhard Monpellier, as Vice Consul. M. Monpellier removed to Bristol, and died there.

[220] Cleland Kinlock was from South Carolina. He spent his summers here, with his family, for a number of years, and died at his country seat, at Statesburg, S. C., September 12, 1823, aged 64 years. At one time, while residing in Newport, he occupied the Kay estate.

ings enjoyed by the Protestant Episcopal Church in Rhode Island, in common with those of the State of Connecticut, during the Episcopal Regency of our departed Rt. Rev. Diocesan, we conceive it our duty at this time to join with you in paying our tribute of Regard to the memory of our worthy Bishop, and to call upon you for a continuance of our common ecclesiastical interest and diocesanal unity. And as it has pleased the adorable Head of the Church to call hence our visible centre of unity, we have to request you to use your best endeavors and influence with the churches which you represent, that they lose no time in making choice of a suitable person to watch over the Doctrines, Discipline and Institutions of our faith and common salvation.

From the paucity of our congregations, we pretend not to any share in your election ; only to be admitted, so far do we request as to homologate your choice, and to give an adjunct suffrage and recommendation in favor of the elect, whom y°, under the direction of Almighty God, may judge worthy of filling the Episcopal chair.

And may God, of his infinite goodness and love for this Church, direct us in all things for the good of the same ; that His Name may be glorified, and the number of the faithful daily increased and rejoice in the salvation of Jesus.

We are, Gentlemen, with every sentiment of love and esteem, and with prayers for your temporal and eternal happiness, your most affectionate and very humble servants, the Standing Committee of the Protestant Episcopal Church in Rhode Island,

   W^M SMITH, Rect. Tr. C., N. Port,
   ROBT. N. AUCHMUTY,
   ABRA^M L. CLARKE, Rect^r St. John's Ch'h, Providence,
   JOHN J. CLARKE.

To the above the following answer was returned. The copy is without date or signatures.

To the Protestant Episcopal Church in the State of Rhode Island :
 Gentlemen :
   Your polite and friendly letter of the 29th of March, last, was received by us in due time. The occasion of your address was truly

a melancholy one. The sudden departure of our late worthy diocesan cast a gloom upon the minds of his numerous acquaintances,
and especially upon the members of his care. We were happy in
being favored with so good a man to fill the Episcopal chair ; and
we sincerely lament the great loss we have sustained.

The delay in answering your Letter until this time did not arise
from any inattention to the subject. But we concluded we should be
better able to comply with your request after the meeting of our
Convention than before. At that meeting your letter was read, the
members unanimously expressing their wish that the union between
the Churches of Rhode Island and Connecticut, which had taken
place under the regency of our late Rt. Rev. Diocesan, might still
be continued. The event of our meeting must, ere this, have been
made known to you by the Rev. Mr. Smith. We trust that our
unanimous choice of the Rev. Mr. Bowden will meet the approbation of our sister Churches of Rhode Island. Mr. Bowden's well-
known abilities and integrity, if he accepts the appointment, will, we
trust, in some measure repair the loss we have sustained, and be a
means of continuing and firmly establishing that Diocesanal unity
which has been so happily begun between us. That God would
preserve, bless and direct his Church in all things, and finally receive
us into everlasting glory, is the earnest prayer of

Your most affectionate and very humble

Servants.

April 5, 1796. Mr. Auchmuty having presented to the Vestry
a lease duly executed by Richard Harrison, Esq., of New York, of
Mr. Kay's estate, agreeably to a vote passed by them, at a meeting
on the 30th day of June last, it is voted and resolved: that the
Wardens sign the counter lease, in behalf of the Minister, Wardens
and Vestry and transmit the same to Mr. Harrison.

The Wardens informed the Vestry that they had received the
three hundred dollars, which he had promised to make them a
present of, in order to shingle the church, and that they had lodged
the same in the Rhode Island Bank.

Easter Monday, April 3, 1796. John Handy and Robt. N. Auchmuty were elected Wardens, and Wm. R. Robinson and Saunders Malbone were added to the Vestry.

Messrs. Christ. Champlin, Geo. Gibbs, Francis Malbone and John Bours, the Standing Committee, Mr. Auchmuty having declined to serve longer as Clerk of the Vestry, Mr. Bours was elected as Clerk, to serve through the ensuing year. John Dyer was continued as Clerk of the Church, and Daniel Vernon was continued as sexton. Mr. Berkenhead having offered to play on the organ, for whatever allowance any of the congregation may be pleased to make him, his proposal was accepted.

April 7th, 1796. The vote and resolve following, after a very full and particular deliberation, passed unanimously :

Whereas, the estate in the Town of Newport, late belonging to Nathaniel Kay, Esq., and bequeathed by him, in his last will and testament, in trust, to the Minister, Wardens and Vestry for the time being, of Trinity Church, for ever, for the support and maintenance of a school-master, Episcopally ordained, to instruct ten poor boys in grammar and the mathematics gratis, and to assist the Minister of said Church ; hath been found from long experience to produce but a small and inadequate income for the benevolent purpose designed by the donor, by reason of the buildings and fences falling into decay, and from other unavoidable causes, therefore, voted and resolved: that the offer made to us by Richard Harrison, Esq., of New York, and accepted, as from the record thereof made of the 30th day of June last on this book of Church records, will appear, to take a lease of the mansion house, outhouses, garden, and lot of land adjoining, containing about seven acres, for the term of nine hundred and ninety-nine years, to commence from the 25th day of March, one thousand seven hundred and ninety-six, at the annual rent of three hundred silver dollars, or silver bullion equivalent thereto, be complied with, and that a proper lease be accordingly executed by the Wardens to the said Richard Harrison. And it is further voted and resolved, that the said annual rent of three hundred dollars, or silver bullion equivalent thereto, together with the rent of several small lots of land, situated and lying at the south part of the town, belonging to and being part of the aforesaid estate, bequeathed by said Nathaniel Kay, be religiously and bona fide applied to answer and fulfil the benevolent design of the said Nathaniel Kay; and that Messrs. Christopher Champlin, George Gibbs, John Bours and John Handy, be and hereby they are appointed a Standing Committee to carry said will into execution, by obtaining a person properly qualified to enjoy said living, who, upon his being approved of by the Minister, Wardens and Vestry, shall receive the whole amount of the rents of said estate, as aforesaid.

But as some time may elapse before such person can be obtained, it is voted and resolved: that the committee aforesaid collect all the rents of said Richard Harrison, from time to time, as they become due, and put the same to interest, upon the best terms they can, at their discretion, and that the principal, with the interest thereon, until said school-master and assistant enter upon his living, as aforesaid, shall be made use of and appropriated (together with such other donations as may be obtained for the purpose) to the building of a school-house on the lot of land where the former church school-house stood, or on some other lot, in the opinion of the committee, more commodiously situated for a school-house.   And that the said committee may proceed in exact conformity to the aforesaid resolves, the Clerk of the Vestry is hereby desired to furnish them an authenticated copy thereof, having first entered them in the Church book of records.

And whereas, there is a considerable sum of money now due for the rent of the several lots of land at the south part of the Town, as aforementioned, it is voted and resolved, that said committee be requested to use their best endeavors to collect the same, together with the future rents of said lots, as they become due, and appropriate the same to the schooling as many poor boys belonging to the Church, under the direction of the Rev. Mr. Smith, as the money collected will allow of.   And that the said committee make report of their doings to the Minister, Wardens and Vestry, on Easter Monday, annually, or oftener, if judged necessary.

Attest,   J. Bours,
               Clerk of Vestry.

In consequence of permission obtained from the General Assembly of the State, to dispose of a lot of land in North Kingston, bequeathed some years past, by Nathaniel Norton, of Newport, to this Church, directing that the yearly rent obtained therefor should be enjoyed by the Rector of the said Church for the time being; and it having been found from experience that said lot, from a variety of causes, had yielded but a trifling sum, it was, therefore, resolved, that the said lot should be disposed of by the Wardens, and the money received for the same, appropriated to purchase a lot of land adjoining, Westerly, the Church burial ground, of Thomas Wickham, agent for the heirs of the late James Honyman; and that the Rector of the Church for the time being, shall be entitled to have the use and improvement of said lot, and shall be entitled also to a fee for every corpse interred within the same.

August 28th, 1796. Whereas, a marble monument, to the memory of the late worthy Rector of this Church, the Rev. Marmaduke Browne and Ann his wife, sent from Ireland by their son, the Honble Arthur Browne, of said Kingdom, hath been received and erected in the Church by Mr. Bours, agreeable to permission heretofore granted for that purpose; it is voted and resolved, by the congregation, that we are highly gratified by having so elegant an ornament added to Trinity Church, to perpetuate the remembrance of two persons, deservedly esteemed while living, and recollected with pleasure by an affectionate congregation; and that Mr. Bours be requested to signify the same to Mr. Browne.

April 12th, 1797. The Rev. Mr. Smith, having informed the congregation that he had accepted a call to the congregation at Norwalk, Connecticut, this day embarked with his family, to enter upon his new charge, after having been paid by the Wardens the balance due to him for his salary.

CHAPTER XIV.

1797-1800.

Easter Monday, April 17, 1797. William Crooke and William R. Robinson, chosen Wardens.

Vestrymen: Francis Brinley, Christopher Champlin, George Gibbs, Henry Hunter, John Bours, Thomas Wickham, Francis Malbone, Benjamin Brenton,[221] Stephen Deblois, Henry Sherburne, John Handy, William Crooke, William Littlefield, Robert N. Auchmuty, William R. Robinson, Saunders Malbone. John Bours, Clerk of Vestry; Joseph Dyer, Clerk of Church; Daniel Vernon, sexton.

Voted: that Messrs. Bours, Handy and Auchmuty be the delegates from this Church at the next annual convention.

Voted: that Messrs. David Olyphant, Francis Brinley, Christopher Champlin, John Bours and Robert N. Auchmuty, with the Wardens, be a committee to consult upon a plan for settling and supporting a minister.

May 14, 1797. The committee appointed on Easter Monday last to consult upon a plan for settling and supporting a minister, having now reported the same, voted: that it be accepted, and that the Wardens use their endeavors to complete the same.

Voted: that Mr. Bours and the Wardens be a committee to write

---

[221] Benjamin Brenton was a direct descendant of William Brenton. In 1758 he was an officer in the Provincial regiment sent to the support of the troops then before Louisburg. In 1796 he was in business in Newport in a small way, and subsequently was taking boarders in the Lopez House, on Thames Street. In 1810 his wife, Rachel Cooke, daughter of Silas Cooke, purchased the small house on Church Street that afterwards passed into the hands of Mrs. Mary S. Hunter, and was recently razed. There he resided with his family till he died, February 23, 1830, at the age of 93 years.

to the Rev. John S. J. Gardiner, at Boston, and request the favor of him to come to Newport, and spend a few Sundays with us.

Resolved: that the fee for the burial of any person in the new burial-ground be, for the future, twelve dollars—eight of them to go to the Rector, and the other four to be applied to keeping the fences in repair.

At a meeting of the congregation on Sunday, August 6, 1797: Whereas, the Rev. John Sylvester J. Gardiner, Assistant Minister of Trinity Church in Boston, in consequence of an invitation from the committee appointed for that purpose at a meeting of the congregation on Sunday afternoon, the 14th day of May last, has come to Newport, and hath officiated this and the last Sunday to our entire satisfaction, it is therefore voted and resolved (*Nomine contradicente*): that the said Rev. John Sylvester J. Gardiner be settled as Rector of this Church, and that he be allowed and paid, as a salary, at the rate of five hundred dollars per annum, in quarterly payments, to commence from the time of his salary ceasing in Boston ; and that he have the use and improvement of the parsonage-house and lot, together with all the perquisites to which our former Rectors were entitled; and that Mr. Bours, with the Wardens, be a committee to wait upon Mr. Gardiner, and deliver him a copy of these resolutions.

September 17, 1797. Voted by the congregation : that a letter received from the Rev. John S. J. Gardiner by the Wardens be entered on the book of records of the Church as follows :

Brookline, September 11, 1797.

Gentlemen :

When I had last the pleasure of seeing you, I was in full expectation of accepting the rectorship of your Church, to which I was the more strongly inclined from the unanimity that prevailed in my election; but as I considered that my future happiness would in a great measure depend on the event, I thought it prudent to weigh all the advantages and disadvantages that might result from my acceptance or refusal of your proposal, previous to any final determination. On the one hand, I reflected that I might prove the instrument in the hands of Providence of organizing a scattered Church, and of reuniting a divided people; on the other hand, I was deterred from the undertaking from a sense of its extreme difficulty, and by the fear that my best exertions would prove abortive. I thought, also, that the salary you had voted was a very inadequate compensation for the greatness of the risk, and that, though it was much to you, in your present situation, to give, it was very little for me to receive. Whilst I was thus wavering in my mind, two circumstances occurred which at length determined me, though with great reluctance, to decline your offer. Mrs. Gardiner expressed stronger disinclination than I expected, to remove to a strange place, where she would have new friendships to form, and new habits to acquire; and the Church, desirous of retaining me, evinced their approbation and attachment by raising my present salary to eight hundred dollars. From every motive of gratitude and interest I am induced therefore to remain where I am, and I doubt not you will acquiesce in the reasonableness and propriety of my determination. I should have declined your proposal with more regret, were there not a very promising young man now ready to accept an advantageous settlement in the Episcopal Church. The gentleman I allude to is a Mr. Dehon, now residing at Cambridge, of irreproachable morals, pleasing manners, a good reader and an animated and an interesting preacher. To these qualities he joins a larger share of ancient and modern literature than is commonly met with in so young a student. He can be powerfully recommended by Dr. Parker, and other respectable characters. Nothing will afford me more pleasure to see your Church flourishing in all its former splendor; and I know no one more able to effectuate this most desirable event than this young gentleman.

I am, gentlemen, with every sentiment of gratitude and esteem, &c.,

Your obliged hum^{ble} serv't,

John S. J. Gardiner

The Church Wardens and Vestry
    of Trinity Church, Newport.

Voted and resolved : that Mr. Bours, with the Wardens, be a committee to write to Mr. Theodore Dehon, at present residing in Cambridge, who has been warmly recommended as a young gentleman of learning, and of an irreproachable character, and who is a candidate for Holy Orders in the Episcopal Church, and invite him to come to Newport and officiate a few Sundays for us, that we may have an opportunity of hearing him, and if agreeable to both him and the congregation, to make proposals for a settlement.

Voted : that the thanks of the congregation [be extended] to the Rev. Mr. Moscrop, for his kindly officiating for us, a number of Sundays past, in our destitute state, and that the Wardens present him on the morrow with a copy of this vote.

Meeting of the congregation, October 8th, 1797. Whereas Mr. Theodore Dehon, in consequence of an invitation given him by the committee appointed for that purpose, at a meeting of the congregation, on Sunday, the 17th day of September last, hath come to Newport and inform him that it is the unanimous will of the congregation, that he would enter into Holy Orders as soon as may be, and become our Rector ; that he be allowed and paid, as a salary, at the rate of $500 per annum, in quarterly payments, to commence at the time of his leaving the Church at Cambridge, and that he have and receive all the perquisites to which our former Rectors were entitled, together with the use and improvement of the parsonage-house and lot, and that the committee assure him the congregation will afford every assistance in their power towards his speedily obtaining Deacon's and Priest's Orders, and that Mr. Dehon be requested to give an answer to these proposals.

September 24, 1797. Daniel Mason[222] died and was buried in the church-yard.

---

[222] *Danl Mason* second son of the late Benj. Mason and Mary (Ayrault) his wife, was born at Newport, in 1755. He was a merchant, at one time engaged in business with

Meeting of the congregation, October 29th, 1797. A letter from Mr. Theodore Dehon, of the 21st, wherein he declines accepting the proposals made to him by the congregation, on Sunday, the 8th inst., being laid before them by the committee appointed to deliver the same, it is therefore voted and resolved: that Mr. Dehon be again appealed to, and that Messrs. Brinley, Champlin, Gibbs, and Bours be a committee for that purpose, and that two hundred dollars more be added to the five hundred voted him as a salary, provided *that* be thought by him a support adequate to induce him to accept the rectorship of our Church.

Meeting of the congregation, November 19, 1797.

In confirmation and addition to a vote passed on the 29th day of October last, it is voted and resolved unanimously: that a vote passed by the congregation on the 8th day of October last, inviting Mr. Theodore Dehon to enter into Holy Orders, and to take upon him the rectorship of our Church, and offering to pay him a salary of $500, be reconsidered; and that we will allow and pay him as a salary, at the rate of $700 per annum, in quarterly payments, to commence on his taking charge of the Church, together with the use and improvement of the parsonage-house and lot, and all the other perquisites to which our former Rectors were entitled; and that the Wardens, with Mr. Bours, be continued a committee to inform Mr. Dehon immediately of these proceedings, by enclosing him a copy of this vote, and requesting from him an answer as soon as may be.

The aforegoing vote having been communicated by the committee to Mr. Dehon, the following letter was received from him in answer thereto:

Col. Francis Malbone, and died a bachelor. His remains were borne to the grave in Trinity Church-yard, by the Artillery Company and the Marine Society, of both of which organizations he was a member.

To the Congregation of Trinity Church at Newport.

Gentlemen :

The convincing proof of your anxiety for my settlement among you as your Rector, exhibited in your renewed application, flatters and affects me. When I answered your former proposals, the predominant objection against a compliance with your wishes was the want of a stipend adequate to the situation. But for this, I should have been influenced by your unanimity, and felt it my duty to comply with your request. This objection being silenced by your second resolve, and the same unanimity of proceeding having continued, I feel it an obligation to accept, with cheerfulness, the Rectorship of your Church; relying for assistance upon that Being who alone is capable of blessing men with endowments equal to the offices which they are called to sustain. I promise on my part to discharge the several duties of that office, which I now accept, as far as I am able, and so long as the providence of God shall see fit to continue me in the same.

It will doubtless, gentlemen, be most agreeable to you, and it will be most convenient for me, that I receive Holy Orders before I meet you at Newport. As a presentation from you will be expected by the Bishop, it is necessary that it should be forwarded by the earliest opportunity ; I shall endeavor to be with you immediately after Orders shall have been obtained, and devoutly wish that we may then commence a long series of years of mutual satisfaction, comfort and joy.

Theodore Dehon.

Cambridge, November 29, 1797.

January 11, 1798. Voted and resolved, unanimously, that Mr. Bours, with the Wardens, wait upon our Rector, the Rev. Mr. Dehon, and assure him that we, as well as the congregation at large, were greatly gratified by his excellent, well adapted discourse delivered on Sunday morning last, upon commencing the duties of his ministry, and request the favor of a copy thereof for the press.[222]

January 16, 1798. Voted and resolved unanimously, that the Rector, Clerk and Wardens be a committee to present to the Rev'd Doct' Parker, of Trinity Church, Boston, a tribute of thanks for his exertions and kind wishes in behalf of our Church, and to request of him a copy of the sermon delivered at the ordination of our Rector, for the press.

Voted: that Mr. Brinley, Mr. Gibbs and Mr. Wickham be a committee to make all necessary examination, and report the most eligible place and method for erecting a vestry-room.

Voted: that Mr. Wickham, Mr. Malbone, Mr. Auchmuty, Major Handy and Mr. Bours be a standing committee to transact the business of the Church, and report their doings, from time to time, to the Rector, Wardens and Vestry.

Easter Monday, April 9, 1798. William Crooke and William R. Robinson elected Wardens.

The Vestry and other officers of the Church remain the same as last year.

Voted: that a vestry-room[223] be immediately built at the north-east corner of the Church, on the outside, and that Messrs. Brinley, Gibbs and Wickham be a committee to have the same done, and that the expense be paid by subscription, provided the money can be raised that way; if not, that the Wardens and Vestry be authorized to dispose of one or more of the pews which have reverted to the Church, in order to obtain the money.

The letter from Rev. James Honyman, under date of December

---

[222] There is no evidence that this request was complied with.

[223] This is the present vestry-room. When first built, and for more than forty years, it was without a door from the street, and was only reached through the Church.

6, 1725, on page 40, had been lost; it was found by Mr. Christopher Champlin, presented to the Vestry April 9, 1798; whereupon it was voted: that the thanks of the congregation be presented to Mr. Champlin for his kind attention to the interest of the Church in procuring and preserving so essential a document as the afore recorded certificate, and also to Mr. Andrew Freebody for his " Book of Musick," for the use of the organist of the Church, this day presented.

Voted: that the tax on all the pews below be ten dollars, except the double pews, which are to be twenty dollars, and those one and a half pews, fifteen dollars, and the gallery pews four dollars, for the ensuing year.

Voted: that the house and lot of land bequeathed by William Tate, late of Newport, in his last will and testament, to and for the use of the poor of our Church, be, in future, under the immediate care and direction of the Wardens, and that the annual rent thereof be received by them and paid over to the Rector, first deducting all necessary repairs, and by him distributed among the most necessitous and deserving poor of the Church at his own discretion; it being of the opinion of the Vestry that the rents hitherto received amount to the sums expended by the Church, from time to time, in repairs on the same.

Meeting of the congregation, July 9, 1798. Voted: that the constitution of the churches in this State, transmitted to this Church by order of the convention[224] for adoption, be adopted, on condition

---

[224] At the Annual Convention of the Church, held that year in Trinity Church, July 11th, Rt. Rev. *Edward Bass.* Bishop of Massachusetts, was elected Bishop of Rhode Island. He was born at Dorchester, Mass., November 23, 1726. He graduated at Harvard, was ordained in London by Rt. Rev. Bishop Sherlock, Bishop of

that the convention accede to the amendments proposed in the returned draft, viz., the alteration of the third article, the erasure of the eleventh and thirteenth, and the alteration of the twelfth article.

Voted: that Messrs. Francis Brinley, Christopher Champlin and George Gibbs be added to Messrs. Bours, J. Handy and Robert N. Auchmuty as delegates to represent this Church in the State Convention, to be held at Newport on Wednesday, the 11th instant.

Voted: that the Wardens and Vestry dispose of one or more of the pews below, which have been forfeited to the Church, at their discretion, in order to defray the expense of new doors, and venetian blinds to the large window in the chancel, and that in the vestry-room, and make any necessary repairs in the Church.

Pew No. 82, late James Clarke's, appearing clearly to have reverted to the Church, was sold to Jacob Smith for the sum of $80, and the same appropriated towards building the vestry-room.

Pew No. 70, lately improved by Thomas Rogers, was sold to Samuel Lawton for $60, and the money appropriated to pay for the new doors and venetian blinds.

N. B. Pew No. 56, late Thomas T. Taylor, was sold by Nich' G. Tillinghast, executor, to Robert N. Auchmuty, with the approbation of the Wardens.

At a meeting of the Rector, Wardens and Vestry, February 5, 1799. Whereas, it appears from the report of the School Committee that they have received the rents of the Kay estate leased to Richard Harrison, as they have become due, agreeably to the lease, and that the sum which will become due on the 25th day of September next being added thereto, there will be a sufficient sum to

London, and on his return to America was elected Rector of St. Paul's, Newburyport, where he resided during the rest of his days. He was consecrated by Bishop White in Philadelphia, May 7, 1797.

build a school-house, voted and resolved: that a school-house be built as soon as may be on the lot where the old school-house stood, and that Mr. Gibbs, Mr. Bours and Mr. William R. Robinson be a committee to consult upon a plan to carry the same into effect, and this meeting to stand adjourned to Monday evening next, the 11th inst.

February 11, 1799.   Voted and resolved: that a school-house be built on the lot where the old house stood; that it be forty feet long and twenty-five feet wide; a tower of eight feet square, rising out of the body of the building, at the east end, eight feet above the roof; that there be a cellar under the whole; that a chimney be built at the west end, in the centre; that there be two arched windows at the west end, of 24 squares of 7 x 9 glass, exclusive of the arch, and three such windows on each side, and that the whole be finished in a plain, neat manner, agreeably to said plan offered by the committee.[224a]

Easter Monday, March 25, 1799.   The officers and Vestry were re-elected.

Mr. Gibbs was requested to write to Philadelphia to make inquiry whether a suitable person conld be had from thence for an organist.

Voted: that Messrs. Brinley, Gibbs, Champlin, Auchmuty and Handy be delegates to the next annual convention.

June 28, 1799.   The building an addition to the parsonage, for the better accommodation of the Rector, was ordered; and in order to defray the expense thereof, the Wardens are authorized to hire the money bequeathed by Robert Wheatley, in his last will and testament, to the poor of the Church, and that they give a bond for the same to the trustees appointed by the said Wheatley to dispose of

---

[224a] The building, corner of Mary and School Streets, is now owned and occupied by the Shiloh Baptist Society.

the same; the congregation to hold themselves accountable for whatever sum is paid on account of said legacy, with lawful interest thereon.

August 24, 1799. Grenville Temple,[225] son of Sir Grenville Temple and Lady Temple, was baptized. Sponsors: Sir Grenville, his Lady and Mr. John Rutledge.

October 20, 1799. Caleb Gardner[226] was married to Mary Collins, daughter of Gov. John Collins.

December 1, 1799. Benjamin Gardiner,[227] of Middleton, was married to Almy Ann Coggeshall, of Newport.

[225] Grenville Temple, the father of Sir John Temple, then the British Minister at New York, had married in Boston, March, 1797, Mrs. Russell, widow of the late Thomas Russell.

[226] who was born at Newport, January 24, 1759, attained to a prominent position. June 3, 1770, he married Sarah Ann Robinson, daughter of Dr. James Robinson, by whom he had five children. She died in 1777, and April 17, 1788, he married Sarah, daughter of Samuel Fowler, who bore him other five children, and died in 1795. Mary Collins, to whom he was married as above, died October 2, 1806, and Mr. Gardner died December 24th of the same year.

During the Revolution Captain Gardner enjoyed the confidence of both the American and French forces, and when peace was established he was appointed French Consul for this district. At his house, now owned by the heirs of the late Dr. Daniel Watson, he entertained the distinguished officers of the allied armies.

[227] Benjamin Gardiner was the son of William Gardiner, and grandson of Joseph Gardiner, of Narragansett. He resided on a farm near Paradise rock, and was a useful member of the Church. His first wife was Elizabeth Wickes, daughter of Thomas Wickes, of Warwick. His second wife was the above-named Almy Ann Coggeshall, who died the following month, and was buried January 8, 1800. March 5, 1801, he married Mary Howland, of Jamestown.

Mr. Gardiner was a vestryman in 1786.

[The news of the death of General Washington reached Newport on Sunday morning, December 22, 1799. The bells of the churches and the State House were tolled throughout the day, save during the hours of divine service, and on the following day there was a total suspension of business. The following Sunday the Fraternity of Masons assembled at the State House, and marched with muffled drums and in suitable mourning, to Trinity Church, where the Rector, Rev. Mr. Dehon, preached a funeral sermon, which was published, with the following title:

"A Discourse delivered in Newport, Rhode Island, before the Congregation of Trinity Church, The Masonic Society, and the Newport Guards, the Sunday following the Intelligence of the Death of General George Washington. By Theodore Dehon, A.M., Rector of Trinity Church in Newport. Printed by Henry Barber. MDCCC."

The pulpits in Trinity Church and the Congregational Church were draped with mourning.

A funeral service was held on the 6th of January, 1800, under direction of Major Daniel Jackson, commandant of this district.

At daybreak there was a discharge of artillery at Forts Adam and Wolcott, and a gun was fired every half hour till sunset. At noon the bier was received on the Parade, in front of the State House, the troops gathered there presenting arms. The procession was then formed, and moved to Trinity Church in the following order, the batteries at the forts firing minute guns till the cortege reached the Church:

Newport Guards.
Newport Artillery.
Music.
(A dead march with muffled drums.)
Artillerists and Engineers, from Fort Adams.

Officers of the Army.

Officers of the Navy.

Militia Officers.

Custom-House Officers.

The Orator of the Day.

Society of Cincinnati.

The Clergy.

The Bier, borne by four Sergeants.

Pall Bearers:

Col. Rogers,	Wm. Channing, Esq.,
Col. Sheldon,	Col. Tew,
Col. Crary,	Col. Sherburne,

each wearing a white scarf tied with a bow on the left shoulder ; in
the centre of the bow a rose of black, and the eagle of the Society
of Cincinnati.

Masonic Society.

Marine Society.

Town Council.

Mechanics' Association.

Citizens.

At the Church, after a prayer was offered by Rev. Mr. Dehon, a
funeral anthem was sung, and an oration was delivered by Major
Daniel Lyman, a revolutionary officer. The procession was then
reformed, and the bier was borne to the place of interment, where
it was deposited with solemn music and volleys of musketry. A
vast concourse of people from the neighboring towns attended the
ceremony, and all business was suspended during the day.]

March 18, 1800. Voted and resolved : that so far as this Church
is interested in behalf of the poor belonging thereto, in the one-half
part of a house and lot in Newport, given and bequeathed to them

by Robert Wheatley,[228] of said Newport, in his last will and testament, we will join with the heirs of the other half part of said house and lot in disposing of the same, and do hereby signify our approbation that Mr. Bours, Administrator to the estate of Mary Wheatley, widow of said Robert, execute a deed to Thomas Hudson, in conjunction with the said heirs to the other half part of said house and lot, for the consideration of eight hundred dollars, the whole sum.

Voted: that Messrs. Bours and Auchmuty be appointed trustees, together with the Rev. Mr. Dehon, in conformity to Robert Wheatley's will, to appropriate the interest money arising annually on four hundred dollars, being the one-half part the house and lot of land said Wheatley bequeathed to the poor of the Church, was sold for; and the said $400, loaned by the said trustees to the Church for the purpose of repairing and enlarging the parsonage-house, agreeably to a vote passed by the congregation on the 30th day of June, 1799, and that the Wardens give a bond to said trustees for the same; and that they, the said trustees, make report of their doings annually to

[228] His will was proved February 1, 1762. His first wife was Mary Young, to whom he was married May 4, 1746. She died, and December 17, 1747, he then married Mary Read. She outlived him. In his will he gave his estate to his wife during her natural life, or until she married, should she take another husband. Then the property was to go to his son William; but if his son died before his wife and without issue, then one-half of the estate was to go to the heirs of John Jepson, and the other half to the poor of Trinity Church, "to be distributed to such persons as the Minister of said Church, and any pious communicants thereto, shall judge the most proper objects." Jepson died during the lifetime of Mrs. Wheatley, leaving a daughter, whose heirs united with the Church in transferring the estate to Thomas Hudson, March 19, 1800, he paying for the same "eight hundred Spanish milled dollars."

the Vestry, the first distribution to commence on Christmas day next.

Voted and resolved: that the Rev. Mr. Dehon and Mr. Auchmuty be a committee to make inquiry for a suitable person to take charge of the Church school, qualified agreeably to Mr. Kay's will, and that they be authorized to assure him the tuition of forty scholars at fifteen shillings per quarter, from his entering upon the charge until the 25th day of September next, from which time he will be entitled to receive $300 per annum, the amount of rent paid by Richard Harrison, Esq., of New York, for the house and land left in trust by the said Mr. Kay, for the support of a school-master Episcopally ordained, to the Rector, Wardens and Vestry, for the instruction of ten poor boys, in grammar and the mathematics, and assist the Rector in some part of the service of the Church, as occasion may require.

April 14, 1800. Mrs. Mary Brett,[220] widow of Dr. John Brett, was buried.

[220] *Mary Brett*—was an exceedingly conscientious and good woman. Her maiden name was Howland, a daughter of Rowland Howland, and she was married to Dr. Brett February 10, 1739. But little is known of Dr. Brett, other than that he was a native of Germany, and a graduate of the University of Leyden. He was a scholarly man, and contributed to the collection of books forming the Redwood Library.

The name of Mrs. Brett is associated with a free school for negroes before the Revolution. A society in London, composed of a number of benevolent clergymen of the Church of England, had taken up the subject, and had offered to furnish means to sustain schools of this kind. Each school was to number thirty pupils, negro children, who were to be taught reading, writing, sewing, etc. Such a school was opened by Mrs. Brett at her residence on High Street, Newport, in March, 1773. At the time of her death she was in her 86th year.

CHAPTER XV.

1800–1803.

EASTER MONDAY, April 15, 1800. William Crooke and William R. Robinson were elected Wardens.

Voted: that the number of vestrymen for the future be thirteen.

Vestrymen: Francis Brinley, Christopher Champlin, George Gibbs, John Bours, Francis Malbone, Benjamin Brenton, Henry Sherburne, John Handy, William Littlefield, Robert N. Auchmuty, William R. Robinson, Saunders Malbone and William Crooke. John Bours, Clerk of the Vestry; Joseph Dyer, Clerk of the Church; Daniel Vernon, Sexton.

Voted: that the Wardens continue the present organist, Mr. John Berkenhead, in his office during good behavior, and that they allow him one dollar and twenty-five cents for every Sunday, and other holy days, that he officiates.

August 3, 1800. Voted and resolved: that Mr. Benjamin Brenton be requested to communicate to the daughters of Capt. Jahleel Brenton, at Leith, in Scotland, the thanks of the Rector, Wardens and Vestry of this Church for the elegant damask table-cloth, spun and presented by them for the altar thereof, and to express to them their admiration of this specimen of female industry, piety and benevolence.

August 18, 1800. Whereas, the Rev. Mr. Abraham Brunson, of Cheshire, in the State of Connecticut, has undertaken the charge of the Church school, on the Kay foundation, voted: that the committee who were chosen in March last to make inquiry for a person

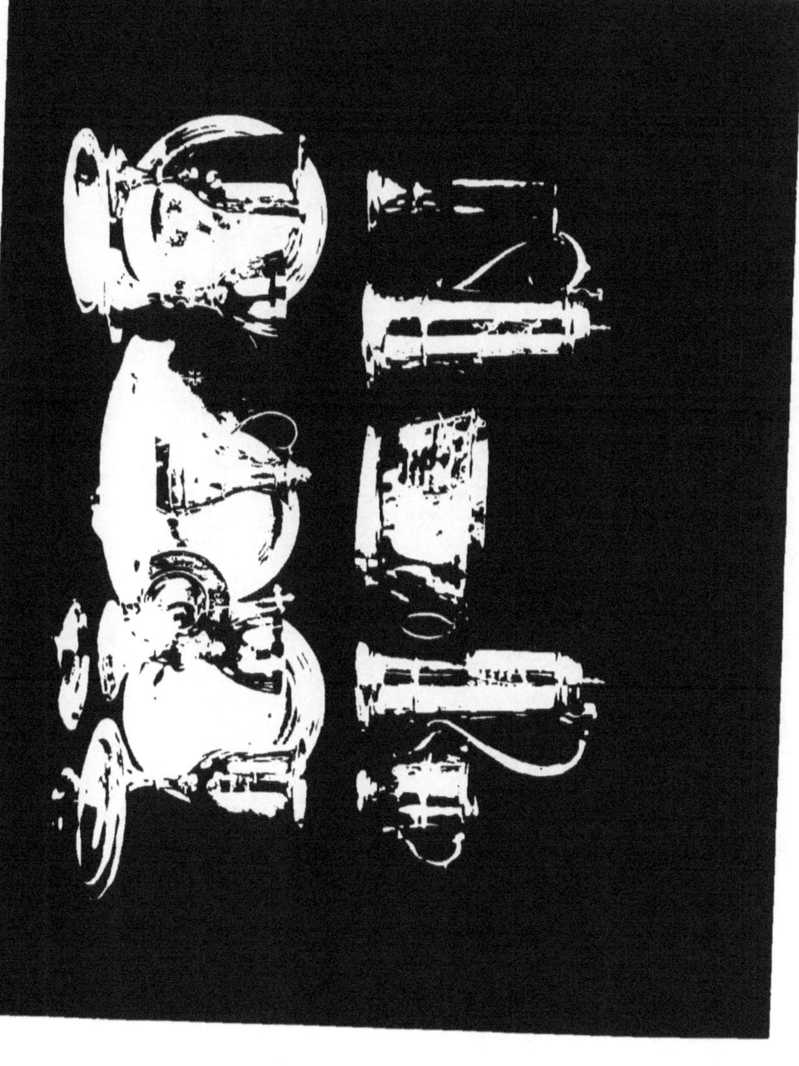

qualified for said office, agreeably to said donation, make the necessary arrangements with Mr. Brunson relative to his settlement, and make report to the next meeting of the Vestry.

Voted: that the Vestry meet in future on the evening of the first Monday of every month, at each other's houses, alternately, beginning with Mr. Brinley, as Senior Vestryman, and proceed through the whole number, according to their standing.

September 1, 1800. Voted: that the Clerk of the Vestry furnish the Rev. Mr. Dehon, our Rector, with the documents necessary for him to present to Bishop Bass, upon his application to him for Priest's Orders, agreeably to the canons of the Church.

February 2, 1801. Voted: that the Rev. Mr. Dehon, Mr. Bours and Mr. Auchmuty be a committee to make inquiry for a suitable person to take charge of the Church school, in the room of the Rev. Mr. Brunson, who has signified by a message to the Vestry this evening, that he proposes to give up his charge on the first day of July next, provided a successor can be had by that time; otherwise to remain until the fall.

Whereas, a deed of a gift of a pew in the Church, being the south half part of pew numbered 86, late belonging to Frances Piper, wife of John Piper, of Colyston, County of Devonshire, Great Britain, to her three children, viz: Stephen Ayrault Wanton, Sarah, wife of Joseph Huntington, and Francis, wife of William C. Robinson, has been presented to the Vestry.

Voted: that the same be accepted.

February 16, 1801. Buried: the Honorable Lucia C. Grattan.[230]

March 16, 1801. Voted: that Mr. Bours and Mr. Malbone be a committee to draw a plan for establishing a fund for the support of

[230] Lady Grattan was the widow of Col. Grattan, cousin-german to the Rt. Hon. Henry Grattan, the Irish orator, and eldest sister of Lord Viscount Falkland.

the Rector of the Church, at a future period, and lay the same before the congregation on Easter Monday next.

Voted: that the report of the Trustees who were chosen on the 13th of March last, to receive from the Wardens a bond executed by them, in behalf of the congregation, for the sum of $400, given by Robert Wheatley, in his will, to the poor of the church, and loaned by the congregation, the interest arising thereon to be paid said poor on every Christmas day, be received and placed on the files of the Church.

At an adjourned meeting Easter Tuesday, April 7, 1801, William C. Robinson and Samuel Whitehorne were chosen Wardens. The Vestrymen and other officers of the Church remained unchanged.

The salary of Mr. Berkenhead, the organist, was raised to $2 for every day that he officiated.

Voted: that the tax on the pews be continued the same; one-third part for the support of the Rector, and two-thirds for the support of the other officers and the repairs of the Church.

Voted: that the committee appointed at Easter last, to consider the expediency of disposing of the lot in the Church lane, be continued, with the addition of Messrs. Benjamin Gardiner and William R. Robinson, and that they sell the same for the most it will fetch, and purchase another lot with the money, covenanting, however, with the purchaser of the lot in the Church lane, that no school-house shall ever be set thereon.

The subscribers, having been chosen a committee by the Rector, Wardens and Vestry, the 16th of March last, to draw a plan for establishing a fund for the support of the Rector, at a future period, to be laid before the congregation on Easter Monday, do report, that we have not, as yet, fully digested a plan, but would beg leave to observe, that, in our opinion, nothing would have a greater tendency to promote and secure the future welfare and prosperity of the Church, than such a measure, and would recommend the previously taking the sense of the congregation upon the practicability thereof; and that a subscription be set on foot to try what sum can be collected to lay a foundation for said fund. All which is re spectfully submitted.

JOHN BOURS,
FRAS. MALBONE.

Newport, April 7, 1801.

In consequence of the above report, which is accepted, it is voted and resolved: that the Clerk of the Vestry and the Wardens be a committee to draft a subscription, and endeavor to obtain as many signers thereto as they can, and make report of their doings within three months, to the Vestry, who will thereupon lay the business, if they judge it expedient, before the congregation.

May 4, 1801. Voted: that thirty feet of the east end of the lot in the Church lane, which was ordered by the congregation to be sold on Easter Monday last, be added to the burial ground, and the remainder only of said lot sold by the committee appointed for that purpose.

Whereas, Bishop Bass has intimated his intention of being at Newport, on a visit to our Church, the second Sunday in June next, voted: that a collection be made on said day, after divine service, in the afternoon, in order to defray the expenses of his journey.

May 7, 1801. Capt. Evan Malbone, of Pomfret, Connecticut, having sold one-half of pew number 79, on the south side of the middle aisle, belonging to him, to Mr. Andrew Freebody, owner of the other half, for $32.50; this record is made by desire of said Freebody.

[July 4, 1801. The use of the Church was granted for the delivery of an oration before the Society of Cincinnati. The following notice of the event is condensed from the Newport *Mercury*, of the ensuing week:]

"The procession after passing through the principal streets of the Town, was received at Trinity Church with the appropriate tune, 'Washington's March.' Rev. Mr. Patten,[231] of the Second Congregational Church, opened the exercises with prayer. The oration, prepared at the request of the Society of the Cincinnati, was delivered by Mr. William Hunter,[232] after which an ode,[233]

[231] Rev. Dr. Patten, born at Halifax, Mass., took his degree at Dartmouth College, in 1783, and, at the suggestion of Rev. Dr. Stiles, was placed in charge of the Second Congregational Church, in Newport, over which he was settled in 1786. In 1833 he retired from the church and removed to Hartford, Ct., where he died in 1839, aged 77 years. He was a Fellow of Brown University, which institution conferred upon him the degree of D.D. For a list of his published works, see Hammett's "Bibliography of Newport."

[232] son of Dr. William Hunter, was born at Newport, in 1774, and died here December 3, 1849. He graduated at Brown University in 1791, went to England and began the study of medicine under Dr. John Hunter, but not liking the profession, he turned to the law, and became the pupil of Arthur Murphy. On his return to America, at the age of 21 years, he was admitted to the bar. His public career commenced in 1799, when he was elected a Representative to the General Assembly of his native State, which office he filled at various times till 1811, when he was elected United States Senator. In 1834 he was appointed Minister Plenipotentiary to Brazil, from which position he retired in 1844, and returned to Newport, where he passed the remainder of his days.

Mr. Hunter married the beautiful Mary Robinson, of New York. Of their numerous family, but one survives, Mr. Thomas R. Hunter, of Newport.

[233] ODE.

Written by William Ellery, a signer of the Declaration of Independ-

written by a young gentleman of Newport—a musical address to
the Cincinnati—was sung to the tune, 'God Save Great Washington.' The dinner, served in the Representative Room in the State

ence, and dedicated to the Rhode Island State Society of Cincinnati, for
the dinner at Newport, 4th July, 1801 :

Hark ! Freedom's silver horn,
Pours on the peerless morn,
   The festive lay ;
Ye sons of bold emprise,
From peaceful slumber rise,
Awake with glad surprise
   To hail the day.

Ye peers of Washington,
Like him and Rome's best son,
   Be peace your aim ;
The plough or falchion wield,
Your native country shield,
The Senate or the field
   Gives equal fame.

No tumults here will thrive,
While hoary vet'rans live
   To guard the State ;
Their swords, for public law
And order, they will draw,
Excite submissive awe
   In Empire great.

Alas ! Columbia weeps,
Her Cincinnatus sleeps
   In Vernon's grave ;
Yet still his spirit guides,
High o'er our State presides,
And on the thunder rides
   With power to save.

House, was presided over by Col. Jeremiah Olney, who had that day been re-elected President of the Society."

September 7, 1801. Voted: that the Wardens, with Captain Littlefield, be a committee to endeavor to ascertain the true bounds of the land whereon the Church stands, to the westward of said land, adjoining a lot of land late belonging to the heirs of Samuel Rhodes, and now belonging to Miss Searing.

September —, 1801. Dr. Benjamin Mason[234] was buried in the church-yard.

November 2, 1801. Whereas, no day has been set apart this autumn by the civil rulers of the State, as a day of Thanksgiving and Prayer to Almighty God, and whereas in the confident expectation of such an appointment the day has elapsed appropriate for that purpose, by the standing order of our Church, in case of no such appointment by the civil authorities, therefore voted and resolved unanimously:

That it be recommended to the congregation of Trinity Church, to observe Thursday, the 26th day of this month, as a day of thanksgiving and praise to the Most High, for the spiritual and temporal,

---

[234] Dr. Benjamin Mason, eldest son of Benjamin Mason and Mary Ayrault (of Daniel 2d), his wife, was born in March, 1762. November 8, 1788, he was married at Narragansett, by Rev. William Smith, to Margaret Champlin, of Christopher. After studying in the office of Dr. Isaac Senter, he completed his medical education in London. At the death of Dr. Senter, who held the appointment at the time, he was made Director and Purveyor-General of the Military Hospital of Rhode Island. He was an honorary member of the Massachusetts Medical Society. His career in Newport was as short as it was brilliant, for he died at the early age of forty years.

public and private blessings of the year past, and of devout supplication for a continuance of His many and unmerited favors.

December 7, 1801. Voted: that the Rev^d. Mr. Brunson be requested to write to Mr. Merriam, at present residing at Brookline, on Long Island, who has been recommended to the Vestry as a suitable person to succeed him as Assistant Minister and schoolmaster, on Mr. Kay's donation, and recommend to him coming on to Newport, as soon as convenient to him, that the Vestry may treat with him with regard to his undertaking the charge.

March 8, 1802. Voted: that Mr. Clement Merriam be invited to take charge of the Episcopal school and perform the duties of the Assistant Minister in Trinity Church, upon the conditions on which the Rev. Mr. Brunson was engaged; and that the Clerk of the Vestry, with Mr. Brunson, be requested to transmit to him a copy of this vote, and explain to him what the said conditions are.

April 6, 1802. Whereas, the committee appointed at Easter last, to dispose of the lot on the Church lane, have reported that they have sold said lot to Simeon Martin,[235] for the sum of $400. Voted: that William R. Robinson, Senior Warden, be requested to purchase a lot of four acres of land on the hill, offered for sale by Samuel Gardiner for $600, provided the said Gardiner will consent to receive in payment for the same the $400 paid by said Martin and a note for the remaining $200, to be signed by the Wardens in behalf

----

[235] *Simeon Martin* was a merchant. In the Revolution he entered the service of the State, was appointed a captain in Col. Lippett's regiment, and was in the battle at Trenton. After the war he was appointed adjutant-general and major-general of the State militia, and repeatedly represented the Town in the General Assembly. In 1811 he was elected Lieutenant-Governor, and held the office till 1816, when he declined a re-election. In 1817 he removed to Seekonk, where he died September 30, 1819.

of the congregation, payable at some distant period, say four or six months, with interest thereon.

At the Annual Meeting, Easter Monday, April 19, 1802, the officers and vestry of the Church were re-elected.

Voted: That Simeon Martin be added to the number of delegates to represent the Church at the next State Convention, and to the committee for ascertaining the bounds of the land between the Church and Miss Searing.

The Rev. Mr. Brunson having been paid his salary to the 25th day of April, and given up his charge, as Assistant Minister and School-master, the Rev. Mr. Clement Merriam is admitted in his room, and his salary of $300, to commence from said 25th day of April, 1802.

[June 21, 1802: St. John's Day, the annual meeting of the Grand Lodge of Free and Accepted Masons was held at the State House; after which the members marched to Trinity Church, where divine service was conducted by Rev. Mr. Merriam, followed by an oration delivered by Hon. William Hunter.]

July 4, 1802. Richard Kidder Randolph[236] was married to Ann Maria Lyman.

August 12, 1802. Whereas, the Rev. Mr. Merriam hath signified to the Vestry, by his note of July 20th, that it is his intention to resign his charge of the school and office of Assistant Minister of our Church, at the expiration of six months from the date thereof. Voted: that the Clerk of the Vestry, with the Wardens, be a com-

---

[236] Mr. Randolph was born in Virginia, October 19, 1781, and was the son of Payton and Lucy Randolph. He graduated at Harvard, and took up his residence in Newport in 1810. He had a seat in the General Assembly, as Representative from Newport, for several years, and died in Newport, in March, 1849. Mrs. Randolph was the daughter of Major Daniel Lyman, and was distinguished for her beauty.

mittee to inform Mr. Merriam, in reply thereto, that they received with concern his so sudden and unexpected notice of a determination to leave us, at a time when our Rector was providentially absent; and to inform him also that it is impracticable for the Church to comply with the terms since personally proposed by him for continuing with us, and therefore, however reluctantly, must accept of his resignation, leaving it entirely to himself to perform whatever part of the service of the Church he may think proper, until his departure, or the return of our Rector.

October 4, 1802. Voted: that Mr. Bours, with the Wardens, be a committee to endeavor to obtain an Assistant and School-master, in the room of Mr. Merriam, by such means as they may judge most advisable.

October 11, 1802. Whereas, the Rev. Mr. Merriam hath again signified to the Vestry, that in consequence of ill health he is unable to attend to the duties of the Church and the care also of his school, during the absence of our Rector, and is desirous of having an assistant in his school; it is therefore voted: that an allowance be made of $25.00 per month, to any proper person he may procure as an assistant, or usher, during the remaining part of the term he has consented to remain with us, agreeably to his note of the 20th of July last.

Meeting of the congregation, December 14, 1802. Whereas, the Rev. Mr. Dehon, our Rector, who has been long indisposed, hath signified to the congregation now assembled for the purpose, by his note of yesterday's date, "that the progress towards a confirmed state of health is so slow and unsteady as to afford but little hope of his performing public service during the cold weather, and being advised by all the medical gentlemen who he has consulted, to try the efficacy of a warmer climate, and is therefore induced, with great reluctance, and after much hesitation, to ask leave of absence during the winter season."

It is voted and resolved: that the so reasonable request of our Rector be granted in its fullest extent, and that his salary be continued and paid as tho' he was present, during his absence, most earnestly praying Almighty God to preserve his life, and to restore him again, in his own good time, in perfect health to his anxious flock.

December 26, 1802. Whereas, the office of School-master and Assistant Minister will become vacant after the 25th day of January next, by the resignation of the Rev. Mr. Merriam, voted: that Mr. Bours be requested to write, by the first opportunity, to Mr. John Reed, Preceptor in the Academy in Plainfield, Connecticut, informing him of the nature of this office, and inviting him to enter on the discharge of its duties immediately after the said 25th day of January, with the view to settlement in said office, provided it shall be found agreeable to both parties; the terms of contract to be settled after conferring with Mr. Reed, and arranging matters relative to his receiving Holy Orders.

Meeting of the congregation, February 1, 1803. Whereas, the time for which the Rev. Mr. Merriam contracted with the Rector, Wardens and Vestry to execute the office of School-master and Assistant Minister expired the 25th ult., and the Church is now destitute of both Rector and Assistant, the Rev. Mr. Dehon, in consequence of ill health, having obtained leave of absence from the congregation and gone on a voyage to the southward; and whereas we conceive it would prove greatly injurious to the welfare and interest of the Church to be deprived altogether of a pastor; therefore voted and resolved: that the Wardens wait upon Mr. Merriam, and invite him to remain with us three months longer, in order to keep the congregation together (independent of the school) by reading the Prayers and performing the other duties of his office, as Deacon, and in a way the most easy and agreeable to himself; and that he be allowed and paid for his services the sum of one hundred and twenty-five dollars, at the expiration of said term of three months; and the Clerk of the Vestry be desired to furnish the Wardens with a copy of this vote, to be delivered to Mr. Merriam.

February 2, 1803. The following answer was this day received from the Rev. Mr. Merriam:

To the Vestry and Wardens of Trinity Church.

. Gentlemen.

The resolution of the congregation, whom you represent, was received with mingled emotions of gratitude and respect—of gratitude for their indulgence towards my past services, and kind invitation to continue longer with them in a more eligible capacity; of regret that their present embarrassment will not permit them to do justice to their feelings in offering a greater pecuniary satisfaction; for I have a higher opinion of their generosity than to suppose they deem the sum which they have offered me an equivalent for discharging the duties of my profession. Impressed with these sentiments, and conceiving with them that it would prove greatly injurious to the welfare and interest of the Church to be deprived altogether of a Pastor, I cheerfully accept the terms proposed: lamenting not that my recompence is small, if it can be paid with the same pleasure with which my duties shall be performed.

I am gent^m with the greatest respect,

Your Most devoted Servt,

Clement Merriam.

CHAPTER XVI.

1803-1806.

EASTER MONDAY, April 11, 1803. Samuel Whitehorne and William Littlefield were chosen Wardens. The Vestrymen were the same, with the addition of Simeon Martin.

Messrs. Champlin, Brinley, Gibbs, Auchmuty, Handy, Bours, Gardiner and Martin be continued delegates to the next State Convention.

Voted: that the Wardens be requested to wait upon the Rev. Mr. Merriam and invite him to officiate for us for two months longer, on the terms allowed him by the congregation on the 1st of February last.

May 1, 1803. William R. Robinson and Wm Crooke were chosen Wardens, in place of Messrs. Whitehorne and Littlefield, who declined serving.

June 27, 1803. Voted: that the Wardens be requested to settle with the Rev. Mr. Merriam, he having notified the congregation that he should leave them this week, and that the money be raised by subscription. Eighty dollars were paid Mr. Merriam, to pay Mr. Jabez Whitaker, as an assistant three months.

Meeting of the congregation, August 7, 1803. Whereas, Daniel Vernon, sexton of the Church, hath resigned said office, voted: that Uriah Gorton be sexton for the remaining part of the year, to Easter Monday, and that he receive the same salary and all other privileges allowed to said Vernon.

September 27, 1803. Voted: that a lot of land, of two acres, situated on the Hill, in Newport, and which is now offered for sale to the Church for $460, be purchased with the money for which the lot in the Church lane was sold to Simeon Martin; the balance of $60 to be made up by subscription, and that the rents and profits be appropriated to the sole use and benefit of the Rector for the time being, agreeably to the will of Nathaniel Norton.

October 19, 1803. Rev. Clement Merriam was married to Elizabeth Hastie.

November 2, 1803. Be it remembered that whereas the lot of land of two acres, purchased by Mr. Francis Brinley at public auction, has been generously given up to the Church for the same money he paid for it, in order to accommodate them; it is to be understood, and it is the intent and meaning of the Vestry, that no buildings may be erected on said lot, whereby his rope-walk, or the adjoining buildings, may be endangered by fire, or in any other way or manner, injured thereby.

Voted: that the Rev^d Mr. Dehon be requested to write to Mr. John Ward, at present residing in the town of Harrinton, Ct., who, we are informed, is a candidate for Holy Orders in the Episcopal Church, and inform him of the situation of our Church, and invite him to come to Newport, as soon as may be, in order that we may have a conference with him upon the subject of settling him as our Assistant Minister and School-master.

November 20, 1803. John Bernard Gilpin[237] was married to Mary E. Miller.

December 5, 1803. Voted: that the Wardens wait upon Mr.

---

[237] The President of the United States issued his exequatur, acknowledging Mr. Gilpin as British Vice Consul for Rhode Island and Connecticut. Mrs. Gilpin died in 1814, and was buried in the church-yard, June 27th of that year. Mr. Gilpin died in Nova Scotia. Mrs. Gilpin was a daughter of Capt. John Miller.

John Ward, who has come to Newport, in consequence of the invitation lately given him, and inform him that the Vestry have agreed to pay him at the rate of $25 per month, being the same sum allowed the Rev^d Mr. Brunson and the Rev^d Mr. Merriam for their services during the absence of the Rector, and until it is ascertained whether a permanent settlement takes place with us, on Mr. Kay's foundation.

February 6, 1804. Whereas, Mr. John Ward, who has officiated in the Church as a Lay Reader, since the absence of the Rev^d Mr. Dehon, has signified to the Vestry that he is under the necessity of returning home within a few days, and that he will soon after arriving there and consulting his friends, resolve whether he will accept of our invitation given him some time past, to a permanent settlement, as School-master and Assistant Minister, on Mr. Kay's donation, voted: that he be paid $100 for his services since he has been with us, including his travelling expenses to and from Newport, out of the rent due from Richard Harrison, Esq., and that he be requested to tarry with us two Sundays more, before he sets out on his journey.

Voted: that Mr. Bours, with the Wardens, furnish Mr. Ward with letters of presentation to Bishop Jarvis,[235] in order to enable him to obtain Deacon's Orders, upon his acceptance of the permanent settlement of School-master and Assistant Minister, which has been offered him.

March 19, 1804. Mr. John Ward having declined the offer made

---

[235] *Abraham Jarvis* — ' Right Revd Bishop Jarvis was born at Norwalk, Ct., in 1739, and died in 1813. He graduated at Yale College in 1761, and was elected Bishop of Connecticut in 1797. He preached the funeral sermon of Bishop Seabury, and became his successor as Bishop.

him, voted: that Mr. Bours be requested to write to Mr. John Reed, at ——— and inquire of him whether he is disengaged, and will, upon receiving a proper and regular invitation, enter into Holy Orders, and become our Assistant Minister and School-master.

Easter Monday, April 2, 1804. Wm Littlefield and Wm Wood elected Wardens. Mr. George Gibbs was added to the Vestry.

April 30, 1804. Voted: that the Wardens, with Mr. Champlin and Mr. Bours, be a committee to make inquiry relative to the procuring a new bell for the Church, in the room of the one which has hung therein and in use for sixty-three years, and now appears of a sudden to be cracked, and is become useless.

The committee appointed on the 5th of December last, to inquire into the state and situation of the lots at the south end of Thames Street, part of Mr. Kay's donation, having verbally reported to the Vestry that they had performed said duty, and are clearly of the opinion that it would be greatly to the advantage of said donation, and much better to answer the design of the pious and benevolent donor, to dispose of said lots and purchase with the proceeds a lot of land, or other real estate, in the Town of Newport; it is, therefore, voted and resolved: that Wm. Hunter, Esq., be requested to draft a petition to the General Assembly, in the name of the Rector, Wardens and Vestry, to be presented at the next session, for permission to dispose of said lots for the most they will sell for, and to purchase other real estate with the proceeds, and that General Martin be desired to present the same

May 31, 1804. Whereas, the committee chosen at our last meeting, to make inquiry relative to the procuring a new bell, have now made report that they have attended to said duty, by applying to the several bell founders in Boston, and the State of Connecticut, to know the lowest terms on which they would undertake to recast the old bell, and whereas it appears from the documents, now laid before us by the committee, that the most eligible terms are received from John Morgan, Esq., at Hartford; therefore voted and resolved; that the said committee be requested to ship the bell by the first conveyance to Hartford, by water, first having her weighed; and that they use their endeavors to have her recast, and returned to us as soon as possible. And the Wardens are further requested to take out a subscription, in order to raise money to pay the expense.

A letter wrote by the committee to Mr. Morgan, at Hartford, requesting his further assistance with regard to the bell, being read, was approved of, and the committee desired to forward the same by the first mail.[289]

July 2, 1804. Whereas, the petition from the Vestry to the General Assembly, for permission to dispose of the lots at the south end of Thames Street, has not been granted, therefore voted: that the Wardens, with Messrs. Sherburne, Bours and Francis Malbone, be a committee to make particular inquiry into the state and situation of said lots, and report as soon as may be to the Vestry their opinion what ought to be done with them, to promote in the best manner the charitable design of the donor.

August 6, 1804. The committee appointed at the last meeting reported that they had caused the lots to be surveyed and a plat

---

[289] In June, 1804, the committee accepted the bid of Fenner & Crocker, bell founders, at Hartford; the work of moulding and casting a new bell to be done by Mr. Doolittle, who had a good reputation in that line. The old bell was to be used as far as it would go, and the new metal to bring it up to the required weight, was to be furnished by the contractors.

In giving their orders, the committee wrote to the contractors: "We are extremely anxious to have another [bell] as near as possible like her; we must, therefore, enjoin it upon the founder that she be *recast* in the same mould and form, of the same metal and thickness, and in every particular as exactly as may be like her: it being the opinion of several persons, who are supposed to be good judges, that its shape in a great measure contributed to its loud and melodious tone."

The bell, when cast, weighed twelve hundred pounds.

made thereof. Voted: that the said committee ascertain what, in their opinion, may be the value of each and every lot to be disposed of for the money, on a lease to be given by the Vestry for the term of nine hundred and ninety-nine years ; and that Tate's estate be included likewise in said estimate, and report their doings to the Vestry at their next meeting for their concurrence.

August 14, 1804. Voted: that the thanks of the Vestry be presented to Mr. Jabez Dennison for his obliging attention to our request to take a survey of the Church lots at the south end of Thames street, and presenting us with a plat of the same, without any compensation for his trouble ; and that the clerk present him with a copy of this vote.

Voted : that the report of the committee appointed at our last meeting to ascertain the value of the lots at the south end of Thames street, be accepted, and that the same gentlemen, with the addition of Mr. Wm. R. Robinson, be continued a committee to dispose of said lots, agreeably to said report, and that they inform the Vestry, from time to time, of their proceedings in the business.

September 3, 1804. Whereas the church bell hath been recast, and is now replaced, as formerly,

Voted : that the sexton ring her as usual, at sunrise, one of the clock, P.M., and at nine in the evening, and that he be permitted to raise money by a general subscription, to reward him for doing the same.

Berkenhead,[40] who has officiated on the organ for several years past, having suddenly left the Town and Church,

---

[40] J. L. Berkenhead, who was blind, and who was far from reliable, was admitted to be a very good organist when at his best. but his habits were such that he was elected organist from year to year "on his good behavior." He had no difficulty in securing pupils, when he chose to give them proper attention. He died in October, 1810.

Voted: that inquiry be made for a suitable person to succeed him.

October 1, 1804.   Voted: that the rent of the church lots at the south end of Thames street, if not previously sold at the valuation reported by the committee, be fixed, after the expiration of their present parole leases, at the lawful interest of the sum they were respectively rated at; except lot No. 1 and half of No 2 together, at $24.

November 5, 1804.   Voted: that the Wardens settle the accounts standing between the Church and Mr. Joseph Dyer respecting the house and lot he has occupied for several years past, which was bequeathed to the poor of the Church by William Tate, and that in said settlement they ascertain what is now due to the poor from the Church on account of said estate.

Voted: that the committee take into consideration the circumstances attending the Tate estate, and make inquiry whether said estate can be also disposed of on a long lease, as well as the lots not yet disposed of in that way.

Voted: that the above committee dispose of one-fourth part of the lot adjoining eastward the lot on which Daniel Ginnedo has a dwelling-house standing, to said Ginnedo, provided he purchase the half lot on which said house stands.

November 26, 1804.   Whereas the church bell, which has been lately recast, has again become useless in consequence of a crack, voted: that Mr. Bours write a letter to Mr. Stanley Carter, a bell-founder at Raynham, State of Massachusetts, and invite him to come to Newport, in order that we may confer with him upon the subject of recasting it at his foundry.

December 3, 1804.   The committee reported the following valuation of the lots at the south end of Thames street, to be disposed of for the money, on a lease of nine hundred and ninety-nine years, and their report agreed to by the Vestry.

No. 1.[241] At present occupied by John Whitehorne, ⎫
 "   2.   One-half.   "   "   "   "   ⎬ $ 335 00

             The other half (No. 2) by Daniel Ginnedo,   80 00
 "   3.   Unimproved. 160 00
 "   4.   Improved by Wm. Gyles' heirs,   . 160 00
 "   5.   "   "   John Howard,   .   . . 140 00
 "   6. & 7.   "   "   John Price, ⎫
 "   8. & 9. Not occupied by any one,   ⎬ all 4, . 258 00
 "   10.   "   "   "   "   .   .   . 67 00

                                                   ———————
                                                   $1200 00

January 14, 1805. A communication being received from the Rev. William Patten, conveying in behalf of the committee of the Second Congregational Church and Society, an offer of the use of the bell belonging to said "Church and Society, to the Rector, Wardens and Vestry of Trinity Church, till the loss sustained in the fracture of their own may be replaced," resolved unanimously that the thanks of this body be given to the said committee for the very friendly and obliging offer, of which we should gladly avail ourselves, if a previous arrangement had not been made for placing the school-house bell in the belfry of the Church, for the present use of the Society.

Resolved also: that the Rev. Mr. Dehon be requested to transmit to the Rev. William Patten a copy of this resolution.

Voted: that the report of the committee, presented at our last

---

[241] Lot No. 1 and half of No. 2 leased to John G. Whitehorne for 999 years, for $335; half of lot No. 2 and lot No. 3 leased to Daniel Ginnedo for $240; No. 4 leased to Charles Gyles; No. 5 to William Howard; Nos. 6, 7, 8 and 9 leased to William Wilder; No. 10 to Arnold Hiscox.

meeting, upon the Tate[242] estate, be accepted; the statement made
of the account between the Church and said estate be entered in the
ledger by the Clerk, and that the sum of ten dollars be paid
annually to the poor of the Church, at Christmas, after this year,
agreeably to said report.

---

[242] William Tate's will was dated June 7, 1758. The following is the
clause in which Trinity Church was interested:

"Item. I give and bequeath to my well beloved wife, Mary Tate, all
my estate, real and personal, for and during the term of her natural life,
to her only proper use and behoof.

"And my will further is, that if my said wife shall think it needful to
sell and dispose of my messuage, or dwelling house, where I now live at
Newport, aforesaid, together with the lot of land whereon the same stands,
together with the buildings, improvements and appurtenances to the same
belonging, then I give her full power and authority to grant, bargain and
sell the same to any person or persons that shall purchase it, and to sign,
seal and duly execute a good deed of conveyance thereof in fee simple,
which shall be for the maintenance of my said wife during her life; and
after the decease of my said wife, what shall be then remaining of my
said estate I give and bequeath the same unto the poor people then belonging to the Church of England, in Newport, aforesaid, to be distributed to and among them, in equal parts and proportions, by such person or persons as my said wife shall nominate and appoint for that
purpose."

William Tate was married to Mary Iverson, May 21, 1731. He was a
blacksmith. Mrs. Tate died in the autumn of 1780, leaving no instructions as to who should distribute the estate. What disposition was made
of the property after her death cannot now be ascertained. The Revolution was not closed, and probably the estate was but of little value for
some time after that date. April 5, 1798, it was rented to Joseph Dyer
at $30 per annum, the Church to keep it in repair. The rent was paid
up to December 25, 1804, and after deducting the expense of repairs, the
Church realized but $164.72 for the six years and more that it had been
so occupied. In 1806 the property was leased to John Yeomans, for 999
years, the consideration being $800, which sum was placed to the credit
of the poor fund. But the Church did not realize more than $700 on
the notes given by Yeomans, which sum was invested in the "Clarke

Feb. 19, 1805. Voted, that the terms proposed by Fenton & Cochran, of New Haven, to cast a bell of new materials, be accepted, and that Mr. Bours, with the Wardens, write to them by the next mail, advising them thereof, and that the cracked bell shall be sent on to New York and delivered to their order, as soon as the weather will admit of the packets passing with safety.

Voted: that the several lots of land at the south end of the Town be advertised in the Newport *Mercury*, to be sold at public auction, on the 25th day of March next, unless previously disposed of at private sale.

Meeting of the congregation, March 3, 1805. The gentlemen of the Vestry having reported that they had made a contract with Messrs. Fenton & Cochran to cast a bell of the same weight of the old one, of entirely new materials, they agreeing to receive the one recast at Hartford in part pay. Voted: that the congregation approve of their doings, and that Messrs. Jacob Smith and Peleg Wood, Jr., be requested to solicit contributions from the congregation to pay for the same.[243]

lot," so called, on Catharine Street. In April, 1822, the Vestry ordered the sale of the "Clarke lot," at not less than $600; but the committee to whom the matter was intrusted, saw fit to lease it to Thomas Harkness, for 999 years, for the sum of $645. The substitution of a lease for a fee simple deed had the tacit approval of the Vestry; which body subsequently made good the loss that had been sustained and passed $800 to the credit of the poor fund. This sum is intact to the present day.

[244] March, 1805. List of subscribers for the new bell:

Francis Brinley,	. $10.00	Thos. Dennis, .	$8.00
Christ. Champlin, .	20.00	Steph. T. Northam, .	5.00
J. Bours, . .	10.00	Saml. Browne, .	5.00
Caleb Gardner,	10.00	Wm. Crooke, .	5.00
Sim. Martin,	8.00	J. Bours, Jr.,	5.00
P. Wood, Jr.,	8.00	J. Gilpin,	5.00
Jacob Smith,	10.00	Edw. Easton,	5.00

March 4, 1805.   Voted: that the Wardens execute a lease for the term of nine hundred and ninety-nine years, of the house and lot given by William Tate, late of Newport, in his last will and testament, for the benefit of the poor of our Church, to Mr. John Yeomans, upon said Yeomans paying the sum of eight hundred dollars, by two notes of hand, payable at one of the banks of Newport, one for four hundred dollars, payable with interest, in one year, and the other for the same sum, with interest likewise, in two years from the date of the said lease.

Voted: that the advertising the several lots of land at the south end of the Town, to be sold at public auction on the 25th of this month, agreeably to a resolve of the Vestry at their last meeting, be omitted as unnecessary.

John Crooke,	$5.00	Edward Brinley,	$5.00
John Wood,	10.00	John L. Boss,	5.00
Tho. Arnold,	5.00	W. Wood,	5.00
Geo. Champlin,	8.00	Mr. Hynde,	3.00
Wm. Miller,	5.00	Mrs. Malbone,	5.00
Mary Gibbs,	20.00	Steph. Deblois,	3.00
Wm. Wilder,	2.00	Wm. C. Baen,	2.00
Tho. R. Gardner,	2.00	Ann Robinson,	3.00
Benj. Gardiner,	5.00	Mrs. F. Malbone,	5.00
Silas Dean,	5.00	Edwd T. Waring,*	5.00

*

Dr. Edmund Thomas Waring was born at Charleston, S. C., December 25, 1779, came to Newport, studied medicine with Dr. Isaac Senter, and here opened an office and devoted himself to his profession, which he followed for more than thirty years. He was one of the founders of the Rhode Island Medical Society, in which society he held an office for a number of years. He died at Charleston, January 21, 1835, and his remains were brought to Newport and laid in the grave in which his wife, daughter of Francis Malbone, had been placed twelve years before.

April 1, 1805. Whereas, the Vestry has been informed through the Rev'd Mr. Griswold, of Bristol, that Mr. John Ward, of Litchfield, Ct., who has formerly officiated in this Church as a lay reader, would, upon receiving an invitation, accept the office of Assistant Minister and School-master.

Voted: that he be invited to said office, and requested to qualify himself by taking Holy Orders, as soon as may be, for discharging

Henry Sherburne,	$5.00
M. Duncan,	4.00
Mrs. B. Mumford,	5.00
Tho. Townsend,	5.00
Wm. Hunter,	5.00
J. E. Scott,	5.00
Nath. Hazard,	5.00
Saml. Lawton,	3.00
S. Malbone,	2.00
M. Scott,	3.00
John Boit,	2.00
Wm. Bretton,	2.00
Freeman Mayberry,	2.00
Mrs. N. Miller,	3.00
William Littlefield,	5.00
Saml. Whitehorne,	3.00

$281.00

Deduct not paid, . 10.00

$271.00

Fenton & Cochran's bill,	$257.03
Freight paid Holt,	6.00
W. Gorton, for collecting,	75

$263.78

Balance carried to credit of Trinity Church, . 7.22

$271.00

Newport, October 21, 1805.

E. E., per J. Bours.

The bell weighed 1375 pounds, and was the one hundred and fifteenth bell that had been cast in the same foundry during a period of ten years. When delivered, it was seen that the metal, in cooling, had shrunk in the upper part of the crown, which disfigured it; and there were some blotches on the rim, caused by the scaling of the mould; but as there was nothing objectionable in the sound of the bell, the committee accepted it.

the duties thereof. Voted also: that the Rev^d Mr. Dehon be desired to transmit to Mr. Ward a copy of this vote, and to require of
him an early answer.

Voted: that the lots at the south end of the Town, which remain
undisposed of, be advertised to be sold at public auction, notwithstanding the resolution of the Vestry to the contrary, at a meeting
February 19th last, and that the Wardens give notice thereof, with
the time and place, in the next Newport *Mercury*.

Easter Monday, April 15, 1805. William Littlefield and William
Wood were elected Wardens.

Vestrymen: Francis Brinley, Christ. Champlin, John Bours,
Francis Malbone, Benj. Gardiner, Henry Sherburne, John Handy,
William Littlefield, Rob. N. Auchmuty, Saunders Malbone, Wm.
Crooke, Simeon Martin, Peleg Wood, Jr., and Caleb Gardner.

John Bours, Clerk of the Vestry; Joseph Dyer, Clerk of the
Church; Uriah Gorton, Sexton.

Delegates to the Convention the same as last year.

May 6, 1805. Whereas, an opportunity presents for purchasing
a lot of land, of ten acres, belonging to Mr. Henry Bliss, with the
money for which the lots at the south end of the Town, part of Mr.
Kay's donation, were rated at, and most of them sold for, voted:
that the Wardens, with Caleb Gardner, Esq., and Mr. Francis Malbone, be a committee to purchase said lot, upon the best terms they
can, and that they, or the major part of them, be empowered in behalf
of the Vestry, to obtain the cash to pay for the same from the banks
in Newport, and that the said committee be indemnified by the
Rector, Wardens and Vestry, as trustees of Mr. Kay's donation, in
transacting said business.

A letter being read from Mr. John Ward to the Rev^d Mr. Dehon,
informing him that he has connected himself with the Church in
East Windsor for five months, at the expiration of which time he
would accept the office of Assistant Minister and School-master for

this Church, voted unanimously: that the Rev^d Mr. Dehon be requested to inform Mr. Ward that we will offer the vacancy to no other candidate, and at the close of his present engagement shall be happy to receive his services.

June 3, 1805. Voted: that Messrs. Sherburne and Francis Malbone be a committee to apply to Wm. Hunter, Esq., now a member to the General Assembly of this State, and request the favor of him to renew an application, which was made to them the last year, for permission to dispose of the Church lots at the south end of the Town, in order to purchase other real estate with the proceeds of the same, and that said committee use their influence to obtain such act.

The following Act was obtained:

State of Rhode Island and Providence Plantation, In General Assembly, June session, A.D. 1805.

Upon the petition of Theodore Dehon, the Minister, and of the Church Wardens and Vestry of Trinity Church, in Newport, praying, for certain reasons therein stated, that they may be authorized and empowered to sell certain lots of land in Newport, heretofore devised by Nathaniel Kay, now deceased, to the Minister, Wardens and Vestry of said Church, for the education of ten poor boys in grammar and the mathematics, and vest the proceeds of said sale in other and more productive lands, to the same use; Resolved: that the prayer of said petitioners be granted, and that the said Minister, Wardens and Vestry be, and they are hereby authorized and empowered, by the advice and direction of the Court of Probate for said Newport, to make sale of said lots of land upon the most advantageous terms they can obtain for the same; provided the said Minister, Wardens and Vestry shall give bonds to the satisfaction of said Court of Probate, that they will, within twelve months after said sale, invest the proceeds thereof in other lands on the Island of Rhode Island, to the same uses, trusts and purposes, as the said lots of land, so to be sold, were devised to, and for, in and by the said will of said Kay; and that a deed, or deeds, made of said lots to any purchaser, or purchasers, shall vest in him, her, them and his or their heirs, or assigns, a fee simple estate therein.

A true Copy.

Witness, SAMUEL EDDY, Secretary.

July 25, 1805. Whereas the purchase of a lot of land, of ten acres, belonging to the late Henry Bliss, was not effected, agreeably to a resolve of the Vestry, on the 6th of May last, Voted: that the Wardens, with Col. Sherburne and Capt. Caleb Gardner, be a committee to look out a suitable lot, and when they find one which they think will answer, to make report to the Vestry.

The committee appointed to examine the Church, with reference to needed repairs and painting, reported, July 28, 1805, "that it be recommended to the congregation to levy a tax on the pews below of $10 each, and on the pews in the gallery $1 each; also, such pews as have become forfeited to the Church should be sold. These modes we think the most eligible for raising the sum necessary to defray the expense of repairing and painting the Church, &c., which we estimate at $1100.

HENRY SHERBURNE,
FRAN. MALBONE,
WM. CROOKE.

Voted, July 25th: that the report be accepted, and that the sum of ten dollars be assessed on each single pew below, and one dollar on each pew in the gallery (a double pew $20,00, and a pew and a half $15.00), the same to be collected as soon as possible.

July 28, 1805. Buried Don Josef Wiseman.[211] Aged 46 years.

September 1, 1805. Whereas, Caleb Gardner, Esq., has reported

----

[211] Don Josef was Vice Consul to the port of Newport from his Catholic Majesty. He came here in 1795, was warmly received, made many friends, and here resided up to the time of his death.

to the Vestry that he has purchased at public auction, this day, the lot of land belonging to the estate of Henry Bliss, Esq., which the Vestry had appointed a committee to purchase before said Bliss's death, but were disappointed in so doing, at the rate of $139 per acre, the same to be surveyed and the number of acres ascertained, Voted: that the thanks of the Vestry be presented to Mr. Gardner for his kind services in negotiating the business, and that he be further requested to assist the Clerk and Wardens in making the necessary arrangements to pay for the same.

Voted: the sum of $300, being one year's rent of the estate leased to Richard Harrison, Esq., becoming due, and to be paid by Mr. Pollock, the present tenant, the 25th day of the present month, be appropriated towards payment of the above mentioned lot.

Voted: that the three-fourth parts[245] of lot No. 3 remaining unsold, be disposed of by the committee for the most they can obtain for the same, as they find it will not sell at the valuation formerly agreed upon by them.

October 7, 1805.   Whereas, the Wardens have reported to the Vestry that they have received a deed of the lot of land which we were about purchasing of the late Henry Bliss, Esq., from his executor, Mr. Clarke Bliss, and after having the same recorded by the Town Clerk, had paid said Clarke Bliss $800 in part; and as some difficulty had arisen with Sarah Bliss, widow of said Henry, with regard to her right of dower, they had retained, in securities, in the hands of the Clerk of the Vestry, the sum of $381.50, for which they have given their obligation payable to said Clarke, with interest thereon, upon his obtaining and delivering to them a quit-claim, or

---

[245] The above-mentioned " three-fourth parts " of lot No. 3 was sold to Daniel Ginnedo for $90, and a deed of it was given to him, together with a deed of the lot that he already held on a long lease, and for which he had paid the stipulated sum.

good and sufficient release from the said widow to her said right of dower.

Voted: that said report be accepted, and the doings of the Wardens in said business approved of and fully ratified by the Vestry.

Whereas, Mr. Moses Seixas hath represented to the Vestry that he, in behalf of the Hebrew Congregation in this Town, is about making an exchange of a small piece of land, which now forms part of the burial-ground belonging to said congregation, for part of the estate leased by the Vestry to Richard Harrison, Esq., June 1, A.D. 1796, and requesting the Vestry to ratify and confirm said exchange.

Voted and resolved: that if such exchange should take place, and the estate leased, as above said, to the said Harrison, should ever by any means revert to us, or our successors, we do, in that case, covenant and engage with the said Hebrew Congregation, for ourselves and our successors, that such exchange shall be fully ratified and confirmed to all intents and purposes for which it was made.

Voted: that if any person who has purchased one of the Church lots, on a lease for 999 years, should apply for a deed in fee simple, it shall be given to him, provided no expense shall accrue to the Church in consequence thereof.

Voted: that Simeon Martin, Esq., be added to the Wardens and Clerk to receive the new bell and settle for it.

October 16, 1805. The new bell, weighing 1375 pounds, neat, was this day received, and immediately hung in the belfry. Payment was made for the same with money raised by subscription, viz.: $263.03, besides the bell which was recast by Doolittle which was credited in part. The whole cost was $504.53.

November 4, 1805. The Rev^d Mr. Dehon having laid before the Vestry a letter he had lately received from the Rev. Mr. John Ward, of Litchfield, and the contents thereof being duly considered; voted unanimously, that the Rev^d Mr. Dehon be requested to reply to said letter, and to inform Mr. Ward that the Vestry will readily receive him as an Assistant Minister to our Rector, and will engage that he shall be paid annually the sum of three hundred and fifty dollars, besides the use or rent of the Church school-house, on condition that he assist the Rector in performing the duties of the Church, in such manner as may be agreed upon by the Rector and himself; and shall instruct, or cause to be instructed, ten poor children in grammar and the mathematics gratis, agreeably to Mr. Kay's donation.

January 29, 1806. Thomas Tromp Tyrrell[216] was buried.

March 3, 1806. Whereas the Rev. Mr. John Ward arrived in Town in December last, in consequence of the invitation given him by the Vestry,

Voted : that his salary commence from the 25th day of said November last, 1805.

Voted : that the Wardens be requested to pay our Rector, as soon as they are in cash, $24, the interest on the Wheatley bond, and the $10 due on account of the Tate estate, to Christmas last, to the poor of the Church, in order that the said two sums be divided among them, agreeably to the design and meaning of said donations.

The money was so paid the following day :

Whereas, the Rev^d Mr. Dehon has informed the Vestry, that at the last Christmas festival he received from Mrs. Catherine Malbone

---

[216] Mr. Tyrrell was born in Jamaica. In his youth he was sent to Newport to be educated. He then returned to Jamaica, where he amassed a handsome property. When he retired from business he returned to Newport, and here married the widow of John Grimes in 1803. Mrs. Tyrrell died in 1830, at an advanced age, and was buried in the same grave with her husband in the church-yard.

a valuable silver cup, for the use of the altar of Trinity Church ; resolved unanimously, that the thanks of this Vestry, in their own behalf, and in behalf of the congregation, be presented to Mrs. Malbone for this generous benefaction; and that the Wardens be requested to have engraved thereon the name of the donor, and the date of the donation, that the remembrance of such distinguished piety and liberality may descend, with the cup, to posterity.

CHAPTER XVII.

1806-1810.

AT a meeting of the Congregation of Trinity Church, on Easter Monday, April 7, 1806, were chosen William Littlefield and William Wood, Wardens.

Vestry. Francis Brinley, John Bours, Francis Malbone, Benjamin Gardiner, Henry Sherburne, John Handy, William Crooke, William Littlefield, Robert N. Auchmuty, Saunders Malbone, Simeon Martin, William Wood, Peleg Wood, Edward Brinley, and John C. Scott.

John Bours, Clerk of Vestry; John Dyer, Clerk of Church; Uriah Gorton, Sexton.

Voted: that the former salary of thirty dollars per annum to the Clerk of the Church be continued and paid; and the same sum of thirty dollars per annum to the Sexton.

Voted: that Messrs. Brinley, Bours, Auchmuty, Gardiner and William Hunter be continued delegates to the next State Convention, and requested to attend whenever called upon.

Voted: that the same tax as the last year be continued, viz.: ten dollars per annum on the single pews below; fifteen dollars on those of one and a half, and twenty dollars on the double pews; and four dollars on each of the gallery pews: the one-third part for the support of the Rector, and the other two-thirds part for paying the salaries of the other officers, and repairs of the Church.

Voted: that the Rector, Wardens and Vestry be requested to use their endeavors to obtain an organist.

Voted: Messrs. Sherburne, Martin and Hunter be a committee

to petition the Legislature of the State to pass an act similar to that granted to the First Congregational Society in New York, to enable our Church to collect the taxes assigned on the pews. Said act was passed at the October session, 1805.

At a Vestry meeting, April 14, 1806, at Mr. Francis Brinley's, Voted: that Messrs. Sherburne, Crooke and William Wood, with Mr. Bours, be a committee to purchase a lot of land, of three and one-quarter of an acre, on the hill, of Lawrence Clarke, provided the same can be had at a rate that will yield six per cent. per annum, interest on the purchase money, and payment made out of the notes received from John Yeomans and Henry Moore, for the Tate lot sold Yeomans.

Voted: That the Wardens proceed in having the fences made about the parsonage-lot, as soon as may be, at the expense of the Church.

At a meeting of the Vestry, May 5, 1806, at Mr. Bours's,

Voted: that Mr. Benjamin Gardiner be added to the committee chosen to lease the lot purchased of Lawrence Clarke.   Voted: that Mr. Gorton, the sexton of the Church, have permission to new shingle the west side of the house he occupies, at the expense of the Church, under the direction of the Wardens.

Voted: that Mr. John G. Whitehorne, who, we are informed, is going to Philadelphia in the first packet, be requested to use his endeavors to obtain in that city, or elsewhere, an organist for the Church, if a person qualified for the office, and of a good moral character, can be had for one hundred and fifty dollars per annum.[247].

---

[247] Berkenhead, the organist, had been discharged, on account of his infirmity. He sent a piteous appeal to the Vestry, begging to be restored, and promising amendment in the future, but he failed repeatedly to make good his promise, and it was decided to secure some one to fill his place. Mr. Whitehorne was probably as well qualified as any one in the Vestry to select an organist. He understood music, and had built a parlor

At a meeting of the Vestry, May 12, 1806, at Mr. Bours, Voted: that the Wardens be requested and empowered, in behalf of the Rector, Wardens and Vestry of the Church, to sign a note of hand to Lawrence Clarke, or order, for the sum of three hundred and forty-six dollars, payable within three years from the date thereof; for the balance due to him for a lot of land purchased of him with money arising from the sale of a house and lot of land in Newport, bequeathed by William Tate, late of Newport, in his last will and testament, for the benefit of the poor of said Church.

At a meeting of the Vestry, May 27, 1806, at Col. Sherburne's:

The Rev⁴ Mr. Dehon having laid before the Vestry a letter received from the Rev⁴ John S. I. Gardiner, Rector of Trinity Church, Boston, upon the subject of our Church joining in convention with the churches in the State of Massachusetts and New Hampshire, for the purpose of choosing a Bishop, Voted: that Mr. Dehon be requested to return answer to Mr. Gardiner, and inform him that his letter shall be laid before our State Convention at its next meeting.

Whereas the lot of land, of which Lawrence Clarke, and Hannah, his wife, have executed a deed of conveyance, bearing date the nineteenth day of the present month, to the Rector, Wardens and Vestry of this Church, was purchased with money arising from the sale of a house and a lot of land in Newport, given by William

organ, which, if it lacked qualities looked for in the work of more experienced hands, bore evidence of mechanical skill and perseverance. He and his brother Samuel, with whom he was in business, were prominent men, both in the community and the Church. Samuel repeatedly served the Church as Senior Warden; and when Zion Church was organized he took an active and leading part in that parish. He married Eliza Rathbone, August 24, 1802, and John married Harriet Greene Malbone, daughter of Col. John Malbone, December 16, 1798.

Tate, late of said Newport, in his last will and testament, to and for the sole benefit of the poor belonging to this Church, Voted, therefore: that the rents and profits of said lot be appropriated to the charitable and benevolent purpose for which it was designed by the testator; and that the same be distributed yearly, and every year forever, among the poor belonging to this Church, at the discretion of the Rector and Wardens for the time being; and that this Resolution be entered by the Clerk of the Vestry upon said deed, and that he be requested also to cause the same to be recorded by the Town Clerk of Newport, as well as in the book of records belonging to the Church, in order that a punctual compliance with the will of the said testator, as far as in the power of the Vestry, may be observed and religiously attended to by them and their successors.

At a meeting of the Vestry, June 2, 1806, at Mr. Saunders Malbone's:

Mr. Benj. Gardiner having reported to the Vestry that he had agreed with Mr. Clarke Bliss upon the division line between the Church lot, lately purchased of said Bliss, and his own land, Voted: that the said report be accepted, and signed by the Wardens on the part of the Vestry, and afterwards entered on the Church book of records; and also on the records of the Town of Newport, to prevent any dispute hereafter with regard to said division line.

The agreement was as follows:

Articles of agreement, made the thirtieth day of May, in the year of our Lord, one thousand eight hundred and six, between the Rector, Wardens and Vestry of Trinity Church, in Newport, of the one part, and Clarke Bliss, of said Newport, yeoman, of the other part, Witnesseth: that whereas a lot of land of eight acres and one-half acre, lately purchased by the said Rector, Wardens and Vestry, adjoining other land now belonging to him, the said Bliss, It is mutually agreed by the parties that they shall make and maintain a good and lawful fence on the line between the said lot and said Bliss land, in the manner following, viz.: The lot belonging to the said Rector, Wardens and Vestry, shall begin at the north end of the said line fence, and extend southerly on said line thirty-six rods, at the end of which, the said Bliss shall begin and extend southerly and easterly about twenty-four rods, to land belonging to Asa Shaw, all which said fence to be made and maintained by the said Rector, Wardens and Vestry, and by their successors in said office; and the said Bliss, his heirs, and administrators, forever, in manner aforesaid; in witness whereof the parties have hereunto interchangably set their hands and seals, the day and year above written.

CLARK BLISS,   [SEAL]

Signed and sealed in presence of
S. T. NORTHAM,
JAMES MOODY HOYT.

July 7, 1806. Voted: that the Wardens, with Mr. Crooke, be a committee to endeavor to obtain an organist for the Church as soon as possible.

August 1, 1806, the anniversary of the founding of the Female Benevolent Society, a sermon was preached in the Church, and the collection taken up in aid of the Society amounted to $132. [The Society owed its origin to the benevolence of Mrs. Osborne, a member of the Congregational Society, which had it under especial care; but its influence for good was wide-spread, and the other churches contributed from time to time, by collections, such as above, preceded by a sermon.]

October 6, 1806. Mr. Edward Brinley was requested to officiate as Junior Warden during the absence of Capt. William Wood, who was going on a voyage to sea.

November 3. The committee having reported that the repairs lately made on the church and parsonage-house amounts to sixteen hundred dollars, which, together with the sum of four hundred dollars heretofore borrowed for the repairs of the parsonage, and for which the Church is now paying interest, making in the whole two thousand dollars; and the sum of ten hundred and fifty having been already assessed on the pews, leaves a deficiency of nine hundred and fifty dollars, to assess which sum immediately is recommended to the congregation.

Some question having been raised as to the power and authority of the Church to make and collect certain assessments, an act explanatory of the charter of the Church was passed at the June session of the General Assembly, 1806.

Be it enacted by this General Assembly, and by the authority thereof it is enacted, that whenever any tax, or proportion of money, shall be assessed by order of said Corporation, upon the pews of the Church edifice and its appurtenances, which are already, or may hereafter be made, such a tax, or proportion of money, shall be paid by the several owners of such pews, agreeably to their respective assessments, and the rules and ordinances of said Corporation. And in case any owner, as aforesaid, shall, for the space of three months, after notice of any tax, or proportion, assessed, as aforesaid, refuse, or neglect, to pay the same, the pews of such delinquents shall and may be sold by order of said Corporation, at public vendue, for the payment and discharge of such taxes and costs; Provided, nevertheless, that such sale shall be previously advertised at least thirty days before such pews shall be offered for sale, and the surplus money, if any, after the payment of such taxes and costs, shall be lodged with the Wardens of said Trinity Church, to be paid over to such delinquents, or their legal representatives, on demand.

November 9, 1806. A tax of nine dollars was assessed on the pews on the lower floor, and one dollar on the gallery pews, agreeably to a recommendation from the Rector, Wardens and Vestry on the 3^d inst., in order to make up the deficiency due for the repairs lately made on the Church edifice and appurtenances.

December 1, 1806. It was voted that Mr. Littlefield be requested to employ Mr. Thomas Arnold to take charge of the Church clock, put her in order, and agree with him for a compensation to keep it so.

It was also voted that the Wardens be requested to have the stove put up in the Church, and that they procure, at the expense of the Church, whatever pipes were wanted, to be made of iron, and that they purchase sea coal sufficient to keep a fire during the winter.[248]

The Rev'd Mr. Dehon was requested, if he could conveniently do so, to go to New York, in order to solicit Bishop Moore to take the churches within this State into his Diocese and charge; agreeably to the unanimous desire of the late State Convention, held in Newport.

January 5, 1807. Francis Malbone and Peleg Wood were appointed a committee to assist the Wardens in collecting the arrearages due to the Church.

February 2, 1807. It having been stated that the subscriptions for repairing the Church not having all been paid in, and the pews of delinquents not having been sold, as contemplated, it was voted: that Messrs. Crooke and Peleg Wood be a committee to loan at

---

[248] The heating of the Church was a problem not easily solved; there was no chimney, and the stoves, first but one, then, in the writer's day, two, were set up, and while they roasted those whose pews were near to them, the congregation in other parts of the Church were smarting with cold. At one time the stoves, two enormous ones, were placed in the middle aisle, and the pipes were led across the Church, right and left, and taken through the windows. The marks where the paint was blistered, both on the inside and outside of the pews nearest to the stoves, can easily be found by one who looks for them. Then the stoves, huge cast-iron box stoves, were placed at the four corners of the Church, and the pipes were gathered into one large vertical copper pipe, that passed up through the ceiling near the centre of the Church, and entered a small chimney built there for that purpose. All these were expedients, and finally the present arrangement, heating by furnaces, was adopted.

one of the Banks in Newport, on account and in behalf of the congregation, as much money as will discharge the balance due from the Church to the Rev⁴ Mr. Dehon, to the first day of January, 1807, as soon as the amount thereof is ascertained; and that the Wardens regularly pay the discount on the same.

At the annual meeting, Easter Monday, March 30, 1807, the following officers were elected:

William Littlefield and William Wood, Wardens.

Vestry: Francis Brinley, John Bours, Francis Malbone, Benjamin Gardiner, Henry Sherburne, William Crooke, William Littlefield, Robert N. Auchmuty, Saunders Malbone, Simeon Martin, William Wood, Peleg Wood, Edward Brinley, Jacob Smith and Stephen T. Northam.

John Bours, Clerk of the Vestry.

Joseph Dyer, Clerk of the Church.

Uriah Gorton, Sexton.

Messrs. Brinley, Bours, Auchmuty, Gardiner and Martin be continued as delegates to the next convention, with the addition of William Crooke and Samuel Whitehorne.

The taxes were to be the same as during the past year; and the Rector, Wardens and Vestry were again urged to "use their endeavors to obtain an organist."

The following report from a committee appointed by the Vestry was read to the Congregation, when it was unanimously adopted, and the Wardens were instructed to carry the same into effect as soon as may be; and if any legal advice was necessary, they were to apply to William Hunter and request his assistance.

Whereas, on an investigation of the accounts for the repairs of Trinity Church edifice, and its appurtenances, it is found there is still a large sum wanting to pay the demands against said Church, and the subscribers having been appointed a committee, at a meeting of the Rector, Wardens and Vestry of said Church, on Monday, the 16th inst., to draft a plan to be laid before the Congregation for their approbation, on the ensuing Easter Monday, in order to carry into effect a law passed by the General Assembly of this State, at their Session, in June last, empowering the Corporation to dispose of any pews in said Church, which are indebted for the repairs thereof, do respectfully report, that it is expedient the Corporation should empower the Wardens, with the advice and consent of the Vestry, to dispose of such Pews as have become forfeited to the Church by the original regulations thereof; and any other pews, in conformity to the above-mentioned act of the General Assembly, and that the money arising from such sales be appropriated accordingly.

It having been stated at a Vestry meeting June 1, 1807, that " a French gentleman, at Philadelphia," had offered to become the organist of the Church, " provided he could receive suitable encouragement," it was voted that one hundred and four dollars per annum be offered him, with an assurance that the Vestry would do all in their power to secure pupils for him.

Delinquent taxpayers having been duly informed of the course the Vestry would pursue if any taxes remained longer unpaid, it was voted August 21st that the following pews on the lower floor be " advertised for sale in the next *Newport Mercury*, agreeably to the original regulations of the Congregation of the Church : Numbers 9, 11, 19, 21, 26, 28, 32, 47, 49, 62, 63, 67, 76.   Half pew of No. 80 and No. 92 ; and in conformity to an Act of the General Assembly of the State of Rhode Island, passed at the June Session, 1806 : pews Nos. 23, 34, 39, 52, 55, 59, 64, 65, 68, 77, 91, 93, 95 and 96, for taxes due for repairs ; and that the said pews be sold at public auction on Wednesday, the 23d day of September next, at 10 o'clock in the forenoon, at said Church."

The sale took place March 30, 1807, and the purchasers were :

No. 9.	Peleg Wood, south half,	$100.00
" "	Edward Easton, north half, .	80.00
" 11.	Robert Robinson, north half,	75.00
" 19.	Francis Brinley, .	55.00
" 21.	Edmund T. Waring,	80.00
" 39.	Samuel F. Gardner,	80.00
" 55.	Robert N. Auchmuty, .	65.00
" 59.	John Boit, .	90.00

Nos. 4, 23, 26, 28, 32, 34, 47, 49, 62, 63, 64, 65, 67, 68, 77, 88, 91, 92, 93, 95 and 96 were purchased by William Crooke, for the Church, at prices ranging from $20 to $50.

June 18, 1807. William Audinet[219] was buried.

At a Vestry meeting, November 2, 1807. Upon motion made by Mr. Francis Malbone, and unanimously agreed to, that twelve cords of wood should be purchased and presented to the Rev^d Mr. Dehon, and Mr. Northam generously offered to advance the money to procure the same. It was also voted that Mr. Northam be requested to purchase twelve cords of good oak wood, and have the same carted, sawed and stowed at the parsonage, and that he be reimbursed by the Wardens as soon as they are in cash on account of pews lately disposed of.

December 7, 1807. The Rector and Wardens were a committee to make enquiry of the Rev^d Mr. Ward respecting the state of the school, and make report at the next meeting of the Vestry.

A proposal being made that another stove should be procured and set up in the church, similar to the one already there, the same

---

[219] " William Audinet was born at Perigueux, France, and for many years was an inhabitant of the island of Guadaloupe. Compelled to fly on account of the civil commotion there, he sought safety and protection in a land of liberty, and twelve years since came with his family to this town, where he has lived in such a manner as to acquire notice and respect from all who became acquainted with him. Abroad he always appeared polite, affable and pleasing in his manner. At home the pious and exemplary Christian, the kind and affectionate husband, and the most indulgent master ; beloved and revered alike by all, they mourn his exit with the sincerest emotions of unfailing grief. His remains, attended by many of the most respectable citizens, were decently interred on the Tuesday evening following. The funeral services were performed by the Rev. Mr. Ward, of the Episcopal Church."—*Newport Mercury*.

Madame Audinet soon after died, which event was thus noticed by the same paper :

On Sunday, October 18, 1807, Madame Mary Catharine Audinet, relict of Mr. William Audinet, whom she survived only four months, and near to whom her remains were placed. Rev. Mr. Matignon, Rector of the Roman Catholic Church in Boston, performed with affecting solemnity the burial service agreeably to the rites of that Church.

was assented to and a subscription immediately opened to purchase a stove and the necessary pipe, and to pay the expense of erecting the same.

At a Vestry meeting, December 8, 1807, the following vote of the Town was ordered to be recorded.

"In Town Meeting, December 8, 1807. It is voted and resolved that the thanks of the Town be presented to the Society of the Episcopal Church for the use of their bell heretofore, and to request of them that it may be continued to be rung, as usual. It is also voted : that the sexton of the Church be the person to ring the said bell, and that he have fifty dollars per year. It is also voted that Mr. Robert Rogers be appointed to present the thanks of the town to the said Society for the use of their bell heretofore.

"Witness, JONATHAN ALMY,

"Town Clerk."

March 7, 1808. The Rev[d] Mr. Dehon having delivered to the Wardens one hundred dollars, the amount of two legacies bequeathed by Mrs. Judith Tillinghast[250] and her sister, Miss Susan Ayrault, in their last will and testament, to the poor in Trinity Church in Newport, and having informed the Vestry of the opinion of Mrs. Mary Scott, the administratrix upon the estates of the donors, that their design would be most extensively and permanently accomplished by making the said donation a part of the poor fund : Voted, therefore, that the same be added to the said fund for the use of the poor, and that Mr. Francis Brinley be requested to purchase with the money a share in the Rhode Island Union Bank.

[250] Judith Tillinghast and Susanna Ayrault were sisters, and daughters of Daniel, son of Pierre Ayrault. Judith, born December 9, 1725, and died November 26, 1806, married Joseph Tillinghast. Susanna, born June 29, 1723, remained single and died a year after her sister. Mary Scott, the administratrix, was the daughter of Stephen Ayrault, son of Daniel, and the widow of George Scott, who died in 1798, and to whom she was married September 16, 1764.

At the meeting of the Congregation, Easter Monday, April 18, 1808:

William Littlefield and Benjamin Mumford, Jr., were elected Wardens.

Vestry: Francis Brinley, John Bours, Francis Malbone, Benj. Gardiner, Henry Sherburne, William Crooke, Wm. Littlefield, Robt. N. Auchmuty, Benj. Mumford, Jr., in place of Saunders Malbone, resigned, Simeon Martin, John Wood, in place of his brother, William Wood, deceased, Peleg Wood, Edward Brinley, Jacob Smith and Stephen T. Northam.

Clerk of the Vestry, John Bours; Clerk of the Church, Thomas H. Mumford, son of John Mumford; and Uriah Gorton, Sexton.

The salary of the Clerk of the Church was raised to $50, but that of the sexton was continued at $30.

The tax remained the same.

The Wardens were enjoined to use their endeavors to obtain an organist.

Voted: that the thanks of the Congregation be presented to Miss Calhoun for her officiating on the organ to this time, and to request a continuance to gratify them, while agreeable and convenient to herself, and that the Clerk of the Vestry furnish her with a copy of this vote.

The thanks of the Congregation were also presented to Mr. Edward Brinley, for kindly officiating as Warden, during the absence of Capt. Wm. Wood, and since his death.

[February 13, 1809. Mrs. Sarah Read, consort of Dr. William Read, of Charleston, S. C., suddenly died here. Her remains were taken to Trinity Church, where the burial service was read by Rev'd Mr. Dehon, after which they were deposited in the family vault of the late Governor Wanton, adjoining the Clifton ground.]

March 6th. Voted: that the lot purchased lately of Lawrence Clarke, and leased to him until the 25th inst., be again leased to him for two years, by the Wardens, and at the same rent, he. giving security for the payment of the same.

Benj. Gardiner was appointed to lease the Bliss lot for a term not exceeding three years, and that a refusal be given to James Mitchell, who had improved it for the past three years.

The Wardens were to have the clock repaired.

May 1.   Col. Sherburne and Mr. Crooke were a committee to wait upon Rev. Mr. Ward, and enquire of him whether Mr. Trevett had given him possession of the school-house, and whether it was in as good repair as when he entered it.

June 2, 1809.   Benj. B. Mumford was appointed to act as Clerk of the Vestry during the absence of Mr. John Bours.

Francis Brinley, Benj. Gardiner, Simeon Martin, William Crooke and Benj. B. Mumford were appointed a committee to digest a plan for a raising a permanent fund for the Church, and to report at the next meeting.

A committee appointed to receive the books and papers belonging to the Church, and in the hands of Mr. Bours, reported August 7th that they had received from Mr. Bours " A chest containing two books of record, two books of account and divers files of papers ; also a mortgage deed of Wm. Howard's house and lot of land for one hundred and twelve dollars and sixty-three cents; a certificate for one share in the Rhode Island Union Bank, John Bours' note endorsed by Stephen T. Northam, payable at said bank in six months, for two hundred and fifty-three dollars and fifteen cents, and also the balance in his hands belonging to the Church Yard Fund, amounting to twenty-four dollars and thirty-two cents."

The plan for raising a Permanent Fund was received, and its further consideration was deferred to a subsequent meeting.

August 21, 1809.   It was voted that a committee be appointed to report another plan for raising a permanent fund, to be laid before the congregation, and the Vestry was to meet the following Thursday at Mr. Auchmuty's to receive the report. Messrs. Sherburne, Gardiner and Northam were that committee.

At a meeting of the Vestry August 24, 1809, the report of the committee for raising a permanent fund was received, when it was voted to call the congregation together on the following Sunday afternoon, to hear it read and take some action upon it. The following was the report:

The Committee appointed by the Vestry of Trinity Church, on the 21st inst., to report a plan for raising a permanent fund for the better support of the Church, do respectfully offer the following, viz.:

That a subscription be opened under the direction of the congregation, for raising the sum of six thousand dollars, payable in one year by quarterly instalments of 25 per cent. after the aforesaid sum of six thousand dollars shall be subscribed.

That an annual contribution be solicited for raising such further sums as in addition to the sum subscribed for (with the interest that may arise thereon) will amount to ten thousand dollars, which contribution might perhaps be made in Church, by having a day, or part of a day, annually set apart for that purpose.

That all money raised by subscription, or donation, be put to interest, or vested in some subscription of permanent stock, under the direction of a committee to be appointed by the congregation for that purpose, and that none of the money raised as aforesaid, or the interest arising thereon, be appropriated or used for any other purpose whatever, until the same amount to the aforesaid sum of ten thousand dollars; after which the annual profit of said fund shall be at the disposal of the Corporation of Trinity Church, and that the subscription shall not be obligatory on any person until the amount of six thousand dollars be subscribed.

Submitted by

HENRY SHERBURNE,

BENJ. GARDINER,

S. T. NORTHAM,

Committee.

At a meeting of the Congregation at Trinity Church, Sunday, August 27, 1809,

Voted : that the report of the Committee for raising a permanent fund be accepted, and that the consideration thereof be for the present deferred."

At a Vestry meeting, October 19, 1809, Voted : that the thanks of this Vestry, on behalf of the Congregation, be made Miss Floride Calhoun, for her goodness in officiating on the organ, and that a silver cup, of the value of thirty dollars, be also presented her, as a token of their respect and esteem, with the following inscription engraved thereon :

" Presented on the 7th of November, 1809, by the Rector, Wardens and Vestry of Trinity Church, in Newport, Rhode Island, to Miss Floride Calhoun, of Charleston, South Carolina, as a testimony of their sense of the obliging manner and excellent skill with which she has performed on the organ of the Church, and a small token of their gratitude and respect."

The Wardens were instructed to procure such a cup, and present it to Miss Calhoun.

At a Vestry meeting, February 5, 1810,

Voted : that it is the opinion of this Vestry, that chanting be continued in the Church, conformably with the rubric, until Easter Monday.

Voted : that the final discussion of altering the organ loft be deferred till Easter Monday ; but in the mean time the Chanters may, under the immediate directions of the Wardens, at their own expense, make such internal alterations in the four pews (two on each side of the organ loft) as may suit their own convenience.

Voted: that the Vestry of Trinity Church thank the gentlemen and ladies for their performance in chanting the service on Christmas days, and request a continuance thereof; and that a copy of this vote be presented by the Clerk of the Vestry.

CHAPTER XVIII.

1810–1811.

[At this time, February, 1810, the Rector, Rev[d] Theodore Dehon, D.D., received a call to the rectorship of St. Michael's Church, Charleston, S. C., and from that city he addressed the following letter to the Wardens, Vestry and Congregation of the Church:]

Charleston, 21 Feb., 1810.

Gentlemen :

When I received an invitation to the Rectorship of St. Michael's Church in this city, I thought it a duty to visit this place before I came to a decision, in order that I might be more fully satisfied of the course which I ought to pursue. I have found here a climate in which my health has been better than at any other time in the last fifteen years of my life, a very numerous Church, among whom it would seem I may minister in sacred things without any diminution of my usefulness, and a body of clergy of our own denomination, such as I have long wished to be associated with. The provision proposed to be made for my maintenance is ample ; and the building in which I am to officiate not disproportioned to my strength. These considerations, combined with others which I need not now mention, presented a body of inducements to a removal which my friends here thought I ought not to resist. But their force has been strengthened in a manner which leaves me unable any longer to doubt which is the path, that a regard to my health and my usefulness in the Church of the Redeemer should lead me to pursue, by an unanimous consent of the Vestry, that I may reserve to myself the privilege of being absent during the summer months, as long as it shall be necessary to my safety.

On this condition, without which I had made up my mind to return to the care of my beloved flock in Newport, I have felt it my duty to accept the invitation given me; and, consequently, to resign the Rectorship of your Church. This resignation, Gentlemen, I hope will be received by you with an assurance that it is not made with any diminution of my regard for your long respected Society, and that it is the result of much serious, prayerful and anxious deliberation. It would have comported more with my own feelings, not to have made it till after my return to the northward; but I have deemed it due to you, as well as coincident with wishes, expressed, when I was about to leave Newport, to make this early communication, in order that any opportunity which may occur of providing your Church with another Rector, need not pass away unimproved. Should you, however, desire it, this arrangement need not go into full separation until the autumn of the year. I shall return to Newport (God willing) in the Spring, and if it will in any way be promotive of the welfare, or convenience, of the Church, my services shall be cheerfully given during the summer to the flock among whom I have so happily lived and labored, and whom I shall leave with emotions which can only be known by him who feels them.

I am, Gentlemen, with the highest sentiments of esteem and regard,

Your Humble and obedient servant,
THEODORE DEHON.[251]

The Wardens, Vestry
   and Congregation of Trinity Church.

---

[251] Right Reverend Bishop Dehon was born in Boston, in 1776, graduated at Harvard in 1795, was called to Trinity Church in 1798, removed to Charleston, S. C., in 1810, where he became Rector of St. Michael's, and was made Bishop of South Carolina in 1812. He died in 1817.

Two volumes of his sermons were published in 1821. They were much read, both in this country and in England. An edition was published in London, in 1823, and a new edition in New York, 1859.

A number of his sermons were also published in pamphlet form. One on the death of General Washington, 1800; one on the death of George Gibbs, 1803; a discourse delivered in Providence before the Female Charitable Society of that city, 1804; and a Thanksgiving Sermon in Newport, 1806.

Bishop Dehon was married to Sarah Russell, daughter of Jonathan Rus-

At the Annual Meeting, Easter Monday, April 23, 1810, the following officers were elected :

Samuel Whitehouse,	Senior Warden.
Edward Easton,	Junior Warden.

Vestry :

Francis Brinley,	Benj. B. Mumford,
John Bours,	Simeon Martin,
Saunders Malbone,	John P. Mann,
Benj. Gardiner,	John Wood,
Henry Sherburne,	Edward Brinley,
Wm. Crooke,	Samuel Whitehorne,
Wm. Littlefield,	Steph. T. Northam,
Rob. N. Auchmuty,	Edward Eaton,

John L. Boss, Senior.

Benj. B. Mumford, Clerk of Vestry.

Uriah Gorton, Sexton.

Delegates to the State Convention : Messrs. Brinley, Bours, Auchmuty, Gardiner, Martin, Crooke and Whitehorne.

No change was made in the tax.

Voted : that Benjamin Gardiner and Simeon Martin, Esquires, be, and they are hereby appointed and empowered, jointly and severally, as delegates from this Church, to meet at Trinity Church in Boston "on the Tuesday preceding the last Wednesday in May next," then and there to vote for a Bishop to preside over this congregation, and to transact such other business as may come before them touching the interest of the Church, and that their expenses be paid by the Church.

sell, of Charleston, October 26, 1813. Mr. Russell was of Rhode Island origin. At one time he was Collector of the Port of Bristol, and at another time Minister from the United States to Sweden.

Voted: that the organ-loft be altered and enlarged, to accommodate the singers and chanters of sacred music.

[The convention met in Boston, in June, and unanimously elected Rev⁴ Alexander Viets Griswold,[252] Bishop of Massachusetts, New Hampshire, Vermont and Rhode Island.]

June 4, 1810, the Wardens, Messrs. Whitehorne, and Col. Sherburne, were appointed to present the name of some suitable person to be settled over the Church as minister.

[The annual meeting of the Grand Lodge of Free and Accepted Masons, in Rhode Island, was held at the State House in Newport, on St. John's day, June 25, 1810. After the installation, the members of the Order marched in procession, with music, to Trinity Church, where a discourse was delivered by the newly elected Bishop of the Diocese.]

July 2ᵈ the following action was taken in regard to the resignation of Rev⁴ Mr. Dehon:

Whereas, the Rev⁴ Theodore Dehon did, by his letter of February last, to the Wardens, Vestry and congregation of said Church, communicate his resignation of the Rectorship thereof, with a tender of his service 'till the ensuing autumn, to which letter no answer hath been given, it is therefore voted unanimously that Francis Brinley, Benjamin Gardiner, and Wᵐ Crooke, Esquires, together with the Wardens, be a committee to wait on him, to congratulate

----

[252] *Alexander V. Griswold* — Rt. Rev⁴ Bishop Griswold, born at Simsbury, Ct., April 22, 1766, was ordained priest, October 1st, 1799. After his ordination he had charge of several small parishes in his native State. In 1804 he was settled at Bristol, R. I., as Rector of St. Michael's. He was consecrated in Trinity Church, New York, in May, 1811, by the Rt. Rev. Bishop White; but his connection with St. Michael's did not terminate till 1835, when he gave his whole attention to the Episcopate.

him on his safe return to this place, to acknowledge the receipt of
the above communication, and to thank him for his kind and
benevolent offer of continuing with us till the ensuing autumn,
assuring him that it is with pleasure that we accept thereof, expect-
ing within that time we shall be so fortunate as to settle a Rector
in our Church.

[The committee addressed a letter to Bishop Jarvis, of New
Haven, asking him to recommend a clergyman to take charge of
the parish. A little later Revd Salmon Wheaton came to Newport
bearing a letter from Revd Bela Hubbard, of New Haven.]

New Haven, July 11, 1810.

Dear Sir:

The bearer is the Revd S. Wheaton, A.M., of Yale College, of
handsome talents, and of much literary accomplishment for his age;
a close student, and who bids fair to make a useful member of
society in general, and of the Church of God in particular. For
some months past he has been assisting me in my church, to universal satisfaction. He makes an exchange with Mr. Seabury, of
New London, and contemplates going to Newport, and would
spend a Sunday in your Church, and, attached, as I know you are,
to our most excellent Church, I presume to solicit your attention
so far to my young friend, as to give him an introductory letter to
such person or persons of that Church as you shall think proper.
I am, dear sir, with sentiments of esteem, your old and affectionate
friend,

Bela Hubbard

John Bours, Esq.,
Mr. Wheaton is in *Priests' Orders.*

[Mr. Bours was at that time in New London, and on the receipt
of the above letter he wrote to the Wardens:]

New London, July 16, 1810.

Gentlemen :

You will be sensible of the propriety of my forwarding to you the enclosed letter by the bearer of this, the Rev^d Mr. Wheaton, from its contents. To add to a recommendation from so respectable and good a character as Doct^r Hubbard, were I able to do it, might, perhaps, be judged superfluous; shall, therefore, only observe, that Mr. Wheaton officiated in the Church here, all the day yesterday, the Rev^d Mr. Seabury being absent on a journey, to universal approbation.

I am extremely anxious to return to my native town once more, and to reunite with you in public worship, in that Church, in whose courts it has been the most fervent wish of my soul to dwell, but the delicate situation of my health is such that I greatly fear it is otherwise ordered.

That the congregation may be united in the choice of a Rector, and our Church again prosper and flourish, and thereby the cause of our holy religion promoted, is the ardent prayer to heaven of,

Gentⁿ your old brother, affectionate friend and Obed^t hum^{ble} servant

J. Bours.

Messrs. Littlefield and Mumford,
    Wardens of Trinity Church,
        Newport.

[With the above there was the following letter from Rev. Mr. Hubbard to the Wardens of Trinity Church :]

New Haven, July 12, 1810.

Gentlemen :

In consequence of your letter to me, under date of the 21st ult., the Reverend Salmon Wheaton makes you a visit, conformably to the wishes you expressed. The testimonials it will be proper for him to submit to your inspection, will inform you of his orders. This letter may serve to certify, as far as I know, that his life and behavior have been agreeable to the tenor and requirements specified in the general canons of our Church. For the relief of the Rector of Trinity Church in New Haven [Rev. Bela Hubbard] the vestry engaged him to officiate in said Church, which he has done for some months past I believe to the approbation of the congregation. I have no cause to doubt the correctness of his principles, and therefore think him deserving of confidence, in regard to soundness in faith, as it may relate to doctrines, government and discipline of the Church.

Commending you and your Church to the protection and blessing of Almighty God,

I am, Gentlemen,

Your obedient humble

Servant in Christ,

BELA HUBBARD.[253]

[Revd John Ward, who had been school-master and assistant minister, and for a short time filled the pulpit after the resignation of Rev^d Mr. Dehon, having closed his connection with the Church at this time, and left the town, the following letter was addressed to him by Mr. Samuel Whitehorne, the Senior Warden.]

Newport, July 26, 1810.

Revd John Ward.

Dear Sir :

I am directed by the Vestry of Trinity Church to pay you for your kind services in officiating in said Church, from the

---

[252] Revd Bela Hubbard died in 1812. "The faithful missionary, the pious priest, the watchful pastor, after a life spent in the service of his Master, was called to his reward on the 6th day of December, 1812. His name is yet green among the children of those who knew and loved him, and enjoyed his ministrations, and is never mentioned by them but with affection and veneration.—*His. of Trinity Church, New Haven.*

resignation of Mr. Dehon until your departure, at the same rate of salary paid him, say seven hundred dollars per annum. After deducting for one month and five days paid you as an Assistant Minister during the time which, as per statement enclosed, you will find a balance in your favor of two hundred and twenty-three $\frac{61}{100}$ dollars, which my brother will hand you, by whom I send this.

The reversed account inclosed, annexing a receipt for the balance, you will please sign and hand him.

I have taken this mode of remitting you the money, not knowing when I should have the pleasure of seeing you in Newport.

I am, Revd Sir,

Your respectful friend,

Sam. Whitehorne, Senior Warden.

[The following letters at this time passed between Rev. Salmon Wheaton and a committee of the Vestry:]

New Haven, Aug. 21, 1810.

Gentlemen :

The importance of the subject and my not returning to New Haven quite as soon as was expected, must be my apology for delaying to write to you.

When I consider the pleasant local situation of Newport, the kindness and hospitality of its inhabitants, the state of your Church, and, above all, the *perfect unanimity* with which I was elected your Rector, I am strongly inclined, I am *very desirous*, to accept your invitation. My friends also, and the friends of our Church, are solicitous that I should.

But on the other hand, there is some difficulty in my own mind, and in the minds of my friends, with regard to the *salary*. I am sensible it would be abundantly sufficient for my support were I to remain a single man. How long that will be I can't say. Like other young men, I am liable to have a family. From a statement of your late worthy Rector, Dr. Dehon, and from the result of many other inquiries, I am inclined to believe that the salary proposed will hardly be sufficient for the support of a clergyman at housekeeping. If I know my own heart, *money* is not the object for which I entered into the sacred ministry. I wish nothing unreasonable, but I *do* wish to be in comfortable circumstances, and I am confident your Church have it in their power to place me in such. May we not then adopt some expedient which will accommodate both the congregation and myself?

I think I should be well satisfied to accept what you have proposed, so long as I might remain unmarried, provided you will agree to raise the salary in case I should marry. How *much* it ought then to be raised you who have families are better judges than myself. Relying, therefore, wholly on your candor and goodness, I respectfully submit it to you to say whether or not such a conditional addition to the salary shall be made and, if so, what that addition shall be.

That God may bless our excellent Church, and especially that part to which you belong, is the sincere prayer of

Gentlemen,
Your most obedient and humble Servt

Salmon Wheaton —

Messrs. Gentlemen of the Committee.

Newport, Augst 24, 1810.

Reverend Sir:

In consequence of your letter of the 21st inst., received last evening, a vestry has been called this day, who consider us a committee appointed by the congregation to invite you to become the Rector of our Church, and to make a specific offer of emoluments to you, in case you accept the office, which they have no power to alter.

The letter from the Bishop of Connecticut to a former committee, and that from Dr. Hubbard to Mr. Bours, both forwarded by you, together with your performance, have hitherto commanded unanimity in our Church; should a congregation be assembled and a majority consent to the terms proposed by you, we know of no compulsory means to bind the minority, and it might tend to discord in the Church. It is our wish, and we believe it to be the general wish, that our Rector should have a decent and competent support, and if, on trial, our present offer should be found insufficient for that end, we trust the congregation, on a fair representation, would not fail to make it such.

The time is now short that we can expect the voluntary benevolence of Doctor Dehon, to keep our Church open ; we therefore wish that, as soon as your decision is made, it may be communicated to
Your Obedient Humble Servants,

FRANCIS BRINLEY,
EDWARD EASTON,
SAM. WHITEHORNE,
Committee.

Revd Salmon Wheaton,
New Haven.

New Haven, September 4, 1810.

Gentlemen :

I have again to apologize for delaying to write you. To leave my friends and near connections, and take the oversight of the Church of God in a land where, but a few weeks since, they were all strangers, you must be sensible is no small undertaking. I have taken time to deliberate on the subject and weigh the contents of your letter. My opinion is still the same, *that the salary is quite too small ;* but I confess there appears to be much propriety in your remarks, as respects calling another meeting of the congregation. I have been in Newport but two Sundays ; of course it cannot be expected that I have the confidence of the people to any very great extent ; and to press at this time an addition to the salary might, as you very justly observe, tend to discord in the Church, especially as you have no law, as in Connecticut, to bind the minority. On the whole I have thought it advisable to come to Newport upon the terms that you have proposed ; and if after being there a sufficient time to become acquainted with the people, I see no reason to alter my mind, shall expect to be instituted your Rector according to the office prescribed by the Protestant Episcopal Church in the United States.

My time to remain here according to contract will expire on the 23d of next month, when I shall be at liberty to be with you. To be sure, I have a right to leave N. Haven at any time; but it will be more convenient for me, and for the people of this Church, to have me stay my time out; and if it is not very material with you, I should by all means wish it. My engagement was with the *Vestry*, and a conditional one, as I told you; but I find it to be the general expectation among the congregation, that I am to remain until the time I have mentioned. It will give them an opportunity to do something about procuring another assistant for Dr. Hubbard. I shall also be able in the mean season to visit my friends and make arrangements for my removal.

With sentiments of respect and esteem I am,

  Gentlemen, your most obedient, humble servant,

       SALMON WHEATON.[254]

Messrs. Brinley & Co., Committee of the Episcopal
 Church, Newport, Rhode Island.

---

[254] In 1808, at the request of Rev. Bela Hubbard, Rev. Mr. Wheaton was engaged as Assistant Minister of Trinity Church, New Haven, where he remained in the active performance of his duties till called to Newport, in October, 1810, as Rector of Trinity Church, which office he held till 1840, when he resigned his charge, removed to Johnstone, New York, became the Rector of St. Michael's Church in that town, and there remained up to the time of his death, in 1844. September 24, 1812, Rev. Dr. Wheaton was married to Miss Ann Dehon, sister of Rt. Rev. Bishop Dehon, by Rev. Dr. Gardiner, in Trinity Church, Boston.

On the right of the chancel in the Church, there is a monument corresponding in details to that on the left, to the Rev. Marmaduke Browne, bearing this inscription :

To the Memory of

SALMON WHEATON, D. D.

An Eminent Christian.

For thirty years the Faithful Rector of this Church,

Who died December 24th, 1844, aged 62 years.

Also to ANN DEHON, his Wife,

Who died December 8th, 1855, aged 73 years.

Their mortal Remains rest in a tomb under

St. Paul's Church, Boston, Mass.

Behold the spirits of the Just,

Whose faith is changed to sight.

The committee replied:

Newport, September 11, 1810.

Rev. Sir: Your esteemed favor, under date 4th inst., was duly received, and was laid before the Vestry, who were much pleased with your determination to come among us.

We shall be happy to see you as early as you can make it convenient, but consider that you cannot, consistent with propriety and sense of duty, leave the Church at New Haven, before the expiration of the time you agreed on, unless a successor to you should in the mean time be appointed.

With sentiments of esteem and respect, we are,

Revd Sir, Your Obed. and h'ble servt's,

EDWARD EASTON,
SAM^{L.} WHITEHORNE,
Committee.

For themselves and Francis Brinley, absent.

July 30, 1810. The Wardens were instructed to borrow two hundred dollars to pay the balance due Rev. Mr. Dehon and Rev. Mr. John Ward. Captain Littlefield was to engage Miss Towle as organist, and to employ Mr. Berkenhead to give her two lessons a week, for one quarter, at the expense of the Church.

October 1, 1810. Voted: that Benj. Gardiner's account for his expenses in attending the convention of the Eastern Diocese, at Boston, Sept. 24th, as a delegate, being $15.91, be paid by the Wardens.

Voted: that the thanks of the Vestry be given Benj. Gardiner,

---

The use of the pew under the monument was given to Miss Ann Wheaton, youngest daughter of Rev. Dr. Wheaton, during her life, and is still known as "the Wheaton pew."

The eldest daughter, Sarah Gibbs Wheaton, became the wife of Dr. David King, a physician prominent in his profession, distinguished for his many sterling qualities of heart and mind, and a devoted friend of the Church. He died March 7th, 1882, and in August of the same year his widow also expired.

Esq., for his faithful service rendered to the Church in his attendance upon the convention of the Eastern Diocese, at their two last meetings, and that the Clerk of the Vestry present him with a copy of the above.

October 25, 1810. The Wardens were requested "to have the Congregation convened on Friday morning, at 10 o'clock, for the purpose of receiving a communication from the Rev. Doctor Dehon."

At that meeting the following letter was read:

Newport, 22d Oct., 1810.

Gentlemen:

Being informed that your Rector-elect will be here on the first Sunday of November, and a convenient opportunity offering for me to embark for Charleston next week, I have presumed that next Sunday will be the last of my regularly officiating with you. I ought to observe to you, Gentlemen, that since the date of my resignation of the Rectorship of the Church, I have not felt myself entitled to the use of the parsonage-house by any formal arrangement. But not having been on the spot at the time, to have removed my family, and there not having appeared any necessity to remove them since, we have continued in it. For the rent thereof I will account with the Wardens, or in any other way that you shall direct. You will also indulge me with observing that although no objection was made to the resignation, yet the customary acknowledgement of the acceptance of it by the corporation, to whom it was addressed, has not been transmitted to me in their behalf. This acknowledgement I could wish to receive before I take my leave of the congregation.

In making this communication to you, gentlemen, I cannot help looking back upon the series of years in which we have jointly, and with the utmost harmony, superintended the concerns of the Church in this place. It is pleasant to me to find nothing in the retrospect which indicates a want of union and fidelity; and while my most earnest prayers are offered to Heaven, that with equal peace, and greater prosperity, you may continue to manage the same important interests, I pray you to be assured, that to me, the most painful thing in the review of my connection with the Vestry, arises from the consideration that it is now to be terminated.

I remain, gentlemen, with esteem and best wishes for your welfare, your obliged and obedient servant,

THEODORE DEHON.

The Wardens and Vestry
    of Trinity Church.

At a meeting of the Wardens, Vestry and congregation of Trinity Church, held at the Church on Friday, the 26th day of October, 1810,

Resolved unanimously, that this Corporation accept the resignation of the Revd Doctor Theodore Dehon as Rector of this Church, as communicated to this Corporation by his letter of February last, and do the same impressed with sentiments of esteem, respect and affection for him personally ; with gratitude for the favors conferred on us for several months past, and with feelings of real regret at taking leave of a clergyman, whose services during his connection with us, have been highly valuable and acceptable, whose conduct and deportment have been uniformly correct, dignified and scrupulously moral, and, as we sincerely trust and believe, influenced by the precepts and example of his and our Lord and Saviour Jesus Christ.

Newport, October 26, 1810.

The Revd Doct^r Theodore Dehon,
    Dear Sir :

    In reply to your letter of the 22^d inst., we beg leave to observe that your's from Charleston, addressed to the Corporation of Trinity Church, is not now before us ; we understand it to be in the possession of Capt. Littlefield, who is absent from town ; we must, therefore, apologize to you for referring to it from recollection only. We believe it to have been dated after the middle of February. The first meeting of the Vestry after that time was on the 13th of March.

We think you mentioned your intention to be in Newport early in the spring ; it was therefore supposed that any answer to it would not arrive in Charleston until after you had left it, and we did not conceive that our acceptance of your resignation at that time was of material consequence to you ; we are much concerned that the omission should have occasioned you any embarrassment. We deem the use of the parsonage-house since your resignation a very inadequate compensation for the valuable services you have during that period rendered the Church. We enclose a resolution of the corporation duly accepting your resignation, and have adopted this form, presuming it to be correct and satisfactory to you. In this resolution, sir, as members of the congregation we have already expressed our feelings—gratitude for your services, and sorrow for your departure ; permit us to say, that as members of the Vestry for so many years associated with you in the superintendence of the concerns of the Church in this place, that we sincerely reciprocate your assurance, " that the most painful thing in the review of our connections arises from the consideration that it is now to be terminated."

With sentiments of the highest esteem and respect, and with best wishes for your welfare, sir, for and in behalf of the Vestry and Wardens of Trinity Church, I remain

Your Obed[t] Humble Serv[t]
B. B. MUMFORD, Clk of the Vestry.

At a special Vestry meeting Oct. 29, 1810,

Voted : that the Wardens, with Benj. Gardiner, Esquire, be a committee to wait on the Rev[d] Doctor Dehon, and present him the thanks of the Vestry for his excellent sermon delivered yesterday, and request a copy of the same for the press.[255]

November 5, 1810. Voted unanimously, That the polite and kind offer of Messrs. Levi Tower and Samuel O. Auchmuty to officiate,

---

[255] This was the last sermon that Bishop Dehon preached in Trinity Church.

the first as Clerk of the Church, and the second as organist, be accepted and acknowledged; and that they be requested to officiate under the direction of the Rector, in said stations, so long as it may be convenient and agreeable to them; or until a permanent Clerk and Organist can be obtained; and that the Clerk of the Vestry furnish each of them with a copy of this vote.

Voted: That Messrs. S. Whitehorne and Wm. Littlefield be a committee to wait on Miss Towle,[256] and acquaint her, that in consequence of the death of Mr. Berkenhead, the offer of two young gentlemen to officiate, one as clerk and the other as organist [had been accepted] and as the Church cannot depend upon her services for any length of time in the Church, the Vestry feels grateful for her past favors and tender her with a ten dollar bill.

Voted: That Capt. S. T. Northam be a committee to inquire into the state of the School-house, now in the occupation of Mr. John Rodman,[257] and report to the next Vestry.

December 5, 1810.   Voted: That the Rector be requested to call the Congregation together on Sunday afternoon next, for the purpose of laying before them the report of the committee to whom was referred the plan for raising a permanent fund for the support and maintenance of the Church and Minister, for their approbation and aid.

Voted: That the Clerk of the Vestry have the leases given to

---

[256] Miss Towle was the daughter of the Moravian Minister in Newport. Lacking the necessary qualifications as an organist, but desirous of perfecting herself, she became a pupil of Berkenhead, the former organist of the Church, the Vestry paying for such instruction; but Berkenhead died at this time, and as it was uncertain how long Miss Towle would remain in Newport, apart from any question of her ability to fill the post, the above arrangement was made.

[257] John Rodman was a Quaker, who devoted his whole attention to teaching, in which he gained the confidence of the public.   He was born in 1785, and died in 1827.

Richard Harrison, Esq., and to Mr. John Yeomans, recorded upon the Town records, agreeable to law, and that he pay for the same and charge it to the Church.

At a meeting of the Congregation of Trinity Church, held at the Church on the 9th of December, 1810:

Voted, unanimously: that the report of the committee to whom it was referred, to report the ways and means to raise a permanent fund, for the better support of the Minister of this Church, dated August 23, 1809, be adopted.

Voted, unanimously: that Benjamin Gardiner, Samuel Whitehorne, Steph. T. Northam, Thomas Handy, and Simeon Martin, Esqrs., be a committee to carry the object of that report into full effect.

At a Vestry meeting, Jan'y 7, 1811. Voted: that the report of Mr. Stephen T. Northam, relating to the School-house be accepted, and that the amount of his account for repairs on the same, $15.99, be paid by the Wardens.

Voted: That Mr. John Rodman continue in the Church schoolhouse, for the term of one year, from the 1st of January, 1811, on the same conditions that he has heretofore had said house, and that Mr. Stephen T. Northam be requested to desire Mr. Rodman to instruct the scholars that are under his care by Mr. Kay's donation, to teach them the catechism agreeably to the Episcopal mode, at least once a week, and that the children that are admitted in said school must produce to Mr. Rodman a certificate from the Rector, the Wardens, or one of the Vestry of Trinity Church.

Voted: That the Wardens be directed to pay the instalments as they become due, for the three shares subscribed by F. Brinley, Esq., for the Corporation of Trinity Church, at the Union Bank in this Town, agreeably to the regulations, as directed by said bank, which installments are to be paid from the monies arising from Mr. Kay's donation.

Voted: That the Rev. Mr. Wheaton be requested to deliver a sermon, as soon as possible, on the subject of the proposed plan for promoting the subscription for raising a permanent fund for the better support of the Church.

February 7, 1811. Voted: That the Wardens be a committee to wait upon Mr. Neupeau and acquaint him that the congregation will employ him as organist on the commencement of Easter, provided he qualifies himself to officiate as such by that time, allowing him the same annual compensation as was paid to Mr. Berkenhead.

[Mr. Samuel Whitehorne had heard of Mr. N'Pau in Philadelphia, as a person who might fill the position of organist, and who, on learning that the Vestry were disposed to give him a trial, wrote to the Senior Warden, as follows. For some reason, probably a want of proper qualifications, he was never appointed as organist. The letter is without date :]

Sir: I thank you for your kind advice of becoming an organist in the Trinity Church at next Easter. I resolved therefore to accept the kind offer of the Vestry of the Trinity Church, if those gentlemen find me qualified for it.

I therefore request you, sir, to inform those gentlemen that I wish very much that they would be very strict in their vote. And should any person of this town be better qualified to it than I, that I should rather prefer to give to real merit the preference, than to take my own advantage.

I am with respect your Obt. Servt,

FRED. N'PAU.

April 1, 1811. Voted: That the custom of carrying around the box every Sunday, immediately after the sermon, be discontinued, and in lieu thereof it be carried round on the last Sunday in every quarter.

CHAPTER XIX.

Easter Monday, April 15, 1811.

Samuel Whitehorne elected Senior Warden, and Edward Easton, Junior Warden.

Vestrymen: Francis Brinley, Saunders Malbone, Benj. Gardiner, Henry Sherburne, Wm. Crooke, William Littlefield, Robt. N. Auchmuty, Benj. B. Mumford, Simeon Martin, John P. Mann, John Wood, Edward Brinley, Samuel Whitehorne, Stephen T. Northam, Edward Easton.

Benj. B. Mumford, Clerk of the Vestry, Uriah Gorton, Sexton.

Voted: that the salary of the clerk be fifty dollars per annum, and that of the sexton be thirty-nine dollars.

Voted: that Messrs. Brinley, Auchmuty, Gardiner, Crooke, Martin and Whitehorne be delegates to the State Convention. The tax was to continue the same.

The Vestry were authorized and empowered to select and appoint a clerk for the ensuing year.

Voted: that Messrs. Mumford, Thos. Handy and John G. Whitehorne be a committee to inquire whether ten scholars can be obtained, and if attainable, the committee to write to Mrs. Clarke, at New York, and propose to her to be the organist of the Church, stating to her the amount of salary (being one hundred and ten dollars) the Church is willing to give.

Voted: that the grateful thanks of this congregation be made to Levi Tower and Samuel O. Auchmuty, Esquires, for their services under the Church, the past year, and that they be requested to continue the same until the committee hear from Mrs. Clarke, at New York.

At this meeting the following note from Mr. John Bours,[258] a member of the Vestry, was read :

" Mr. Bours presents his best and most affectionate regards to the Rev. Mr. Wheaton, Rector, and to the Wardens and Vestry of Trinity Church, and requests that he may not be re-elected at the choice of Church officers, on Easter Monday next, as the infirmities incident to his period of life, added to very ill health, render him utterly unable longer to discharge his duty as a member of the Vestry.

Newport, April 13, 1811."

June 11, 1811.   Voted : that Thomas H. Mumford be and he is hereby appointed clerk of the Church for the remaining part of the year, at the rate of $50 per annum.

July 2, 1811.   Voted : that Mr. Manchester be instructed one quarter, by Miss Towle, at the expense of the Church, and that the Wardens pay the same.

---

[258] There had been no more prominent and efficient layman in the Church, for a period of forty-six years, than Mr. Bours ; and there is abundant evidence in the records that he was an exemplary Christian. It has been said that he was the leader of those who were opposed to Rev. James Sayre.   The writer at one time entertained the same views, but he is now constrained to say there is no warrant for it.   From what has since been brought to light in regard to the character of Rev. Mr. Sayre, it is evident that his mind was then diseased, and it is known that he was insane at the time of his death.

At the time of these troubles in the Church, Mr. Bours was clerk of the Vestry, and it is to his credit that there does not appear on the records any evidence of any misunderstanding between the pastor and the people.

That Mr. Bours led a godly life we may reasonably believe, for had it been otherwise the congregation would not have urged him to take orders and become their settled minister.   He died July 26, 1815, in his 81st year.

August 5, 1811. Voted: that the Wardens wait upon Samuel O. Auchmuty, Esq., and make him the grateful thanks of this Vestry for his past favors, and request him as a particular favor conferred upon them, to officiate upon the organ until a permanent organist can be obtained, and that he be requested to accept the salary assigned to the organist.

August 19, 1811. Voted: that the resignation of Thomas H. Mumford be accepted as clerk of the Vestry.

Voted: that Captain Easton be authorized to wait upon Levi Tower, and request him to set the psalms until an organist can be procured.

September 2, 1811. Voted: that Mr. Tower be requested to set the psalms in his pew, and that he be allowed and paid at the rate of $55 per annum for the time he may serve.

October 13, 1811. Married, at Trinity Church, by Rev. Dr. Dehon, Thomas William Moore. [His Britannic Majesty's Vice Consul at Philadelphia, to Mary, daughter of George Gibbs. She died October 14, 1813.]

November 11, 1811. Whereas, Mr. Mallet, an organist from Boston, has been recommended to the Vestry as a gentleman well qualified to officiate in the Church, and whereas, the Easter meeting restricted the salary of the organist to $110, voted: that Colonel Sherburne, be, and he is hereby authorized, to write to Mr. Mallet and acquaint him that the salary cannot be exceeded by the Vestry, but a number of gentlemen will make up that salary to $133, equal to £30 sterling.

Voted: that notice be given in the next *Newport Mercury*, by the Senior Warden, to the proprietors or owners of pews in the Church, unless they pay up the taxes and assessments now due, they [the pews] will be sold by public auction, agreeably to the law in such cases made and provided.

At a meeting of the congregation, held at the Church, December

16, 1811. Voted: that the report of the committee appointed for the purpose of obtaining subscribers for the fund of the Church be received, and that the subscription paper, with the report, be recorded verbatim in the Church record book.

Voted: that the congregation present to the Bishop of the Diocese $100, and that a collection be made in Church on Sunday next for that purpose; and if the above sum is not collected, that the balance be raised by subscription.

REPORT.

We, the undersigned, being appointed a committee by the congregation of Trinity Church, on the 9th of December, 1810, for the purpose of raising by subscription the sum of $6000, to be appropriated for a permanent fund, beg leave to report: that we have by our united endeavors accomplished the desirable end proposed, and are happy to state that the sum of *six thousand and fifty dollars* is now subscribed for the aforesaid, and that the subscription was completed on the 5th day of December, instant. All of which is respectfully submitted by

SIMEON MARTIN,
BENJ. GARDINER,
THOMAS HANDY,
STEPHEN T. NORTHAM,
SAM^L WHITEHORNE,
Committee.

Newport, 16th December, 1811.

Whereas, it appears by the report of Benjamin Gardiner, Simeon Martin, Thomas Handy and Stephen T. Northam, a committee appointed by the congregation, December 9th, 1810, to solicit subscriptions for raising a permanent fund for the better support of the Church, that they have accomplished that desirable object, by obtaining subscriptions to the amount of $6050, being the amount stipulated by the conditions of said subscriptions, in order to make it obligatory on the subscribers, in order to carry this laudable means into full effect. Voted: that the Vestry of the Church be, and they are hereby authorized and empowered to take such measures as they may think best for the collection of said monies, and for vesting the same whenever collected in such way and manner as they in their best judgment may think most promotive of the interest of the Church, agreeably to the conditions of the subscription; said subscription being completed on the fifth day of December instant.

It is further voted: that the first instalment, of twenty-five per cent. be paid on the 5th of March next, the second on the 5th of June next, the third on the 5th of September next, and the fourth and last, on the 5th of December next, and that the Vestry report their proceedings to this congregation on the first Tuesday in January, 1813.

The committee appointed by the Vestry of Trinity Church in the Town of Newport, in the State of Rhode Island, on the 21st of August, 1809, to report a plan for raising a permanent fund for the better support of Trinity Church, did respectfully offer the following, viz:

That a subscription be opened under the direction of the congregation for raising the sum of *six thousand dollars*, payable in one year, by quarterly instalments of 25 per cent., after the aforesaid sum is subscribed; and that the first payment be made in three months after the said sum of six thousand dollars shall be subscribed.

That an annual contribution be solicited for raising such further sums as, in addition to the sum subscribed for (with the interest that may accrue thereon) will amount to *Ten Thousand Dollars*, which contribution might perhaps be made in Church, by having a day, or part of a day, annually set apart for that purpose. That all money raised by subscription, contribution or donation, be put to interest, or vested in some description of permanent stock, under the direction of a committee to be appointed by the congregation for that purpose; and that none of the money raised as aforesaid, or the interest arising thereon, be appropriated or used for any purpose whatever, until the same amount to the aforesaid sum of *Ten Thousand Dollars;* after which the annual profit of said fund shall be at the disposal of the Corporation of Trinity Church, and that the subscription shall not be obligatory on any person until the amount of six thousand dollars shall be raised.

Now we, whose names are underwritten, being appointed the said committee, respectfully solicit the aid of all who have at heart the prosperity of the REDEEMER'S KINGDOM, and are desirous of promoting the immortal interest of man. We ask the assistance of all for the support of that religion which deeply affects the happiness [of] individuals, and on which the welfare of civil society greatly depends, that religion whose divine Author was ushered into the world by the acclamation of the heavenly hosts, proclaiming " Peace on earth and good will towards men."

Our brethren of the congregation of Trinity Church, and others who are disposed to support the gospel, are confidently invited to co-operate with us for the establishment of the proposed fund. Its sole object is the support of our excellent Church, a Church built upon the foundation of the Apostles and Prophets, Jesus Christ Himself being the chief corner-stone. According to our ancient Liturgy many of our fathers have here worshipped. They have left an inheritance which we cannot be so insensible as not highly to appreciate. Shall we not, then, exert ourselves to transmit to our children the blessings which we have the happiness to enjoy? Shall we not cheerfully contribute, according to the ability which God has given us, towards the accomplishment of what would doubtless very much tend to promote the prosperity of our Zion? We trust there are none who do not feel the propriety and justice of providing liberally for such as may labor among us, *in the Lord, even so hath the Lord ordained, that they who preach the gospel should live of the gospel.* Let us, then, enter with earnestness upon so important an undertaking. Let us accomplish an object whose beneficial effects will happily be felt by many in our own time and to prosperity.

SIMEON MARTIN,
BENJ. GARDINER,
STEPHEN T. NORTHAM,
THOMAS HANDY,
SAMUEL WHITEHORNE,
Committee.

For the purpose of raising a permanent fund for the better support of Trinity Church, in the town of Newport, we, the subscribers, agree and voluntarily bind ourselves and our heirs to pay the sum annexed to our respective names, by quarterly instalments of twenty-five per cent. The first payment to be made within three months after the subscription shall be completed. This subscription not to be binding, unless the sum of six thousand dollars shall be subscribed within two years from this date. Newport, 21st January, A.D., 1811. Witness our hands.

Simeon Martin, ...	$300
Benj. Gardiner, eight shares of the Newport Insurance Company, ...	400
Stephen T. Northam, ...	300
Edward Easton, ...	200
Samuel Whitehorne, ...	200
Francis Brinley, ...	200
Robert N. Auchmuty, ...	100
Samuel A. Auchmuty, ...	100
John G. Whitehorne, ...	300
Robert Robinson, ...	200
S. T. Northam, for Thomas Dennis, ...	200
Benj. B. Mumford, ...	100
Jnᵒ R. Sherman, ...	200
Francis Robinson, ...	100
John Wood, ...	100
Mary Gibbs, ...	300
John Banister, ...	100

Christopher G. Champlin,[259] $100
Margaret Champlin, ... 200
Robinson Potter,   .   . 100
Edward Martin, ... 100
John H. Wheelwright,   . 100
Henry Sherburne,   .   .   . 50
William Littlefield, .   .   . 100
John P. Mann,   .   .   . 100
Mary Scott,   .   .   .   100
Edward Brinley, ... 50
Edmund Thos. Waring,   .   .   . 50
John Bours, ... 100
Joseph Wood,   .   .   . 50
George W. Martin, ... 50
Benj. Gardiner, for Wm. Britton, ... 100
William Shaw, ... 20
Polly Miller, a pew in the Church, ... 20
Benj. W. Wood, ... 20
Jeremiah Lawton, ... 20

---

[259] attended the Congregational Church. He was the son of Christopher Champlin, was born in Newport, April 12, 1768, graduated at Harvard, travelled in Europe after completing his studies, and April 14, 1793, married Martha Redwood Ellery, daughter of Benjamin Ellery, and granddaughter of Abraham Redwood. In 1796 he was elected a Representative to Congress from Rhode Island, but resigned before he had completed his second term. In 1809 he was elected U. S. Senator, to fill the vacancy caused by the death of Francis Malbone, but an affliction that befel him in 1811 (the death of his son) led him to retire from public life. In 1803 he joined the Artillery Company, served in the ranks, then as Lieutenant, and finally as Colonel. March 28, 1840, full of years and respected by all who knew him, he passed from earth, dying in his own house in Newport. Mrs. Champlin, who was born March 13, 1772, died February 22, 1847.

John C. Phillips, .	$50
Daniel W. Barker,	20
Henry Shaw,	20
George Wanton, .	20
Chas. Baring, Jr., .	200
Samuel F. Gardner,	100
Jonathan Almy, .	5
William Crooke, .	100
Silas Dean, .	50
John L. Boss,	50
William Hunter, .	50
Benj. Hazard,	25
S. Malbone,	20
Wm. C. Gardner, .	100
Mrs. Jane Stewart,	20
Miss Nancy Stewart, .	20
Francis Brinley, 2d subscription, .	20
Simeon Martin, do do	20
Stephen T. Northam, 2d subscription, .	20
Edward Easton, " "	20
William Littlefield, " "	10
Henry Sherburne, " "	5
Samuel Whitehorne, " "	10
Cash, .	10
William Crooke, 2d subscription,	5
George W. Martin, " "	5
John R. Sherman, " "	20
John H. Mumford,	4
James Mumford, .	4
Edw[d] Brinley, 2d subscription, .	12
Edw[d] Martin, " "	10
John P. Mann, " "	20
John P. Mann, for Mary Scott, 2d subscription, .	10
John C. Phillips, " "	10
Katharine Skinner, .	50
John H. Wheelwright, 2d subscription,	5
	———
	$6050

February 3, 1812. William Littlefield and William Crooke, appointed to collect the first instalment of the above subscription, and they are directed to deposit the money in the Rhode Island Union Bank, to the credit of Trinity Church.

Easter Monday, March 30, 1812. Samuel Whitehorne elected Senior Warden, and Robert Robinson Junior Warden.

Vestrymen: Francis Brinley, Benj. Gardiner, Henry Sherburne, William Crooke, William Littlefield, Robert N. Auchmuty, Benj. B. Mumford, Simeon Martin, John P. Mann, John Wood, Edward Brinley, Sam¹ Whitehorne, Stephen T. Northam, Edward Easton, Robert Robinson, John G. Whitehorne, Silas Dean.

Benj. B. Mumford, Clerk of the Vestry. John Springer,[260] Sexton, with a salary of $50 per annum.

The selection of an organist was left with the Vestry.

Messrs. Francis Brinley, Auchmuty, Gardiner, Northam, Martin and Sam¹ Whitehorne, delegates to the convention.

The thanks of the Congregation were extended to Levi Tower and Samuel O. Auchmuty for their respective services during the past year.

April 1, 1812. Samuel O. Auchmuty was elected organist, with a salary of $150 per annum.

[260] From the time of his election as above, Mr. Springer performed the duties of sexton of the Church down to Easter, 1840, without interruption. At that time he addressed the following note to the Vestry. He was born March, 1770, and died November 4, 1850.

To the Wardens and Vestrymen of Trinity Church, Newport.

Gentlemen:

I have served as Sexton of Trinity Church for the past thirty years, and have endeavored faithfully to perform the duties of said office, and would most cheerfully continue so to do, did not my age prevent it. I am now seventy-one years old, and feel that I ought to withdraw, and I therefore respectfully request that you will not consider me a candidate for said situation.

May 12th, 1840.

May 20, 1812. Voted: that John G. Whitehorne and Capt. Northam have the trees around the Church-yard trimmed and cut agreeably to their judgment.

August 3, 1812. Voted: that $20 be presented to Mr. Levi Tower, for his services while Clerk of the Church.

December 21, 1812. Baptized Richard, the property of Margaret Nowell.[261] Sponsors, Cudgo Gibbs, Harry Vaughn and Margaret Bours. Also Sarah Wilson, daughter of James and Sarah Danzell; Sponsors, Cudgo Gibbs, Catharine Nowell and Margaret Bours.

February 8, 1813. Voted: that in future no person shall be allowed to order the sexton to dig any grave in the church-yard, nor shall the sexton dig any grave in the church-yard without the direction of the Wardens, and in their absence, by the order and direction of the Clerk of the Vestry.

April 12, 1813. The Senior Warden laid before the Vestry Mr. Wheaton's, the Rector's, letter, praying for an increase of salary, and it being addressed to the congregation as well as to the Vestry, Voted: that the Rector be requested to request the gentlemen of the Congregation to remain after divine service in the afternoon of Sunday next, to take into consideration the subject-matter of the Rector's letter.[262]

---

[261] The Nowells, of South Carolina, were much in Newport. Elizabeth Warden Nowell "lovely in person and amiable in manners," daughter of Edward Brown Nowell, and granddaughter of Dr. Lionel Chalmer, of Charleston, died here in 1820, at the age of 19 years. Her oldest brother, Edward Saville Nowell, lieutenant of marines, U. S. N., also died here. They were both buried in the church-yard.

[262] Newport, 12th April, 1813.

To the Wardens, Vestrymen and Congregation of Trinity Church in Newport, in the State of Rhode Island.

After a residence among you of two years and nearly six months, it is with pleasure I can say, that the utmost harmony has continually prevailed in the Church; that much attention and kindness have been shown

April 18, 1813.   At a meeting of the congregation, the Rector's letter was read, and after mature deliberation it was

Voted and resolved : that it is inexpedient to raise the Rector's salary during the present year.

Easter Monday, April 19, 1813.   The Wardens, Vestry and other officers of the Church were re-elected.

---

me, and that my salary has ever been paid with scrupulous punctuality. Exertions, too, have not been wanting to perpetuate the temporal interests of the Church by the establishment of a *permanent fund.*   While I congratulate you on those pleasant events, it is with pain I behold the gloomy state of our political affairs, and the consequent distresses and calamities with which this town is visited.

Under all these circumstances, it is not without much reluctance I feel myself obliged to make further demands upon your goodness, in order that according to divine appointment, I may *live of the gospel.*

You will no doubt recollect the conditions on which I accepted the rectorship of your Church were : that if on trial my present salary should be found insufficient for a decent and competent support, the congregation, on a fair representation, would not fail to make it such.

I find, since I have been at housekeeping, that my expenditures have exceeded my income, which obliges me, at this difficult time, to make this statement to you, that it may "*stir up your minds by way of remembrance.*"

With sentiments of esteem and respect,

I remain your obedient, humble servt.,

S. WHEATON.

The following letter, in reply to the above, was addressed to the Rev^d Mr. Wheaton :

Newport, April 23d, 1813.

Revd Sir:

The undersigned, a committee appointed by the Congregation of Trinity Church, to communicate to you their determination in relation to your request for an increase of salary, do themselves the honor to enclose the vote of the congregation on that subject.

We did ourselves the pleasure yesterday of waiting on you for the pur-

Charles Manchester was elected organist, to be paid at the rate of $55 per annum.

Delegates to the Convention: Francis Brinley, Benj. Gardiner, Stephen T. Northam, Simeon Martin and Samuel Whitehorne.

Voted: that seven members shall form and constitute a quorum, at their meetings, and that they are hereby empowered to transact all business that may or shall come before them, and the business so done and transacted by them shall be obligatory upon the congregation, as if done and transacted by a greater number.

October 5, 1813. Charles Welles,[263] of the privateer Dart, a native of St. John's, was buried by Rev⁴ Mr. Wheaton.

December 6, 1813. Voted: that the Rector, Rev⁴ Mr. Wheaton, be and he is hereby requested to preach a sermon for the benefit of the Church at Greenfield, Massachusetts, after the Holy Days having expired, agreeable to their letters and the Bishop's recommendation.

January 10, 1814. Voted: that Samuel Whitehorne, Stephen T. Northam and Silas Dean be a committee to investigate the state of the permanent fund, and that they devise some method for completing it as speedily as possible, and also to consider and form a plan for the better support of the Church in the meantime, till the fund can be brought into operation.

pose of announcing and explaining to you the vote, and the views and motives of the Congregation in adopting it. It was a vote passed without a dissenting voice; and our object in waiting on you was to make you sensible that the distress of the times justified the proceeding on the part of the congregation.

We are, with sentiments of great respect,

Your obedient, humble servants.

The above is from an unsigned draft of a letter.

[263] The Dart, a British privateer, was captured off Point Judith by the U. S. Revenue Cutter Vigilant, and brought into Newport. Welles, her first lieutenant, was killed in the action.

February 7, 1814. Voted : that Mr. Benj. Hazard be requested to draft a petition to the General Assembly of this State, to raise by lottery $8000, clear of all expenses, which sum, when realized, be added to the permanent fund of the Church.

Voted: that Mr. Hazard[264] be requested to present and advocate the same in the Legislature.

Voted: that this Vestry cannot approve of the request of the Rector, to call the congregation together, for the purpose of increasing the tax on the pews.

March 7, 1814. Voted : that a subscription be opened, and that a sum be raised (more or less) and be presented to the Rector, as a compensation from the subscribers, and that his correspondence will be laid before the congregation and a decision had upon the same.

April 4, 1814. Voted: that Messrs. Northam, S. Martin and S. Dean be a committee to wait upon Benj. Hazard, Esq., and obtain his legal opinion relating to the lease given by Richard Harrison, Esq., of New York, to this Church, and whether Mr. Harrison is not bound to keep the said estate in as good repair, and to prevent it from falling into a yearly decay, as when he received it.

---

[264] Benjamin Hazard, son of Thomas G. Hazard and Mary Easton, his wife, was born in Middletown, September 9, 1774. He graduated at Brown University in 1792, was admitted at the bar in 1796, commenced the practice of law in Newport, and here followed his profession with honor during the rest of his days. As early as 1809 he was elected a Representative to the General Assembly, and only retired from that position in 1840. His ability was marked, and his integrity was never questioned. He married Harriet Lyman, daughter of Major Daniel Lyman and Mary Wanton (the beautiful daughter of John Wanton) his wife. In the Wanton house on Broad street, now Broadway, he resided, and there died, March 10, 1841, aged 67 years.

CHAPTER XX.

1817–1821.

EASTER MONDAY, April 11, 1814. Wm. C. Gardner elected Senior Warden and Henry Shaw Junior Warden.

Vestrymen: Francis Brinley, Benj. Gardiner, William Crooke, Wm. Littlefield, Benj. B. Mumford, Simeon Martin, John Wood, Edward Brinley, Samuel Whitehorne, Stephen T. Northam, Edw. Easton, Robert Robinson, John G. Whitehorne, Silas Dean and Edw. Martin.

Benj. B. Mumford, Clerk of the Vestry, and John Springer, Sexton.

Charles Manchester was continued as organist, with a salary of $75 per annum.

Delegates to the Convention: Francis Brinley, S. Martin, Benj. Gardiner, Stephen T. Northam, and William C. Gardner.

Voted: that whereas, Miss Ruth Gibbs, in behalf of her family, has prayed by letter, permission to erect a monument in the Church-yard, that the prayer of said letter be, and is hereby referred to the consideration of the next Vestry, and that their opinion and decision thereon shall be binding upon the Congregation, as if voted this day.

Voted: that whereas, the Rev^d Mr. Wheaton, the Rector of this Church, has requested an increase of salary, and that the letter of the Committee, dated August 24, 1810, who were authorized by this Congregation to invite him to take charge of this Church, be laid before the Congregation, which being done, after duly considering the premises and knowing the limited circumstances of the Church revenue and the impracticability of augmenting the taxes on the pews, that it is at the present moment inexpedient to raise his salary.

Voted: that the grateful thanks of this Congregation be made Col. Henry Sherburne, for twenty-one years of faithful services as a vestryman of this Church.

May 2, 1814. Voted: that the Senior Warden be requested to furnish the Rector with $100, to meet his expenses, to attend the General Episcopal Convention, to be convened in the city of Philadelphia.

June 6, 1814. Voted: that the thanks of this Vestry be, and they are hereby made to Benj. Gardiner, Esq., for his attending the General Convention, and for his correct report of its proceedings.

June 21, 1814. Voted: that the application of Major-Gen. Sheldon for permission to ring the bell, and to suspend several lighted lamps in the lantern, in case of an alarm, under the immediate direction of the Church Sexton, be and is hereby granted, provided that Maj.-Gen. Sheldon shall cause one or more discreet persons to be stationed in the Church lantern, there to remain so long as the lighted lamps shall continue burning, to prevent the steeple from taking fire.

July 4, 1814. Voted: that whereas Mrs. Mary Gibbs having requested this Vestry for liberty to dig a vault in the west end of the Church-yard, for the purpose of interring her family therein, be and is hereby permitted and authorized to dig a vault 16 feet by 12 feet, she paying for the same $100, and that the ground covered by said vault remain to her, her heirs and assigns forever, in fee simple.

September 5, 1814. Voted: that the sum of $30 be paid by the Senior Warden to the Rev^d Mr. Wheaton, for his attendance at the convention of the Diocese, to be holden at Portsmouth.

October 17, 1814. Voted: that the Senior Warden be authorized to hire a sum of money sufficient to purchase ten cords of wood, including the cost of sawing and piling, and present the same to Mr. Wheaton, the Rector of the Church.

Voted: that the Wardens be requested to take around the box every Sunday afternoon, immediately after the sermon, to collect such donations and pew rents as may be given and paid to them.

March 13, 1815. Voted: that in consequence of the application of the Rev^d Mr. Wheaton, stating his pressing necessities, the Senior Warden be, and he is hereby authorized to advance him $50, and that this Vestry will lay the same before the Congregation on Easter Monday next, for their approval.

Voted: that whereas, the Rev^d Mr. Wheaton having made a verbal communication to this Vestry, stating, in purport, that an increase of salary is desirable, that Benj. Gardiner, Esq., Wm C. Gardner, Senior Warden, Henry Shaw, Junior Warden, and Benj. B. Mumford, Clerk of the Vestry, be a committee to wait upon him, and receive his request in writing, stating fully his views upon that subject, for the purpose of laying the same before the congregation on Easter Monday next.

March 20, 1815. The Vestry having taken into consideration the communication of the Rev^d Mr. Wheaton, of the 6th inst., did present him with $50, are obliged from various circumstances, candidly to inform him, that they can do no more, and that they cannot pledge themselves to supply him with his wood for the ensuing winter.

Easter Monday, March 27, 1815. The officers of the Church and the Vestrymen were re-elected, and Henry Shaw and Levi Tower were added to the Vestry.

Voted: that seven members of the Vestry shall form a quorum.

Voted: that the Trustee of the permanent fund shall make a

statement of all outstanding notes and subscriptions due to said permanent fund, together with the amount collected and funded, Easter Monday next.

Voted: that the tax due from Mr. Levi Tower,[265] on his pew, No. 11, in consideration of his service, by directing the organist and setting the psalms, be remitted; but the amount thus remitted extends to the claims the Church has upon Mr. Tower since his occupancy of said pew, but does not extend to any demands against said pew previous to that time.

May 1, 1815. Mr. Manchester was elected organist on a salary of $75 per annum; but on the 5th of June the Wardens were instructed "to pay off Mr. Manchester, and acquaint him that the Church has no further need of his services as an organist."

Baptized, May 4, 1815, William and Mary, both the property of Charles Baring, Esq. Sponsors, Joseph, Thomas and Nancy Baring, and Nancy, a free woman of color.

June 12. Voted: that the Wardens, with Wm Crooke, Esq., wait upon Miss Mary Towle and thank her for her polite and kind offer to officiate upon the Church organ, and request she would be pleased to accept $100 per annum for the same.

Voted: that the Wardens, with Samuel Whitehorne, William Crooke, Edw. Brinley, Benj. Gardiner and Simeon Martin, Esquires, be a committee to devise ways and means for the better maintainance and support of the Church, and that they report in writing at our next meeting.

----

[265] Levi Tower graduated at Brown University in 1800, and found employment as assistant in Robert Rogers's school, in which school he became the successor of Mr. Rogers. For many years he was a prominent and successful instructor, until the infirmities of years made it necessary for him to give up teaching. He died June 4, 1854, aged 78 years.

June 27, 1815. Voted: that the report of the committee appointed at our last meeting, be accepted.

Voted: that S. T. Northam and J. G. Whitehorne be a committee to call upon each owner of a pew in the Church, and procure their consent in writing, to relinquish the use and occupation of their pew or pews to the Church, for the sole and exclusive purpose of having them hired out yearly at public auction, for five successive years, on each Easter Monday, from Easter Monday, A.D., 1816, to the highest bidder, and the rent that may accrue by their hire, shall be applied for the support of the Church and its officers, and at the expiration of the said five years, the pews shall revert to their present owners, or their heirs or assigns, free of all incumbrance whatsoever, that may accrue within that period, and that said committee report as soon as may be convenient.

October 2, 1815. Voted: that a committee be appointed to repair all the damage to the Church and steeple, occasioned by the recent violent gale of wind, and that the Wardens be requested to hire $200 to meet these necessary expenses.

November 6, 1815. Voted: that ten cords of oak wood be purchased by the Senior Warden, and presented to the Rev^d Mr. Wheaton, and that he pay for the carting, sawing and piling, charging the whole expense to the Church.

December 6, 1815. Voted: that all accounts against the Church, that shall or may hereafter lay dormant and unclaimed for six successive years, agreeable to the statute of limitation, of this State, shall not be allowed or paid, but be considered as given to the Church.

Voted: that the Vestry recommend to the congregation to give on each Sunday one cent to each individual of their families attending Church, to be deposited in the contribution box ; and that this laudable practice commence the first Sunday in January next.

AT A VESTRY MEETING,

Holden on the 6th day of December, A. D. 1815.

Voted, Unanimously, That the Vestry recommend to the Congregation to give One Cent on each Sunday, to each individual of their Family attending Church, to be deposited in the Contribution-box, when the same shall be brought round immediately after the Sermon, and that this laudable practice commence the first Sunday in January next.

Voted, That the above Vote be printed, and a Copy placed in each Pew of the Church.

A true Copy, as extracted from the Records :—

Attest,   *BENJAMIN B. MUMFORD,*
                                              Clerk of the Vestry.

February 5, 1816. Voted: that the Vestry recommend to the Rector, to cause the bell in future to ring but ten minutes, and to toll but ten minutes.

Voted: that pews No. 6, 10, 24, 55, 56 and 60 be disposed of at auction to the highest bidder, on the third Monday of May next, unless the amount due on them be paid previous to that day.

Easter Monday, April 17, 1816. Edward Brinley elected Senior Warden and Stephen T. Northam, Junior Warden. The Vestrymen were re-elected, with the exception of Henry Shaw.

Voted: that a tax of ten dollars be assessed on the pews below, and that a tax of two dollars be assessed on the pews above stairs.

Voted: that Levi Tower be clerk of the Church, at a salary of $50.

Voted: that no money belonging to Trinity Church, in Newport, shall be hereafter expended by the Vestry, for any other purpose

than to comply with the appropriation made on the previous Easter
Monday ; for such necessary expenses as may occur for the Rec-
tor's attendance on Convention and for all necessary repairs to the
Church property.

May 6, 1816.   Voted unanimously : that the proceedings of this
Vestry forever hereafter be kept a profound secret, and that no
communication whatever shall be made known, either of opinions,
arguments or form of vote, to any one out of the Vestry ; except it
be to a member of this body who may happen not to be present at
a Vestry meeting.

Voted unanimously : that this Vestry accepts with sentiments of
real pleasure and esteem, the kind and generous offer of Miss
Catharine Tweedy, of placing the portrait of our late venerable
pastor, the Rev^d Mr. Honyman,[266] in the Vestry room; and that
the Clerk of the Vestry furnish Miss Tweedy with a copy of this
vote, as a mark of our sincere attachment to so amiable a character,
and to her for her politeness and attention.

May 26, 1816.   A copy of the Constitution for the Church in
this State being submitted and compared, article by article, with the
old Constitution now in force; thereupon voted : that Articles Nos.
1 and 2 be approved.

Voted : that the 3d Article be and the same is hereby approved,
with this amendment, that the words " not exceeding four " be
added after the word " delegates."

Voted : that Articles 4th, 5th and 6th be approved.

Voted : that Article 7th be approved, with the amendment, that
the words " by any two members " be added, and the words " two
votes " be stricken out.

---

[266] This picture is the one referred to in a notice of Rev. James Honyman, page 95, where the gift is erroneously credited to Mrs. Malbone.

Voted: that Article 8th be approved.

July 1, 1816. Voted: that the Rector, with Messrs. Brinley and Samuel Whitehorne, be a committee to attend quarterly the examination of Mr. Rodman's school, and see that the charity scholars are taught those rudiments of learning as prescribed by the will of the late Mr. Kay, and that they report quarterly to the Vestry the progress of said children in their learning.

October 2, 1816. Voted unanimously: that the thanks of this Vestry be presented to the Rev^d Mr. Morrice A. Lance, for officiating in our church during the absence of our Rector, and that the Clerk of the Vestry be directed to transmit to him a copy of this vote, as a testimony of our gratitude and esteem.

October 2, 1816. Buried Godfrey Wainwood, aged 77 years.

October 7, 1816. Voted: that the Rector, Messrs. Benj. Gardiner, Samuel Whitehorne, William Hunter and Wm. Crooke, be a committee to prepare a new charter for the Church, and as soon as it is prepared, to report the same to this Vestry.

October 20, 1816. Voted: that the charter reported by the committee, consisting of ten sections, having been distinctly read over, section by section, be, and the same is hereby adopted.

Voted: that the Rector be requested to notify the Congregation to meet at 12 o'clock, on Monday next, for the purpose of laying before them the aforesaid charter for their approval, amendment or rejection.

Meeting of the Congregation, October 28, 1816; the Rector being absent, Voted: that the Hon. Benj. Gardiner be moderator for this meeting,

Voted unanimously: that the Charter of Incorporation, consisting of ten sections, being read over, section by section, be, and the same is hereby received, approved and adopted, and that it be presented to the Honble General Assembly at this, their present October Session, for ratification and enactment.

Voted: that the petition addressed to the Honble General Assembly, praying for the adoption of the aforesaid charter[265] of incorporation, being read over by the Clerk of this Congregation, be, and is hereby approved, and that he, as Clerk of the Vestry and Congregation, sign the same, expressive of the sentiments and wishes of this congregation.

Voted unanimously: that the Honble Benj. Gardiner, Wm. C. Gardner and Benj. Hazard, Esquires, be a committee to present the charter and petition to the Honble General Assembly for a new incorporation, and press its adoption.

To the Honble General Assembly, to be holden at Providence, R I., on the fourth Monday of October, 1816.

The petition of the Minister, Church Wardens, Vestry and Congregation of Trinity Church in Newport, R. I., respectfully sheweth:

That from experience and the occurrence of difficulties and inconveniences, they find that their present charter of incorporation, granted them in the year 1769, is inadequate in its powers and provisions for the proper and beneficial management of their business and concerns; and they pray that a new Act of Incorporation, substantially in conformity to the draft of the act herewith presented, may be enacted by the General Assembly; and they, as in duty bound, will ever pray.

By order and in behalf of the said Minister, Wardens, Vestry and Congregation of Trinity Church, Newport, R. I.

BENJ. B. MUMFORD,
Sect'y of the Vestry and Congregation.

Newport, 28th October, 1816.

November 4, 1816. Voted: that the Secretary of this Vestry

---

[265] See appendix.

be, and is hereby required to procure a large sheet of vellum parchment, and have written thereon, in a strong, legible hand, the new charter, and have the same duly authenticated by the Secretary of this State; the whole expense to be paid by the Senior Warden out of the Church funds.

Voted: that William Hunter, Samuel Whitehorne, Esq'rs, and Benj. B. Mumford be a committee to draw up a code of By-Laws, for the future government of this corporation.

Voted: that Samuel Whitehorne, Esq., and Benj. B. Mumford be a committee to purchase a new set of books for this corporation.

Voted: that the Secretary of this Vestry be requested, and he is hereby authorized to procure a brass seal, of a reasonable size, for this corporation, and have the same handsomely engraved on the outer circle: "Trinity Church, Newport, R. I., Incorporated 1769," in the centre to have a raised cross, the head of the cross to be encircled with these words: "God Send Grace."

Voted: that the Revᵈ Rector be requested to commence the Evening Service in future, till the spring commences, precisely at half past two o'clock, and that he would be pleased to notify the congregation from the desk next Sunday.

December 2, 1816. Voted: that a note be addressed by the Secretary to the Revᵈ Rector, and request that he would be pleased, should it meet his approbation, to instruct the clerk to omit the afternoon chaunt, at least during the winter season.

January 6, 1817. Voted: that the grateful thanks of this Vestry, in behalf of the congregation, be made to Miss Sarah Freebody, for her present of a large bible to the Church, and that she be furnished with a copy of this vote.

Meeting of the corporation at Trinity Church, January 13, 1817. Voted: that the new charter, adopted by the General Assembly of this State, at their October session, 1816, consisting of ten sections, having been carefully read over, section by section, and after mature deliberation, the same be and is hereby fully approved and adopted as the charter of this corporation.

Voted : that Samuel Fowler Gardner be and is hereby elected Treasurer of this corporation till Easter next.

January 14, 1817. Voted : that Samuel Fowler Gardner, Esquire, the Treasurer, be and he is hereby authorized and empowered to dispose and to sell the three shares in the [Rhode Island] Union Bank, owned by this corporation, for the most they will command, and apply the proceeds, first, to reduce the note of $400 to $300 and, secondly, the surplus to the discharge of those debts that now exist against the Church.

March 3, 1817. Voted : that Messrs. Benj. Gardiner and Stephen T. Northam be a committee to wait upon Mr. Searl, and obtain his opinion in writing upon the responsibility of Mr. Harrison, arising upon the lease given by this corporation to him, and whether Mr. Harrison is not bound to indemnify the corporation for the destruction of the house, stable, out-houses and fences, that have occurred.

Voted : that the Vestry coincide with Rev^d Mr. Wheaton in sentiment, upon the utility of having divine service performed in the Church exclusive of Sundays, and they hope he will open the Church every Sunday evening, and on such other evenings as he may deem it conducive to the interest of the Church and the promotion of piety.

March 6, 1817. The committee appointed by the last Vestry, to obtain Mr. Searl's opinion in writing, upon the lease given to Mr. Harrison, of the Kay Estate, having presented and read the same, it is therefore voted : that the report of the committee, and also Mr. Searl's written opinion, be and is hereby received and accepted.

Voted : that the Vestry deem it absolutely expedient to prosecute Mr. Harrison upon his lease, for the waste and destruction made upon the Kay Estate, leased him by the " Minister, Wardens and Vestry of Trinity Church,"

Voted : that Messrs. Benj. Gardiner, Silas Dean, and Steph. T. Northam be a committee to carry into execution the preceding vote, at any time they may deem it most expedient.

Voted : that the committee employ as attorneys, to bring this suit, and defend the same, Messrs. Searl, Hunter and Hazard.

Easter Monday, 7th day of April, 1817.   Meeting in the Church.

Present : Edward Brinley, Silas Dean, James Mumford, Levi Tower, Robert Robinson, Wm. C. Gardner, Samuel Whitehorne, Samuel Fowler Gardner, Thomas White, Edward Martin, Henry Shaw, Dr. Charles Cotton, Stephen T. Northam, Benj. B. Mumford.

The following officers were elected :

Edward Brinley, Senior Warden.

James Mumford, Junior Warden.

Benj. B. Mumford, Secretary.

Levi Tower, Clerk, to set the psalmody.   Salary, $50 per annum.

Elizabeth Fowler, Organist.   Salary, $100.

John Springer, Sexton.   Salary, $40.

Vestrymen : Benj. Gardiner, Benj. B. Mumford, Stephen T. Northam, John Wood, Samuel Whitehorne, Robert Robinson, Jno. G. Whitehorne, Silas Dean, Levi Tower, Samuel Fairweather Gardiner, Robinson Potter.

Dr. Charles Cotton, Treasurer.

Hon. Simeon Martin, in consequence of his removing from town, declined a re-election as vestryman.

Delegates to the State Convention : Samuel Whitehorne, Steph. T. Northam, and Benj. B. Mumford.

May 8, 1817.   Voted : that the committee authorized at a former meeting to prosecute Mr. Harrison for the destruction and waste committed upon the Kay Estate, employ such counsel as they may deem expedient, either in or out of the State.

Voted : that the Sexton be directed, under the direction of Messrs.

Wood and Brinley, to set and erect all the gravestones that have fallen down in the church-yard, and cause such trees to be cut down as they may think proper.

May 12, 1817. The Treasurer was directed to pay to the Junior Warden, and he to the Rev^d Mr. Wheaton, $40, for the purpose of defraying Mr. Wheaton's expenses to the Episcopal General Convention, to be holden in New York on the 20th inst.

Messrs. Robinson and Potter were a committee to have the bell immediately repaired.

June 2, 1817. Voted: that the committee heretofore authorized to prosecute Mr. Harrison, be and is hereby directed to request Mr. Wells, counsellor-at-law, of the city of New York, to effect, if possible, a compromise with Richard Harrison, Esq., of the same city, for the waste and destruction committed upon the Kay Estate; and if no settlement can be effected with him, then to commence a suit against him for damages and reparation for the misimprovement of the estate aforesaid.

July 8, 1817. Voted: that the thanks of this Vestry be made to John Wells, Esq., Counsellor-at-Law, in the city of New York, for his distinguished attention, for his law information, given gratuitously to Benjamin Gardiner, Esq., in behalf of this Church; and that the Secretary be and he is hereby directed, to furnish him with a transcript of this vote, as a testimony of the great obligation they feel themselves under for the essential and important services rendered this Society.

Voted: that the Secretary be directed to purchase a folio Prayer Book, for the use of the Church, of Messrs. J. & T. Swords, at New York, not exceeding the cost of $20.

August 4, 1817. Benj. B. Mumford, a committee to inquire for and select a suitable person for organist.

Voted: that Miss Towle be paid all that is due to her as organist, previous to her leaving Newport.

Voted: that whereas Miss Mary Towle being about leaving Newport, and she having been so kind as to officiate for several years past upon the organ of the Church, the Secretary be, and he is hereby directed, to furnish her with a copy of this vote, as a testimony of our respect and esteem for her personally, and as approbatory of her judicious deportment during our acquaintance with her.

August 18, 1817. Whereas, the Revd Samuel Wydown,[269] a Baptist Minister, having applied to this Vestry for testimonials, for the purpose of obtaining Holy Orders, and we having been acquainted with him for these two years past, it is therefore voted: that we believe him to be a moral and pious character, and that he is attached to the doctrines and discipline of the Episcopal Church.

September 11, 1817. Buried at Bristol, R. I., by Rev^d Mr. Wheaton, Mrs. Elizabeth Griswold, wife of Revd Alexander Viet Griswold, Rector of St. Michael's, Bristol, aged 49 years.

September 17, 1817. Miss Eliza Davis was elected organist, with a salary of $60 per annum.

Voted: that the four first pews, on the west side of the broad aisle, be made into two pews, painted on the inside, and labelled on the outside " For Strangers," and kept for that purpose.

[The usual vote for the purchase of wood for the Rector was passed at this meeting.]

October 6, 1817. Voted: that the Church edifice be given to the members of St. Paul's Lodge, for their installation; and that

---

[269] The Standing Committee rejected the application of the Rev. Mr. Wydown, and the Vestry, on the 2d of February, 1818, realizing that they had been hasty, and had not with sufficient care looked into the character of the applicant, acknowledged their mistake in a vote passed at that time.

Messrs. Northam and Potter be a committee to wait upon Mr.
Wheaton, for his approbation.

Voted: that the vote passed the 14th of May, 1797, be so far repealed as relates to the collecting the $12 therein mentioned, and
that the Senior Warden in future collect that amount for all persons interred in the new burial ground.[269a]

November 24, 1817. Voted unanimously: that the grateful
thanks of this Vestry, in behalf of the congregation, be made to the
gentleman who so generously and unsolicited, gave to the Permanent Fund of this Church *Five Hundred Dollars;* and that the
Rev[d] Mr. Wheaton be requested to transmit a certified copy of this
vote to Wm. Dehon, Esq., of Boston, and by him to the benevolent
donor, who requested his name might be kept secret; but if it be
consistent with the feelings of the donor, the Vestry would be happy
to record his name, for so disinterested and kind act.

Voted: that the thanks of this Vestry be made to William
Dehon, Esq., of Boston, for the distinguished service rendered this
Church, by receiving and transmitting five hundred dollars, pre-
sented to the Permanent Fund of this Church.

January 6, 1818. Voted: that the Rev[d] Mr. Webb take the
school-house, upon the same terms that Mr. Rodman had hitherto
done; that he take immediate possession of the same under the
direction of the Rector and Wardens, and at the end of his term to
return the school-house in as good order, wear and tear always ex-
cepted, as he receives it.

Easter Monday, March 23, 1818. Present: The Rector, Oliver
H. Perry, Edward T. Waring, Silas Dean, James Mumford, Saunders Malbone, Samuel F. Gardiner, Charles Cotton, Samuel Fowler

---

[269a] The new burial ground was a small strip of land added to the graveyard, by purchase, at the extreme west end.

Gardner, Levi Tower, William Crooke, Benj. Gardiner, John B. Lyon, Samuel Whitehorne, John G. Whitehorne, Wm. Shaw, Benj. Hazard, William C. Gibbs[270] and Richard K. Randolph.

Dr. Charles Cotton elected Senior Warden.

S. Fowler Gardner, Junior Warden.

Vestrymen: Benj. Gardiner, Edw. Brinley, Benj. B. Mumford, Steph. T. Northam, Silas Dean, William Crooke, Saml Whitehorne, John G. Whitehorne, John P. Mann, Levi Tower, Robinson Potter.

Richard K. Randolph, Treasurer.

John B. Lyon, Sec'y to Corporation and Clerk to Vestry.

Miss Eliza Davis was chosen organist, salary $60, whose duty it shall be to attend and perform on every Sunday, Christmas and Good Friday.

Delegates to the State Convention: Benj. Gardiner, Samuel Whitehorne, Stephen T. Northam, Benj. B. Mumford.

Voted: that the tax of $10 on each pew be continued.

On motion of Stephen T. Northam it was voted: that a committee of five, Wm. C. Gibbs, Benj. Hazard, Edw. Brinley, Wm. Crooke and John P. Mann, be appointed to take into consideration the expediency of revising our present charter, and report to the corporation on the first Monday in May next.

Voted: that the practice of carrying the contribution box round the Church on Sundays be discontinued, but the quarterly collection be continued.

---

[270] William C. Gibbs was the son of George Gibbs. He was born February 10, 1790, and died February 24, 1871. His wife was Mary Kane, daughter of Charles Kane, of New York, to whom he was married in 1822. In the political excitement in 1821 he was elected Governor of the State of Rhode Island, and held the office till 1824. He had also represented Newport in the Legislature, and for many years was a prominent citizen of Newport.

April 7, 1818. Voted: that the fence around the two-acre lot be immediately repaired, at the expense of the Church.

Voted: That the committee who were to attend to the above be requested to make an arrangement with the Rector, by allowing him $24 per year for the rent of the said lot, and the Church take the lot under their own direction.

Voted: that in consideration of services rendered the Rector and his family by Doct. Edmund T. Waring, that the tax now due from him be relinquished.

Voted: that the owners of the following pews being in arrears for taxes, that the pews be advertised for sale immediately—Nos. 35, 50, 52, 60, 61, 70 and 89.

Meeting of the Corporation, May 4, 1818.

The committee appointed on Easter Monday made report in part; thereupon it was

Voted: that the following amendments be made to the Charter, viz.:

"Be it enacted by the General Assembly, and by the authority thereof it is enacted, that the election of officers by the Corporation of Trinity Church shall be by ballot without nomination."

Voted: that the committee heretofore appointed upon the subject of amendments to the Charter be continued, and directed to ascertain the powers and duties of the Rectors of this Church previous to the charter last granted, and also the powers and duties of Rectors of other Episcopal Churches in this State, and to report to the congregation on Thursday next, at eleven o'clock, A.M.

The following motion was made by James Mumford, and referred to the committee on the revision of the charter: "That the charter be so far altered that no pew shall be sold or held responsible for the payment of any other charges or expenses, except the actual repairs on the church edifice.

May 18, 1818. The committee to make an arrangement with the Rector respecting the two-acre lot, made a verbal report, that they had, with the consent of the Rector, rented the lot for five years, at an annual rent of $24, the tenant to be at the expense of fencing.

Voted: that the Wardens be authorized to have the steeple repaired and secured immediately.

Voted: that the Rector be requested to furnish annually, on the first of December, a list of the poor of the Church for the use of the Vestry.

Voted: that the Sexton be directed not to deliver the keys of the Church to any person except the Wardens or Vestry, without an order from one of the Wardens.

June 3, 1818. Voted: that the Wardens be empowered to have the spire painted and the balls and vane gilded.

June 5, 1818. At a meeting of the corporation, the committee appointed at Easter, on the revision of the charter, made a verbal report, and recommended the adoption of the following:

" That in the election of any Minister of this Church, as provided by the sixth section of the charter, the vote of three-fifths of all the members of the corporation shall be required to make a choice, and by the same number of votes any Minister of said Church may be removed by the corporation; three months' previous notice of said removal having been given to him; and upon similar notice, any such Minister shall at all times be at liberty to withdraw from s^d Church."

Whereupon it was voted: that the above bill be passed, and that Benj. Hazard and Wm. C. Gibbs, Esquires, be a committee to present the bill passed at the Corporation Meeting, May 4th, and the above bill, to the General Assembly at their next session, for their sanction, as amendments to the constitution.

A motion was made that the Charter be so far amended as that the Rector shall be admitted into the Vestry, which motion was negatived.

Voted: that the Wardens be authorized and directed to have the organ removed as far back as they shall think proper.

July 1, 1818. Voted: that the Church edifice be painted, without and within, and whitewashed; that the trees within the Church-yard be cut down below the earth; that the fences be put in perfect repair, and that a committee be appointed to solicit subscriptions to defray the expense: O. H. Perry,[271] Wm. C. Gibbs, Stephen T. Northam and Robinson Potter to be that committee.

August 5, 1818. Voted: that the floor of the Church be sheathed and painted.

August 21, 1818. Voted: that the Wardens be authorized to have the outside of the pews painted stone color; and they were instructed to purchase six yards of silk velvet and gold fringe for the desk, etc.

---

[271] with his family, occupied the Champlin pew, No. 14, north aisle, which pew is still in the possession of some of his descendants. On the wall over it there is a marble tablet, bearing this inscription:

"To the Memory of Commodore OLIVER HAZARD PERRY, U. S. Navy: Born at South Kingston, Rhode Island, August 23, 1785. Died while on a Diplomatic Mission to Venezuela, Aug. 23, 1819.

"His Remains were brought to this Place by order of the Government, in the U. S. ship Lexington, and Re-interred by his Native State, in 1827.*

"History records his Public Deeds and Private Worth.

"This Tablet is erected by his Widow, ELIZABETH CHAMPLIN PERRY, August, 1855, as a mark of her continued Affection and Respect for his Memory."

* An error; it should be 1826.

September 2, 1818.   Voted: that the Wardens be authorized to have the under part of the benches painted light lead color, and the Creed, Commandments, and Lord's Prayer, on the Altar, painted, lettered and gilded.

Voted: that in future no colored people be allowed to sit down stairs.

Voted: that owing to the numbers of the pews being altered, that a new register of the pews, as they now are, with the former numbers, be recorded on the Vestry books.

Voted: that the pews belonging to the Church be exposed for sale on the 5th inst. at public auction, and if they bring the price appraised, or over, to sell them.

October 12, 1818.   Voted: that the Vestry will not allow the carpenters, for their work on the steeple, over $1.50 per day.

October 18, 1818.   Voted: that the Corporation present the Rector with ten cords of wood.

November 4, 1818.   Voted: that the Vestry grant for the use of the Sunday School the belfrey of the Church; the same to be put in repair under the direction of the Wardens.

December 9, 1818.   Voted: that the Wardens be authorized to purchase a foot-stove for the Rector.

February 3, 1819.   Voted: that the Wardens be authorized to purchase a foot-stove for the organist, and direct the sexton to furnish fire for the same.

Voted: that Mr. Samuel Whitehorne, the Treasurer of the Permanent Fund, be authorized to give Isaac Winslow and Saunders Malbone, Executors of the estate of the late Mrs. C. Malbone, a bond of indemnity in case any demands should be presented against the estate, to bear an equal proportion, according to the amount given by Mrs. Malbone to the Permanent Fund.

Easter Monday, April 12, 1819.   Present: John G. Whitehorne, Samuel Whitehorne, William Hunter, E. S. Hunt, Henry Potter,

E. T. Waring, Thos. Bush, John P. Mann, Wm. Shaw, Wm. Crooke, John Wood, Benj. Hazard, Levi Tower, Benj. Fry, Robinson Potter, Henry Bull,[272] Edward Brinley, Charles Cotton, Saunders Malbone and Stephen T. Northam.

Robinson Potter was chosen Senior Warden. Wm. H. Rathbone, Junior Warden. Richard K. Randolph, Treasurer. John B. Lyon, Sec'y of Corporation and Clerk of the Vestry.

Vestrymen: Benj. Gardiner, Edward Brinley, B. B. Mumford, Steph. T. Northam, Silas Dean, Wm. Crooke, S. Whitehorne, J. G. Whitehorne, John P. Mann, Levi Tower, John Wood.

Miss Eliza Davis was chosen organist, salary $80. John Springer, Sexton.

Delegates to State Convention: Benj. Gardiner, John P. Mann, Steph. T. Northam.

Voted: that the tax of ten dollars on each pew be continued.

Voted: that in consequence of the indisposition of Mr. Wheaton in the year ——, which caused him an extraordinary expenditure, that the sum of $96 be and is hereby voted him.

June 13, 1819. At a meeting of the Corporation held in the Church,

------

[272] *Henry Bull.* was born at Newport, August 29, 1778, and died October 12, 1841. He was of the fifth generation from Governor Henry Bull, one of the original purchasers of Aquidneck, now the island of Rhode Island. Thrown upon his own resources in early life, he began business in Newport at the age of sixteen years, and in 1803 was both master and supercargo of a vessel bound for the West Indies. In 1807 he was in business in Newport, and continued to be engaged in commercial pursuits up to the time of his death. For nearly twenty years he was a leading and useful member of the General Assembly, and in 1836 he was chosen a Presidential Elector. To the history of the State and town he gave much attention, and he wrote a valuable series of papers known as "Memoirs of Rhode Island," which were published in the *Rhode Island Republican.*

Voted : That the Minister be reinstated in the Vestry and placed in the same situation he was before the last revision of the Charter.

Voted: that Wm. Hunter, W. Crooke and J. P. Mann be a committee to make what alteration is necessary in the charter for carrying the above vote into effect, and that they present the same to the next meeting of the State Legislature for their sanction.

July 12, 1819. The Senior Warden reported that Mr. Harrison had made a proposition to pay the Church $2000 on account of lease of the Kay Estate—$1000 in one year, and $1000 in two years, and renew the lease, so that the rent shall be in proportion to the old lease;

Voted : that the proposition be acceded to.

Voted : that in future there shall not be any collection in church of the pew taxes, but that the Wardens be directed to have receipts. printed, and give them to each proprietor on their paying their dues.

August 4, 1819. Voted : that the application of the Rev^d Mr. Webb for the use of the Church school-house once or twice a week till the first of October next, for the purpose of the meeting of the singers of the Methodist Congregation, to practice singing therein, be, and the same is granted.

October 10, 1819. Voted : that the Senior Warden be authorized to purchase ten cords oak wood for the Rector, and have the same sawed and piled in the Parsonage cellar, and pay for the same out of the funds of the corporation.

December 1, 1819. Voted : that in future no fire be taken out of the stoves on Sundays or Prayer-days.[273]

---

[273] It had been the custom for many years for elderly ladies and persons in feeble health, to send a foot-stove to the Church just before the hour of service, where it was filled with live walnut coals from the stoves and placed in the owner's pew. An occasional gratuity made this extra work

Easter Monday, April 3, 1820.   Robinson Potter chosen Senior Warden, W. H. Rathbone, Junior Warden.

James Mumford, Treasurer; John B. Lyon, Secretary; Eliza Davis, Organist.

Vestrymen: Edward Brinley, Benj. B. Mumford, S. T. Northam, Wm. Crooke, Sam' Whitehorne, J. G. Whitehorne, John P. Mann, Levi Tower, J. Wood, Chas. Cotton.

John Springer, Sexton.

Voted: that the tax of ten dollars on each pew be continued.

Delegates to the State Convention: Messrs. Edward Brinley, John P. Mann, S. Whitehorne.

April 5, 1820.   Voted: that Benjamin Hazard be requested to draw up such a deed, to be made by the Corporation to Mr. Harrison, as he shall think will be proper for this Society to make and execute, and report the same to this Vestry.

Voted: that the tax now due, and that may hereafter annually accrue and become due upon Dr. Waring's pew, in consideration of his professional services rendered, and to be rendered, the Rev⁴ Rector and his family, be remitted.

Voted: That the Sunday-school that now assemble in the organ-loft be requested not to meet there in future, and that the same be exclusively reserved for the accommodation of the organist and singers.

July 8, 1820.   Voted: that the Society of which John G. Whitehorne is a member, be and they are hereby authorized and permitted, to meet in the Church and use the organ in their perform-

anything but a hardship to the sexton, who, to oblige all callers, frequently so reduced the quantity of coals in the stoves as to rob the congregation of the heat they had a right to look for.   This abuse led to the above order,

ances, and that the Senior Warden be requested to make known to the Rector the object of this vote.

August 2, 1820. Voted: that Robinson Potter, with either Benj. Hazard or Wm. Hunter, be a committee to make the arrangement with Mr. Harrison immediately.

September 11, 1820. Voted: that the Rector and Samuel White-horne be a committee to make such arrangements for the accommodation of the Clergy, that may attend the Convention, as they may think expedient.

October 4, 1820. Voted: that the organist be requested to accompany the organ with her voice in the voluntaries.

November 19, 1820. At a meeting of the corporation, voted: that six cords oak wood be purchased for the Rev^d Mr. Wheaton, and the same be sawed and piled in his cellar.

December 8, 1820. Voted: that the indenture and the terms and conditions thereof be and the same are hereby agreed to and confirmed, and that Jas. Mumford, Treasurer of the Corporation, be and he is hereby directed to affix thereto the common seal of s^d corporation and to sign the same in his said capacity, agreeably to the charter, to deliver the same to the said Richard Harrison, Esq., and to receive in exchange his part of s^d indenture, duly executed.

February 7, 1821. Voted: that the subject of the music be postponed until the next meeting of the Vestry, and that Doct. Mann be specially notified to attend.

Voted: that a pew be selected by the Wardens for the accommodation of John Handy's family, which shall be free of tax.

April 4, 1821. Voted: that the trustee of the Permanent Fund, the Senior Warden and the Treasurer, be directed to make out their accounts and inform the Auditors when made out and ready for their examination, so as to enable them to report thereon on Easter Monday.

April 11, 1821. Voted: that the Rector be requested to direct

the organist to sing the morning and evening hymns, if it meets
his approval.

Annual meeting of the corporation, Easter Monday, April 23,
1821.

Present: The Rector, Henry Bull, S. Fowler Gardner, Wm. H.
Rathbone, Henry Potter, Levi Tower, John G. Whitehorne, C. S.
Hunt, James Mumford, S. H. Cahoone, Robt. Robinson, Rob'n
Potter, H. S. Newcomb, Saml Whitehorne, Wm. Hunter, Chs.
Cotton, Wm. Crooke, Edw. Brinley, Wm. C. Gibbs.

The following gentlemen were duly elected officers for the year
ensuing:

Stephen T. Northam, Senior Warden.

Wm. H. Rathbone, Junior Warden.

Vestrymen: Edward Brinley, Benj. B. Mumford, Wm. Crooke,
S. Whitehorne, J. G. Whitehorne, John P. Mann, Levi Tower, Rob'n
Potter, Rob. Robinson, John B. Lyon.

Steph. H. Cahoone, Secretary; Jas. Mumford, Treasurer; Miss
Eliza Davis, Organist; salary, $80 per annum.   John Springer,
Sexton; salary, $40 per annum.

Voted : that the tax of ten dollars on each pew be continued, and
that the Wardens rent the gallery pews.

Delegates to the State Convention: E. Brinley, S. T. Northam,
J. P. Mann and S. Whitehorne.

Auditors: J. G. Whitehorne, S. Fowler Gardner.

The Treasurer of the Permanent Fund made the following report, which was received and ordered to be recorded:

PEWS IN TRINITY CHURCH, EASTER, 1821.

No.	Owners.	Occupants.
1	Church,	George Cox, one-half pew.
2	do	John Tew, one-half pew.
3	do	
4	do	Mrs. Lawton and Miss Burdick.

No.	Owners.	Occupants.
5	Thomas Bush,	Thomas Bush.
6	David King,[274]	{ David Melville, John B Lyon.
7	Mrs. Wickham,	{ Mrs. Wickham, Mrs. Miles.
8	Mrs. Gardiner,	{ Mrs. Gardiner, Mrs. Penrose.
9	Esther Freebody,	{ Steph. H. Cahoone, W. Norris.
10	Estate of Jona. Almy,	David Coggeshall.
11	Estate of Benj. Gardiner,	B. Gardiner's family.
12	Sarah Wood,	Almy Wood.
13	Margaret Champlin,	Margaret Champlin.
14	Margaret Champlin,	Sarah Greene.
15	Steph. T. Northam,	{ Steph. T. Northam, Mrs. Burdick.
16	Church,	Benjamin Brenton.
17	Mrs. John Langley,	Mrs. John Langley.
18	Church,	{ Mrs. McKenzie, Mrs. Morgan.
19	Estate of Silas Dean,	Miss Mary Dean.
20	William Crooke,	{ James Gardiner, Edw. C. Gardiner,
21	Church,	Mary Easton.
22	Miss Dillon,	Miss Dillon.
23	H. S. Newcomb,	H. S. Newcomb.
24	Thomas White,	Thomas White.
25	Robinson Potter,	Robinson Potter.

---

[274] *David King* — Dr. David King was born at Raynham, Mass., in 1774, graduated at Rhode Island College in 1796, became the pupil of Dr. James Thatcher, of Plymouth, Mass., and in 1799 began the practice of medicine in Newport, the field of his usefulness during the rest of his days. The first person vaccinated in Rhode Island, Walter Cornell, was vaccinated by Dr. King. Dr. King was one of the first promoters of the Rhode Island Medical Society, and held in turn the offices of Censor, Vice-President and President. Stricken with paralysis in August, 1834, he gradually failed till November 14, 1836, when he passed away. Mrs. Ann Gordon King, his widow, survived till November 9, 1852, when she died at the age of 70 years.

No.	Owners.	Occupants.
26	Samuel F. Gardner,	Samuel F. Gardner.
27	Henry Sherburne,	Henry Sherburne.
28	Samuel Whitehorne,	Samuel Whitehorne.
29	Charles O. Handy,	Thomas Handy.
30	{ Mrs. Wickham,	Mrs. Wickham.
	{ Mrs. Stewart,	Mrs. Stewart.
31	Edward Stanhope,	Edward Stanhope.
32	Church,	M. Sherman, one-half pew.
33	do	
34	do	
35	do	
36	do	Mrs. Townsend, one-half pew.
37	do	{ Russell Coggeshall,
		{ Catharine Thurston.
38	do	
39	do	
40	do	
42	do	Thomas W. Brown.
43	do	{ Miss Nicholi,
		{ Miss Mayberry.
44	Bannister Estate,	Sarah Freebody.
45	W. H. Rathbone,	W. H. Rathbone.
46	Nicholas Geoffroy,	Nicholas Geoffroy.
47	Henry Bull,	Henry Bull.
48	Robert Robinson,	Robert Robinson.
49	Estate of F. Malbone,	{ William Douglass,
		{ Susan Atkinson.
50	Edmund T. Waring,	Edmund T. Waring.
51	William Crooke,	William Crooke.
52	Estate of F. Brinley,	Mrs. Fry.
53	Permanent Fund,	Mrs. Moore.
54	Church,	Rector's Family.
55	do	
56	Permanent Fund,	Lieut. Lyon.
57	Estate of F. Brinley,	Mary Staunton.
58	Miss Susan Mason,	Mrs. O. H. Perry.
59	William Hunter,	William Hunter.
60	Estate of F. Malbone,	Mrs. Breese.
61	Levi Tower,	Levi Tower.
62	Thomas Dennis,	Mrs. Reece.

No.	Owners.	Occupants.
63	Estate of Peleg Wood,	Sarah Wood.
64	John G. Whitehorne,	John G. Whitehorne.
65	Benj. B. Mumford,	Benj. B. Mumford.
66	Henry Moore,	Henry Moore.
67	William Crooke,	James Mumford.
68	Church,	John Handy.
69	do	
70	do	
71	do	, William Rider.
72	do	{ Paul Mumford, C. Bannister.
73	John L. Boss,	John L. Boss.
74	Andrew V. Allen,	Andrew V. Allen,
75	Richard K. Randolph.	R. K. Randolph.
76	Edward Brinley,	Edward Brinley.
77	John P. Mann,	John P. Mann.
78	Estate of George Gibbs,	{ Charles Cotton, P. Johnson.
79	Stephen T. Northam,	S. T. Northam.
80	Estate of George Gibbs,	{ Wm. C. Gibbs, Mrs. Greene.
81	Jacob Smith,	Jacob Smith.
82	John G. Whitehorne,	Edward Martin.
83	Church,	
84	Sarah Freebody,	Mrs. Mason.
85	Church,	John W. Davis.
86	do	Henry Tisdale.
87	do	
88	do	John B. Gilpin.
89	Mrs. Gibbs,	Wm. C. Gibbs and Miss Greene.
90	William V. Taylor,	Wm. V. Taylor.
91	John R. Sherman,	John R. Sherman.
92	Estate of F. Robinson,	Henry Potter.
93	do do do	Benj. Hazard.
94	John R. Stanhope,	John R. Stanhope.
95	Jeremiah Lawton,	Jeremiah Lawton.
96	Church,	
97	do	Mary Wallace.
98	do	John B. Atkinson, one-half pew.
99	do	

TRUSTEE'S REPORT.

EXPENDITURES AND RECEIPTS ON ACCOUNT OF THE PERMANENT FUND
TO APRIL 21, 1821.

Dr.

To 61 Shares Union Bank, cost,	$6745.00
" 14 " Newport Bank, cost, . .	924.00
" 8 " Bank of Rhode Island, cost,	816.00
" Sundry expenses, . .	6.82
" Cash on hand, .	508.70
	$9000.52

Cr.

By Subscriptions, notes, collections at church, legacies and donations, ...	$5933.76
By Interest on shares in bank and on notes paid and renewed,	3066.76
	$9000.52

Note.—Amount received as per account above, . $9000.52

Sundry notes on hand, . . $841.93

Interest to April 21. 1821, . 227.00

1068.93

Amount due on subscription list, 165.00

Interest to April 21, 1821, . 86.00

251.00

Pew in church given by Mrs. Miller, valued at 50.00

Total amount of Permanent Fund, $10,370.45

I do not consider that more than nine thousand, three hundred and fifty dollars of the above can be estimated as good.

Signed,

SAMUEL WHITEHORNE, *Trustee.*

RECTORS OF TRINITY CHURCH.

Rev. Mr. Lockyer,	1698	to	1704
Rev. James Honyman,	1704	"	1750*
Rev. James Leaming,	1750	"	1754
Rev. Thomas Pollen,	1754	"	1760
Rev. Marmaduke Browne,	1760	"	1771*
Rev. James Sayre,	1786	"	1788
Rev. William Smith,	1789	"	1797
Rev. Theodore Dehon,	1798	"	1809
Rev. Salmon Wheaton,	1810	"	1840
Rev. Francis Vinton, D.D.,	1840	"	1844
Rev. Robert B. Hall,	1844	"	1846
Rev. Darius H. Brewer,	1846	"	1855
Rev. Alexander G. Mercer, D.D.,	1855	"	1860
Rev. Oliver H. Prescott,	1861	"	1863
Rev. John H. Black,	1863	"	1866
Rev. Isaac P. White, D.D.,	1866	"	1875*
Rev. George J. Magill,	1876	"	

SENIOR WARDENS OF TRINITY CHURCH.

Nicholas Lange,	1709	to	
Daniel Ayrault,	1719	"	1721
Nathaniel Newdigate,	1721	"	1722
Adam Powell,	1722	"	1723
William Coddington,	1723	"	1724
Henry Bull,	1724	"	1725
Godfrey Malbone,	1725	"	1726
William Wanton,	1731	"	1732
Jonathan Thurston,	1732	"	1733
James Martin,	1733	"	1734
Jahleel Brenton,	1734	"	1735
John Gidley,	1735	"	1736
Samuel Wickham,	1736	"	1737
Edward Scott,	1737	"	1738
Daniel Ayrault, Jr.,	1738	"	1739

---

* Died while at the head of the Church.

William Mumford,	1739	to	1740
Joseph Wanton,	1740	"	1741
John Bannister,	1741	"	1742
Peleg Brown,	1742	"	1743
Philip Wilkinson,	1743	"	1744
Stephen Ayrault,	1744	"	1745
Thomas Wickham,	1745	"	1746
William Paul,	1746	"	1747
Walter Chaloner,	1747	"	1748
Evan Malbone,	1748	"	1749
Charles Wickham,	1749	"	1750
Walter Cranston,	1750	"	1751
Robert Sherman,	1751	"	1752
Jonathan Thurston,	1752	"	1753
Thomas Vernon,	1753	"	1754
Edward Cole,	1754	"	1755
Metcalf Bowler,	1755	"	1756
Robert Jenkins,	1756	"	1757
Joseph Wanton, Jr.,	1757	"	1758
Charles Handy,	1758	"	1759
Andrew Hunter,	1759	"	1760
Isaac Stelle,	1760	"	1761
John Mawdsley,	1761	"	1762
Benjamin Mason,	1762	"	1763
Benjamin Brenton,	1763	"	1764
Samuel Bours,	1764	"	1765
John Jenkins,	1765	"	1766
John Bours,	1766	"	1767
Simon Pease,	1767	"	1768
Francis Brinley,	1768	"	1769
Francis Malbone,	1769	"	1770
Peter Cooke,	1770	"	1771
John Bours,	1771	"	1786
Samuel Freebody,	1786	"	1789
John Handy,	1789	"	1797
William Crooke,	1797	"	1801
Wm. R. Robinson,	1801	"	1803
Samuel Whitehorne,	1803	"	1804
William Littlefield,	1804	"	1810

Samuel Whitehorne,	1810	to	1814
William C. Gardiner,	1814	"	1816
Edward Brinley,	1816	"	1818
Charles Collins,	1818	"	1819
Robinson Potter,	1819	"	1821
Stephen T. Northam,	1821	"	1823
Samuel Whitehorne,	1823	"	1828
Edward Brinley,	1828	"	1832
George C. Mason, Sr.,	1832	"	1835
Benjamin Finch,	1835	"	1838
Robert Johnston,	1838	"	1839
George C. Mason, Sr.,	1839	"	1842
Samuel Fowler Gardner,	1842	"	1843
John H. Gilliat,	1843	"	1845
Samuel Fowler Gardner,	1845*		
John H. Gilliat,	1845	"	1847
Edward King,	1847	"	1849
Marshall C. Slocum,	1849	"	1855
George C. Mason,	1855	"	1859
John H. Cozzens,	1859	"	1861
Marshall C. Slocum,	1861	"	1863
George C. Mason,	1863	"	1889
LeRoy King,	1889	"	

JUNIOR WARDENS OF TRINITY CHURCH.

Thomas Lillibridge,	1709	to	
William Gibbs,	1719	"	
Adam Powell,	1721	"	1722
William Coddington,	1722	"	1723
Henry Bull,	1723	"	1724
Godfrey Malbone,	1724	"	1725
John Freebody,	1725	"	1726
Jonathan Thurston,	1731	"	1732
James Martin,	1732	"	1733
Jahleel Brenton,	1733	"	1734
John Gidley,	1734	"	1735

---

* Mr. Gardner met with an accidental death in the summer of the same year.

Samuel Wickham,	1735 to	1736
Edward Scott,	1736 "	1737
Daniel Ayrault, Jr.,	1737 "	1738
William Mumford,	1738 "	1739
Joseph Wanton,	1739 "	1740
John Bannister,	1740 "	1741
Peleg Brown,	1741 "	1742
Philip Wilkinson,	1742 "	1743
Stephen Ayrault,	1743 "	1744
Thomas Wickham,	1744 "	1745
William Paul,	1745 "	1746
Walter Chaloner,	1746 "	1747
Evan Malbone,	1747 "	1748
Charles Wickham,	1748 "	1749
Walter Cranston,	1749 "	1750
Robert Sherman,	1750 "	1751
Jonathan Thurston,	1751 "	1752
John Jepson,	1752 "	1753
Edward Cole,	1753 "	1754
Metcalf Bowler,	1754 "	1755
Robert Jenkins,	1755 "	1756
Joseph Wanton, Jr.,	1756 "	1757
Charles Handy,	1757 "	1758
Andrew Hunter,	1758 "	1759
Isaac Stelle,	1759 "	1760
John Mawdsley,	1760 "	1761
Benjamin Mason,	1761 "	1762
Samuel Brenton,	1762 "	1763
Samuel Bours,	1763 "	1764
John Jenkins,	1764 "	1765
John Bours,	1765 "	1766
Simon Pease,	1766 "	1767
Christopher Champlin,	1767 "	1768
Francis Malbone,	1768 "	1769
Peter Cooke,	1769 "	1770
Thomas Wickham,	1770 "	1771
Isaac Lawton,	1771 "	1781
Francis Malbone,	1781 "	1789
Robert N. Auchmuty,	1789 "	1797

Wm. R. Robinson,	1797	to	1801
Samuel Whitehorne,	1801	"	1803
William Littlefield,	1803	"	1804
William Wood,	1804	"	1808
Benj. Mumford, Jr.,	1808	"	1810
Edward Easton,	1810	"	1812
Robert Robinson,	1812	"	1814
Henry Shaw,	1814	"	1816
Stephen T. Northam,	1816	"	1817
James Mumford,	1817	"	1818
Samuel Fowler Gardner,	1818	"	1819
Wm. H. Rathbone,	1819	"	1826
Stephen A. Robinson,	1826	"	1828
Stephen H. Cahoone,	1828	"	1838
Christ. Grant Perry,	1838	"	1845
Walter Nichols,	1845	"	1848
John H. Cozzens,	1848	"	1859
William G. Seabury,	1859	"	1861
Charles Hunter,	1861	"	1862
James Birckhead,	1862	"	1863
Samuel Engs,	1863	"	1886
Rodman Cornell,	1886	"	

OFFICERS OF THE CHURCH.

1889.

Rector.

REV. GEORGE J. MAGILL.

LEROY KING, *Senior Warden.*

RODMAN CORNELL, *Junior Warden.*

Vestrymen

BENJAMIN FINCH.
JOHN H. COZZENS.
WILLIAM E. DENNIS.
HENRY D. DEBLOIS.
WALTER L. KANE.
PHILIP RIDER.
JOHN IREYS.
THEODORE R. HELME.
V. MOTT FRANCIS.
GEORGE GORDON KING.

WILLIAM E. DENNIS, *Secretary.*

PHILIP RIDER, *Treasurer.*

WM. IRVING LYON, *Organist.*

W. G. SCHWARZ, *Sexton.*

SILVER OWNED BY TRINITY CHURCH.

	Oz.	Dwt.
One Chalice, silver gilt,	17	6
One Paten,	11	19
One silver gilt Paten,	5	16

The above from the Society for the Propagation of the Gospel in Foreign Parts, 1702.

	Oz.	Dwt.
One Baptismal Basin,	52	12

The gift of Nathaniel Kay, 1733.

	Oz.	Dwt.
One Flagon, from Mr. Kay, 1733,	39	8
One Flagon from Richard Perkins, 1733,	39	8
One Chalice, with handles,	23	0

Not marked ; probably the piece given by Mrs. Catharine Malbone.

	Oz.	Dwt.
One Alms Basin,	22	3

From Johannes Mulderi D. Guilielmi Bright.

	Oz.	Dwt.
One Alms Plate from Mrs. Sarah Jones,	12	17
Another Alms Plate, from the same,	11	04
Two Chalices, from Rev. A. G. Mercer. Each,	11	12

One gold-lined jewelled Chalice and Paten, in memory of Daniel LeRoy.

One gold-lined jewelled Chalice and Paten, in memory of Samuel Engs, late Junior Warden.

Two Patens.

One small Flagon.

One gold-lined Spoon.

CHARTER OF TRINITY CHURCH,

WITH AMENDMENTS.

STATE OF RHODE-ISLAND & PROVIDENCE PLANTATIONS,
IN GENERAL ASSEMBLY, OCT. SESSION, A.D. 1816.

WHEREAS, the *Minister, Church-Wardens, Vestry and Congregation of* TRINITY CHURCH in NEWPORT, have preferred a Petition unto this General Assembly, and for the reasons therein assigned, have prayed this Assembly to alter, amend and enlarge their original Charter of Incorporation, granted them in the Year 1769, and to extend the powers and provisions thereof, so as to suit the present state of the concerns; to enable them, with greater convenience, to manage and secure the Property and Funds of which they are now, or may be hereafter possessed, and to promote and establish the Worship of ALMIGHTY GOD, according to the discipline, rites, canons, usages, ceremonies and liturgy of the Protestant Episcopal Church, in the United States of America:

SECTION I.—*Be it therefore Enacted,* That the Minister, Church-Wardens, Vestry and Congregation of said Church, be, and they and their successors forever are hereby made and constituted, and confirmed to be, a body corporate and politic, with perpetual succession, by the Name of *The Minister, the Church-Wardens, Vestry and Congregation of Trinity Church, in Newport,* and by that Name shall be able and capable in law, to sue and be sued, to plead and be impleaded, to answer and to be answered unto, to defend and to be defended against, in all Courts and places, and before all proper Judges whomsoever; to take, receive and hold all monies and other property, real or personal, by voluntary subscription, contribution, donation or otherwise, and also all legacies and devises of real and personal estate; and also to have, acquire, hold, occupy, possess and enjoy lands, tenements and hereditaments, goods and chattels, and property of every description, not exceeding in the whole Forty Thousand Dollars, and all and singular the estate and prop-erty aforesaid ; to lease, grant, convey or dispose of in such manner as they may judge best for the interest of said Corporation, to have and use a common seal, and the same to alter, or renew at pleasure, with full power and authority to make and ordain all such laws, rules, and ordi-nances, for the government of the Corporation, and the better manage-ment of the affairs thereof, as they or the major part of them, who may be present on due notification, may deem necessary and proper, provided the same be not repugnant to the laws of this State, and Constitution and Laws of the United States.

SEC. II.—*And be it further Enacted by the authority aforesaid,* That all the Funds and Property now owned or possessed by said Corporation, be and the same is hereby vested in, confirmed to, and continued in the same Corporation.

SEC. III.—*And be it further Enacted by the authority aforesaid,* That there shall be an Annual Meeting of said Corporation on Easter Monday, yearly and every year, at which meeting there shall, and at any other legal meeting there may be, if vacancies should happen, elected two Church-Wardens, who shall be *ex-officio* Vestry-men ; eleven other Ves-try-men, a Secretary, who shall also be Clerk of the Vestry, and such other Officers as may be judged necessary. And that legal meetings of said Corporation may be called at any time, by the Minister of said Trinity-Church, by either of the Church-Wardens, by any five Vestry-men, or any ten members of said Corporation ; and at any of the meet-ings aforesaid, any of the affairs and business of said Corporation may be attended to, transacted and performed.—And although said Corporation should not, from any cause or circumstance whatever, hold their Annual Meeting on Easter-Monday yearly, and every year hereafter, yet this Act shall nevertheless continue and be in full force, and Officers may be elected, and the affairs and business of said Corporation may be trans-acted and performed at any subsequent meeting which may be called in either of the modes before stated.

SEC. IV.—*And be it further Enacted by the authority aforesaid,* That the Church-Wardens and Vestry-men elected by said Corporation, shall for the time being, have the entire and sole control, management and disposition of all the property and funds of said Corporation, in trust nevertheless, and for the use of said Corporation, for the sole support and promotion of the public worship of GOD, as in the preamble of this Act expressed, for defraying the incidental expenses thereof, and for the

repairs of the Church edifice and its appurtenances.—That the said Corporation shall on Easter-Monday annually, or oftener if it should become
necessary, for the security of the property and funds aforesaid, elect a
Treasurer, who shall keep fair and accurate accounts of the Property and
Funds aforesaid, and of the management and disposition of the same; and
shall attend when required, and shall have a right at all times to attend
the meetings of the Vestry, and shall at every Annual Meeting on Easter-
Monday, make a written statement, or report of the same, to the said
Corporation ; and shall, when required by a vote of said Corporation, or
by a vote of said Church-Wardens and Vestry-men, make further statements and reports of the same, and shall produce the books, vouchers
and documents, containing the accounts and statements of the property
and funds aforesaid, and the use, management and disposition of the
same, which shall be open to their inspection and examination.—And
the Treasurer, previous to entering on the duties of his Office, shall
annually give satisfactory bonds to the said Corporation, for the faithful
discharge of the duties of his said office.

Sec. V.—*And be it further Enacted by the authority aforesaid,* That
each Male Owner of a pew in Trinity-Church in Newport, or lessee or
hirer of the same for One Year, or a longer time, and who professes to
attend public worship therein, shall be a Member of said Corporation,
and be entitled to appear and vote in all Corporation Meetings, and that
in all such Meetings, eleven members shall be necessary to constitute a
quorum.

Sec. VI.—*And be it further Enacted by the authority aforesaid,* That the
Minister of said Church, shall be elected by the Corporation aforesaid,
at a meeting of said Corporation legally called ; and the Minister by
them thus elected, shall, as soon as may be instituted Rector, according
to the office set forth for that purpose by the General Convention of the
Protestant Episcopal Church as aforesaid.

Sec. VII.—*And be it further Enacted by the authority aforesaid,* That
the minister so elected and instituted Rector, shall thereafter, while he
continues such, be *ex officio* a member of said Corporation, and when
present, Moderator thereof at all meetings of the same.—That he shall
have a right at any time, to inspect the Books and Records of the Corporation.—That it shall be his right and duty, from time to time, to state
verbally or in writing, the condition of the affairs of the Corporation, and
to recommend such measures as he deems advisable for its benefit, to the
meetings of the Wardens and Vestry-men, at which meetings one of the
Church-Wardens, or Senior Vestry-men present, shall be Moderator;

and in all meetings of said Wardens and Vestry-men, seven Members shall be necessary to constitute a quorum, each Member being entitled to one Vote, excepting the Moderator, who shall only be entitled to give the casting vote.

Sec. VIII.—*And be it further Enacted by the authority aforesaid,* That all donations made, or that may be made to said Corporation, or that ensue, or may ensue to their use, shall be strictly used and applied according to the intentions and directions of the donors ; and that all deeds and conveyances made by said Corporation, shall be made by the Treasurer thereof for the time being, when authorized by a recorded vote or resolution of the Wardens and Vestry, to which said deeds and conveyances the seal of said Corporation shall be affixed.

Sec. IX.—*And be it further Enacted by the authority aforesaid,* That whenever any tax or proportion of money shall be assessed by order of said Corporation upon the pews of the said Church edifice, for the repairs of said edifice and its appurtenances, which are already or may hereafter be made, or for the expenses of said Corporation, such tax or proportion of money shall be paid by the several owners of such pews, agreeably to their respective assessments, and the rules and ordinances of said Corporation ; and in case any owner as aforesaid shall, for the space of three months after the notice of any tax or proportion of money assessed as aforesaid, refuse or neglect to pay the same, the pews of such delinquents shall and may be sold by order of said Corporation, at public Auction, for the payment and discharge of such taxes and costs : *Provided nevertheless,* That such sale be previously advertised, at least thirty days before such pews shall be offered for sale, and the surplus money (if any) after the payment of such taxes and costs, shall be lodged with the Treasurer of said Corporation, to be paid over to such delinquents, or their legal Representatives, on demand.

Sec. X.—*And be it further Enacted by the authority aforesaid,* That the Charter aforesaid, of one thousand seven hundred and sixty-nine, granted to the said Minister, Wardens and Congregation of said Trinity Church, and the subsequent amendments thereto, be, and they hereby are, with the assent and at the request of said Minister, Wardens and Congregation, repealed, abrogated and annulled.—*Provided nevertheless,* That all acts legally done, and all responsibilities legally incurred, and all by-laws, resolves and regulations passed under said Charter and amendments, shall be and remain in full force and virtue.

A true Copy :—Witness,

SAMUEL EDDY, *Secretary.*

AMENDMENTS.

On the Petition of the Minister, Church-Wardens, Vestry and Congregation of Trinity-Church, in Newport, *It was Voted and Resolved*, That the Charter of Incorporation of said Church be so altered and amended, as the Minister or Rector of said Church may attend and be present at the Meetings of Wardens and Vestry of said Church, and when so present, shall be the Moderator of said Meetings;—anything expressed or implied in the present Charter of Incorporation of said Trinity-Church to the contrary notwithstanding.

A True Copy:—Witness,

HENRY BOWEN, *Secretary*.

June, 1827.

An Act providing for the investment of certain Funds, belonging to Trinity Church, in Newport.

Be it Enacted by the General Assembly, That the fund heretofore raised by subscription, donations, legacies or otherwise, and intended by the subscribers, donors, &c., to be a permanent fund for the better support of Trinity Church, in Newport, and Now, with the interest thereon, amounting to the sum of ten thousand five hundred dollars, par value, being invested in some safe and profitable stock or stocks, or real estate, in the Name and right of the Minister, Church-Wardens, Vestry and Congregation of Trinity Church, in Newport, shall remain so invested, together with all sum or sums which may hereafter be raised in the way or manner aforesaid, permanently and untransferable, except by the act of the Corporation at a regular meeting, with Notice of the business to be transacted; which act, to be valid, shall require the presence and the concurring vote of at least three-fourths of the whole Male members of said

Corporation, who shall at the time be owners of pews in said Church, or part owners, with authority in writing from a majority of all the part owners, to act in their stead; one vote only to be given by any one member, or in behalf of any number of members owning one pew: and the said fund, in whatever manner the same may at any time be invested, shall remain unimpaired and undiminished by any act of said Corporation; and the accruing interest, dividends or profits thereof only, shall be at the disposal of said Corporation, agreeably to the terms of the original subscriptions.

JUNE, 1828.

AN ACT IN AMENDMENT OF THE CHARTER OF TRINITY CHURCH, IN NEWPORT.

SECTION I.—*Be it Enacted by the General Assembly and by the authority thereof it is enacted,* That each white male owner of a pew or pews on either floor of Trinity Church, who professes to attend public worship in said Church, and whose pew or pews aforesaid qualify no other person holding a lease of the same, or in the occupation thereof, to vote according to this Act—And also the lessee or hirer of a pew on the lower floor of said Church, who professes to attend public worship therein, shall be a member of said Corporation during the time he continues so qualified, and be entitled to appear and vote in all Corporation meetings: and at all such meetings fifteen members at least shall be necessary to constitute a Quorum for business; that no member shall be entitled to more than one vote, and that no pew shall entitle more than one person to vote at the same time: *Provided, nevertheless,* That no lessee or hirer of a pew or pews as aforesaid, shall be entitled to vote unless he is, at the time of voting, and has been for the term of one year at least, previous to such time of voting, possessed and in the occupation of such pew or pews, or some other pew or pews in said Church, and shall have paid all taxes that have been lawfully assessed and become due against the pew or pews that may qualify him as aforesaid; and also the rent that may have become due; provided such pew or pews belong to said Church or Corporation.

SEC. II.—*And be it further Enacted,* That all future special Meetings of said Corporation shall be notified by reading the notice audibly and publicly on the Sunday previous to said meeting, at said Church, when the congregation is assembled for public worship, in the usual manner as heretofore, at least four days previous to such Corporation meeting; which notice shall state the time and place of meeting, and the business pro-

posed to be transacted; and no business at such meeting, except what is
so proposed in said notice, shall be legal ; *Provided, nevertheless,* That
nothing herein contained shall affect the right to meet by adjournment of
any legal meeting.

And be it further Enacted, That the fifth Section of the said charter of
Trinity-Church be and the same is hereby repealed.

JUNE, 1847.

AN ACT IN AMENDMENT OF THE CHARTER OF TRINITY CHURCH.

SECTION I. *It is Enacted by the General Assembly as follows,* That each
owner of a pew in Trinity-Church, Newport, who professes to worship in
the Protestant Episcopal Church, shall be a member of said Corporation,
and shall be entitled to vote either in person or by proxy in all Corporation Meetings, and in all such meetings not less than fifteen members
shall form a quorum for the transaction of any business. *Nevertheless,* no
person shall be entitled to vote except all taxes legally assessed and become
due upon the pew which qualifies such person to vote shall have been first
paid.

SEC. II. That all Special Meetings of said Corporation shall be called
by reading in said Church a public notice thereof, on the Sunday next
before any such meeting, and not less than four days previous thereto,
which notice shall state generally the business to be transacted.

SEC. III. That the fifth Section of said Charter and all acts in alteration or amendment thereof, are hereby repealed.

JANUARY, 1865.

AN ACT IN REPEAL OF AN ACT AMENDING THE CHARTER OF "TRINITY CHURCH IN NEWPORT."

It is Enacted by the General Assembly as follows :

SECTION I. So much of the Act entitled an Act in Amendment of the
Charter of Trinity Church, in Newport, passed at the June Session of the
General Assembly A. D. 1842, as authorizing the voting by proxy in all
Corporation Meetings is hereby repealed.

NOTE.—There appears to be no Record among the acts of the General Assembly of
any Act passed in June, A. D. 1842, referring to Trinity Church. The date A. D. 1842
is evidently erroneous, and should be A. D. 1847.

LIST OF SUBSCRIBERS.

Arnold, Mrs. Edmund S. F.,	.	$10.00
Belmont, Mrs. August,	. .	20 00
Berry, Mrs. R. P.,	. . .	5.00
Brown, J. Nicholas,	. .	25.00
Bailey, Miss Annie S., .	. .	5.00
Bailey, Miss Josephine I., .	.	5.00
Bliss, Mrs. Wm. B.,	. .	5.00
Beach, Mrs. C. N.,	. .	5.00
Collins, George, .	. .	10.00
Clarke, Mrs. Mary H., .	. .	1.00
Clark, Rt. Rev. Thomas M., .	.	5 00
Chace, Henry J., .	. .	5.00
Cornell, Rodman,	. .	55.00
Cushing, Robert M.,	. .	10.00
Cornell, Rev. John,	. .	5.00
Carr, George H., .	. .	5.00
Dennis, William E.,	. .	5.00
DeBlois, Henry D.,	. .	5.00
D. S., .	. . . .	1.00
Douglass, Rev. Geo. W., D.D.,	.	10.00
Fearing, Daniel B.,	. .	10.00
Francis, V. Mott, M.D.,	. .	5.00
Gibbs, Theodore K., .	.	50.00
Garner, Mrs. Thomas, .	.	10.00
Griswold, John N. A., .	.	5.00
Gibbs, Geo. W., . .		50.00
Goodwin, Rev. Daniel, .	.	5.00
Handy, Miss M. C., .	.	2.00
Hunter, Wm. R., .	.	5.00
Henshaw, Rev. Daniel,	.	5.00
Ireys, John, . . .	.	5.00
King, LeRoy, . .		75.00
King, George Gordon, .	.	75 00
King, Mrs. Edward, .	.	125.00
Kane, Walter Langdon,	.	10.00

Klapp, Lyman, .	.	$15.00
Lorillard, Louis L., .	.	30.00
Magill, Rev. George J.,	.	10.00
Magill, Rev. Geo. Ernest,	.	5.00
Malcom, Rev. Charles H., .	.	5.00
Moore, Rev. Wm. H., D.D.,	.	25.00
Metcalf, Mrs. Alfred, .	.	10.00
McA., Mrs., . . .	.	5.00
Matthews, Mrs. Nathan, Jr.,	.	5.00
Miller, George MacCulloch, .	.	5.00
Norris, William, . .	.	25.00
Nightingale, Geo. G., Jr.,	.	12.00
Nichols, Walter, . . .	.	5.00
Otis Library, Norwich, Conn., by		
Jonathan Trumbull, .	.	5.00
Potter, Rt. Rev. Henry C., .	.	5.00
Powel, Mrs. Samuel, .	.	10.00
Pell, Mrs. Duncan C., .	.	5.00
Pierce, Moses, . .	.	5.00
Riggs, William, .	.	5.00
Rider, Philip, . .	.	5.00
Richmond, F. E., .	.	5.00
St. Stephen's Guild, .	.	25.00
Shields, Prof. Charles W., .	.	5.00
Sheldon, Frederick, .	.	5.00
Sheffield, William P., .	.	10.00
Tyler, George F.,	.	10.00
Tuttle, Rt. Rev. Daniel S., .	.	5.00
Tompkins, Hamilton B.,	.	5.00
Vanderbilt, Cornelius, .	.	100.00
Vestry of Trinity Church,	.	100.00
Wetmore, Geo. Peabody,	.	75.00
Woolsey, Miss Theodora W.,	.	5.00
Zabriskie, Lansing, .	.	5.00

INDEX.